THE ADAMANTINE HEART

I0671323

WILLIAM RUSSELL SHERIDAN

THE GERMANIA PRESS
Bavaria, Germany and California, USA

The Germania Press

Bavaria, Germany and California, USA

First Germania Press edition August 2016
Emended November 2020

Jacket design by Laura LaRoche of LLPix.com

Manufactured in the United States of America
Library of Congress Cataloging-in-Publication Data

Sheridan, William Russell.
The adamantine heart: a novel/William Russell Sheridan

ISBN: 978-0-9909682-0-7

ACKNOWLEDGMENTS

My dearest and most persistent readers deserve my gratitude:

In the United States and in Germany, my parents Bill and Helga for tolerating these diversions from my other career work.

In California, Janet and Dick Immel; William Clark. Tom McDowell for his trust and faith that I could do it. All my generous handball buddies who have promised to chip in and buy one copy of the book. My two favorite literati Mike Miller and Willy Bruijns.

In the Mid-west, Steve Doty and Marlene Ciorba for their nearly infinite patience and acceptance; Steve and Judy Schultz for caring; Abu Timbo for sharing his knowledge of Sierra Leone.

In Bavaria, Germany, Erster Hauptkommissar Roland Rüssel, my inspiration; and special thanks to Martina Rüssel for her encouragement over the years. A special thanks to Marlies Reuther-Rüssel for the exceptional care and consideration she provides me. My gratitude to Ernst Baur for graciously providing friendship and a place to write at Villa Ernesto in the Italian Alps high above Cannobio on the Lago Maggiore.

And, of course, whether at home in Bavaria or California, Nancy Clark for her timely and gentle insistence to quit writing and get the damn thing published.

"He who finds diamonds must grapple in mud and mire because diamonds are not found in polished stones. They are made."

Henry B. Wilson

Contents

Chapter One: The Hauptkommissar

A PHONE RINGING in the next room awakened him from a fitful sleep. He had been dreaming of his mother. She wanted to know why he had been demoted in rank, why he had lost a star. He tried to explain and he was angry that once again she would not listen to him. In his dream, just as he was about to persuade her that it was not his fault, a phone rang. He refused to answer. It could only be his boss, Polizeirat Steinmetz, wanting to take away yet another star. As he let the phone ring, the incessant pulse from silence to noise moved from inside his head to outside and pulled him by the ears into a semblance of consciousness. Now awake, he was angry that he had lost control of the dream. He opened his eyes but could not see. He blinked away the vestigial fog of sleep and closed his mouth. He had been sleeping on his back with his mouth open. He struggled through a swallow. He lay on the couch in the living room, dressed in wrinkled slacks and a polo shirt from the day before. He could see his feet, still in socks. Someone had removed his boots and covered him with a blanket. Konstanze.

Empty wine bottles of Rotgold and Ruländer stood on the coffee table; one lay sleeping on its belly as the others stood watch around it. The smell of wine from the bottles now had an acidic undertone. He raised an eyebrow as he counted. She certainly could hold her wine. He saw the ashtray littered with cigarettes, some half-smoked as if the fire had gone out prematurely, others bent and twisted from the force of being stubbed out against the glass, some a prelude to a kiss. All hers. He did not smoke and despised the habit. He saw the lipstick that kissed the ends of the smokes and remembered its strawberry taste. He tolerated her smoking for the sex. He got his feet to the floor as the ringing continued. This could only mean someone who knew him or his habits; otherwise, they would have given up in frustration and hung up long ago. The ringing hurt his head and he knew the only way to stop it was to answer the damn phone. He coughed his throat clear, opened the smoked glass door to the vestibule and picked up the receiver from the black phone on the desk. He hoped no one would be at the other end.

"Rieger."

The caller hesitated before speaking. "I'm sorry. Did I wake you, sir?"

It was his partner, Sylvie Schumann.

"What time is it, Lieutenant?" He did not mean to be brusque. He did not know the time.

"One o'clock, sir. In the afternoon," she added.

"It's my day off."

She paused before she spoke again, as if carefully weighing her words, or the decision to use them. "There has been another murder, sir. We're needed at once."

He considered what she had told him. There was one hope for them both. "We're not the only investigative team in the Kriminalpolizei. Who assigned us this case?"

"Kriminalpolizeirat Steinmetz himself."

2

"Wonderful. That explains it."

The chief had also assigned Lieutenant Schumann to him against his wishes to the contrary and against his threat to resign forthwith. He withheld the letter only because he knew the immense satisfaction it would give Steinmetz to finally drive him from the department and force him off the Job. It was not his fault that Steinmetz's eighteen-year-old daughter had fallen in love with him. Rieger knew the affair eventually would run its course, and it had, because like any normal teenager, she had outgrown her infatuation with her Hauptkommissar and was now interested in pursuing her male physics teacher at the local Gymnasium where she went to school.

No doubt, she once had loved him; at least she had said so often enough to convince herself, but he was more inclined to believe the forbidden relationship was a convenient way to get back at Papa. And it worked, all too well. Rieger was now stuck with the consequences of first sticking it to Konstanze and then indirectly, her father, Chief Steinmetz. Last night had been their farewell evening and Rieger knew that the sex had been passionate enough to predict a return. He had feigned just the right amount of hurt to inflame her ardor.

Now he was stuck babysitting a young lieutenant fresh from her university training in criminal investigation and stuck with an assignment to a case that involved a series of murders no detective in the Bavarian criminal police had been able to solve. That was his punishment. He took a deep breath, sighing it back into the phone's receiver. The break-up sex with Konstanze last night had been worth it. Now it was time to pay up.

"Where are you calling from, Sylvie?"

The question startled her. She assumed he knew. "My office at Headquarters." She was learning that Hauptkommissar Roland Rieger preferred conclusions derived from facts, rather than unsupported assumptions.

"Pick me up at two. Ring when you arrive."

"Very good, sir. Sorry to disturb you. I know today is your day off." She was genuinely contrite.

"Don't worry about it, Sylvie. It's not your fault. This is between Steinmetz and me. You can brief me in the car as we drive to the scene."

She blew an involuntary sigh of relief back through the line. She knew Hauptkommissar Rieger's reputation as an investigator was unequaled, matched only by his reputation with women, or so her colleagues whispered around the office. This, more than anything, left her nonplussed. She considered herself reasonably attractive and certainly fit. In fact, she had a great body, an opinion supported by her previous boyfriends. Why then had he not come on to her? She knew he was reluctant to work with a partner, and she believed that his hesitancy had everything to do with her being a female officer recently graduated from the police university. She had not come up through the ranks like Rieger or so many other commanders on the Job. She attributed his lack of interest to that fact.

Recently, she had learned from the scuttlebutt behind the desks that she had been assigned to him as a form of retribution and the last thing she wanted was for the assignment to be a punishment for them both. In the three months they had worked together, she was surprised by his behavior. To her consternation, not once had he made an advance. He was consistently professional and maddeningly polite and this made her both angry and frustrated that she was being tolerated. She was therefore determined that she would perform her duties to the highest

4

possible standard until once and finally she earned his respect. She did not yet understand that this, of course, was exactly his purpose.

As he replaced the receiver, he knew that at the stroke of two his door buzzer would ring. Sometimes it is good to be German, better to be Bavarian, he thought, as he went directly into the bathroom and tried to repair the damage wrought by too much wine, too much sex, and too little sleep separating the two. Broken capillaries from the evening's exertions mapped his brown eyes; his tongue dry as a buried bone. With fifteen minutes to spare, dressed in everything but his coat, he stood before the full-length mirror propped against the wall in his spare bedroom. He checked the action of his service pistol, a Glock 20 ten-millimeter. He still missed the nine-millimeter Walther PPK, known to him as the Polizei Pistole Kurz, later Kriminal, which he had carried for so many years despite the weapon's shortcomings. Changing to a new weapon was like getting a new girlfriend. No matter how good looking and exciting the new one might be, there were things you missed about your former flame. Mostly a matter of comfort and familiarity, he thought, like the way she lay in the hand. Besides, it had never failed to impress women when he informed them that this was the same pistol once carried by James Bond. But even Bond eventually gave up the Walther for a Beretta. Unfortunately, the added stopping power of the Glock was no longer a luxury these days, and given the rise in terrorist activity in the Fatherland, for additional firepower, he carried a Heckler and Koch MP5 submachine gun in the trunk of the BMW.

He snugged the pistol with its practically indestructible grip into the holster under his left arm. He had time for a cup of tea. As he waited for the water to boil in the silver teakettle, he took the water can from the kitchen table into the living room and doused the elephant ear begonia and the dieffenbachia, both looking a bit neglected. He misted the flowering cactus smuggled out of Sardinia during his last vacation. The dried soil was the color of his tongue. He thought about giving himself a squirt but decided against it.

He pulled the band to raise the wooden louvers covering the door to his balcony and they clattered up out of the way. The bright light of the early afternoon hurt his eyes and he shielded them as he stepped out onto the balcony and into the day. Beyond the rise of his apartment complex, he was pleased to see the rise of the Alps where, as a younger man, he had so often climbed with his brother Erik and Bill, the husband of his sister Hannelore. Those had been wonderful times and he remembered them with fondness. He missed both men and thought often of his sister, now living in the United States. The cool air did him good. To be honest with himself, he admitted that he would miss the amorous attention of the eager if somewhat imperfectly schooled Konstanze. He drew a breath of mountain air deep into his lungs and accepted the inevitability of relationships doomed to failure by cultural taboo. His time to reminisce shortened, sweet and memorable, and now gone—like an affair with an eighteen-year-old—he returned to the kitchen, made his tea in the English style with a little cream to cut the tannins of the cheap blend, and took the warmth of the liquid into the queasiness of his stomach. Halfway into the cup, the buzzer at his door sounded, a signal that someone had pressed the button downstairs outside the door to the apartment complex. He looked at his watch. Exactly two o'clock. Good girl. She was relentlessly on time.

He poured the rest of the cup into the sink—he had made it too sweet to finish anyway—rinsed it, and set it upside down to dry on a paper towel. He closed the kitchen window and reset the mechanism that allowed it to open in from the top for ventilation. He closed the door to the small kitchen behind him so the wind would not blow it shut. He shouldered into his uniform coat, patted his breast pocket for his sunglasses, checked the angle of his hat in the mirror, brim polished to a mirror-like sheen, and pulled on his leather gloves. Ready. Under normal circumstances, he worked in plainclothes. But he had not done the laundry this week. And he still required Lieutenant Schumann to work in uniform until he decided she had earned the right to work as a criminal detective in plainclothes. It was more than simply a matter of discipline: it was a matter of honor.

The stairwell echoed from the fall of his polished black boots as he descended the three flights to the ground floor. He pushed through the common door and stepped out into the parking lot. She had taken the time to reverse the BMW so that the nose of the green and white cruiser pointed back out onto the road. She waited outside the car by the driver's side. He knew she wanted to drive, but she knew better than to ask. She came around the front of the car to greet him and she waited as he acknowledged her with a nod from beneath the brim of his officer's hat. His inspection was brief but thorough. Her uniform was as immaculate as his and well-tailored to her figure. Her make-up was understated; she was one of those lucky women who could afford to highlight instead of hiding. Her hair had been done the day before and it was once more under her control. The shorter cut suited her face and the use of a henna shampoo had introduced additional highlights to her soft blonde curls. She was surprised when he mentioned the cut. He could not, however, understand why she insisted on dyeing her nearly white blonde hair a darker shade of blonde. Then he understood. It had nothing to do with vanity. It made her look a bit more mature. He took a step closer.

"I approve of your perfume, Lieutenant..."

"Thank you, sir."

"...But I suggest you use it more judiciously. Perfume is designed to allure and invite one closer, not to overpower and stupefy the senses."

She was shocked and blushed into her cheeks so deeply that it seemed she had also misapplied her rouge. He had not meant it as a rebuke; rather, he wanted to teach her. She was young and eager enough to learn and he appreciated her enthusiasm for the Job.

"A woman as pretty as you requires very little perfume, Sylvie."

She was stunned. In the three months they had worked together, this was his first personal compliment to her. She smiled like a young girl freshly kissed at her first festival dance under the beer tent. He smiled to himself and got in behind the wheel. She had already forgotten about wanting to drive. He keyed the ignition, adjusted his mirrors, and fastened his seatbelt. He watched her ready herself for the climb into the car. The seat was too far forward and her freshly pressed, worsted wool skirt slid up to the top of her thighs. The seatbelt, as she pulled it across her chest, redefined her breasts. He caught a glimpse of her white bra as the shirt bloused and this time he grinned openly. He was certain her mother still bought her underwear for her. Under the sheen of the expensive pantyhose, she had good legs, he noticed, long and sleek. On such legs, pantyhose were superfluous. He asked how her running was going.

"I'm up to ten kilometers a day, sir," she said, with obvious pride. He had this uncanny ability to mention things she was certain he could not know about her, damn him. How did he do it? She pushed the seat away from the dash to make her long legs comfortable and said, "Ready."

"If it's not too much bother, you might want to tell me where we are headed," he reminded her.

Chagrined, she told him "Mooshütte, on the trail behind the little Gasthaus. The Schutzpolizei are waiting there for us."

"Thank you," he said. "I know it well." He released the handbrake, shifted the cruiser into gear and drove them out of the city. "By the way," he said to her, "if you have no objections, plainclothes for duty after today, uniform for official functions only." She had no objections behind her relentless smile.

They reached the outskirts of the city of Kaufbeuren where the concrete buildings and asphalt parking lots gave way to clover fields, sweet-milk dairy cows, and honey wagons that sprayed their pungent effluent across the redolent grasses so green they hurt the unprotected eye. He picked up speed in an effort to drive out of the barnyard smells. Sylvie reached to the back seat for her black leather satchel where she kept her papers, a graduation present from her mother. This was not to be confused with her handbag, where she kept an extra pen or two and her truly important necessities such as lipstick, tissues, keys, 4711 eau de toilette, coin purse, compact with mirror for quick touch-ups, nonoxynol-9 birth control inserts in case she lost control impulsively, her official canister of mace, badge and identity papers. She rummaged past the handcuffs, which she had tried on herself once, at the urging of her last boyfriend, pushed through a scattering of clutter she simply had not taken the time to clear out, and only then found a pen that worked. She arranged her notes on top of the satchel and waited. He rolled his window back up and nodded, convinced that the air was once again country but not farm fresh. She briefed him as they traveled.

"The Forstmeister for the region around Kempten, Horst Neckermann, found the body, what appears to be a young adult female, earlier this morning; no identification. He called the SCHUPO and they secured the crime scene..."

He interrupted. "How did the forester happen to find the body?"

She thought for a moment, trying to understand the intent of the question. She reasoned that the Hauptkommissar was exploring the possibility that the forester might be a suspect.

"He was cutting wood, taking down some diseased trees when he saw a flash of white from within one of the slash piles he was going to burn later this afternoon. He said," and here she referred to her notes, "that if he had not seen the exposed hand, he would have burned the pile to the ground."

"And instead of the discovery of a body we would have had an inadvertent funeral pyre."

"Yes, sir."

"Eliminate him as a suspect."

"Yes, sir." She made a show of striking through a name on her notepad.

"No, Lieutenant. Make an argument convincing me to eliminate Forstmeister Neckermann as a possible suspect."

"Ach, forgive me, sir."

"And Sylvie, let's dispense with the 'sir' and the formality. When we are working together like this you may call me Roland."

She smiled, and then gathered herself. "If he were the murderer, he would have set fire to the woodpile as a matter of course and we would have no report of a body."

"Very good. One more question. Does the crime fit the man?"

She repeated the question: "Does the crime fit the man? No, sir... excuse me, no Roland, in this instance it does not."

"Why not?"

"The victim is unknown to the warden, so he reports. There is no relationship established between the two. He knows that part of the forest as well as you know your kitchen. His discovery of the body was evidently due to coincidence. I say that because if he truly wanted to kill someone and dispose of the body, he could do so where we wouldn't find it in a hundred years, even if we were standing on the grave."

He noticed her confidence growing as she continued her analysis. She pursed her lips and knotted her eyebrows as she thought aloud.

"For him to commit a murder, sir—oops, sorry." She tried to hide her gaffe like a young girl covering her mouth with her hand to hide a little burp. He waited for her to continue.

"For him to commit a murder would be out of place with the character of the man, at least from what my preliminary investigation of his background tells me. I see what you mean by the question now. It definitely would not fit the man. He has no reason to kill her."

He turned the nose of the BMW onto a small road barely wide enough to accommodate both tires, the track scarcely larger than a paved bicycle path. He drove on into the forest beyond the hay fields.

"Are all murders motivated, Sylvie?"

"I'm not sure, but I would say yes. What do you think?"

"I can tell you this much, Lieutenant. Every murderer I have ever investigated has been a highly motivated individual."

"What about crimes of passion, Herr Hauptkommissar?"

He knew the use of the title here was to signal the stroke, the capstone of the rebuttal like the announcement of 'checkmate!' to end the chess match. He looked over at her after he pulled the vehicle in behind another cruiser and switched off the ignition. "You don't consider passion a motivation?"

"Sorry," she admitted, as if she had just been shown that her move was illegal. "I spoke without thinking. I was looking at it in terms of the impulse."

"I know what you meant. But don't confuse impulse with random action. Even an impulse is a motivated action. This is our edge, Sylvie, our advantage. The act of killing someone is first and foremost an effect. Our job is to find the cause of the effect. Let's go to work."

They walked another six hundred meters or so into the green mix of pines and fragrant cedars. Rieger stopped before they reached a clearing and put out his arm to block his partner. "Tell me what you see."

"I see a crime scene. The photographer is taking pictures. Two officers of the SCHUPO are sitting on tree stumps drinking beer and smoking cigarettes. The Forstmeister is also waiting, impatiently I might add, amidst the disruption of his work."

He stopped her. "Details, Sylvie, give me the details. Look deeply into the scene."

She did not hide her consternation. She thought she had given an excellent description. She tried again, determined to see what he saw. "Aha. I see log piles, freshly cut logs, some carefully stacked and one just being built or left unfinished. I see the sawdust; in fact, I can smell the sawdust. Between the sawhorses I see a log with a saw buried in the middle."

"As if the sawyer stopped in mid-stroke?"

"Yes!" Now she was genuinely excited. Her perception sharpened and she saw more deeply into the details of the scenario. "Yes. As if he

12

suddenly spotted something out of the ordinary, something so strange that it drew him away from his work. He stopped and walked to the slag pile and saw the body. He took only enough time to remove his gloves before he ran back to his car parked on the path."

"How do you know he hurried?"

"The gloves are not placed one atop the other as you or I would do when we remove our gloves and put them down. They were thrown to the ground next to the pile of sawdust below the sawhorses."

"Why there?"

"So that in the commotion of what had happened and what probably would happen, he would not forget them?" Now she was a bit uncertain.

"And why would this be important to him?" That stumped her.

"I don't know, sir."

"They are a present from his young wife. She objects when he caresses her with his calloused hands. He is recently remarried, something you could not have known. One last thing for your notebook before we examine the body. Please note that from here we cannot see the cars parked on the access road. The killer would have been able to take his time without fear of discovery."

She dutifully recorded the observation, which she had missed, but she was confounded by the part about the Forstmeister caressing his young wife. Before she could ask for an explanation, the Forstmeister noticed them standing on the verge and walked up to meet them.

"Roland. It's been a while. I see that the KRIPO is finally recruiting a better class of officer." He intended the compliment for Sylvie.

"Gallant as ever, Horst, you old gnome of the woods. Nothing escapes your eye. Forgive me, my partner Kommissar Sylvie Schumann.

Lieutenant, master of the woods Horst Neckermann. This area is part of his responsibility."

He first touched his fingers to his Alpine hat, then stepped forward and offered his hand. She immediately noticed the blisters.

"Stupid of me," he explained. "I started cutting in this section yesterday and like an idiot forgot my gloves. This is the result of my absentmindedness." He offered both hands palms up for inspection like a schoolboy just back from the lavatory.

"You would think, dear Horst, that as hard and as often as you grip a beer bottle, your hands would be covered with a pad of callous thick as pine bark."

"It's the hand cream my wife makes me use," he admitted with some embarrassment. "Nivea," he stated, as if the brand name would be useful to them. "Keeps them silky smooth, she tells me. I knew I better not forget the gloves again today."

Sylvie stared at Roland with unabashed amazement. Now she got it. He placed a finger under the point of her delicate chin and gently closed her mouth.

The younger of the two Schutzpolizei stood and greeted Roland by name and rank. The older sergeant scratched a two-day stubble of beard and remained seated. The SCHUPO were responsible for securing the crime scene and making certain that no evidence was disturbed. So far as he was concerned, his job was done now that the criminal police had arrived to begin their investigation. He reached back behind the stump supporting his ample rear end and held up a bottle of beer for Rieger to take.

"Generous of you, Schutzpolizei Hauptmeister Doppelmayr." Rieger unhinged the rubber cap stoppering the bottle and took a long pull. He pointed at his partner with the bottle and introduced her.

14

Sergeant Sepp Doppelmayr did not stand to greet her either, nor did he offer her a beer, but he did push the brim of his hat back with the tip of his beer to get a better look. She was good looking enough to merit a "Good day."

"Lieutenant, why don't you take Corporal Franz Schmidt here and go examine the body," Rieger suggested.

She was confused. "Aren't you going to look at it too, sir?"

He nodded. "I'll pay a little visit after you've finished your initial examination and have taken your notes," he assured her. "I don't want to get in the way."

The young corporal was eager for something to do and gladly took the lieutenant to the body.

Chapter Two: Observation and Analysis

ROLAND LAID HIS handkerchief atop the short stump before he sat gingerly, trying not to tip it. He removed his hat and put it on his knee. "So Sepp, what's up? What's with this disorderly desecration of our beloved Bavarian forest?"

During the early years on the Job, Sepp Doppelmayr had been his partner as they patrolled the Autobahns around Munich. When Roland was selected for the KRIPO, Doppelmayr was left behind to do the ordinary, routine police work that had turned him into a functioning alcoholic. Although a reasonably intelligent man quite capable of passing his exams for promotion, the excess of beer and wine long ago destroyed the memory and motivation required to sit and read and study. He had tried twice, three times, and each time had given up, gotten up, and headed for the local Gasthaus. He was a man who had come to grips with his limitations, and the alcohol that kept him happy, long ago had diluted the residues of bitterness still in him. The gradual destruction of his liver was only a secondary concern. Roland knew that his old friend would likely be dead within five years. He had seen it happen to many of his colleagues while on the Job.

Sepp, like a man who has seen his future, got right to the point. "Please tell me you are on that girl day and night, front and back."

Roland looked at him carefully. The rivers of booze were wearing him just as surely as the wind and rain eventually wears away the peaks of an alp. "Just exactly what do you think I have hanging between my legs, an ice pick?"

Doppelmayr guffawed and spit, then leaned over to slap him on the shoulder. He appreciated the constancy of an old comrade. "That's a good one, Rolli. An ice pick for the ice maiden." They clicked beer bottles to toast the joke.

"She's young and inexperienced but she's smart. Graduated head of her class, you know. And she certainly is eager, I'll give her that."

Doppelmayr mulled this over. "Now if she were my partner," he offered, "I'd crack that icy wall by getting her good and thoroughly drunk and then I'd introduce her to some authentic Bavarian Braunschweiger. That would heat up your snow queen."

Roland could tell the sergeant was impressed by something apparently more noticeable than her intelligence. He nodded at his old mentor. "We had some good times, didn't we, Sepp?"

"That is an indisputable royal Bavarian fact. However, near as I can tell, we still have not drunk up all the beer in southern Germany, although I hear stocks are running dangerously low these days."

Now they had reason to drink another toast to the days of fast pursuits, fast fights, and fast relationships, and then one to the Job back when it had still been good duty. Now the scum of the drug trade pouring in from the east and the bureaucrats who tied their hands had fucked up what had once been a good thing. As they commiserated, they watched the Forstmeister and the corporal pull branches from the log pile covering the corpse. With enough of the detritus cleared, they stepped back for a moment to give the forensic photographer access.

"What do you know about this one?" Roland asked the sergeant, as they stepped closer to the crime scene.

"Ugly. The bastard must have been a frustrated butcher. He carved up a pretty kid. He used a knife to cut the cunt open but that's not what killed her, if you ask me. Apologies for my use of language, Fräulein," he said in deference to Sylvie's rank, which did not impress him in the least.

The lieutenant, as she stepped in closer to view the remains, saw the mutilation between the victim's legs and blanched, hand to mouth.

"Well, she won't be any good for fucking tonight, not with that image seared into her retinal memory," observed Sepp.

Sylvie stepped over a tangle of branches and they heard the rip as she tore her pantyhose on the run into the woods. They could hear her gag and retch as she gave up her lunch to the forest floor. Roland and Sepp watched the little drama with amusement, and Sepp said she had lasted longer than he had expected, and Roland remarked that this was most likely a function of the high quality of training investigators received at the university these days.

"What do you think killed her, Hauptmeister? I'm asking."

"Garrote. Ligature marks around the entire neck. Windpipe severed, trachea severed, larynx severed. He practically cut her head off, if you really want to know the gory details, you pervert. This was either a very strong man, Rolli, or a very angry one, or both. No. She was dead before he began to sculpt her."

"Strangulation could have been post mortem," Roland suggested.

Doppelmayr shook his head and pursed his lips, letting Roland know that there was no chance whatsoever of that being the case.

"Petechiae. I checked inside the eyelids for broken capillaries."

Roland nodded. He had suspected the same. "Is the modus operandi the same as the other two cases?"

"Wouldn't know about that, Herr fucking Hauptkommissar of the asshole criminal police and the huge vocabulary, but the MO is the same."

Rieger grinned from ear to ear. He missed his old friend. Lieutenant Schumann, finished with her regurgitation, walked up sheepishly, eyes on her shoes.

"That was quite the lunch you had, Sylvie," Roland observed. Sepp did not laugh but the effort forced tears from his eyes as he shook. She could not decide whether to be angry or ashamed and she lost control of a grin.

"What got you?" Rieger asked.

"The smell," she admitted, as she wrinkled her nose at the memory.

Rieger nodded and reached into his back pocket for his handkerchief and offered it to her. "Spray this with your eau de toilette and cover your mouth and nose with it. Time to take a look."

He saw a young female in her death repose, her body lacerated by branches and crisscrossed with knife cuts. She had been killed and dumped, trash thrown on the heap. Her hair was blonde and long, matted with pine needles, and the dirt from the forest floor had dulled the shine. She was naked except for her shoes. He gently moved the head from side to side. The left earring was in place; the right had been torn out through the lobe and was missing, a result of the struggle, no doubt, and not an attempt to steal it, or the other would have been taken too. He asked the corporal to search for it after they finished. He gently pulled down the skin beneath the eyes and saw the red dots there, broken capillaries that signaled severe strangulation. Sepp Doppelmayr, the old pro, was correct. He examined the cut marks at the throat. They completely encircled the neck. This caused him to think more deeply about the garrote. In his mind's eye, he envisioned the thin

19

circle of wire lasso the neck, silently, snug tight, a second loop following the first, and then the violent mortal twist of the fists that cut and killed. He looked up at the corporal watching the Hauptkommissar intently. He could hear the rasp of his breathing as the young man hyperventilated. He saw the spark of intelligence in his eyes.

"Did you find the wire, son?"

"No sir. I searched thoroughly, at the Hauptmeister's request, but we did not find anything." His breathing returned to normal.

"Thank you, Corporal Schmidt, you did well. But there is a good chance we will find the earring." He knew the earring was unimportant but it would serve to occupy the young man.

Sylvie glared at Roland but he ignored her, returning to his examination. He pushed on the jaw below the lower lip along the plane of the chin and the mouth creaked open. On the back molars, the tips of the crowns had been chipped. He searched for the penlight on the inside breast pocket of his jacket but could not find it.

"Evidence bag." He reached back and Sylvie handed one to him. He snapped on the latex gloves, wrinkling his nose at the smell. "Penlight and pencil."

She opened her handbag, rummaged a bit, and found both. He inverted the pencil, holding it by the lead end, and used the eraser to fish out the tiny bits of broken tooth. He sealed these in the plastic bag and she initialed them. He motioned her down for a closer look. Her pantyhose were already ruined before she dropped to her knees. She would learn not to wear them to crime scenes. She looked into the mouth of the dead woman.

"What do you see?" he asked, holding the penlight steady for her.

"Chipped teeth."

"What caused it?"

"Happened in the struggle?" she guessed.

"Don't guess. If you don't know, say so. If you make a claim, be sure you can support it with evidence." He turned the woman's head slightly to the side and tilted the chin up. Just below the chin and along the jaw line there was a bruise and a dent in the center of the bruise. He had her feel the line of the jaw with her finger.

"My god," she said, "It's fractured. So that's why the jaw creaked when you first opened her mouth."

He nodded. He indicated the mouth again. "Something's missing." He directed the question to Sylvie and the corporal and let them mull over the physiology of the oral cavity as they took inventory. In the meantime, he studied the dead young woman's bare chest. Both breasts were crisscrossed with lacerations that had lightly bled out, indicating that the disfigurement had occurred after death. Both nipples were missing. Time was up. He waited for one or both to answer. They shrugged in unison. Nothing seemed missing as they compared her mouth with their own. The missing nipples seemed too obvious.

"No semen. Help me roll her over. Note the lividity where the blood has pooled in the body, drawn there by the force of gravity into what appears to be those black bruises." He gingerly separated the buttocks with the gloved thumb and forefinger of his left hand, the right holding the penlight steady.

"No semen," they said as one.

"No semen outside the rectal sphincter, to be precise. We'll leave the internal investigation for the pathologist in case the killer climaxed inside her." He carefully repositioned the body. "Note that the stomach is starting to bloat due to internal decomposition."

The young corporal let out a low whistle. He thought she might have been four of five months pregnant and was glad now that he had held

21

his tongue instead of showing off, more for the Hauptkommissar than for the pretty lieutenant.

Roland picked up each hand of the deceased woman and held them in his as if he were asking the dead woman for one last dance. "What do you see here, Lieutenant?"

"She cares about her nails. They are nearly perfect and freshly painted and the color is the same as mine. I would say, looking at the condition of her nails, she probably had them done less than two days ago."

"I agree. Make a note to canvas the beauty shops. Get a head shot from the photog and have him photoshop the neck so that the garottage does not show." He waited for her to finish writing. When she looked up he asked, "What don't you see?" He let them each take a hand.

"No skin under the nails," the corporal said, beating her to the punch.

Damn, she thought, that's what I was going to say, but to be generous she simply nodded in agreement. Then it hit her. No rings. "It's possible she is single."

Roland smiled at them both. "It's certainly possible. It's also possible that any rings were stolen. However, what we don't see are any marks on the fingers indicating that she wore rings. And with that tan, we would have noticed." He directed her to take scrapings from under the nails just to be certain no DNA from the killer had been left there.

He moved to the dead woman's feet and observed her open-toed shoes. "Why did the killer leave her naked except for shoes?"

He waited but no one answered. "Given the other evidence we have observed, there is a strong likelihood that the killer is male. If this is a correct conclusion, why did he leave this fit and attractive young woman in shoes?" He posed the question for Sylvie, looking directly at her. Hauptmeister Doppelmayr knew. The corporal did not. When the answer hit her, Sylvie blushed again, much to the Hauptmeister's

22

amusement. "She looks sexier with her shoes on," Sylvie said, thinking about the last pair of heels she had bought for herself, despite the fact that they barely fit.

"I certainly agree," said Sepp.

Roland smiled to himself, and then continued his analysis: "She buys her shoes at least a size too small, but she demands a heel, suggesting a certain degree of vanity. This is supported by the meticulous condition of her toenails. She has the money and the time for manicures and pedicures. You might also have noticed that she flossed after her last meal. She cared about how she looked and what other people thought about the way she looked. We might conclude she was between relationships, not unexpected, given her age and her attractiveness. She used a pumice stone to control the callus on her feet. I would suggest she has some degree of back trouble, particularly if she often wore high heels, and I think she did, given the malformation of the toes and the slight hyper development of the gastrocnemius."

The corporal looked puzzled.

"The calf muscles are bigger than they are supposed to be," Sylvie explained.

Roland continued. "She is obviously nulliparous." This time he looked at Schumann and grinned.

From the look on her face, the university graduate was stumped. "I don't know that one."

"Good of you to say so. That admission is your first step to becoming a competent detective. She has never given birth."

Sylvie was incredulous. "How could you possible know that, given the mutilated state of the vagina? He slit her open all the way to the bellybutton."

Roland knew she was thinking about the hymen, but its absence would not necessarily indicate a birth. "The aureoles of the breasts indicate she has not carried a pregnancy to full term. They remain relatively small and round and lightly colored. However, this too is not an infallible sign, but all the evidence together suggests she has never given birth."

Sylvie flushed. She thought of her own nipples and aureoles and she could tell Rieger knew exactly what she was thinking. She glared at him, but he merely smiled. The young corporal, fortunately, had no idea what was going on between them. The Hauptmeister looked thirsty, excused himself and walked back to the stumps and an unopened beer, which he shared with the Forstmeister as he sat, nearly falling from the stump as it rocked back and forth beneath his considerable weight. The Forstmeister was good enough to steady him with a hand on the shoulder, a professional courtesy.

"No stretch marks on the breasts to indicate lactation or nursing. No stretch marks or scars on the belly to indicate birth by caesarian section. By the way, how old do you think she is, Lieutenant?" Rieger asked.

"Thirty-five or forty."

He laughed. She was being deliberately catty. "Twenty-three or four at the most."

"How can you tell that, sir?" the corporal asked. "I mean she looks young and everything but how can you really tell?"

"The teeth. The general wear-and-tear and the fact that she just got her last set of molars." He gently separated her legs. The entire vaginal area was a bloody mess. "The pathologist will earn his money today."

"No semen again, sir?" the corporal suggested, interested in maintaining his advantage.

"Most likely. No bruising of the inside of the thighs to suggest forced sex..."

"Which is not to say he didn't sexually violate the corpse after death while wearing a condom?"

"Point taken, Lieutenant."

She beamed at the corporal like a young girl who has just been invited to move to the front of the line.

"But I don't think this is a case of necrophilia. Nor do I believe it is a sex crime. Do you need to see anything else?" he asked abruptly. He intended the question for Sylvie but both nodded no. "If not, I am finished—excuse me, we are finished here. Sylvie, if you would be so kind as to finish your notes and transcribe your recording of our investigation and see that I get copies on my computer tomorrow. Corporal, please see to it that the body is not disturbed and is treated appropriately and with respect when the coroner arrives. She deserves at least that much from the State." He rose and brushed the dirt from his creaking knees, grown stiff from the rigor of bending, and put the penlight back into the inside breast pocket of his forest green coat. Sylvie frowned at the loss of her penlight but did not mention it.

"Sir, if I may just say that I was honored that you let me participate...."

"Thank you, Corporal Schmidt, and if I may offer you just a bit of advice."

"Of course, sir, anything."

"Get in the Hauptmeister's back pocket and stay there."

The corporal grinned to his ears. "They already say we're connected at the hip, Herr Hauptkommissar."

They walked back to the stumps by the sawhorses where the forest warden and Hauptmeister Doppelmayr waited.

"Rolli, I see you're finished with the dirty work. I hope my cub hasn't been too much of a pest."

"Not at all. He's got some potential. If only we could find him a decent partner to develop his raw talent." He put his arm around his old mentor. "But you're right about this being a filthy job and my throat is parched. The Lieutenant needs to finish her notes and write her field report, so you and I will let the good Waldmeister lead us to our favorite Gaststube in Mooshütte and we three will drink to old times. First round is on you. Sylvie, Corporal Schmidt will be happy to drive you back to Headquarters in his car after the coroner has done his work."

There was no disagreement.

CORPORAL SCHMIDT DROVE Kommissar Schumann to the Landesamt of the Kriminalpolizei, the state office of the criminal police in Kaufbeuren. They chatted about the case as he negotiated the twisting turns through Marktoberdorf and then on to Kaufbeuren, once a medieval center of trade and commerce. He pulled the green and white BMW to a stop directly in front of the steps leading up to the Headquarters building. He was nervous during the ride and made a deliberate attempt to keep their talk pleasant but professional. He knew she noticed his discomfort but as they bid each other goodbye, he went through the motions of asking for her telephone number. He was polite enough and certainly not unattractive, so she gave him the number out of courtesy, certain that he would not call despite the fact that he was obviously attracted to her. By now, she was used to it and did not take it personally. No SCHUPO officer in the state of Bavaria would dare date the new partner of Hauptkommissar Roland Rieger.

She took the marble stairs up to the second floor, scuffing her black leather pumps into the highly polished finish of the stone, and let herself in to Roland's office, a suite of two connecting rooms. Her desk, with phone, computer, and file cabinets, occupied the first room. A framed door with smoked glass occupied the second room and served as the office of the Hauptkommissar. Roland had given her complete access to and use of the interior office, and her own key to the door. At first, honored by his show of generosity, she soon realized why he had made the offer. She was barely able to make a working space for herself atop a desk buried under manila files, some closed cases, some pending, official forms, and unread inter-office memos. In the three months they worked together, she had seen him in the office exactly twice. He occasionally came into the Headquarters building, but only to consult with other officers working on cases. He did not attend staff meetings and he most certainly did not answer email. She preferred working at his desk for the additional privacy it afforded her, the exterior office too close to the hall and leering eyes. The interior office also contained the fax and printer, which she loaded with paper before turning on the computer. The screen showed 138 unread messages for his account, for which she had the password. As she rewound the cassette in her micro-recorder and opened a new word processing file on the computer, she thought about the two different routes that had brought them together in the KRIPO office.

Rieger was definitely old-school, but only in the sense that he had come up through the ranks. There was nothing old-school about his investigative methods or his abilities to solve difficult cases, the only sort the captain ever assigned him. As a young man, he had done his service in the elite Border Patrol Police, the Grenzschutzpolizei, and from there entered the ranks of the Schutzpolizei as a Patrol officer. After three years of training and rapid advancement, he was selected for advanced training as a detective in the criminal police, Kriminalpolizei. In those days, promotion to Kommissar, the lowest rank in the criminal division, required four weeks of exams, twenty written and one oral. Successful

27

completion led to one year of training for the final exam. Passing the exam qualified him for university work where he received three more years of study in criminal investigations. Half the year was spent at school and the other half on duty.

My god, she thought to herself, no wonder these guys act the way they do. No wonder they resent the new system. Now there was a social and political push in West Germany to bring more women into all branches of the service and the system was reworked to accommodate the new social directives. She was one of the first to come up the new way. She had gone to college after receiving her Abitur, a degree equivalent to an Associate Arts degree from an American junior college. This qualified her for a new three-year program at university where she studied specifically to qualify for acceptance in the Criminal Investigation Department. After her years of intensive study, she graduated as a Lieutenant Detective and was assigned to Group One of the Criminal Police.

Group One detectives were trained to investigate violent crimes and crimes of high danger. Within Group One, she had been assigned to Office KK11, which handled investigations in cases of death. This office worked closely with KK12, which handled sex crimes and missing persons. Because of staffing reductions, Hauptkommissar Rieger worked cases in both offices. After her graduation from the Polizeifortbildungsinstitut, the Institute for special advanced training for detectives investigating violent crimes, and despite the fact that she had graduated first in her class, she was partnered with Rieger, a name already familiar to her from the Institute. Hauptkommissar Roland Rieger had a reputation as a rogue detective, one unwilling to play by the bureaucratic rules that often hamstrung an investigation. He also had problems with authority that were legend among the Institute's teachers. Supposedly, after work one evening, he punched out a judge—reviled among the force—that had released a known sex offender on a technicality and this action resulted in a temporary demotion in rank.

She understood now that Kriminalpolizierat Ludwig Steinmetz had teamed her with Rieger as a means of punishing him. Steimetz, she learned first-hand, was a leering, offensive sexist who detested the addition of female detectives to the force. She refused to submit to the man and this was her punishment. It was a petty and vindictive act and she hated men and their stupid political games, she thought to herself. She just wanted to do her job and bust bad guys, and avoid all the testosterone-fueled power plays. She wondered to herself if, after all, perhaps she had gotten lucky with her assignment. For reasons she could not yet fathom, Rieger seemed highly respected by officers in the division who were not outright allies of Steinmetz.

Finished with her transcription of the recording, she saved the file, printed three copies, shut down the computer and after a last glance around the chaos of the office, which she damn well was not going to clean up, she walked home for dinner. She ate alone as she studied the transcripts. The young SCHUPO officer, to whom she had given her telephone number, as expected, did not call.

Chapter Three: The ADAMAS File

LIEUTENANT GENERAL MARKUS Johannes Wolf sat in the garden of his mistress's house on the outskirts of Potsdam. The specially built high walls and cleverly designed shrubbery concealed the backyard from prying eyes on the ground. The gate at the back wall opened onto the local forest, where he enjoyed taking walks in the evening after supper. Recumbent on his chaise longue Wolf, whose family had long practiced nudism for its myriad health benefits, was naked under his dressing gown, taking the morning sun. Gretel, his mistress of the last two years, lay on the grass completely naked atop a beach towel. Her skin glistened from the sun and baby oil and he could smell her as the gentle breeze followed the sun across the tops of the eastern wall. For once, the weather was cooperating as the summer months appeared on the calendar. A breath of wind peaked the nipples atop her still perfect breasts. She propped herself up on a bent elbow, shielded her eyes from the sun, and watched him watch her.

Without a word between them, she picked up the bottle of oil and sat next to him on a low stool at his hip. She knew he was having problems with his back again, a chronic condition he managed with exercise and massage. She pulled his robe open further, drizzled the oil into her palm, and stroked him until he was erect. She waited for him to relax the incline of the chaise longue, prop the pillow behind his head so he could watch her, and then she bent over and took him into her mouth. The sharp intake of breath that was not quite a gasp pleased her. She worked him with diligence and skill, alternating her hand with her mouth, shifting the position of her body so that he could cup her breasts and gently pull her nipples, which she loved. The attention made her wet and she opened her legs for his hand and his middle finger. Now he was no longer watching her and she felt the head of his penis swell just before he came in her mouth. She used her hand to milk the semen from the length of the penis, careful not to over-stimulate him. Only after his belly fell and his breathing relaxed did she release him from her mouth. He paid her the courtesy of keeping his eyes closed as she pulled a cloth napkin from the table next to them and quickly and quietly spit the fluid into the unfolded white square. "Wait here, darling," she told him, jumped up and ran through the open French doors of the bedroom and into the bathroom. She came back with a white bath towel and a matching moistened washrag, which she used to clean the oil from his glistening penis, once again grown small and still. He smiled at her as she cleaned him. "There," she said with a sense of satisfaction. "Nice and clean again. You won't have to take another shower before you leave for work."

He shook his head in disbelief. "Gretchen, you are a true asset of the State. On behalf of the Party, the Committee, and our ever present Soviet advisors lurking in the bushes behind the wall, I thank you."

She laughed good-naturedly at their private joke. It was not improbable to think that one of the ubiquitous agents, with their darkly accented and grammatically imperfect grammar, might indeed be crouched on the other side of the garden wall. Warts on the hands of the service, Wolf often remarked to her. Nevertheless, she knew all too well that one disparaging word from Wolf, second in command of East Germany's secret police, the Stasi, and she would never be seen again, ever. Such was the power of this man in East Germany. The realization chilled her more than the morning breeze caressing her breasts. "I'll leave you to write now." He held her hand, letting it slip through his as she walked away. He would show his appreciation later in the evening, when he returned home from headquarters in East Berlin. He would do the cooking.

He allowed himself the luxury of reminiscing a bit about the early years, before he refocused on the problem at hand. Markus Johannes Wolf steepled his fingers, closed his eyes for a moment, and rehearsed a history of the Stasi he was preparing for his future memoirs. He took his favorite pen, purchased from the west, a lined yellow notepad, and began to write.

"I was born in Hechingen in southwestern Germany in 1923, in the state now known as Baden-Württemberg. My father, considered a free spirit, was a doctor, a playwright, and a noted intellectual. When the Nazis took power in Germany, our German-Jewish family fled to Moscow in 1934. After education at the Communist International School, the Comintern at Kushnarenkovo—an elite school for students from countries previously occupied by the Nazis—I returned to Berlin in 1945. Shortly after the war ended, the Soviet Occupation Zone was emplaced and German personnel such as I were repatriated to help build the new communist state that would become the German Democratic Republic, the DDR. With the help of Soviet advisors, a People's Police force was empowered to protect the citizens and the property of the newly emerging Soviet satellite. In 1946, two old guard communists, Bruno Heidt and Franz Dahlem put together East Germany's first espionage service under the auspices of the People's Police. Called the Fifth

Department of the People's Police (K-5), the agency was charged with internal security and suppression of dissidents."

Wolf made a mental note to himself. This previous fact would re-emerge in the development of his historical narrative. He remembered that K-5 lasted about four years and served as the foundational building blocks for what would later be termed the Stasi.

"October 7, 1947, (who could forget that date?), the DDR became a sovereign state. The fledgling government, with the advice and consent of the Soviets, created a Ministry of the Interior (MDI). In February of 1950, K-5 became the Ministerium für Staatssicherheit, the Ministry for State Security, subsequently called the Stasi. Most of the officers of the new MfS were former officials of the K-5. At its head were Minister Wilhelm Zaisser and Deputy Minister Erich Mielke, who would later become my boss."

Wolf paused for a moment and sipped from a cold bottle of sparkling water. The morning sun and the attentions of his mistress had left him parched. Thinking about Mielke was distasteful. The man had never liked him and as a counter-intelligence officer, saw himself as Wolf's rival. As a result, the two never got along. But he was getting ahead of himself. Now the story was becoming a bit more complicated, and he forced himself to refocus his thinking as he simplified the narrative.

"I became a spy in 1951. The political party in control of the DDR, known as the Socialist Union Party of Germany is, in fact, a politically expedient union of two other parties. It controls the DDR."

Here Wolf wrote a note in the margins. He translated Sozialistische Einheitspartei Deutschlands (SED) into its English equivalent: the Socialist Union Party of Germany, anticipating an international readership. He returned to his narrative.

"The Party previously had sent me to the Comintern school, used me for propaganda services in radio stations in Moscow and Berlin, and had sent me to Moscow as a diplomat, where I first met Stalin. Now they needed me for intelligence work and I was honored to be called. In 1951, SED member Anton Ackermann, whose real name was Eugen Hanisch, was the East German foreign secretary. He had been tasked with creating a foreign political intelligence service, the Aussenpolitischer Nachrichtendienst, or APN, and Ackermann assigned me to it in his new role as its first minister. The cover name given our service was the Hauptverwaltung für Wirtschafts-Wissenschaftliche Forschung, which the west knew as the Main Directorate for Economic Scientific Research, or the IWF. Because the IWF reported directly to the SED central party leadership and, of course, to our Soviet advisors, it worked independently of the MfS. Its purpose was espionage and intelligence gathering with information reported directly to the Soviets and the SED."

The Lieutenant General fondly remembered his early days there working for six months as deputy chief of analysis before an important career opportunity presented itself. Wolf took up his pen again.

"In December of 1952, East German leader Walter Ulbricht informed me that my boss, Anton Ackermann, who had led the foreign intelligence service from its beginnings, was resigning for health reasons, which I found curious, knowing that Ackermann's health was fine. The true story is that Ackermann, head of the APN/IWF, was fired for not doing his duty and alerting the Soviets of impending dissension in East Germany. Without asking me, Ulbricht appointed me to take Ackermann's place. I was not yet thirty years old. Accordingly, I was made Head of Department for the APN/IWF, answering only to Ulbricht, who later ceded control to Wilhelm Zaisser.

"And then, around Easter 1953, things began to go very wrong. That year saw the near destruction of my country, my service department, and my career. That year saw the defection of an agent to the west, revealing for the first time the existence of the IWF and its true mission. Many of my agents were compromised and subsequently arrested. In June of the same year, (he sighed heavily as he remembered those times) the labor party of the DDR started a revolt that spread throughout the country, overwhelming the police. Much to their chagrin, DDR leadership was forced to call in Soviet troops to suppress the uprising. Without the assistance of Moscow, I am now firmly convinced that my country would have fallen, disbanded, and reunited with West Germany."

Wolf sweated a bit as he recalled these dire events and he took another drink of the sparkling water next to the lounge chair. Those had been difficult days indeed.

"Then came the cataclysmic organizational fallout from the political turmoil. Zaisser, who was head of the Ministry for State Security, the MfS, was purged for failing to anticipate and control the labor unrest that tore our country apart in 1953. He also made the mistake of trying to depose SED General Secretary Walter Ulbricht, who had him removed as he ruthlessly consolidated his power in the DDR. Ernst Wollweber was appointed to take his place but suffered the ignominy of seeing his bureau demoted from ministry status to a secretariat. Rebadged as the Secretariat for State Security, it was placed under the control of the Ministry of the Interior. Because of its poor performance and the defection of Gotthold Kraus from the APN/IWF in 1953, I reorganized my department and instituted new procedures to assure that this could not happen again. The APN was then transferred under the control of the SfS, but was permitted to operate independently of them. In 1955, things began to improve. An internal informant network was established; the Secretariat for State Security regained some measure of trust with the SED and its party leaders, earning an upgrade to Ministry status again. As a further show of confidence in our hard work, the SfS was once again entitled to call itself the Ministry for State Security (MfS). And in 1956, I was promoted to Head of Main Department X5 within the APN, which subsequently was renamed the Hauptverwaltung Aufklärung (HVA) or the Main Intelligence Directorate."

He chuckled to himself. He wondered if his American counterparts in the CIA had suffered through as many reorganizations, renamings, and retaskings of its intelligence and counter-intelligence departments.

"In 1959, the HVA merged with MfS, the two units collectively known as the Stasi thereafter. Former Deputy Minister Erich Mielke became Minister of the MfS after Wollweber, like his predecessor Zaisser, was fired for opposing SED party members. Now Head of the HVA, and promoted to Lieutenant General, I controlled all internal security, secret police, and foreign intelligence operations."

Wolf was aware of his growing reputation as a spymaster, but as a matter of humility, did not allude to it in his narrative. He had been particularly effective in setting up intelligence gathering operations against West Germany and her NATO allies. Some of his successes were already legendary within the intelligence communities and his failures were few, although noteworthy.

"The second major defection from the MfS/HVA in 1959 resulted in the subsequent loss of many of my prized deep cover assets in the west. To this day, the loss of the agent who operated under the code name Baroness in the 1960s still disturbs me. It has taken years to undo the damage wrought by that particular failure."

He made a note to himself that one day someone would write the history of this particularly galling episode, but it would not be him. He still did not understand the endgame of an espionage match he had designed, initiated, and to the very end, thought he had won for himself and East Germany. Oh well, he mused, like his favorite football team Dynamo, you can't win all your games. Ultimately, you will be judged on your overall record.

He paused and put the pen and notebook down. Enough of writing history; the present demanded his immediate attention. The time was right for a new intelligence coup; one he hoped would surpass his previous success of introducing agents deep within the governmental hierarchy of West Germany. This would be his magnum opus and solidify his reputation as the greatest spymaster of all the intelligence and espionage services in the world.

This is what he knew: embargo against his country by the western Allies was proving especially effective. East Germany had managed to stay abreast of scientific and technological advances only because of his highly successful infiltration of agents into West Germany. His "Romeo" agents and their female equivalents were procuring enough classified western documents to keep the analysts in his technical division working full-time and crying for more personnel. No, that was a good problem. For an additional moment more, he remembered the Baroness with fondness. She had been a favorite and one of his most productive field agents until the Bundesnachrichtendienst, his intelligence counterpart in West Germany, had taken control of her without her knowledge. Once her secret had been discovered, the BND and CIA working in concert had fed her technical misinformation that seriously undermined efforts to advance East Germany's fledgling nuclear program. That fiasco had almost cost Wolf his career and his head. Now that they were finally on track again and certain of their information streaming in from the west, the problem of hard currency once again reared its ugly red head.

East Germany could not buy the diamonds it needed so desperately for its secret defense programs. The damned Soviets were largely to blame. Not only did they bleed the DDR of practically every mark of hard currency they produced, they also hoarded every diamond they could get their hands on for their own industrial and military uses. They simply were not able to satisfy the voracious appetite for diamonds consumed by their profligate military-industrial complex. It was time to take control of the matter. He could not count on the Soviets for help. He knew that it was Chairman Walter Ulbricht's dream to make East Germany a viable nuclear power independent of the Soviets, and diamonds were an essential component of the strategic missiles being designed to carry the warheads. The problem had been dumped in his lap, in no uncertain terms, and he had opened a file to support the top secret nuclear development program, code-named MIJOLNIR, the hammer of Thor. Until they had the requisite number of diamonds, the scientists and engineers working on the MIJOLNIR Project could not proceed. It was time, he decided, for East Germany to enter the diamond trade.

At precisely 9:45 in the morning, Markus Wolf's car, a specially prepared black Mercedes-Benz, arrived at the front door of the country house held in his mistress's name. Wolf, already in the foyer, briefcase in hand, kissed Gretel goodbye. She tasted of mint toothpaste. She smoothed the handsome greatcoat across the slope of both shoulders, squared the knot of his tie, and then stepped back to admire the drape of the cashmere coat. She could tell his mind was already occupied with some problem of State, which he never discussed with her, and so she hurried him out the door to his waiting car. She looked forward to stealing back another hour or two of sleep from her bed. Wolf was an indefatigable and insistent lover and as much as she appreciated the attention, the visits from the Lieutenant General left her fatigued in a most pleasant way.

The Head of HVA greeted his driver with a nod. The man held the door open but did not salute. It was enough for the neighbors to wonder about the limousine; they did not need to speculate about the rank or position of the man in back. It was enough that they thought him a rich businessman. Wolf exchanged pleasantries and once settled on the polished black leather of the back seat, asked about the man's wife and their two-year-old daughter, who he knew by name. Little Annika had kept both parents on sleepless watch for the last three nights with a howling ear infection. He could see the effects in the young officer's sleep-bagged eyes but his driving was precise and smooth enough to permit a sip or two from his coffee cup as they headed for East Berlin. In the mobile sanctuary of the bomb and bullet-proofed limousine driven by the young Special Forces Kapitän trained in tactics for high-speed evasion and anti-terrorist combat, Wolf was able to do some of his most productive, uninterrupted thinking. Once out of Potsdam, where the German Democratic Republic housed its training facilities for Stasi officers, the traffic thinned. This Wednesday he was more pensive than usual. Heavy lies the head that wears the crown, he thought. Such are the vagaries of responsibility. He wondered if he could ever trade the trappings of the job—the luxuries afforded the elite class within the system, the cars, clothes, housing, and perhaps most importantly, the status—and regress to the old days, when things were infinitely less complicated. He decided such thinking was counter-productive to the needs of the State.

THE ADAMANTINE HEART

The car arrived at Stasi headquarters in East Berlin. He stepped out onto the sidewalk fronting Klosterstrasse and accepted the salute from his driver. As he walked away toward the building housing the offices of State Security, he suddenly stopped and turned back, as if he had remembered something. "I will not need the car further today, Kapitän. You are relieved of duty until tomorrow. Go home and take care of your child."

"I could certainly use the rest, sir, but I am fully prepared to do my duty."

"Of course you are. But you have your orders." He smiled so the orders would be taken as intended, and then hurried up the marble stairs of his agency's building. His legs were none too fresh after last night's romp with Gretchen. He was pleased with what he had done—in bed and on behalf of the young soldier. It was a simple thing, really, pleasing a woman and giving a man a little extra time to be with his sickly daughter. For these reasons and others, he was admired and revered by his subordinates and viewed with suspicion by his superiors.

Out of his coat, which was too heavy for the warming day and into his chair, the first call of the morning was to Albrecht Gottschalk, head of KoKo, the Division of Commercial Coordination, and State Secretary for the Foreign Trade Ministry. Wolf considered Gottschalk to be the German Democratic Republic's chief finance wizard, responsible only to party leader Erich Honecker, who had taken over from Walter Ulbricht after he resigned for health reasons in 1971. So much bad health in our political system, Wolf thought to himself, as he waited for the call to be routed through. He checked the score of his favorite football team, Dynamo. The sports section of the newspaper lay atop his desk, neatly folded to the appropriate page, made ready for him by his secretary. He expected, appreciated, and rewarded such kindly efficiencies, which

40

made his job all the more tolerable. On the intercom, his secretary announced that the call had connected and he put the phone to his ear as Gottschalk grumbled his name into the receiver.

Wolf laughed. "I thought you were at the office, Colonel, not at home."

"If you must know, I'm taking this call in my bed. Why must you call so damnably early?"

Wolf looked at his Swiss-made wristwatch, a benefit of the travel he was required to do outside the country.

"It's almost noon, Albrecht. Your lunch should be ready soon."

After the small talk, Wolf could tell that the head of Commercial Coordination was lucid enough to conduct business. Gottschalk, in addition to being the finance wizard of the DDR, also held an appointment in the elite OIBE, and was designated as an officer in special operations assigned to the Stasi. This was their connection and their grounds for working together on numerous past occasions. Besides, Gottschalk was one of the very few bureaucrats Wolf respected. Between the two, they were responsible for most of the hard currency available to the DDR. It was not uncommon for one to help the other.

"Thanks for the wake-up call, Mischa. But you know what a travail it is attending all those diplomatic parties...."

Wolf was fully aware of Gottschalk's sacrifices for the homeland and he let him ramble on a bit.

"Anyway, how can I help you?"

"I need a man."

"What kind of man?"

"Should be around thirty, well-educated, must speak excellent English and French. I would like a man who has served abroad and has recently returned. That should whet his appetite for travel outside the country again."

Gottschalk chuckled into the phone. They both understood the personal privations required to further the solidarity of the State.

"Dark features are required and he should be able to pass for Jewish, although medical services can help us there. Being reasonably attractive, a definite plus."

"What in the world are you planning?" Gottschalk wondered aloud.

"Tell you in a minute. Our man should be a quick learner and absolutely loyal to our cause." He emphasized the word "our" for the colonel. 'Loyal to our cause' was a private code phrase between the two suggesting that the work would require a man who could be trusted to remain loyal to his superiors even if the mission required him to suborn the philosophical orientation of the State. "A man in the OIBE would be ideal." He heard Gottschalk shift the receiver to the other ear, leaving his right hand free to write a message.

"I think I have the man for you. About twenty-eight, a captain in the OIBE, an excellent head on his shoulders. If I remember correctly..."
Wolf heard the snap of fingers and knew Gottschalk had an aide with him.

"If I remember correctly, yes, his mother is half-Armenian. He just returned from a tour of the United States with the Women's Olympic swimming team. He is without doubt one of my best men, Mischa. What's he worth to you?" Business, after all, even between cooperating agencies and friends, was still business. Wolf had expected as much.

"Half," he said into the phone.

"Half of what?"

"Half of all the currency we make."

"What in the world are you getting into, Mischa?"

42

"Diamonds. We are going into the diamond business." He waited for the laughter of respect to end and then filled him in. They finished the conversation by asking about each other's wives, as a professional courtesy to the wives, and then confirmed the dates of their next hunting trip together on the taiga of Siberia. Breshnev and head of the KGB, Andropov, would also be there. Colonel Albrecht Gottschalk, head of KoKo, promised Lieutenant General Markus Johannes Wolf, head of the HVA, that he would have his man within the week, replaced the receiver and accepted the breakfast tray from his waiting aide.

Wolf looked once more at the newspaper on his desk. Dynamo's win was indeed a good omen.

THE CAPTAIN STOOD before him at full and correct military attention. He had shaved so closely his cheeks gleamed. Across the desk, Wolf could smell the man's aftershave, distinctively French with a citrus note not at all offensive to his nose. Few of his officers had the means or the knowledge to use such a scent correctly. He closed the dossier on his desk. The man before him confirmed the record. He combed his black hair straight back from his forehead and wore it slightly longer than regulations allowed. His brown eyes might have been warm during his youth but there was now a dark edge at the rim of the iris, an element of carefully controlled cruelty, perhaps. Wolf did not doubt that this one could kill on order. The captain was not quite as tall as Wolf, but thicker through the chest. He was not an unattractive fellow, Wolf conceded, but the uniform drew attention from the man's distinctive nose. It was slightly larger than it needed to be for the proportions of his face, and it curved from brow to tip, the legacy of his mother's Armenian heritage. In profile, the nose appeared more prominent than when viewed head-on, a curious trick of the eye. Given the man's dark complexion augmented by a good tan, Wolf had no doubt the man could pass for a Jew.

He put the captain at ease and invited him to sit. He rang for his aide who brought sandwiches and coffee. "What I am about to tell you Captain Hain, is top secret. Only two people in the Republic are aware of its existence: Gottschalk and I. I am the architect of the plan, which we will call the ADAMAS File, after the Greek word for diamond. You, sir, are going to infiltrate the diamond cartel and become the principle diamond merchant for KoKo and the Stasi. I have developed a dummy corporation for you to lead and will provide you with all the requisite paper work. In other words, we will build your history for you, giving you entrée into the world of the diamond industry."

The captain swallowed his last bite of the dainty little fish and cucumber sandwiches. "A challenging assignment, sir, but to be honest, I know nothing of diamonds and very little of the diamond world." He took the linen napkin from his legs, refolded it and placed it on the tray. There were also individually wrapped Belgian chocolates in a crystal dish, but he waited for the Direktor of the Stasi to offer him one.

"An indulgence which I allow myself at this age." Wolf patted his flat stomach for emphasis and offered the dish to Hain.

As he unwrapped the delicacy, the captain said, "I have seen special forces soldiers less fit than the Herr Lieutenant General." He rolled the gold foil between his thumb and index finger and placed the little ball on the tray next to the chocolates.

Wolf nodded. It was true. His daily regimen of swimming and exercise and visits to Gretel kept him exceptionally fit. "I need time to establish your bona-fides and set up the operation. In the meantime, I must send you back to Moscow for advanced training, but not at the KGB school. I'm sending you to my dacha outside Moscow instead."

"Very kind of you, sir."

"Don't be impertinent. Your training officer is Dr. Kristal Petrova. She holds a doctorate in the study of precious gems. She happens to be an asset of ours. You must do nothing to compromise her, is that understood?"

"Understood, sir."

"Moreover, she is your superior officer."

"How so, Herr Direktor?"

"She also happens to be a colonel in the KGB, Ninth Directorate, if memory serves."

The captain's expression did not change but Wolf detected the twitch of a jaw muscle. "As of today, you are temporarily promoted to the rank of major. If you successfully complete your training, and I will be receiving weekly reports from your education officer, you will return to Berlin with the full rank of major. Your Aeroflot flight for Moscow leaves in two hours."

As newly promoted Major Rudiger Hain stood and saluted, Wolf permitted himself a vestigial smile, born just at the corners of his mouth. To limit knowledge of his plan, Wolf had taken extraordinary measures. He knew that the more people his young agent contacted during the essential training phase, the greater the risk of speculation at the Institute in Moscow. These were, after all, highly intelligent men and women, whose job was to do exactly that sort of speculation and then develop scenarios of explanation. This he wanted to avoid at all costs. Therefore, he made the sort of decision for which he was famous. He assigned his new major not to the KGB institute for espionage training in tradecraft, but posted him to his personal dacha at Kushnarenkovo, near Ufa, on the banks of the Belaya river. This allowed Markus Wolf to control a variety of factors. Contact with others would be limited. The

KGB doctor and the Stasi major would be together twenty-four hours a day, thus ensuring high-intensity immersion in the subject, thereby decreasing the time needed for mastery. More importantly, it would focus the idle gossip and speculation exactly along the lines Wolf intended.

Wolf opened the dossier once more and had another look at Kristal Petrova, Ph. D. Judging by the attractiveness of the pretty woman in the photograph, he expected that the gossip would be limited to romantic issues, if he were any judge of Russian character. The mysterious couple most certainly was highly placed or they would not have access to a dacha in the woods, a luxury usually reserved only for those who had achieved a certain rank and membership within the party. Their limited interaction with others in the community could mean only one thing: theirs was a private and, most likely, an illicit affair. This was a romantic assignation between two very important and highly placed party apparatchiks very much in love, and that they wanted and needed their privacy was understandable to all. Anything less might prove dangerous for those who intruded or interfered. Smart people looked the other way and held their tongues; others disappeared in the middle of the night. Wolf had no doubt that his scheme would work.

Chapter Four: The Semiotician

WILL SHERIDAN WAS first made aware of the power of semiotic analysis in a graduate class at Washington State University that had nothing whatsoever to do with semiosis, the analysis and interpretation of signs and symbols. The class, in fact, pushed him farther from the subject matter before them, the study of iconography, and forced him to consider other more immediate, mundane interests for the sake of his sanity. He diverted his attention from the professor, a sweating toad of a man whose rigid, authoritarian manner—a substitute for his inability to teach—had reduced most of the female graduate students to tears at one time or another during the semester. This was his way of separating the wheat from the chaff, and a class of eighteen, by mid-semester had been badgered and reduced to half its original size. Professor Frosch also practiced the affectation of snorting snuff—the poor man's cocaine—into each nostril before every class. He pulled a handkerchief from the sleeve of his houndstooth coat and blew his nose to clear out the leaking pipe to his brain. He kept the snuff In a small enameled box. He opened the hinged lid, pinched the scented cut tobacco between thumb and index finger, and snorted the load into first the left nostril, repeated, then the right. His eyes watered, he sneezed into the handkerchief, thankfully, and brushed the remnants of the tobacco off the seminar table back into the case. The nicotine of the shredded black leaves shot into his brain as if it had been delivered there by a hypodermic syringe. He shivered, he swallowed the honey sweet taste of the weed, his eyes cleared, and then he addressed the class.

There she sat: the object of the budding semiotician's distorted attention. Will centered both eyes on her but kept one ear tipped to the croaking of the Toad on the off chance that he might accidentally offer information or insight not previously covered in their iconography textbook. So he practiced his powers of observation and read her like a mystery novel. She was both a sign and a symbol for something, he guessed, and he took it as his mission to discover the meaning of her. Everything she did was of a purpose; therefore, motivated and meaningful. He would discover the text of the young woman; decipher the code of her being, the sense of her existence. He would resolve the ambiguity of her presence and in so doing, achieve understanding without speaking one word to her. That was the challenge, knowing her in the absence of the confusion wrought by language. Therein lay the primary reason for the breakdown in communication between men and women, he reasoned. The babble of language, the most intricate semiotic system created by human beings, so complex and convoluted in its potential for alternative interpretations, had driven an artificial wedge between the sexes. He chose, therefore, not to allow language to complicate his analysis. He would center his analysis on the meaning of her actions.

The meaning is in the action, he thought. It's what she does that's important, not what she says. The frog professor continued to stupefy the other students, thereby making for him Will's point about the confusion wrought by language. He watched the other graduate students slavishly taking notes as if knowledge were somehow contained in the act of transcription. To appear scholarly, and not to invoke the wrath of the learned Toad, who was forced to sweat through the exertion of simply speaking, Will feigned taking notes dutifully like the other future amphibians surrounding him at the lily pad of the seminar table.

He recorded his observations of her. Observe and describe first, he reminded himself. Pre-mature theorizing is dangerous. Empirical observation is the key. Every detail is meaningful and the part is related to the whole. The challenge comes when the whole is greater than the sum of the parts. This is what made understanding another human being so difficult. One could learn the cardiovascular system, the neuromuscular system, the endocrine system, the skeletal system; in fact, one could study every system in the human system and still not understand why the female system across from him wore the same brown sweater to class almost every day. She was a first-year, first-semester master's student, as was he. She had a research assistantship, as did he. Admitted to an elite program with the tuition waiver that came with it. Seemed very smart and probably graduated at the head of her high school class and then with honors from the small private university where she excelled. A reader then, as an English major in a master's program, someone who probably spent more time with books than with people. But why? Ah ha. Too smart for most boys and unwilling to do the things most girls practiced to be popular. Shy then, because of inexperience and not a little frustrated by it. Channeled those energies into her studies and this made the cycle vicious. He grunted a bit, satisfied with his preliminary hypothesis. The reptilian professor showed his tongue as he stumbled into his next enervating tangent, mistaking Will's grunt as a sign of comprehension of a particularly relevant and cogent point. Will wondered exactly how the professor, greasy hair parted to show the middle of his white scalp, would interpret an inadvertent fart.

She was prettiest in the eyes and mouth. Her lips were red without lipstick. Her hair was the lightest tawny brown and fine, as if she had never lost her baby hair. She was medium height, too short for him really, if they were to dance dirty and close, and she was slim. Her clothes were new. They had been bought the summer before leaving for the big university, but she generally wore conservative colors and styles. Sweaters and shirts, usually some shade of tan or khaki. It couldn't be that her favorite color was brown, could it, to match her hair and her eyes? Probably a boy in high school had paid her some silly compliment that brown accentuated the color of her eyes and she had never forgotten it. He shook his head at the precise moment when the professor posed a rhetorical question he himself believed could only be answered in the negative, noted with satisfaction that at least one of the dimwits out there had enough on the ball to reach the same conclusion. He turned his back to the board and began to write in his nearly indecipherable scribble. Will heard the audible sigh of students relaxing and pushing back in their chairs to get comfortable. Some even put their pens down and flexed the rigor from their fingers, hoping the crease forced into the tip of the index finger would not be permanent or disfiguring. Others chewed the butt-end, still nervous, and thirsty others sipped instead from coffee mugs or sodas gone flat like their enthusiasm.

He knew this much: she smiled when he greeted her, more from the eyes than the lips, but small talk evidently made her uncomfortable. And it was an incontrovertible fact, at this point in the semester, with so many places now open at the long seminar table, she sat every Monday, Wednesday, and Friday directly across from him. And she never missed class. At some primal, unconscious level then, she was interested in him. This hypothesis demanded testing. On Wednesday, he sat one seat to the left of his normal position at the table. She sat directly opposite. Friday, he returned to his original seat, and as expected, she matched his move. There is a synchronicity here, he thought. She follows my lead like a dancer. She dances with me in her unconscious sense of self. But he needed to know how powerful the attraction was. Did she, in fact, dance with him in her dreams just before she fell asleep? He needed further substantiation before he would act. A week later it came.

She was late. The professor in her previous class had kept them over. She usually checked her mail in the foyer where the graduate student and faculty mailboxes, with their brass-faced tiny windows and black numbers, lined up against the wall as in a post office. She fumbled with the mass of keys, shook the correct one out of the jumble, opened the square long box stuffed with the blizzard of paper produced by administrations, keyed the box closed, and without sorting through the pile, hurried into the small seminar room five minutes late. With a sense of relief, she noticed that she had arrived ahead of the professor, who was just now switching off his computer in his office upstairs. She knew she had five minutes to compose herself as he hopped down the stairs to the seminar room. Will was already there, already writing something.

Her arms were full of books from her English Romanticism class, the mail, the iconography text, notebooks, purse and keys, so she dumped the load on the table. The pile spilled in different directions and she blew her bangs off her forehead in frustration. What a mess. Will smiled but did not speak. He noticed with interest that most of her stuff had encroached onto his side of the table. Her jumble of keys almost touched the back of his writing hand.

Significant action, he thought. He studied her like a professional black-jack player sizing up the dealer. What would her actions tell him next? He could tell she was frustrated and a bit disordered by the delay. So what, he thought. This isn't grade school. Something else is causing the frustration. He did not help her with the pile and she frowned. She had recovered most of her things and brought order to the chaos of her place just as the Toad huffed in to claim his ritual place at the head of the table. They suffered through his routine of wiping his sweaty face with the handkerchief, edged in lace, drawn from his sleeve like some nineteenth century fop. He took a new, pearl-inlaid snuffbox from his briefcase this time, probably a present from his wife, pinched the tobacco and placed it in the valley of his thumb pressed against the edge of the index finger. He snorted the load into first the left nostril, repeated, then into the right. He sneezed, to the horror of those sitting closest to him, a burden they endured for the privilege of conspicuous placement, but this time he was too late to contain most of the sneeze in the folds of the handkerchief, which blew out like a sail filling with wind. He sniffed a mumbled apology to those he had sprayed and then the tedium began. Will noticed that her unrecovered and forgotten keys sat so close to his right hand that he could distinguish each. The car key to the Ford, the apartment key to graduate student housing, room 206, he made a note, her office key, mailbox key, building key, computer room key, and so on.

He waited, but she made no move to retrieve them. He could not wait to kiss those naturally reddened lips. He was not prescient or psychic nor was he possessed of some supernatural power that allowed him to read minds. He was a semiotician and could read signs, symbols, and signals. Keys are symbolic. Keys provide access. They open locked doors. Here were the keys to her life, practically given to his hand. She was tired of waiting for him, frustrated that he would not act; herself too shy to initiate an interaction. Her unconscious had acted for her; her primal, instinctive self had had enough of this inaction. If only he were smart enough to decipher the code. Here are the keys to my heart, she silently screamed.

After class mercifully ended, she reached across to collect her keys, surprised to find them there and not in her purse. When her hand accidentally brushed his, she blushed but did not speak. He seemed not to have noticed. As she stood and turned to walk out, she wished him a good weekend and he stopped her for a moment. She immediately said yes when he asked her to study together that evening.

They worked the pretense of studying for an hour in her small room back at graduate student housing, and then put the books away and happily drank the wine he had brought along. He kissed her wine-darkened lips and purple tongue as they danced in the cubicle of her room. Later that night she traded her virginity for the pleasure he gave her. Finally, finally. She sighed into his ear and held him tightly. As they spooned and cuddled, he teased her, asking why she had waited so long, wanting to know why a smart attractive female would wait until she was almost twenty-four years old to lose her virginity. Instead of answering, she asked why he had waited so long. When he asked her what she meant, she said I don't know, it just popped into my head, you know, foolishly, how people sometimes talk without thinking. He kissed her vigorously because she needed it right then, and he told her about the keys. She thought he was absolutely nuts and even laughed a little at his analysis and then she was ready for him again. At that point, he was absolutely and irrevocably convinced of the power of semiotic analysis.

They broke up only when he was accepted into a doctoral program in semiotic theory the next year and she returned home with her master's degree to teach English at the local community college. Her favorite color was brown.

NOW IN HIS early thirties and firmly entrenched within the world of academia, Will was rapidly tiring of the university. He was at the point in his life where he felt he needed to weigh the negatives against the positives. Each year within the state university system he found his list of negatives growing and the list of positives shrinking. He despised committee work, for example, and considered it a waste of long hours given over to endless debate about the most insignificant issues. He was tired of hearing the faculty pontificate or tear apart irrelevant issues like bull terriers pulling at the play rag. Each had a need to grab hold and amidst the growling and gnashing of teeth, the rag would first move toward one dog, and then toward the other. They would worry it and tear at it and finally shred it so that each ran away happy, streaming a mouthful of shredded rag. At faculty meetings, the professors talked and argued and vacillated and did everything possible to avoid the inevitable: making a damn decision. More often than not, the decisions they did make did not serve the students, usually the last consideration in their decision-making process.

Often he was exasperated to the point of frustration. He was hired to teach semiotic theory, there being no such course currently available within the department. Three years later the course was officially listed in the university catalog. He had to endure presenting and defending the course first to the Department Curriculum Committee, some of whom acted as if it were a complete surprise that the department would even consider offering such a subject. Then he had to face the College Curriculum Committee, composed of members who had not one iota of understanding for what semiotics was in the first place. Finally, he had to go through the whole mess again before the University Committee on Curriculum and make the same presentation, answer the same questions, a complete waste his time since they had his formal proposal at hand. He was forced to present to faculty who had learned early on in their careers that teaching or doing substantive research was hard work; it was much easier to find and sit on committees where nothing substantive was ever done or required of them. In a curious twist of irony, service on such committees was not only valued but rewarded. He avoided them.

So for three years he taught the very same course described in the curriculum proposal on an "experimental" basis, whatever that meant. More troublesome in the eyes of certain faculty members, was the fact that his students considered him an excellent teacher because he had the courage to challenge them in the classroom. This earned him the respect of his students and he was invariably with someone during his office hours. This further served to alienate him among the faculty who trembled at the mere thought of having to speak directly to a student who might be so impertinent as to ask them a question they could not answer. His courses were oversubscribed with waiting lists of students wanting the course. This, however, only served to deepen the jealousy and envy of his colleagues who had insufficient enrollments to fill their pet courses taught at times convenient mostly to college professors. This resulted, in the new era of fiscal responsibility and self-sustaining departmental budgets, in the cancellation of their courses and re-assignment into the lower-level general education courses the university required all students to take. There was no greater shame in all the university than having to teach a course filled with freshmen who didn't know anything and who resented having to take a course because the university required it. For this reason, most of those courses were foisted off on the graduate teaching assistants.

Since he had made the decision to avoid the stultifying committee work and enervating faculty meetings where everything was discussed but nothing was decided, his actions were considered tantamount to treason. In spite of his outstanding teaching evaluations and excellent record of publication, he received yearly reports from the department head and the dean of the college suggesting that he was not a team player. This struck him as rather a curious assessment coming from two people who had never played an organized sport or been chosen for a team and subsequently had not the faintest notion of what being a team player actually entailed. It was noted that his actions were contrary to and served to denigrate the sense of community they were trying so desperately to develop instead of working to see that the students within the college were actually being taught something useful. Fortunately, he grew in stature as a scholar, in spite of their best efforts, and so they chose to ostracize him, which was not surprising, since he had done essentially the same to them. He had the misfortune of belonging to a faculty, most of whom were intolerant of anything that smacked of individuality, or creativity, or, god forbid, excellence. In other words, they could tolerate nothing that might reflect badly on the mediocrity they had so carefully and painstakingly nurtured for themselves and their students.

Rather than fight the inertia of those who were politically correct and professionally mundane, he began to consult. During the summers when he was not given a teaching assignment, he took on the challenge of solving "dead files," that is, cold cases of unsolved murders, still open and on file but with little or no hope of being closed. He dedicated his time and his professional skills as a trained semiotician, expert in the analysis and interpretation of the information collected by the detectives. After he solved his third dead file case, criminal investigation departments around the country began to seek him out. He wrote up his casework and explained the methodology of semiotic analysis in respected, peer-reviewed journals. Shortly thereafter, he was contacted and engaged as a consultant by both the FBI and Interpol. The FBI granted him special agent status in exchange for the courses he taught at Quantico. Subsequently, his fame and reputation grew within the criminal investigation community. Moreover, against the express wishes of those faculty who considered such a course an academic perversion, once a year he offered a graduate course wherein the students took on a local or regional case and tried to solve it by applying their theoretical training in semiotic theory.

For his primary texts he used the works of the great Italian semiotician Umberto Eco, also famous worldwide for writing such popular novels as "The Name of the Rose" and "Foucault's Pendulum." But those were not required reading in his seminars; Eco's brilliant academic work "Sign of the Three" was. In this book, Will's students learned how some of the great detectives of fiction used semiotic techniques to solve their most perplexing cases. Poe's great detective Auguste Maupin came to mind, but the man most students recognized was none other than the redoubtable Sherlock Holmes himself. They were thrilled to learn that a detective as famous and enduring as Holmes, his fictional character notwithstanding, practiced the science of semiotics in solving his most difficult cases. The students were often more eager to read A. Conan Doyle's accounts of the exploits of his great criminalist than listen to the actual cases solved by Will. And then the inspiration hit him. The advanced graduate students would take a special projects course wherein they were required to apply the theory they learned in their texts and from lecture and discussion. As he took on a new case, he brought the graduate students along. This became one of the foundational experiences of their graduate education.

When the official letter came he was torn. He would miss the interactions with the students and the role he played in their intellectual development. But he was tired of the incessant politics and posturing that polluted the collegiality within the department. It had not occurred to him that professionals so highly trained and learned as to rank in the top one percent of the world's educated elite could be reduced to acting like children jealous of each other's accomplishments. With the semester two weeks from its end in early May, he walked into the Head of Department's office and presented him with his letter of resignation. He could not be dissuaded. That evening he answered his uncle's letter, placing himself and his talents at his service for however long it would take. As far as he was concerned, the university had seen the last of him.

Chapter Five: Direktor Hauptmann

E STEPPED OUT into a mid-morning that was bright and cool against his cheek. He wore Adidas running shoes and an old polyester jogging suit that smelled of the cedar drawer. The suit looked new because he had not worn it much and could not bring himself to throw away something so unused, no matter how old or outdated it seemed. He couldn't explain his sudden desire for exercise; he stayed fit swimming through the indoor pool at the Sporthalle or working on the speed bag hanging in his living room. All his friends, male and female alike, made fun of him for that but each and every single one could not resist giving it a punch or two. Half an hour on the bag kept his reflexes sharp and the fat off his middle. But this morning, for reasons he could not fathom, he wanted to run. He walked across the street and waved to the owner in the new beverage store. There he redeemed the monthly beer ration given to the teller at the bank where he kept his monies. Every month when he went in to deposit his check, she slipped him the ration chit, good for a case and in return, he visited her once a month at her apartment across town. He did not sleep over. He walked briskly past the new houses where only two years before there had been a lush green field. Once on the path that bridged the river Wertach, he picked up the pace and before he knew it, was actually jogging. Still fit he told himself. Five minutes later he had to stop and spit the burn from his lungs. Recovered, he decided there was no need to sprint, and walked back into a shuffling run. His pace took him out into the country and along the river. At the little dam, he dropped back into a walk and crossed the iron catwalks atop the water that spilled over the artificial height of the concrete dam. He was sweating now and he flicked the moisture from his eyebrows and his mustache. Roland determined that if he was going to make it back, he had better walk the rest of the way out and since he was not ready to give up his nature walk, he ambled on. Now and then a bicyclist passed, ringing the bell on the handlebars. The riders were mostly women from the outlying areas riding into town to do the shopping before the noon meal. On the return, their baskets over the back wheel would be full of rolls, cold cuts, beer bottles, and maybe a pound of Leberkäs. All this sporting activity was making him hungry. He jog-walked on.

At the edge of a field, he spotted three deer, pulling at the grass. They stood stock-still as did he, each watching the other. The only movement was the flick of the buck's tail. They gave up their brunch and filtered back into the woods. This is what he had come for. Roland walked in after them and found to his surprise an unmarked path. His curiosity piqued, he followed it. Half a kilometer or so later he flushed a hawk from its perch atop a dying pine. He was close enough to hear the beat of the wings as the bird flew back into the seclusion of the forest. Around the bend in the path he came upon a clearing. A knee-high fence, hand-made of rough limbs and boughs, lined the perimeter. He closed the gate behind him. He saw a small cottage, so small it almost seemed a child's house but when he looked in the window he could see it was outfitted and ready for use. He walked over to the gazebo, just large enough to hold a bench. A path led from the gazebo to a little pond. He felt he was trespassing now when he spotted a sign nailed to one of the posts supporting the domed roof of the gazebo. In Bavarian dialect the sign read: "This is my sanctuary and I invite you to share it with me. I ask only that you enjoy it but leave it as you found it. Please do not reveal its whereabouts. I want others to experience the joy of its discovery as you and I have." It was not signed. He sat on the rough wood of the bench and relaxed, listening to the birds in the trees sing their brief melodious songs. He thought he heard a lark. An owl hooted and he hooted back. The forest fell silent. He decided his owl call needed work.

All the signs pointed to a serial killer. He had worked two such cases before. He reviewed the present case in his mind. A classic serial killing. Lieutenant Schumann, fresh from her books and her theory would no doubt corroborate his conclusion. Classic serial killing. Three young women, three mutilated corpses, the result of the killer's psychopathology. A textbook case, she would tell him. He felt the old familiar pang in his stomach, the short note of panic, like a bird's song, when he looked in the mirror and saw more gray among brown. The same pang in the instant just before the bra came off to show the truth of a woman's breasts. The same thing he felt when he knew there was something not right about a case, in spite of his conclusions. Or, he was hungry. He took in one last deep breath of the solitude and thanked the person who was willing to share so graciously something so simple yet so important. Bavaria, all the way back to Ludwig, was renowned for its eccentrics and to his mind only added to the allure and mystique of the land he felt so close to. Now there was danger in his beloved forests and the peace and harmony of the place had been disrupted. The burden of taking care was heavy on his shoulders and he knew he would not rest until the evil in the woods was driven out. He made his decision and started back. He ran the last kilometer home to impress all the neighbors who saw him.

SHOWERED, SHAVED, AND in dress uniform, he walked from the apartment complex past the elementary school. On the other side of the large windows that opened out, students sat at their desks, learning their lessons. He walked past the soccer field, empty now. He stopped for a bit to remember the times when he could take the long passes out of the air on the instep of his foot, fake a step and shoot a left-footed curling shot high into the left corner of the net past the diving goalie. He ambled by the church, also empty and into St. Peter's Stube, down the stairs and through the heavy oaken doors, salvaged from a fourteenth century barn, old metal hinges and all. The noon crowd had already eaten and returned to work so he had the place mostly to himself, which he preferred. Frau Gutknecht, wife of the owner, came out from her washing up in back, drew down a glass of Bitburger Pils and placed a coaster under the glass at his table.

"Are you losing weight?" he asked the fat, sweating woman. She pushed a limp strand of hair bleached blond, straightened by the perspiration, back from her brow. She beamed.

"Herr Hauptkommissar, if you could have seen me even fifteen years ago..."

"I've seen pictures, Trudi. Heinrich was lucky to capture a beauty such as you. You were much too good for him, you know." She blushed so violently that the crimson spread into her throat. "Now if that lucky scoundrel can keep his hands off you long enough to fix me a little something to eat, I would enjoy a bowl of the oxtail soup to start, and the sauerbraten with spätzle, I think."

"Hungry today, Hauptkommissar Rieger."

"You have fired my appetite, Frau Gutknecht." As she pushed herself back to the bar and yelled his order to her husband at the grill, he

62

noticed she had not marked the first beer against him on the cardboard coaster beneath his pilsner glass.

Lieutenant Sylvie Schumann pushed through the massive doors as he was enjoying his soup with the freshly baked Bavarian bread rolls from the basket Frau Gutknecht had brought him. She wrapped her skirt tight to her legs and scooted across the bench to sit. She seemed a bit breathless and preoccupied even as she greeted him.

"And how is your mother, Sylvie?" he asked with emphasis on the verb.

She looked at him with false exasperation. "Honestly, Roland. How do you do that? How can you possibly know what I'm thinking? Did my mother call you?" she asked, more exasperated than suspicious. He shrugged his shoulders with false humility.

"You're late and I know you never to be late. Something or someone held you up. Your right ear is red, as if you had pressed something against it for quite some time. A telephone?" He sipped from the spoon. "Who would call you at home just after the lunch hour? A lover, making arrangements for the evening?" He looked deeply into her eyes. "No, not Kommissar Schumann of the KRIPO. She calls him," he teased.

She glowered at him and helped herself to a fresh roll. Trudi had already brought her a half-liter glass of beer and glanced at Roland, approvingly. But the beer was charged against him. "Go on," Sylvie told him.

"A business call, then? No. You would have handled it quickly and been on your way. A mother, then, who has lost her husband and whose daughter, because of her career, doesn't visit as often as she should, calls every Wednesday and talks for at least an hour."

"Sometimes an hour and a half," Sylvie corrected with the world-weary sigh of all daughters struggling with overprotective mothers.

"And today was a long one because she wanted to know if you had found anyone yet."

"Again," she interjected.

"Because she wants you to get married."

"Enough. Working with you is like having the most intimate details of my private life taped on my forehead for everyone to read."

He shook his head as he pushed the soup bowl away. The sauerbraten was coming, and a fresh beer. "Just for me to read, Sylvie, and only because you are my partner."

This positive bit of news encouraged her. She reached into her satchel and removed an evidence bag. He put down his knife and fork and took the bag.

"Corporal Schmidt and I found it after you left yesterday. I have no idea what it is, nor could anyone back at the office hazard a guess. No prints, so it's safe to handle."

He did not remove it. He knew what it was. "Excellent police work, Lieutenant. That blue-white piece of paper is used for one purpose only: to wrap and transport diamonds in the pocket of a merchant known as a "sight-holder." The fact that it is a slightly oversized plaquette indicates one thing and one thing only." He did not wait for her to offer a guess.

"It is Russian."

AT THE LANDESKRIMINALAMT (LKA) in Munich, Roland and Sylvie, in full uniform, were shown into Leitender Kriminaldirektor Bruno Hauptmann's office, and sat before the immense, highly lacquered desk. A polished brass reading lamp stood in the middle of the desk. The high-backed stuffed leather chair was empty, and swiveled off to one side. A window behind the chair admitted light but little or no noise from the busy street below. The desk was an imposing structure of red mahogany and golden brass and Roland guessed it must have taken six men to carry it into the room. A ship, masts erect, sailed into a bottle on the flat, calm of the desk. The entire office, as he looked around, given its nautical pretensions, would have made Admiral von Dönitz feel at home. Roland heard the swish of Sylvie's expensive panty hose as she scissored her legs for the third time. Roland knew she was nervous. He told her, "I think I'm getting seasick," and she had to stifle her smile as Hauptmann entered the room from a private side-door. He was dressed in a rather severe English-cut suit, probably Saville Row, Roland guessed, dark-blue with pinstripes, robin's egg blue shirt, Italian silk Hermes tie, French-cuffed shirt sleeves which he shot to correct their length on his arm. He stood before the chair and acknowledged them with a cursory nod as he gathered himself to sit. He was the sort of man who sat carefully to preserve the press of his elegant suit, the sort of man who did not spend much time at his desk. This might explain why he was not in a good mood. He greeted his two officers by rank, removed the handkerchief from his breast pocket and polished the glass in the gold wire rims.

"I've just returned from a meeting with the Minister himself. It did not go well. To say the least, he's not very happy with the present situation and he informed me in no uncertain terms that this case is to be solved forthwith. As Director of the Bavarian State Investigative Bureau, I assured him that it would be. I am here to receive your assurances to the same effect." His glasses cleaned and inspected, he returned them to the bridge of his nose and pulled his chair forward to the desk. "And that is why I assigned you to this case Hauptkommissar Rieger, over the express and rather adamant wishes to the contrary of your immediate superior.

"He is an incompetent bungler, sir," Roland said quietly, and Sylvie swallowed loud enough for him to hear the gulp.

The Direktor swiveled his chair and pulled a folder from a side drawer. "Of course he is. And you antagonize him by screwing his daughter." He said it as a matter of record, without recrimination. He drew his finger down the length of a paper in the thick folder. "He cost you a star. Charged you with brutality for nearly beating a man to death." He looked across the ocean of his desk. "I knew your father and had the pleasure of serving with him shortly after the war, although he was Wehrmacht and I was Navy".

This surprised Roland. The man looked fit and trim and could not have been much older than sixty. But it was possible. Late in the war, boys as young as 14 and 15 were pressed into service. It was not Roland's intention to offer an explanation for his conduct but the Direktor had specifically provided him with the opportunity.

"The man was driving drunk. His license had already been pulled by the SCHUPO for a similar offense. This time he smashed head-on into a Ford, killing the mother and her young daughter. I was the third car in the line to arrive at the scene and when I approached him and presented credentials he was ranting at the dead woman, yelling that the bitch had ruined his new Mercedes. He said he would have my job when I placed him under arrest after he could not produce a license. He then called me a Gestapo pig, a Nazi, and an asshole and then he took a swing at me, sir. I took offense at being called an asshole and was forced to defend myself."

Sylvie was aghast that the Hauptkommissar would be so flip with the Direktor, despite the shadow of a smile on his lips.

"He was in the hospital for three weeks," noted the Direktor, dryly.

"I gave him the opportunity to think about the two innocent lives he destroyed."

The Direktor turned three or four pages over. "Here's a citation and medal for bravery in the line of duty."

"Circumstance again, sir. I was investigating a murder scene with my partner in a warehouse and two idiots decided to break-in and rob the office. One surprised my partner, mortally wounding him, but Sepp killed the man, even as he fell bleeding. As I ran to the shots, the second man fired at me and I stopped him with a bullet to the shoulder. He had a machine pistol on automatic and was bringing it up to fire again and I put one in his knee. He dropped the weapon and started to crawl away..."

"And you fired one into his ass for good measure."

This time Sylvie could not stifle a laugh as she pictured the scene in her mind.

"He was crawling away at a high rate of speed, sir."

The Direktor permitted himself a full-on smile. "I see you got your star back shortly thereafter, although, I might add, over the objections of your superior."

"He does not have a medal for courage. And thank you, Direktor, for intervening in the matter."

Hauptmann did not say anything. He pushed back from his desk, crossed his legs and steepled his fingers. "Tell me about this case."

Sylvie cleared her throat, pulled her notebook from her valise and opened it atop her lap. She took a deep breath. "Three women dead, sir. Ages twenty-three to thirty, young, relatively pretty, all teachers, but no connection there."

"Explain."

"One is a university professor; one teaches at the Gymnasium level; the third is an instructor at the technical Realschule. Each from a different school district. They could not have known one another."

The Direktor nodded.

"Each victim found brutalized and brutally mutilated. Breasts and vaginal area severely lacerated. In each case, death by strangulation— Hauptkommissar believes by garrote—all other wounds inflicted most likely post mortem. Our supervisor has adjudged this case to be the work of a serial killer, a sexual psychopath engaged in the ritualistic slaughter of young German school teachers."

"Do you concur, Lieutenant?"

She swallowed and reached for a glass of water. "May I?" she asked.

"By all means. Feel free to serve yourself. Roland?"

Roland shook his head no.

"A whisky perhaps?"

"If you will join me, sir."

The Direktor went to a cabinet and opened a new bottle of Canadian Club. He poured it next into two gold-rimmed shot glasses. He did not ask Roland if he took ice. They drank to the job, King Ludwig the Second, and the free state of Bavaria. Sylvie, her throat sufficiently lubricated, was ready to proceed.

"There is not yet sufficient evidence to warrant such a conclusion."

The Direktor looked at her with interest. She was directly contradicting the report of her supervisor, Captain Steinmetz. Roland smiled but did not look at her. Good girl.

"The only physical evidence we have, sir, is a piece of paper used to transport diamonds. It is an anomaly sir; it simply does not fit the case. What would a sexual psychopath be doing with papers used to carry diamonds?"

The Direktor sipped his whisky. Good question. He thought for a moment. "You're using the anomaly as the basis for changing the direction of the investigation." He looked at Roland to confirm his conclusion.

"Exactly, sir. My intuition tells me that there is something wrong about the case. One thing I can tell you sir, I cannot solve the case given the evidence we now have."

The Direktor nodded. This is not what he expected to hear, but he appreciated the honesty of the assessment. He expected nothing less from his officers. "So we're stuck with an unsolvable case."

"Not exactly, sir. I can't solve it, given the paucity of evidence at hand. But I know who can."

The Direktor was genuinely surprised. "Explain."

"The successful resolution of this case, Herr Direktor, requires someone who can think outside the box, so to speak, someone who can give us a fresh perspective. I know such a man. He is a university professor in the United States, a professor of semiotics trained in the interpretation of signs and symbols. He is a consultant to the FBI and assists police jurisdictions with dead file cases. I have read his papers, sir, and his method of interpretation has resulted in an excellent record of solving so-called unsolvable cases. We need this man, sir."

There was merit to what Rieger suggested. He vaguely recalled mention of this American professor solving cases using semiotic analysis. Now he remembered. "Don't they call him the Semiotician?"

Roland raised his eyebrows. "They do, sir."

The Direktor made a decision. "You'll have your man, detectives." He made a note to himself. "Roland, see to it that Liselotte is given the pertinent information."

Sylvie was shocked to hear the Direktor call Rieger by his first name.

"But there is one condition."

Roland and Sylvie knew there were always conditions.

"Your chief has already petitioned me for the use of a forensic psychiatrist, what the Americans call a 'profiler'."

"Let me guess, sir, he wants that arrogant bastard von Eltz."

The Direktor grinned to himself. This is exactly how he referred to von Eltz, in private, of course, and then only to his secretary, Liselotte. "Those are the conditions, Hauptkommissar. If you want your semiotician, you will also have to accept the appointment of Professor Doktor Osvald von Eltz to the case. There are political considerations if you expect me to take such extraordinary measures."

Roland understood the politics all too well. Unfortunately for his career, he had decided early on to avoid as much of it as possible, choosing instead to spend his time solving his cases and becoming a better detective. He had seen men of lesser qualification and poorer records than his own advance because they got along, didn't rock the boat, and got their tickets punched at the right time and place by the right people. The fact that they were indifferent and ineffective detectives was not considered an impediment to their promotion to the administrative ranks. Roland considered them Arschlecher, ass lickers, and he avoided them.

"Perhaps von Eltz will contribute to solving the case, sir."

"I doubt it," the Direktor stated as a matter of fact, "but your full cooperation will give him every opportunity to do so." He buzzed for his secretary and Roland handed Liselotte the information she needed to process the paperwork. They shook hands with the Direktor, and he pulled Roland aside for a moment. As he gave the man his ear, he could smell the cedar and sea of his expensive cologne. "Invoke my name, but only when you absolutely must. And call me at home. You have my private number."

Roland nodded. It was because of men like Direktor Bruno Hauptmann that he remained on the force.

As they walked out the building and to the car Sylvie said, "You never cease to amaze me, Hauptkommissar." He let her open her own door to the green and white BMW. "If you don't mind my asking, how did you learn about this so-called semiotician?"

"He's my nephew."

Given everything that had happened today, she was not the least bit surprised. But Roland had yet another surprise for her.

"Up for a trip to the Munich airport?"

Why in the world would they need to go to the Munich airport? "Are we taking someone there?"

"Just the opposite. We're picking someone up."

"May I ask whom?"

"Certainly. My nephew; as we discussed." He drove the car with sure, quick shifts, keeping an ear to the purr of the engine instead of an eye on the tachometer to engage the clutch. He peeked at her out of the corner of his eye. She was staring at him unabashedly. He knew what she wanted to say. He had only just received permission to bring the Semiotician on board and now he was due to land at Franz Josef Strauss airport outside of Munich that very afternoon.

Chapter Six: The Major

A T THE INSTITUTE in Moscow, he was assigned to Dr. Kristal Petrova, a KGB colonel in the Training and Technical Services Directorate. Wolf had contacted the Institute under the auspices of sending a senior officer for instruction in the curricular and pedagogical development required to teach new field agents. The dossier that Wolf forwarded showed that Major Rudiger Hain was slotted to head Stasi training and indoctrination in Potsdam. Also a professor at the university in St. Petersburg, she held a doctorate in gemology and was director of graduate studies in earth sciences. Her work, and the fact that she was a double-agent, covered Wolf's needs perfectly.

Hain was impressed with the woman upon first meeting. She had shoulder-length red hair, which she straightened by ironing, but to her great despair, even this could not fully control its waviness; her eyes were water-color blue and her lips a full cherry red, two shades darker than her hair. Her skin was white as Siberian ermine and there was only one flaw in her otherwise perfect face: a faint track of freckles lay across the nose and bled into each cheek. She considered the freckles a disfigurement and detested them. Fortunately, Western makeup was able to hide the irregularities of her complexion but she used it sparingly because of its expense and scarcity. Major Rudiger Hain of the East German Secret Police thought she was the most beautiful Russian he had ever seen. He decided to become a diligent and industrious student. He looked forward to developing their student-teacher relationship. But with this one he knew it was best to proceed with extreme caution. She was the kind of woman who, forced to rebuff constant sexual come-ons, had become inured to them. Accordingly, she judged all men the same and disavowed them. Instead of relationships, she developed her mind and her career.

SHE DROVE THEM to Ufa in one of those ridiculous cars the Soviets had modeled after an Italian Fiat. It smoked, the transmission resisted each shift of the gears and there was no power steering. In fact, there was no power anything. Hain was thankful the brakes worked but doubted the heater was of much use during the famous Moscow winters. Unlike most Soviet women, she was a capable enough driver, given her academic travels abroad, and with the map in his lap they made good time to the dacha in the forest. Wolf had called ahead and everything lay in readiness for them. Limited to one suitcase apiece and a carry-on bag, it did not take them long to unpack. They agreed to a routine. Work together started after breakfast. They stopped for lunch and then separated until three o'clock. They worked together without interruption until dinner. A cook from Ufa had been hired to look after the preparations, and after serving, returned to his duties in town. They had their evenings to themselves. She preferred classical music on the short-wave radio; he, rock and roll. When they played chess together, classical music it was, but no opera. She permitted rock when they read newspapers or magazines or picked-up after themselves to keep the dacha livable until the maid came in to clean on Saturdays. During this time, if the weather permitted, they walked in the woods or paddled on the Belaya River. An avid outdoorsman, Wolf kept the dacha outfitted with fishing tackle, rods, reels, bait box, nets, fillet knives, hooks, sinkers, and even spools of extra line. The hunting rifles were locked in a handsome cabinet, and they did not have the key. On Sundays, when she did not care to drive into town, she would go fishing with him, although she usually took a book along if the action was too slow.

Saturday morning was test day. They sat shoulder-to-shoulder at the oak table and from her valise she pulled a white envelope. She opened the rectangular plaquette and placed five diamonds on a sheet of white paper. "Please identify each," she said.

He loved testing days. She sat close and almost always wore her short skirt and white blouse, as if the formality of her attire somehow contributed to the seriousness of the examination. He had no doubt she wore the same outfit when testing her students at the university. Except they didn't get to sit close enough to smell her perfume or watch the rise and fall of her breasts as she breathed. He focused his concentration on the task at hand. He had already decided what his reward would be this weekend if he passed his tests.

He reached up and switched on the table lamp. He was becoming adept at fitting the jeweler's loupe into the bony orbit of his right eye. The 10x magnification allowed him to look into the adamantine heart of the gem. To the naked eye the gems appeared relatively similar, cut the same and each about a half-carat. He picked up the first diamond. "This one is pique. It has a blemish visible to the naked eye."

She nodded that he was correct. He used the tweezers to pick up the next stone. He looked into the geometric planes of the diamond and discovered a cleavage crack. "This one is feathered." In the third, he could discover no inclusions. The diamond was loupe-clean. He looked into her blue-eyes and said "flawless." She blushed, but he was correct again. She took the tweezers and loupe from him. Two diamonds remained. He carefully picked up the first between index finger and thumb, examined it visually, and replaced it. The second diamond, upon visual examination, appeared identical to the first, except for one detail. "This one is real, the other is an artificial," he declared.

"Why?" she asked him

"You know," he teased.

"You're right. I do know. But do you know?"

"A real diamond is oily to the touch."

She smiled and refolded the diamonds in their paper plaquette. She pulled another from the valise and opened them for inspection. He examined each of the four through the loupe and then re-ordered them. He removed the loupe and thought for a moment. "The first four are colored gems, or fancies. The first, with the rosy tint, is the result of manganese. The next is blue, caused by the existence of boron. The yellow-hued diamond is the result of nitrogen. The last has no color that I can detect. It appears chemically pure, indicating that it is carbon only. White light enters it and leaves unaltered."

"Very good." She was impressed. "What causes the coloration?"

"Colors are caused by the chemical impurities I noted."

"And what are those called technically?"

He sighed and turned away, looking out the window of the front room at the pines and cedars that flanked the walkway up to the house. He shook his head. "Something chromatics." He remembered that chromatics referred to color.

"Allochromatics." She enunciated the word for him to repeat.

"Allochromatics."

"Describe the colorless diamond correctly and we will stop for today."

He nodded and reexamined the diamond. The light seemed to burst from the stone in a dazzling eruption of fire. "This diamond is as near to being colorless as I can determine. Thus it contains no nitrogen or other allochromatics. A spectroscopic examination would reveal no band at 415.5 nanometers in the absorption spectrum and thus verify that it is indeed chemically pure. I would grade it therefore as an exceptional white plus, a D, a River, or in German, a Hochfeines Weiss, all used to denote the highest color scale on the International Scale of Colors when compared against a master diamond."

He sat back and looked at her, awaiting her judgment. She studied the black hair, neatly combed, and the dark eyes set above the nose, just a bit too large for the proportions of his face. His lips were full and sensuous and against her better judgment and in an impulsive act that surprised her, she kissed him hard and long on those very same lips. When they broke the kiss to breathe he asked, "Did I pass?"

"You passed, you idiot," and the test was over.

STILL A BIT shy in her bikini, she made herself comfortable in the bow of the old flat-bottomed boat. The oarlocks creaked against the thole pins as he put his back into it and moved them upstream against the gentle current. He enjoyed the exercise of each long pull at the oars and she enjoyed watching the muscles of his back distend and relax. The exertion was making him sweat and he had his shirt off, liking the cool breeze off the humid river. She trailed a hand in the tepid water. They rounded a bend where the river broadened and pushed itself up under the hanging canopy of the maples and oaks that lined its banks. A bed of underwater vegetation emerged from below the surface, laying an irregular moving carpet of green atop the water.

"Throw out the anchor," he told her, "and when it hits, tie it off."

The anchor set against the pull of the current and the little boat swung in closer to the weed bed but below it.

"Perfect. Time to catch supper." He had the larger open-bail spinning rod rigged up with heavier line and a steel leader. From the end dangled a red and white spoon with a large treble hook at its rear. Today he was after pike, but it was early yet. In the shade, they were protected from the rays of the early-afternoon summer sun. He reached for a beer; she had brought him the luxury of an authentic Czechoslovakian pilsner.

"We've got time for a lesson, if you're up to it."

"Sure," she said, taking the opened beer from him. She waited until he had his own opened and tasted. "A little geography today, given the occasion. Diamonds were originally found near mounds or hills of a distinctly yellow soil. Such hills are called kopjes."

"What makes the soil yellow?"

"Don't interrupt," she scolded. "I was about to tell you. The yellow soil is the result of eroded kimberlite pipes." She made a defiant face at him.

"I give up; what's a kimberlite pipe?"

"Kimberlite is a blue rock that has solidified as it pours from the earth's core and hardens; it turns yellow when exposed to air. The shafts or tunnels it oozes from are the pipes. This solidified pipe of blue rock is where diamonds are found. The tip of the pipe exposed to the elements is eroded in alluvial washes."

"So that's why it's possible for people to find diamonds just by walking along and looking down."

"That's right. But such diamonds are usually a considerable ways downstream of the pipe. The trick is to find the kimberlite pipe where the majority of the diamonds are just waiting to be mined. As you have learned, De Beers controls most of the world's diamonds. You are being trained as a diamantaire, that is, a professional in the diamond industry. Diamonds are called the goods unless they are smuggled, and by smuggled I mean beyond the control of the South African cartel. These are called outside goods. Almost all the stones we handle at Russelmag are outside goods."

"Russelmag?"

"You didn't know?" she laughed, and hid a little beer burp behind her hand. He shook his head.

"Most of the diamond trade is closed and highly regulated. And most diamantaires are Jewish. And it's a business kept in the family, so it's hard to break in to. Here's how it works. Once every five weeks, three hundred or so of the world's top diamond merchants meet in Antwerp to buy rough gem diamonds; unfinished stones are called rough," she explained. "De Beers determines who gets what based on your reputation and what you can sell, but each and every diamond merchant has to take what he gets. The Central Selling Organization (CSO), also known as the Syndicate, thus controls the marketing of eighty percent of the world's rough diamonds."

He shook his head. "They sound better organized than we are."

"And harder to infiltrate," she assured him.

"That's why the KGB established Russelmag on Pelikaanstraat in Antwerp. No exchange or customs controls there either. We sell our polished goods directly to market, bypassing De Beers."

"That probably doesn't make them very happy, to say the least."

"This is why most Russian diamonds are outside goods, smuggled by diplomatic courier from Angola or Zaire."

He finished the last of his beer. She constantly amazed him with the depth of her knowledge. But now it was his turn. The trees on the bank threw shadows more deeply into the river and cooled those waters by a few degrees. The baitfish, in order to escape the killing light of the sun, moved into the weeds for protection. The predators moved up from the deep and followed and thus a pattern emerged. He cast the spoon into the pockets of the weeds. He let it pulse across the weed tops, pushing water as it wobbled and jerked, and at the weed-line let the red and white spoon flutter down like a wounded bait fish.

The strike, when it came, was brutal and vicious. She saw the fish slash at the artificial bait with such speed and accuracy that she inadvertently gasped. He snapped the rod up, setting the hook, and the fight was on. He had been smart enough to set the drag but the bend in the rod convinced him he had better loosen it or he would soon be reeling in nothing more than disappointment hanging from a slack line. He loosened the drag and the fish stripped line from the reel as it ran for the deep water of the channel. As she saw the flash of the green flank, she covered her mouth. He pivoted in his seat, keeping the rod tip up. This was good; the fish had chosen the deeper water instead of running into the cabbage of the weeds where he might never pull it free from the mess. The fish suddenly stopped its run and the line went slack. He stood, raising the rod above his head and reeled like a mad man. The boat rocked and she grabbed both sides.

"He's running straight to the boat," he hollered in excitement. If the fish ran beneath the boat the fight was over. He caught up to the fish and pulled it in the direction of the bow. Its strategy defeated, the fish ran again for the deep. He blew out his checks in relief and slowly cranked down the drag. The fish was tiring. He sat again. Now as he gained line back he knew that he was making headway against the creature. And then it stripped off every inch of line that he had won, the drag singing in protest. He loosened it further, preventing a break off.

This time the pike ran toward the shore, intent on burying its nose in the tangled green miasma of ropy stems and twisted growth. But now the strength of the fiberglass rod dominated the struggle and with one last mighty effort to free itself, the fish leaped into the air, shaking its massive head in an attempt to dislodge the treble hook. As it geysered out of the water its entire length, it twisted and thrashed and tail-walked across the water before it slapped back to the surface, still twisting.

"Oh my god," she cried, pointing at the fish. "What in the world is it?"

He pulled the exhausted fish alongside the boat. He said the name for her first in German. "Wasserwolf. The Water Wolf, also known as the pike. This is a dangerous fish because of his teeth. I'll need your help if I'm to get him in the boat."

"Me? I don't want to touch it," she said, her eyes wide.

He handed her the rod, bail open and showed her how to pinch the line against the base of the rod with her index finger. "If he decides to make another run, just release the line and let him go, but I think the fight is out of this one." He made sure the stringer was handy, and then he did something that she would never forget.

First he wetted his hand and then he grabbed the fish across the raised bony ridges that protected the pike's eyes. He pressed his fingers into the eye sockets and she watched the eyes of the fish sink inward under the pressure. He stood and pulled the fish up out of the water and over the side into the boat. She was shocked to see its length. It hung from just below his chin to well below his knees.

"Hand me those pliers," he commanded. He pried open the rounded jaw of the cavernous mouth and pulled the treble hook from the gristle and cartilage of the maw. She reeled the lure in and put the rod out of the way. "Come here and take a look." He held the mouth open for her to see. Her entire fist would have fit into the mouth, lined with rows of needle sharp teeth angling back toward the throat. "When this guy locks down, nothing escapes."

"I can see why." She looked at Hain. His breathing was shallow and fast but she was equally excited. He used his left hand to grip the predator beneath the gill plate, sliding his fingers carefully up to the rounded edge of the jaw. Grabbing the gill plates could cut him like a knife; the teeth could slice like a razor. Every aspect of the front of this fish posed a danger. He released his grip from the eye ridges and the fish thrashed. He felt its enormous power but he had an invincible grip.

"Grabbing them by the eyes paralyzes them. I only do it if I'm going to keep the fish."

"What are you going to do with this one? Don't you think we should let it go?"

He shook his head. "We're going to eat it." He said so with finality and she knew there was no arguing. He thrust the metallic point of the stringer up through the white flesh of the under-jaw of the green fish, incandescent where the light hit its mottled flank, and returned it to the water, secured at the end of the stringer.

"Whew. That was a fight." He washed the slime of the fish from his hands and motioned for another beer. He was sweating. "Dinner is on me tonight."

She wasn't entirely convinced if that was a good thing.

Back at the dacha he found a whetstone and carved a fresh edge on the fillet knife. She watched with fascination as he inserted the tip of the blade into the pike behind the flat skull where the bony spine began. With a surgeon's skill he essentially extirpated the fish, driving the point into the tiny brain, killing it instantly. He moved the fish, almost four feet in length, to the countertop next to the sink. He cut a line along the backbone almost to the tail, then returned to the head. He cut down hard from the top in an arc behind and along the bony gill plate to the bottom of the fish. With the tip of the knife he sliced back along the white belly down to the tail, careful not to open the gut sack.

He returned to the second cut behind the gills and angled the length of the knife toward the tail. He carefully cut a huge slab of meat from the fish and put it in the sink. He flopped the fish over and filleted the other side. She held the plastic sack for him as he folded in the carcass of the fish. It seemed such a shame. Only moments before it had been a living, swimming creature, ruler of its domain. But what a ferocious, powerful creature it had been. She was afraid of it still and afterwards double-tied the ends of the bag closed. She took it out back and put it carefully in the trash barrel where they burned their garbage. He had cleaned up most of the blood and slime while she was gone and he was waiting for her.

"The reason most people don't like pike is because of these bones here." He let her touch the points that protruded through the flesh. "These are called the Y bones and they give the fish its power and speed. That's why it looks and moves like a torpedo through the water." He cut a wedge about an inch and a half from the top third of each fillet and discarded the bony rope of flesh containing the Y-bones. He placed the huge fillet skin-side down and grabbed the tail with his left hand. He razored the knife into the flesh at a flat angle and pulled the meat from the skin. "We've got probably three kilos of fillet here." He next cut the firm flesh into squares, rinsed and dried them. He set aside enough for dinner and lunch for the next day and put the remainder in the freezer, wrapped in plastic and butcher paper.

He made up a beer-batter, seasoned with salt, pepper, and paprika. On the stove, she had readied a heavy deep-sided cast iron skillet and measured in about four inches of oil. From the day before, the cook had prepared them a potato salad in the German style. She decided they would eat at the wooden table in the back under the conifers and she brushed the pine needles from the top and then covered the rough oak boards with a tablecloth. She opened an Alsatian wine and drew the fruity, perfumed scent into her nose. White and dry, the wine had what the French called a goût de terroir, a flinty taste of the earth underlying the fruit that would match the fish perfectly. He brought a basket of golden brown fillets, tinged red from the paprika seasonings and served her. They toasted the catch and their time together. She carefully forked a piece of fillet into her mouth, chewed and swallowed. Her eyes opened in surprise. "Absolutely delicious."

"Told you so," he mumbled through a mouthful.

The flesh under the delicate coat of the fried batter was white and firm and juicy. She practically gorged herself; the fillets were as addictive as candy. Finally, she could eat no more and pushed her plate away. He grinned at her appetite and her indulgence. He liked this side of her and told her so. After they cleared the table they sat for a while and finished the Pinot Gris. The wine, the coming of evening, and her day in the sun on the river, was making her melancholic. She knew better than to involve herself but she was also a woman.

"You have such a beautiful smile when you're happy," he said, and his compliment had the desired effect. She showed him her perfect white teeth. He knew a walk would restore her and burn off the sadness of the alcohol. At the end of the little path that ran from the back of the timbered house through the forest and down to the river, she stopped and let herself be kissed. She gave him her hand on the walk back. His lovemaking was powerful and toward the end, a little bit cruel and this was what she needed before her release came.

THE TWO MONTHS allotted for his training were almost over and KGB Kristal Petrova looked up from the assessment report she was writing to watch him through the open curtains of the window in the living room. He had his shirt off and she was mesmerized by the detail of his muscles as they worked to swing the heavy axe. Through the open window she could hear the chunk of the sharp blade as it split the hardwood into kindling. He bent to pick up the two pieces and threw them on the growing pile. He placed another log on the stump, rested the blade atop it to gauge its center, then neatly split the short log in two, the axe blade biting into the stump where he left it, handle vibrating. His exertions had forced him into a clear sweat and he flicked the beads of perspiration from his forehead before he tossed the kindling on the loose pile of chopped wood.

Working at the oak table where they did most of their training, Dr. Petrova of the 9th Directorate for Training and Technical Services, re-read his fitness report. He had been an avid and intelligent student, surpassing even the best of the graduate students she taught at the university. She understood now why the East German Stasi were held in such high regard by her fellow officers in the first and second directorates (foreign and counter-intelligence) of the Komitet Gosudarstvennoi Bezopasnoti of the Soviet Committee for State Security. She wrote a measured but supportive analysis and critique of Major Rudiger Hain, and deemed him worthy of taking on the task of redeveloping training courses and curricula at the institute in Potsdam.

Even so, Petrova debated whether to give him the last lesson she had prepared. Doing so could place her at risk; the information was still highly classified and she doubted that it had been disseminated widely even within her own directorate. He came in at that moment, using his shirt to towel off his chest, smiled a greeting, and headed for the shower in the bathroom. She decided to handle the problem like a bureaucrat or a dean: she would share the information with him because the advantage it might provide him outweighed any potential risk to her career in Intelligence. She could afford to do so because there would be no record of the last lesson in her report to Andropov, who would pass it along to Wolf. She signed her name and dated the document and put the papers away. He startled her from behind, nuzzling at the hollow of her neck where she had touched it with Chanel No. 5. She smelled the western shampoo in his hair and felt the brush of its cool wetness against her cheek. He came around to the other side of the long table and sat across from her. He was trying to be good. He was ready for his last lesson and she was ready to give it to him.

She went to her bedroom and returned with a brown case about the size of an attaché but twice as deep. She carried it by the handle and laid it gently on its side atop the French polish of the oak table. She popped the clasps at either end of the case and opened it flat. She took out a velvet cloth folded into a rectangle and then a ten-power jeweler's loupe. Embedded in the protective white Styrofoam that lined the case, he saw additional lenses of varying powers, a diamond tester, and a series of stoppered tubes containing an unknown clear liquid. She pushed the case aside to make room. "What I'm about to show you is top secret and not three weeks old. One of our field agents working in the United States got hold of what I'm about to show you and it was sent to me for analysis and appraisal." She paused to unfold the soft cloth. Three stones radiated fire into his eyes. "I would like you to identify each, please."

He sat still for a moment, letting his eye take in the radiance produced by the cut of each stone. Their shape was identical, all three emerald cuts of similar weight. Using the tweezers she gave him, he rotated the stones through various planes and angles, watching the brilliant play of light reflected through the facets. He fitted the ten-power loupe into and against the orbicular ridge of his right eye and looked deeply into the adamantine heart of each stone. His visual analysis completed, he asked for the tester, a standard heat-conductivity probe that any reputable jeweler in Antwerp or Amsterdam or New York would use to test for authentic diamonds. In turn, he checked the thermal properties of each stone. He set one aside, grouping the remaining two in a pair. Next, she removed a Plexiglas tube from its bed in the case, carefully uncapped the stopper, and handed it to him.

"The liquid is rather toxic, so don't spill," she warned.

Using the tweezers again he dropped the first stone in—the one he had set aside—and watched it float, suspended within the clear liquid. Gingerly, he tweezed it back out and dried it with the cloth she supplied. The second and third stones floated slowly to the curved bottom of the vial, one at a time. He knew that the fluid in the tube allowed him to test for the specific gravity of the stones. He recapped the vial and handed it back and she replaced it in the case. He was almost ready to offer his assessment but he deliberated, reviewing his mental checklist of criteria before he spoke.

With confidence he said, "The first is a cubic zirconia. The other two are not."

She was pleased. The cubic zirconia was such an excellent example of its type that it would fool the eye of most sight-holders. "Correct," she acknowledged, "but what about the other two?"

"They are diamonds," he replied, equally certain.

She shook her head. "One is, but one is not." She watched the surprise register in his face. It pleased her that she could evoke this sort of response in him. She was also flattered that he trusted her enough to share his surprise. It was time to teach again. She popped out another vial in the series stored in the Styrofoam. "The fluid in this tube is calibrated for a specific gravity of 3.52." She carefully placed the first of the two remaining stones in the mouth of the tube and released it. The pull of gravity on the stone was directly balanced against the viscosity of the fluid in the tube. The stone hung there as if suspended in space and time.

"That has to be a diamond."

She nodded. The next stone dropped to the bottom.

"I withdraw my earlier conclusion. The last stone appeared to have all the properties characteristic of a diamond. I do not know what it is."

"Don't feel bad, Rudi. Fewer than twenty people in the world know what this stone is."

"What in the world is it?"

Before she answered she removed yet another tube. "The density of the liquid in this vial is calibrated to suspend a stone at a specific gravity of 3.32." Sure enough, now the stone floated. She dried it after taking it out, placed it in the center of the velvet cloth by itself and let him study it as she replaced the vial. "This is a synthetic moissanite."

"A synthetic moissanite?" he repeated.

"Yes. Named after Henri Moissan, the French chemist who discovered moissanite. Actually, he discovered silicon carbide, to be exact, and it was re-named in his honor. Moissanite is exceedingly rare in nature and found most often in meteorites. On the Mohs' hardness scale, it's second only to diamonds, 10 versus 9.25." She paused for a moment, rotating the stone so that it radiated an almost otherworldly brilliance from the various angles of its make. She continued her exposition.

"An American scientist has figured out a way to artificially produce large, single crystals of silicon carbide. One of the prototypes lies before you. It possesses virtually the same thermal conductivity of a diamond, and our initial tests show it to be as tough as or tougher than a diamond. Its refractive index and dispersion factors are slightly better than a diamond's. At this time, the only way to distinguish synthetic moissanite from real diamonds is the specific gravity test. But that can only be done for loose stones. A gem already placed in a setting will fool anyone. And our experts suggest that the Americans will be able to manufacture it for less than half the cost of a diamond of similar weight." She refolded the three stones into the velvet cloth and left him to ponder the possibilities of what she had shown him. She knew he would file the information into that prodigious memory of his and save it for use at some later time as circumstances warranted.

The last lesson was completed and their time together was growing increasingly short. They were required to leave the next morning. She stood from the table and stepped back just enough so that he could see her full length. She unzipped her skirt at the hip and let it fall around her sandaled feet. She unbuttoned her blouse slowly and deliberately and let him stare as she took out the combs holding her long auburn hair in place. She shook it out around her shoulders, using her fingers to comb out any tangles. They did not make even the short trip to his bedroom. Instead, they tested the load-bearing capacity of Markus Wolf's magnificent polished oak table, and with the exception of a few creaks and groans where the joints were tightly fitted, found it more than sufficient to withstand their rigorous challenge.

When the time came and he was ready, their good-byes were professional and correct, without promises. She did not expect him to write and he knew he could not. Neither expected to see the other again.

THE MAJOR

Three years later she was unexpectedly called into the office of her department head at the University of St. Petersburg. A package had arrived for her in care of the department and he passed it along. His professors often received packages from the West, items unattainable in the Soviet Union and given as gifts by colleagues from research universities. The postal censors at customs had already gone through the package and given it clearance.

She opened the package in her office, cutting the twine and the brown wrapping paper that had been shoddily rewrapped by the customs agent. She did not recognize the return address, curious that the package had originated with the West German Bundespost. Inside a stout cardboard box were four large tubes of Crest toothpaste, nearly impossible to get, even for officers of the KGB, unless they were posted as Residents in the West. She grinned ruefully and wondered if someone was trying to tell her something. On the morning of the third day of use, in spite of meticulously squeezing and rolling the tube from the end, she was unable to force any more of the paste from the opening. She looked at it in consternation and got a safety pin. She stuck the pin into the open end of the tube and through the white, minty, fluoride-added paste, touched something hard. As she pushed it back away from the bottleneck of the opening, toothpaste again curled out.

"What in the world?" she wondered. She walked into the tiny kitchen of her flat and got her sharpest knife. She cut the tube open like a fish and found the impediment. "Aha." She had it and rinsed the white goop from it under the tap. She held to the light a near-flawless, pure-white, grade D diamond of almost three carats. In each of the other three tubes she found the same. Her smile that day was brilliant.

Chapter Seven: Sierra Leone

THE AEROFLOT FLIGHT from Moscow was, thankfully, only partially full and this afforded him the luxury of taking all three seats in his row. Palliated by the free drinks, most of the other passengers were huddled under blankets, sleeping or reading or talking quietly. A relatively mixed group was aboard: Africans in brightly colored robes and headgear returning home from diplomatic missions, Russian military officers assigned to training rebel guerilla units, and a small number of tourists heading for the beaches, Dutch, German, and British taking advantage of the reduced fares. He stretched out, back against the bulkhead, supported by the ubiquitous small white square pillows found on aircraft, pushed the button for the small light above his seat, and prepared to go over the material prepared for him by Research. In an attempt to clear some of the hazy fog blown forward by the incessant smoking of the Russians on the flight, he opened the nozzle of the air vent that hung above him like a nipple on the belly of a sow. He studied the map of Africa.

Sierra Leone was in West Africa, that part of the massive continent that bulges like the overdeveloped deltoid of a shoulder as he looked at the map face-on. About the size of Scotland, the West-African country exposes its western flank to the Atlantic Ocean. Here lay the prized and relatively undiscovered beaches, some of the best and cheapest in all of Africa. Catering to the tourist trade, three or four decent hotels were built right on the sands of the peninsula where the capitol of Freetown had sprung up. To the north and east, Guinea wrapped itself around Sierra Leone like a kidney. To the south and east, it perched atop Liberia like a golf ball atop a tee. Portuguese sailors were the first European presence and in 1460 their man Pedro da Cintra came and left the name Lion Mountains. Sir Francis Drake landed during his explorations of the Dark Continent and opened the door for the British presence that would follow, seeking to export slaves during the eighteenth century.

The country had three distinct geographic zones. The coastal zone was comprised of excellent beaches and eerie mangrove swamps as one traveled inland. These gave way to the central plateau as the land undulated and rose ultimately to the heights of the Lola Mountains. In the humid central plateau, which once had been heavily forested, the farmers had burned and slashed and dug out as much of the rain forest as they could manage, and placed the scoured land under agricultural production. The gem of the Lola mountain range was Mount Bintumani, 1948 meters high, supposedly the highest peak in all West Africa. The major took the time to read a footnote from the editor who had prepared the monograph for him. He argued that this claim was specious and depended on a rather liberal definition of which countries and which mountain ranges actually lay in West Africa. It was this sort of attention to stultifying detail that made the Stasi great, he decided.

Major Rudiger Hain turned next to a report prepared by the agency's geologist. At this point, the flight attendant offered him another Scotch, and he accepted. She pulled two small bottles from the voluminous front pocket of her serving apron and handed them to him with a conspiratorial wink. He broke the sealed cap on the miniature bottle and poured the liquid over the ice in the plastic cup. He let the ice cool the amber drink exactly thirty seconds by his watch before he took his first sip. Single malt Highland Scotch whisky was his preference but he rarely had access to such indulgences unless he was posted abroad. Field duty had its share of compensations.

Three hundred and sixty kilometers east of Freetown and east of the Lola Mountains lay the diamond fields of Koidu-Sefadu, commonly called Kono. Fifteen kilometers west of Kono at Yengema, the National Diamond Mining Company had its headquarters. There they received and processed the diamonds mined at Kono and in the rich deposits of the Tongo fields fifty kilometers to the south. Large-scale mining of this sort had begun in the 1930s, but large diamonds still were being found in the rich alluvial deposits washed down from the mountains over the eons of time. The third largest diamond in the world was found at Kono in 1972, a monster of 969.8 carats quickly appropriated by President Stevens in the name of national security. The major shook his head. Politicians were the same everywhere, a bunch of greedy, self-serving bastards. The précis ended with the statement that a considerable percentage—the Stasi author placed the estimate at nearly 90 percent— of the diamonds mined in Sierra Leone were smuggled out of country. And it was this fact above the many others that had convinced him Sierra Leone was the prime location for establishing a pipeline that would run from West Africa to East Berlin.

He turned next to the political assessment. He looked again at his watch and reminded himself to remove it before they landed. He had been briefed to wear no jewelry or show any signs of wealth. The thieves, pickpockets, and muggers would prey instead on the stupidity of the tourists who flaunted their Western wealth in the face of the destitute Africans. Not much more than an hour left. He didn't know if he could stand even that much more in the poorly padded seats of the Aeroflot jetliner. Politics and history are incestuous bedfellows and the major made certain the report briefed him on both. He was glad to see that the three different sections in Research responsible for compiling the briefing were consistent with their facts.

The Portuguese were the first Europeans to land on the peninsulas of the coast around 1460 where Sir Francis Drake also landed for a time 120 years later during his voyages. The sailors found there an indigenous people mixed with the Mandingo tribes of the southern Mali Empire. In the eighteenth century, the British came in their high-masted sailing ships and the slavers followed soon after. A major slave center was established on Bunce, a small island nestled safely in the harbor protected between the fingers of the peninsulas on which Freetown sat. After slavery was abolished in Britain in 1787, Freetown became a sprawling shantytown of nearly one hundred ethnic groups, each living in their own section of town. Non-indigenous Blacks, many Christianized by the missionaries, were called Krios and considered themselves superior to the others. Some were educated at Fourah Bay College, the first English-speaking university in Africa, and the British showed them favor by appointing many of them to key civil service positions. The major did not consider this much of an advantage.

In the latter part of the nineteenth century, war broke out between the Krios and the indigenous peoples and many Krios were killed. He noted that their sense of superiority evidently did not extend to warfare. By World War I, the Lebanese merchants who came to trade with the tribes of the interior largely supplanted the Krios. Britain granted Sierra Leone independence in 1961, a western-style democracy was instituted, and social and economic conditions in the country went progressively and rapidly downhill. Hain chuckled to himself and sipped from his Scotch. According to the CIA World Book, cited by the Stasi writer in a wicked touch of irony, Sierra Leone now had the distinction of being the world's poorest country. So much for the power of capitalism and democracy, Hain thought. English, however, remained the national language. If ever there was a country in need of Father Marx's good tutelage...he thought to himself. What this country needed was socialism for the collective good of the people. The example of Angola came to mind.

The current head of state was a man named Siaka Stevens, a former trade unionist and head of the party he had founded, the APC or the All Peoples Congress. Aha, thought the major, there is hope for them yet. Stevens had replaced the corrupt Albert Margai, brother of Dr. Milton Margai, Sierra Leone's first Prime Minister, dead in office in 1964. In the late sixties, Stevens had returned from exile in Guinea where he was preparing a group of rebels for an invasion. Fortunately for him, Sierra Leone had just staged its third coup within 13 months, a record for instability even in Africa, and he was handed the reins of power. He brought some political stability to the region but not much, given the ethnic division of the country's two political parties. The southern Mende tribes supported the Sierra Leone People's Party (SLPP). The APC, founded by Stevens, was identified with the Temnes of the north. The Krios, who had once aligned themselves with the British and actually resisted the move for independence, chose incorrectly once more by throwing their support behind the SLPP, whose leader was Milton Margai.

Brother Albert Margai repaid their allegiance by replacing them with Mendes throughout the government. A great deal of Stevens' popularity stemmed from the claim that his family was represented in one way or another by almost each and every one of the eighteen major ethnic groups in Sierra Leone. However great his popularity, it was not sufficient to deter two assassination attempts on his life on a single day in 1971, at which point he took the extreme measure of requesting bodyguards from Guinea, with whom he had made a military pact. Perhaps there were twenty major ethnic groups, thought Major Hain.

The pretty attendant returned for his empty cup and the pilot announced they would be landing in Freetown in about twenty minutes. He replaced the papers in his briefcase and sat up in his chair. He could feel the pressure change in his middle ear as the plane began its gradual descent over the ocean. He could see now the small islands of Sherbo, Banana, and York, lying just off the coast. He saw the only coastal range in West Africa lining the southern peninsula. They actually flew over the city of Freetown on Freetown peninsula, crossed the bay and headed for Lungi airport. It was clear enough today to see Mount Bintumani in the distance at the center of the Lola Mountains. Nestled just below Mount Aureol of the coastal range, he saw Freetown, a curious admixture of modern hotels on the beach and the shanty town sprawl of loose hovels cobbled together of just about any material that was flat, could hold a nail, and was easy to carry on the head. He saw Bunce Island off to his right at the mouth of the Sierra Leone River and in the protected bay of the surrounding peninsulas. The captain raised the nose of the big plane, the wheels chirped as they contacted the concrete runway and they were down, welcomed to Sierra Leone across the intercom in four languages. As they rolled to the terminal, the major wondered what he had gotten himself into.

He considered Lungi International Airport a grandiose and pretentious misnomer. There was only one other jet of size on the ground, a humpbacked 747 of the Royal Dutch KLM fleet, recently arrived from Amsterdam. Most of their passengers were mining engineers headed for the Kono or Tongo diamond fields. Three other stumpy twin-engine aircraft waited on the tarmac, one unloading passengers, two taxiing into position for take-off. A Sierra Leone jet was accepting passengers for Accra, and the Nigerian Airways plane, second in line, was returning to Lagos and then on to Port Harcourt. The Air Gambia aircraft brought its engines up to full power, released its brakes and powered down the runway before lifting into a flight destined for Banjul.

After the massive Aeroflot jet lurched to a halt, he allowed the high-anxiety types to rush forward and wait in line standing as the wheeled stairs were pushed up to the forward and rear exits. This necessitated half the crowd turning about-face. After the clogged artery of his aisle cleared, he gathered his raincoat and briefcase from the overhead bin. As he deplaned, he again thanked the flight attendant for being so overly generous. She said she looked forward to seeing him again soon and he got the strange feeling that she meant it. Under the diplomatic cover of a Soviet economic fact-finding mission, he was there to investigate the possibility of establishing a direct link between their diamond business in Idar-Oberstein, West Germany and Sierra Leone. His forged papers in order, khaki clad officers in British-style tropical uniforms waved him through customs. He was struck at how truly black the customs officials were. He was more used to the café-au-lait skins of the Cubans he had worked with during a posting to Havana. The diplomatic cover saved him the trouble of having to bribe his way through.

Half an hour later, his two travel bags in hand, he boarded the airport bus for the Tagrin ferry. The Aeroflot flight crew, captain, co-pilot, engineer, and five attendants were already aboard. He nodded to the pretty Georgian, a little too old for him really, although fit and tight under her uniform, but she was seated next to a comrade-in-flight. Lungi Airport had been built on the northern peninsula above Freetown and thus required a forty-minute ferry ride across the bay to Kissy terminal on the south peninsula. A shared taxi or bus ride, given the conditions of the potholed roads, took the better part of three hours to circumnavigate the bay and reach the city center. The ferry was cheaper, quicker, and the bus drove right on and off and dropped passengers at the Paramount Hotel where the flight crew stayed. Hain's flight attendant looked back just before she stepped off and it wasn't to check for left baggage. He pretended to look out the window at the sea.

His hotel, the Drake, was across the street on Hill Street, near Victoria Park, and the bus driver took him there although he was not required to. The major handed the man a pack of Marlboro cigarettes. The Drake was a modern hotel in the British colonial style. Eight white columns fronted the façade and a white fence linked each to the other. On the veranda were wrought iron tables and chairs painted black. The flag of Sierra Leone flew from above the massive oak double doors, also painted white and trimmed in black iron and these doors opened into the hotel lobby. The charm of the hotel for him was the multi-colored apartment blocks, individual cabanas of self-contained studios with kitchens. This gave him the privacy to come and go as he needed and afforded him walking distance to Barclays Bank, where Lieutenant General Markus Wolf deposited by wire transfer the venture capital required to set up their diamond enterprise.

After he checked in at the main desk, he was taken to his cabin by a young man in a crisp, starched white shirt, white shorts, calf-length white socks, and polished black shoes. He sweated under the burden of the major's bags, walking gingerly as if his new shoes were too tight or he was not yet accustomed to the habit of wearing them. He followed the young man along the paved path lined with rocks painted white and bordered with carefully pruned and gardened tropical greenery. They continued through this faux rain forest up to a row of cabins whose opposite sides faced toward the Olympic-sized pool. He was let into the room and the cold air from the air conditioning unit was a welcome relief from the humidity coming off the sea. The boy placed the bags at the foot of the queen-sized bed, made a show of turning down the covers and opening the curtains to the sliding glass door that opened out to a patio that faced the pool. He walked to the front door and stood at attention. He was pleased with the tip the major gave him, announced that his name was William and assured Sir that if anything was required, he should be called immediately. The major was already out of his shirt. What he needed now more than anything was a shower and a change into fresh clothes.

Refreshed from his shower and still early in the afternoon, he took the time to make his arrangements. He called Barclays for an appointment, then his man in Kono, and finally, the bus station. The telephone work done, he studied his maps, brought along from Europe. Maps were scarce in Freetown and a luxury exceedingly hard to come by. He gathered copies of his passport and other important papers, the originals stowed in the hotel's substantial safe. He stepped out into a West African day. Mount Aureol was due east, Victoria Park just ahead to the north. He walked past the five-hundred-year-old Cotton Tree, a city landmark old as some of the towns in Europe, then found Siaka Stevens Street, the main thoroughfare running north-east and south-west. A short walk away, Barclays sat at the corner of Charlotte and Stevens. He was shown immediately into the office of the vice-president only because the bank president was in Nigeria attending a financial conference.

The vice-president was a pleasant Krio, educated in London, and he was visibly impressed with the monies the major had brought to his bank. He was both informative and instructive and conducted their business efficiently. When the arrangements were deemed satisfactory and concluded, he recommended Minnie's for supper and apologized that he would not be able to dine with the major today, given the President's absence. It occurred to the major that more likely than not, the President's trips abroad allowed the vice-president to straighten out much of the bank's business, and accepted the man's offer for a later dinner date. His directions to Minnie's had been careful and precise because the establishment was unmarked, not an unusual situation in West Africa where reliable signage was as scarce as maps.

The chophouse was only a few blocks southwest of the bank on Lamina Sankoh Street, less than a hundred meters from Stevens. He found the place without too much trouble and ordered a drink. As he studied the ridiculously low prices for the authentic African dishes, he smelled her perfume even before he looked up and saw her. She held her little Aeroflot handbag in one hand, her drink in the other, patiently waiting as if she were standing in line back home. He did not recognize her at first, out of uniform, but the detail of the purse gave her away. He invited her to dine with him. In so doing, he learned the rather lengthy but sweet story of the young Georgian girl who ran away at eighteen in search of adventure to escape a life of pushing her father's vegetable cart through the narrow streets of her village. Now, years later, she traveled the world to exotic locations, pushing a beverage cart up and down the long, narrow aisles of an aircraft. Sometimes, no matter how far we go, he observed, we wind up where we've been. She did not allow him to pay—that's what expense accounts were for—but she did allow a walk along the beach at Kroo Bay, past the bustling and busy King Jimmy Market where she permitted him to take her hand. On the walk back to his cabana, they were arm-in-arm, and later she let him find that secret part of her no pilot had ever been able to reach. He delayed his trip to Kono by three days, the length of her layover.

THE ADAMANTINE HEART

HE CARRIED AN unmarked day bag on a strap slung over his shoulder. He would miss his Georgian beauty, clumsy in bed but willing to try new things. However, the matters of State required his attentions now and as much as Wolf would enjoy reading his attempts at recruiting a new agent for the service, he would be more interested in learning of his progress on the ADAMAS project. William, the boy at the Drake, told him to be at the bus station at six o'clock on the day he intended to travel, but there was already a considerable queue as he walked up. The polyglot of languages he heard was disorienting. Many spoke Krio, the Creole admixture of English and any number of native tribal dialects. Others spoke Temne, Mende, and Limba, depending on their origin or their destination. The clothing worn by the persons in line was as mixed and diverse as their dialects. Some wore dashikis, some sub-Saharan robes, some western style pants and short-sleeved shirts but everything was colorful and some of it matched. Some wore shoes and some did not; those who did were in some sort of sneaker, usually Nikes; he was in Pumas today.

He had come to Sierra Leone in November and this month had been carefully selected for him. He was still ahead of the harmattan, the desert wind that blew off the Sahara and left much of West Africa in a surreal golden haze of suspended sand and dust before it settled out of the sky to the ground and the sky became blue once more. Despite the yearly harmattan, Sierra Leone was one of the rainiest countries in Africa. The inundating rains were behind him, the worst of the torrent coming in July through September, although the rainy season could last from May to November. The winds of the harmattan blew from December through January and he hoped to be long gone before the first coating of dust precipitated out of the atmosphere.

SIERRA LEONE

At eight o'clock employees began to hand out ticket vouchers to everyone standing in line. William told him this was only the first step. Once everyone was in possession of a voucher, an official with a megaphone called out the destinations. The lines dissembled as those traveling to Makemi, for instance, walked to the ticket office and exchanged their vouchers, paid, and were issued a ticket for their destination. He heard Kono called through the cardboard cone of the megaphone and with six or seven others went to purchase his ticket. He paid the man behind the desk enough Leone for a round-trip and accepted the ticket. His seat number was printed on the chit but given the size of the diesel buses he had seen, getting a seat wouldn't be a problem. An older Mercedes bus, spewing black smoke from the exhaust pipes, chugged up in front of the Sierra Leone Road Transport Corporation; as the rest of his group boarded, he followed. He showed his ticket to the driver and was thumbed to the rear.

He waited as passengers stowed their possessions and collapsed into their seats ahead of him. The bus was uncrowded, as he had anticipated, and he took the unassigned window seat in his row. The bus was not air-conditioned and others were already dropping the big windows for ventilation, so he did the same. The ride, once the excitement of leaving town dissipated, was hot and dusty, long and bumpy, but the scenery compensated for the damage his kidneys were taking. Once out of Freetown and off the boulevards, most of the track was unpaved and riddled with holes and riffles dug into the hard pack of the road by the trucks, buses, and four-wheel drive vehicles.

He noticed that the insufficiency of the road did not deter the native drivers who navigated the route at speeds that bordered on the suicidal. Their Toyotas and Datsuns flew past, out-racing the dust cloud kicked up by their oversized tires. Sometimes, if they recognized the bus driver, and many did, these black brothers of the transportation industry honked their horns and waved as they slewed past. Almost all had taken the time to hand paint one slogan or another on the sides of their vehicles. He learned that "Allah is the Greatest," information that the Communist Party had not yet released to East Germany. One driver was convinced that "The more you hate, the more God bless." One lorry was owned by Okapi the Great, another by the Black Zorro, and one evidently headed in that direction was styled the Mabonto Express. But the slogan he took to heart was the one that read "Your best friend is your secret enemy." Amen, my African brother.

As they lurched east and south, after some twenty kilometers he judged, the land changed significantly from a swampy coastal geography to rolling hills of forests and farms. The forests were an exotic African mix of palm trees and even those were of different varieties. Here and there he saw stands of tall mahogany and less often, more precious teak. The farms produced mostly rice but he also saw millet and sorghum and cane sugar. Tethered to a pole outside the farm huts he saw the occasional goat; and in the fields where grass supplanted the native trees, cattle showing more rib than meat, milled about swatting flies with their agile tails while complacent sheep cropped the green. In the distance, he saw the spine of the Lola range and the rise of Mount Bintumani.

About half way into their journey of 360 kilometers, the bus slid to a stop next to a ramshackle building that posed as a chop bar, convenience store, gas station, and post office. It was time to stretch the legs and rub the back and get some blood back into his rear end. Most of his sweating, stinking, fellow travelers had brought lunch along tied up in red and black scarves or bought something from the bobos, the boys selling drinks, candy bars, cigarettes, or carved ritual masks, and even bolts of brightly colored cloth. Evidently, deodorant was not for sale. He bought a candy bar and stood outside with the others. He had brought bottled water from the Drake Hotel and washed the Snickers bar down with the lukewarm Evian. The driver, having relieved himself, came around from the back of the building, recovered his head with his official transportation cap, the cloth cap stained with sweat to the bill, and jumped aboard. This was the signal for everyone to reclaim their place and with a grind of the gears and a punch on the horn they were once more underway on the road for the twin cities of Koidu-Sefadu.

Chapter Eight: The Warlord

THERE WAS ENERGY at Kono missing in Freetown; he noticed the same when he moved from East Germany into the West. Among the dilapidated cars and trucks, many pieced together with mismatched parts cannibalized from other vehicles, he saw the incongruity of a Mercedes, a BMW, and in one instance, a huge white Cadillac running up and down the street. The difference here was diamonds and the wealth it afforded the men who mined, loaded, and sorted the stones for the companies who controlled the men. The energy he felt was the power of men with money in their pockets and the will to spend it.

Kono was fast becoming a classic boomtown much like the gold mining towns he had read about in Alaska and California. The large-scale operators moved in and started mining in the early 1930s. In the light alluvial soil washed down by the torrential rains in the Loma Mansa range, diamonds were still relatively easy to find and a rush to the fields at Kono and Tonga characterized the Fifties. Although the National Diamond Mining Company tried to control diamond production in Sierra Leone with the aid and assistance of De Beers in South Africa, more diamonds were illegally smuggled across the border to Liberia or Guinea than were legally handled. Any stone found outside the purview of the NDMC could not be legally sold without a government document. This created a robust and lucrative underground market for both gem-quality stones and industrial-grade boart. Major Rudiger Hain was here for both.

He walked from the bus terminal to the market, glad to stretch his legs and breathe fresh air. He heard the calls of the sellers who hawked their hand-hammered silver and gold jewelry, authentic Bondo ritual masks, mahogany carvings of hippos, elephants, and lions for the tourists, baskets of rice and cassava and kola nuts for the locals. He moved through the buyers and sellers, through the noise and the taped native music playing at variable speeds on cassette recorders that boomed the songs at customers as they passed. He moved through the dust and the flies congregating on the meat and chickens hung to cure in the stalls. He decided not to try the smoked snake.

The bobos pestered him like flies the whole way, pimping for money or trying to sell him their cheap goods, and he ignored them with good humor. Soon enough they swarmed a white South African from De Beers, resplendent in his safari shirt and pith helmet. He was foolish enough to hand out a ten Leone bill to one or the other who pressed him, only to discover that this generosity merely renewed their efforts to mine this movable, mobile repository of scrip. As he watched the little drama play out, Samir Ayoub found him, introduced himself, and they exchanged a prearranged verification code. The major relaxed a bit then. Everything about Sierra Leone was strange to him, from the climate to the culture to the color of the people. Although they were friendly and, for the most part, left him alone, with the exception of the young bobos who were just trying to make a buck, he had never felt so out of place in his life.

Samir was the son of a Lebanese diamond merchant who had come to the fields immediately after World War II and sought his fortune in the blue kimberlite that hid the black stones. He found enough gems to stay alive and what he found he sold to smugglers. He became rich enough over the years to attract a lighter-skinned Krio girl, the daughter of a chop bar owner. Following the natural flux that produced the rampant diversity of Africa, he mixed her Creole blood with his Arabic, her Christian religion with his Islamic, her African culture with his Middle Eastern, and the union gave them Samir, an only son. More enterprising than his mother and more intelligent than his father, he grew up in the diamond fields, was sent away to England for school, and trained in terrorist guerrilla warfare with the Cubans and the KGB in Angola. It was this sense of independence that made him the perfect man for the major's venture. Samir invited him for a drink at the Sierra Leone Mining Company club where he was a member. The major was glad for a chance to cut the dust from his throat. They drank the locally produced Star beer cool and fresh from the bottle and surprisingly good, admitted the major.

Samir Ayoub was affable from the start and eager to show off his excellent command of English. He briefed the major on his background. His father, after experiencing the diamond rush in the Fifties, used the profits from his smuggled goods to buy himself a government license to deal in diamonds legally. He prospered, developed a reputation as a fair and honest merchant, and his prosperity elevated him to the ranks of the middle class. He made the critical mistake of taking his status and his money into politics and supported the SLPP, the party that put Margai into power. For a while, things were good. In the coups that followed and eventually emplaced Stevens, there was fighting, murder, and brutality. One moonless night a squad of Stevens' goons rounded up the businessmen and political leaders who supported the SLPP, and drove them out into the forests in the back of their military trucks. All were killed with pistol shots to the back of the head and buried in unmarked mass graves. After killing the men, the thugs were indiscriminate in their butchery, murdering women and children as well. Only the fact that Samir was still in school in England at the time spared his life. He returned to stand in the rubble of his father's looted shop and the next day joined the rebels.

After their second and last beer, they made ready to leave. The major offered to pay the tab and Samir accepted. They stepped back out into the afternoon, into the bright African sun, and walked to Samir's Toyota Landcruiser. The truck was rigged with a row of headlights across the top of the cab, a powerful winch sat on the front bumper, and a roll bar protected the cab. Samir flipped a coin to the young boy sitting guard atop the front right fender and he slid off the hood with a smile. Samir said be with you in just a minute, popped the hood release, propped it open, and popped loose the hold-down clamps to the distributor cap. From the front pocket of his pants he pulled out a rotor, seated it onto the cam, replaced the distributor cap, pushed the clamps back in place and gave the engine a once over visually. Satisfied, he replaced the hold-up bar and clicked it into its plastic holder before he dropped the hood. He came around to the driver's side, got in, fired it up, listened to the engine rumble through the pipes, released the emergency brake and the clutch and they took off. The major asked him if he had to disable the engine every time he parked and Samir said yes with a grin. The truck had been stolen three times previously and each time he had tracked the thief down, administered local and personal African bush justice, and recovered his truck.

Ayoub drove them west to Yengema where he showed the major the massive layout of the National Diamond Mining Company and then headed south for the rich deposits at the Tongo fields. They ran the sixty kilometers in good time and Samir slowed as they neared a single-pump gas station that also served as a chop bar and tavern. The shanty was powered by its own generator and was therefore independent of the local utility. This was more a matter of necessity than convenience as the electricity failed more often than not during the violent storms of the rainy season. The gas-powered generator also established its worth when bandits commandeered the power station, cut the electricity, and held the manager for ransom. He pulled the vehicle around to the rear of the building and as they got out into the dirt, a face peered out through the dark over the half-door set in the wall at the back of the shack. Samir threw this man his keys and explained that the owner of the establishment was a trusted friend who would look after the truck.

They walked around to the front and Samir opened the door to the refrigerator humming on the wooden porch and offered the major a beer. They sat, drank their beer and waited. About ten minutes later a World War II vintage Willys jeep slid to a stop in the dust and two men jumped out, U. S. Army issue Colt .45s at the hip, military caps on their heads, blindfolds in hand. They seated Ayoub and the major in back, tied the blindfolds but kept their hands free, which was a good thing or they would have been bounced right out of the back of the jeep. The trip, to judge from the rush of the wind over the open vehicle was at a high rate of speed while on the blacktop, but slowed somewhat as the potholes and poor condition of the dirt track they turned onto roughed up and overpowered the suspension.

The air turned colder and Hain could tell they were gaining altitude. The driver had to shift more frequently into lower gears and their direction changed more often as if they were winding their way up through the hills. About an hour later they were moving slowly enough that he could smell the distinctive note of a hardwood forest and the old jeep was occasionally slapped by vegetation or brushed by limbs as they motored on. At one point, they slowed and he heard the rush of water as they forded a considerable stream that pushed against the side of their vehicle. As they pulled out onto the other bank, he could hear the slap of mud and gravel from under the wheels as the rear-end fish-tailed up the slippery slope. Ten minutes later they stopped and he heard the engine die, cough, rumble on a revolution or two, and backfire before dying once more.

The driver came around and removed the blindfolds. They sat for a minute or two, getting their eyes used to the light, and tried to get their bearings. He looked over at Samir to determine how he had weathered the trip. He did not seem the least bit worried. He looked at the major and said welcome to the temporary headquarters of the Revolutionary United Front.

The major stretched and looked around the enclave as Samir walked off to meet someone. He wasn't very impressed with what he saw. The camp was light and mobile and most of it looked like it could be quickly torn down, loaded up, and moved out. From what he could tell, they were in what once had been a small mountain village, set on the flat top of a hill ringed by a forest. Tactically, it was a good position for observation but there was only one road in and out. Ten or so native huts with their conical tops of thatched palm fronds had originally housed the villagers but they were now displaced, he assumed. Most likely, the village had been liberated and its inhabitants relocated. Military tents were thrown up amidst and between the huts. Here and there a campfire smoldered, remnants of an earlier meal, and he was perturbed by this obvious lack of discipline. Nothing would give the position of the camp away more quickly than smoke from the fires. But this was not his revolution. He had his own insurgencies to look after.

He noticed that there were enough trucks and vehicles to move about a hundred men but today the camp held only a fraction as many. Samir had disappeared into the largest of the tents in the compound, what looked to be a round circus tent with a high center pole supporting the structure and its guy-lines. Two armed soldiers stood guard at the entrance. He recognized it as a British commander's field headquarters tent and guessed it housed the leader of the guerillas. About the time Samir and a smaller man behind him ducked out through the front flap, three more jeeps roared into the camp. In the back of each a single black man sat blindfolded as he and Samir had been. These men, however, had their hands tied behind their back and they were bloody and swollen in the face as if they had been beaten with rifle butts. The captives, each shoeless and shirtless, were led to the center of the camp at the point of rifles and jabbed into submission. A blow to the back of the neck from the sergeant's rifle butt chopped each terrified man to his knees. The major watched the smaller older man next to Samir unholster his pistol, a Beretta it seemed, and chamber a round. He calmly walked up behind the kneeling men, trembling and begging for their lives, and shot each man in the back of the head. As the last dead body pitched forward, he stepped back, face grim, and holstered his firearm.

The soldiers who had transported the unfortunate prisoners kicked the corpses over on their backs at the toe of their jump boots. The sergeant dropped to his knees at the side of the first dead man. He removed from the pocket of his camo shirt what could only have been a set of dentist's forceps. Another soldier tilted the dead man's head back, careful not to get his hands bloody, opened the dead man's mouth and pushed the tongue aside. The man with the forceps reached in and methodically and with great force extracted the bottom back molars from the dead man's jaws.

At one point the extraction of the second tooth required such effort that he braced his foot against the dead man's chest, grunted, twisted, and pulled. When the roots tore loose from the bone with a sickening pop, he nearly pitched over backward before he regained his balance. On the dead man's chest he placed the two molars, white as elephant ivory against black skin still shiny and moist with the sweat of fear. He repeated his grisly dentistry twice more. Finished with the third, he wiped the tool clean, replaced it and reached for the pair of pliers handed to him by his dental assistant. He returned to the two molars on the first man's chest, cleaned them of blood and gristle with a dirty rag and then cracked them within the steel jaws of the heavy pliers as if they were hazelnuts. From the middle of each tooth he extracted a rather large, rough diamond. He cleaned all six, handed them to the man who had killed the prisoners, saluted, and ordered his men to dispose of the bodies. They were loaded up and taken to the nearby river where the crocodiles would finish the gruesome work of extermination.

The jeeps slid down the road out of the camp and disappeared into the forest, the bodies bouncing in back, arms flailing over the sides as if making one last desperate attempt to escape. Like dust from the wheels of the jeeps, quiet settled over the camp once more and the only evidence that three men had lost their lives was held in the hand of the man responsible for the killing. He stepped forward and introduced himself. "I am Captain Joseph Konema," was all he said as if the mention of his name and rank were sufficient information. He extended his hand and Major Rudiger Hain of the East German Staatssicherheitsdienst—the Stasi—shook it. He used his cover instead of his real name. Konema asked him if he was a KGB operative. The major complimented his host on his excellent perception but neither denied nor confirmed his association with the KGB. The captain was a small man not five and a half feet tall and he was nearly bald. His hands and his feet were small. His handshake had been both cool and delicate and the major wondered if he powdered his hands to keep them dry. The only hair left on his head, which gleamed in the sunlight, was a fringe that ringed his pate like a Roman Caesar's laurel crown.

"Sammy has told me much about you." He opened his left hand and pushed through the stones with the index finger of his right hand. He shook his head. "Strange, isn't it, that in this state they seem so much like pieces of frosted glass." The major stepped closer for a look. "Ah" said Konema, "This is what you have come for. And those three men died for these six pieces of pressurized carbon."

"Hopefully not on my account," the major suggested.

Konema laughed a dry little laugh as if the desert wind of the harmattan had disturbed the fallen, curled leaves under the mahogany tree. "Don't let your conscience worry you. These are my diamonds," he said, looking the major directly in the eye. "Those men were trying to smuggle my diamonds across the border to Liberia." Again he held up the diamonds in the showcase of his pale palm, each diamond about ten carats in weight. "Theirs was not a simple act of greed. Oh, no." He shook his head for emphasis. "In trying to enrich themselves, they risked impoverishing our movement and ultimately, the people of Sierra Leone. Their actions were therefore treasonous, and now you understand why they were executed. The penalty for treason is death, nothing less."

The major nodded his agreement. "I'm sure they were aware of the consequences." The justification for the killings was irrelevant to him. He understood power and, for whatever reason, the small man who stood before him with a fistful of diamonds was nothing less than a powerful man. This was the man he had come to see and the man who had the wherewithal to make his mission a success.

As a powerful man, he had the luxury of audience and explanation and he took it. "I had no choice, really. They gambled their lives against the stones and they lost. For me not to have executed them would have resulted in a loss of face. Perception of power, my Russian friend, as you are well aware, is often more important than actual power itself." With that, Captain Joseph Konema, his cause richer by nearly sixty carats of raw diamonds, invited his two guests to come out of the sun and join him in the cool of his tent.

They sat on yellow and red woolen tribal blankets surrounding a charcoal brazier in the center of the large tent. The captain handed the major a kebab, passed one to Samir, then took one for himself and placed it upon a bowl of rice. Without asking what he was eating, Rudiger Hain took a bite of the first cube at the end of the spit. It had a smoky tang from the marinade and he could taste the salt of the soy sauce. He enjoyed the exotic taste. Captain Konema informed him they were eating wild bush pig he had shot that morning. He poured each man a cup of poyo palm wine. This was not to the major's taste, his palate used to the flowery, delicate wines of the Mosel and the Rhine, but he proposed a toast. "To the success of the revolution."

They drank and ate, each assessing the other. Finished with the meal, the rebel leader patted the bulge of his belly with satisfaction. Except for the potbelly that distended his brown shirt, he seemed fit enough. He turned to the major. "My country is in economic chaos. My people starve while Stevens and his goons loot the treasury and strip our people of their legacy." He took one of the diamonds from the unbuttoned pocket of his shirt. "The irony is that there is enough wealth in the ground to make this one of the richest countries in Africa."

Samir and the major agreed.

"My revolution does not rely on the support of all the people. The SLPP and the APC have far greater numbers than our small movement here in the hills. It is my intention, therefore, not to fight for the hearts and minds of my countrymen. They will follow later." He took a sip from his cup and licked the sweet wine from his lips. "No, my intention is to gain control of the diamond fields. We have already made good progress toward that end; good enough, in fact, that I need buyers for my goods."

"That's why I'm here," the major said. "We can help each other."

The captain nodded his agreement and set his cup down. This was the sort of simple truth he believed in. His reality was hard and cold, like the diamonds in his shirt pocket. If a man steals another man's property, he dies. In this instance, he could see the wisdom of a partnership between the two men. It would be economically beneficial for both. But it was too soon to give away his position. "Why should I sell to you and not some dealer in Tel Aviv or Bombay, or even Brussels for that matter?"

"A fair question," the major replied. "Anyone with sufficient monies would be of benefit to you. But I can give you two things they cannot." Now he paused and finished his wine. The captain was intrigued. Samir had indeed promised that this white man could deliver more than just the promise of money. "What is it exactly that you think would contribute to the just cause of our revolution?"

Now was the time for brutal honesty. "You are undermanned and poorly organized. You lack matériel and the means to obtain it. You are equipped with a hodgepodge of outdated, slipshod, antiquated surplus military gear. You have no supplies, no logistics, and no combat arms to speak of. But I will grant that you have a plan and your assessment of your tactical mission is dead on correct. If you control the diamond fields, captain, your next promotion very likely will be to President or Chief of State or whatever you designate."

Captain Joseph Konema, leader of the Revolutionary United Front and undisputed warlord of the region, permitted himself a smile.

"Your greatest need now before anything else is arms for your men to consolidate and then increase your tactical gains. What you need Captain Konema, if you will permit me to tell you, is an easy to handle, simple but dependable assault rifle."

The rebel leader leaned forward. This was exactly what he needed.

"My contacts have empowered me to offer you a first shipment of one hundred Kalashnikov assault field rifles, model 47."

Konema pulled his fingers along the edges of the goatee that framed his chin. "As much as I appreciate the 47, I prefer the 1959 model. In my experience it is a superior weapon."

"It is a superior weapon and I will personally see to it that you get the AKM, chambered for the M43 7.62 by 39-millimeter cartridge."

Samir asked, "What does the AKM actually stand for? We received training with that weapon in Angola but the Cubans did not know what the letters meant."

"Automat Kalashnikova Modernizirovannyi, also called the AK-47, but technically it is the 1947 model retooled and modernized. Now that I think of it, given the conditions here in Sierra Leone, I will see to it that your weapons come with the chromed bore."

Again, despite his guerilla training, Samir Ayoub looked puzzled.

"Humidity will quickly rust the standard barrel. And the M43 round is somewhat corrosive. The chromed barrel aids in cleaning and will significantly extend the life of the rifle in the field."

"An extremely attractive offer," allowed the captain. "Will you also supply us with ammunition?"

"We will. We feel that we have presented a generous offer, indeed. However, it is not the intent of my backers to be momentarily generous. We are sincere in our efforts to establish a long-term relationship for the mutual benefit of both our interests. We understand your needs, and now permit me to share ours with you." He reached into his trousers pocket and produced a document. "This is an official government license, signed by the Minister himself, re-establishing Samir Ayoub as a legally entitled diamond broker."

Konema examined the document with interest, not a little surprised to see it. "Your connections and resources seem to be greater than I had imagined."

The major nodded but did not comment. It was time to deliver his demands. "We ask that a certain proportion of the diamonds you control be channeled to Samir. He will 'sell' them exclusively to us at our legal business establishment in Idar-Oberstein, West Germany. There the stones will be cut, polished, and sold on the open market. These profits will be used to buy additional diamonds from you. We will pay you in the currency of your choice, German Mark or American dollars, if you prefer. These monies will provide you with the financial resources necessary to raise and properly train a revolutionary army. We ask only that when the revolution comes and you take control of Sierra Leone, you will continue to favor us with access to the diamonds we require."

The captain sat back and uncrossed his legs, rubbing circulation back into the right, where he carried the fragment of a round. What the major offered was nothing less than the means for realizing his dream of one day ruling Sierra Leone. The automatic rifles would enable him to accomplish his goal at a much more rapid pace than he had envisioned.

Once he controlled the diamonds at Kono and Tongo he would be ready to move toward Freetown. With Samir brokering the diamonds to the European, they would have an uninterrupted source of currency with which he could finance the push north and west to the Capitol City. It was in his best interest to establish and maintain a longer-term relationship with the young white man. He turned to Ayoub but spoke to the major.

"You have chosen a good man in Samir. I trust him and I cannot say the same for many others. I would also like to see him marry my daughter one day when we once and finally stabilize this chaotic country of ours."

He reached forward to take the major's hand in his own. "With this handshake our deal is done. You will have your diamonds as long as I am able to give them to you."

It was a simple declaration as when he had first introduced himself with only his name and his rank. Nothing more was needed. The deal was done.

"I hope you will forgive me sir, and I do not wish to appear presumptuous…. However, your first shipment of arms will land in Freetown tomorrow, aboard a Liberian oil tanker out of Havana." He handed the shipping manifest to the captain.

Again the European had the advantage of surprising him. "But these are for barrels of kerosene."

"Exactly. The components for the AKMs are wrapped and stowed in each of the drums. The barrels have been specially constructed so that the kerosene floats above a false bottom. Only a third or so of each barrel contains liquid. The rest is packed with parts and ammunition."

"Very clever," admitted Konema as he handed the manifest to Samir. "We will need trucks to receive the shipment."

"I will see to it," Ayoub assured him and the men prepared to stand.

"One last item, Captain Joseph, if you will permit?"

"There is always one last item in such negotiations, but your actions today and your friendship for our cause require that I listen." He sat back down.

Major Hain took another document from is pocket. "A gift, Captain Joseph Konema, on behalf of my clients. I was instructed to present it when the deal was finalized. It is a gesture of good will on our part, to be precise." He did not wish to place on the captain the onus of having to accept a gift that might cause embarrassment.

Without looking at the sheaf of papers, the guerilla leader said, "I will accept it on behalf of my people and in the cause of our revolution." Only then did he peruse the document.

"As you read sir, I will take the liberty to explain, given the technical analysis in the paper. Diamonds, as you know, are a finite commodity. Once the lode is depleted, there are no more. The resource is exhausted and the wealth they bring in dries up. In time, the diamonds of Sierra Leone will be gone. What you are reading is a highly confidential geological assay prepared by our staff geologists. We recommend that as the number of diamonds diminishes you begin to invest in the mining of rutile."

Samir and the captain looked at each other, puzzled. Neither had heard the word before.

The major took their silence as a sign to continue. "Rutile is the primary source of titanium." He looked at the warlord. "Under the guidance of the right man, your country will have a bright and prosperous future long after the diamonds run out. In fact, our geological assessment shows that Sierra Leone is sitting on potentially the largest deposits of unmined titanium in Africa."

Samir and the captain looked at each other again, this time in unabashed disbelief.

"Rutile?" the captain said.

"Titanium," the major assured him.

Chapter Nine: The Arrival

THE SEMIOTICIAN LANDED in Munich after a short layover in Geneva. An unusually crisp and clear day in early June presented the Swiss Alps in all their snow-capped glory to the passengers, noses pressed against the Plexiglas windows of the aircraft. The stop was brief. He and two or three other passengers did not bother to deplane. Swiss officials came aboard and thoroughly checked the cabin for contraband, controlled substances, and more importantly, bombs. He was glad he had thought to leave his personal explosive device at home this trip, he thought to himself. The taciturn men and women in crisp, tailored dark blue uniforms going efficiently about their business did not seem in the mood to appreciate any attempt at dry humor. At their request, he identified his belongings, his carry-on, allowed it to be searched and thanked them for their professionalism. Five minutes after they were gone, passengers flying on re-boarded and those flying from Geneva to Munich came aboard to locate their seats. Shortly afterward they were underway, the wings of the jet cutting into the wind as they rose to climb above the towering heights of the Alps. It wasn't long before he could identify the Bavarian town of Lindau below, and the sapphire blue waters of Konstanz, the great lake of Germany shared with Switzerland. He thought he could make out the pair of large stone lions standing guard at the mouth of the bay on the German side, protecting what once had been the royal principality of the Bavarian state. On the descent into Munich, mountains gave way to forest, forests gave way to lakes, and lakes gave way to houses and the Autobahn.

His uncle, whom he had not seen in—what was it—four years now, waited for him as he cleared customs. With his suitcase in tow, he passed through the pneumatic glass door as it pulled back to release the passengers into the public area. Amongst the obedient Germans standing patiently behind the reception line, he caught sight of a rather tall, lanky blonde with hair cut pageboy short, waiting at his uncle's side, curious to meet her partner's nephew. Will was always glad to see Roland whether the circumstances were business or pleasure. Roland greeted him with a warmth and unabashed joy that surprised Lieutenant Schumann. She had not yet experienced this side of the Hauptkommissar and she was inwardly delighted that he had responded to the arrival of his nephew with such personal feeling. He introduced his nephew to her formally, using the semiotician's title of Professor Doktor in the German fashion. Dr. William Russell Sheridan's size, his good looks, and a title for which he seemed much too young, surprised her. He was fully a head taller than she, who prided herself on her height, which she accentuated with heels whenever possible for an even greater effect.

Roland offered to pull his largest suitcase, and Sylvie took his carry-on, leaving him with his laptop case. They walked out of the international Terminal 2 to Roland's BMW, illegally parked but unticketed as a professional courtesy, and heaved the baggage into the trunk, the laptop stored more carefully. Sylvie gave up her position in front to sit behind Roland, the shorter of the two men. His nephew's long legs required the seat all the way back to the stops; he was forced to recline the seatback so that his head did not touch the roof of the car. As Roland

121

maneuvered them out of the airport and onto the Autobahn for Munich, they asked the usual questions about the flight, family, and work, and Sylvie was shocked at how good his German was until she remembered that his mother, of course, was German and he had, in fact, been born in Bavaria. She was eager to try her university English and so they made conversation in two languages until they reached the famous Hofbräuhaus brewery in downtown Munich where they sat down to a late lunch.

The Hofbräuhaus was cavernous by design and they walked by row upon row of oaken tables and benches where men and women from all over the world would come to sit shoulder-to-shoulder, drinking and singing lustily during the Germanic ritual drunken brawl of Oktoberfest. It was warm enough to sit outside and they took a table in the warmth of the sun. Will fondly remembered some of those early days with Roland. Others he could not remember. One night they practically crawled home so drunk that between the two they could not fit the key to the lock of the apartment door. They lay on the cold tiles of the hallway floor laughing tears from their eyes at their collective ineptitude. "What do we do now?" Will gasped through the laughter and the hiccups. He was not quite ready to spend what remained of the evening curled up on the doorstep like two bad dogs put out for the night. It was undignified for a doctoral student in semiotics and a newly minted Hauptkommissar to be found sleeping together in public. Roland, as usual, had a plan.

"We call for back-up." He managed to bring his booted foot off the floor high enough to slap the door. He was dissatisfied with his effort, and perturbed by the failure. Will laughed at his inebriated consternation. "Give me that boot," he directed his uncle. He unzipped it and pulled it from the Hauptkommissar's foot, taking most of the black sock with it. Will took the boot by the toe and held it over his head like a hammer. As he pounded the heel against the metal door, Roland hollered in his best command voice, "Open up in the name of the Royal Bavarian State Police!" The effort was too much for them and they collapsed again, one pushing the other off. Five minutes later, Roland's girlfriend at the time, angry but beautiful in her pink nightgown, dragged them one at a time into the foyer. She was disgusted with the work and with them both and looked quickly to see that the neighbors had not been roused enough to come to the door.

"We were hung over for three days," Will told Sylvie.

"You were hung over for three days," Roland corrected. "Once you get over your jet lag, we'll get you into proper drinking shape again." He lifted the liter glass of beer in a toast, a perfect half-inch of foam floating atop the golden yellow liquid. "Welcome home. It's good to have you back." They touched all three of the heavy, thick glass mugs together and drank down through the foam. He could not help but smack his lips, the beer tasted so good. It never ceased to amaze him how good a real beer could actually taste. Perhaps it was the purity of the brew, no chemicals or preservatives, or perhaps it was the setting, a beer garden in a world-famous brewery in a world-famous beer town drinking with a stunning blonde and life-time friend.

The sun warmed the tablecloth; ivy stretched along the wooden slats and the wind rustled the new leaves of the chestnut trees that gave them shade. People laughed and joked as they ate and drank and the waiter appeared from inside, plates lined up his arm like a meld of cards, just as they started to look for him. After lunch was finished and the plates were cleared, the second round of beers arrived and Roland presented Will a recording of arias by his favorite German tenor, Fritz Wunderlich. This surprised Will as Roland was not in the habit of giving presents, but not half as much as his astonishment at Sylvie's attack on her second liter of beer. She was doing Germany proud. Will reached down to his shoulder bag and pulled out a fifth of Crown Royal, bought at the duty-free shop, Roland's favorite Canadian whisky, bar none. He was speechless but obviously pleased as he opened the carton and pulled out the bottle sacked in a royal purple and gold bag that protected the cut glass of the whisky bottle. He loosened the golden cord at the neck and pulled the cloth down over the shoulders of the bottle as if he were taking the peasant blouse from the white shoulders of an Alpine maiden in Oberjoch.

The waiter brought them shot glasses and Roland poured them each a finger of the amber liquid. Roland sniffed his, sipped it, and lingered over the smooth bite of the whisky. Sylvie coughed and choked a bit, unused to the fire in the liquid, but she appreciated the sophistication of its taste. Roland screwed the cap back on the bottle, drew up the sack and snugged the cord around the neck before he replaced it in its proper carton. Sylvie's cheeks were flushed in the late afternoon sun dappling the tables where they sat. She had allowed herself to drink much more than her usual. There was something about being in the presence of these two men that allowed her to drop her guard and just be herself. She was suddenly conscious of the way she looked and she fingered the button of her blouse just above the swell of her breasts. She asked Will, "Do you mind if I ask you a question?" She enunciated the words carefully to show them she was still in control of her tongue.

"Go right ahead."

"What exactly is a semi, semio, damn! semiotician?" She stuck her tongue out to give it a little air. "Let's try that again. I mean, I know all about your record for solving previously cold cases, but I'm not exactly sure how you do it." She slurred her esses now and that flustered her.

She blew her bangs off her forehead. The two men looked at each other and smiled at her effort to understand.

"You've asked a good question, Ms. Schumann, and I want to explain. But to do so I have to give you some definitions first and I don't want to sound like I'm lecturing."

"Oh, don't worry about that," she said, graciously waving his concern away. You go right ahead. Your uncle lectures me all the time."

Will couldn't help but laugh and Roland merely raised his eyebrows. Sylvie wondered what was so funny. As Will began, Roland pushed back his chair, crossed his legs at the knee and got comfortable.

"A semiotician is a person who studies semiotic theory. According to the American philosopher Charles Sanders Peirce, semiotics is a Greek word that means the study of signs, roughly translated. A sign is something that stands for something else to some observer. There are basically three types of signs: icons, indexes, and symbols. Most of the signs I interpret are in fact, symbolic. By definition, a symbol is a sign that has an arbitrary relationship to the thing that it stands for."

"What do you mean by arbitrary?" Sylvie asked.

"Just that there is no necessary or natural reason for the connection between the symbol and the thing it stands for. For instance, take the color of the purple sack that Crown Royal uses. The color purple might symbolize royalty in some cultures. In others, it does not. Why purple? At some point, someone arbitrarily decided to link purple with nobility or royalty. When others accept the association, the symbol becomes meaningful. So, within the context of its use, purple becomes a conventional symbol that represents royalty."

"A diamond ring symbolizes love," Roland suggested.

"I see," Sylvie acknowledged. "Clues in a murder case can be symbolic."

"Yes, but they can also be indexical. Indexical signs point to something else. An exit wound points to the caliber or type of weapon. But the use of a knife instead of a pistol may be symbolic. Each sign then requires interpretation within the context of its use. For me, and the reason I have been successful in my work as a special agent for the FBI in the U.S., is that I treat each homicide or rape as an interpretable text. My job is to take all the available signs and read them. This requires interpretation and interpretation depends on deductive and inductive logic."

"We were taught deduction in philosophy class at the Uni," she said. "Isn't that what Sherlock Holmes used to solve his cases?"

Will smiled. "Holmes was famous for making deductions but he arrived at them by first using inductive logic, to be precise. He would make a specific observation and arrive at a general conclusion. Holmes, after observing Mr. X, says to Dr. Watson that the man smokes cigarettes. Watson is amazed, as usual, because he knows that Mr. X. is in fact a chain-smoker. But he has never smoked in Holmes' presence. So how could he know? His conclusion is actually the end result of a chain of reasoning based on a single observation. Mr. X's fingertips are stained yellow. Holmes remembers that all of the cigarette smokers he has observed in the past have had fingers stained yellow from the nicotine. Mr. X has yellow stains on his fingertips. He infers, therefore, that Mr. X is a smoker."

"But not all smokers have yellow stains on their fingers," Roland noted. It depends on how you hold the cigarette."

"Exactly." Will agreed. "That is why Holmes would have to amend his conclusion to state that most smokers have fingertips stained yellow from the nicotine in the cigarettes they smoke. By the way, nicotine turns yellow when exposed to oxygen."

126

"If that's an inductive argument, what's a deductive argument?" Sylvie wanted to know.

"All blondes are pretty girls. Sylvie is a blonde. Therefore, Sylvie is a pretty girl. In the case of a deductive argument, the reasoning is from the general to the specific but again, the truth of the conclusion often rests in the validity of the premises. For the conclusion to be correct, the premises within the logical argument must also be correct."

"Aha," said Roland. "Not all blondes are pretty."

"Precisely. So, logic alone may not be sufficient to solving a case. But it can be a powerful tool, if used correctly." He paused for a moment, and took a drink from his beer. "Sylvie, would you allow me to take a personal liberty?"

What harm could it do, she thought? "Go ahead. It might be fun."

"I will offer two claims based on semiotic analysis, the second is related to and is a consequent of the first. First claim: you worked very late last night on the case, for the third night in a row. Second claim: the color of your panties does not match the color of your bra. Am I correct?"

Without saying a word, Sylvie Schumann blushed all the way into her ample chest. Roland nearly spit out his beer. Then he noticed Sylvie's bloom of red. "By god, I think he's right."

Sylvie could only nod, dumbfounded. How could he have known and how could he possibly know that the two were related?

"Not by god," Will gently corrected his uncle, "but by semiotic analysis and interpretation. What I have given you is a conclusion based on a complex chain of observation and logical reasoning."

She frowned and he laughed as he explained.

"OK. Here goes. I know that you are recently graduated from university into the Kriminalpolizei. As a young female on a predominately male police force, you feel the need to prove yourself. Working with my uncle, who has very high standards of competency, you feel doubly pressed to make a good impression. So, you work late on your cases and this one is no exception. Today is Thursday, and although you have been working on the case during the weekends as well, you can sleep in those days. By the third night of working late during the week, you are considerably sleep deprived. Those signs of fatigue are evident in your eyes and in your face. You have made an attempt to cover those signs with make-up, but it was hastily done.

"This morning you slept through your alarm after the fourth day of sleep deprivation and this put you behind your normal schedule. You were running late and you felt that it would not be a good idea to keep the Hauptkommissar waiting on the day he is to meet his nephew arriving from the United States. You live alone, you are single and not currently in a serious relationship. There was no one to wake you when you slept through the alarm. You had just enough time to shower but not to blow-dry your hair. You toweled it and combed it and let it dry naturally. You stepped into fresh panties but put on the bra you wore last night. You have not had time to do the laundry lately and find a fresh bra. It does show a bit through your blouse, as you have been worrying, and on occasion you have unconsciously fidgeted with the third button of your blouse. The bra is red; the blouse is blue and so shows a bit. Were you not rushed, you would have chosen another color. But you had not yet done your make-up and it was almost time for Roland to arrive."

"But how does that tell you what color my panties are?' she wanted to know. "And what color are they? There's no way you could guess," she said with certainty, her legs tightly crossed at the knee, one above the other.

"Elementary, my dear Sylvie," he teased her. "Your panties are white."

Incredulous, she shook her head. "Everything you said has been correct, but I still can't figure out how you knew the color of my panties or that they were mismatched."

"You still wear the panties your mother bought for you. Mothers who buy underwear for their daughters typically buy white. Red would be an acknowledgment of the daughter's sexuality, which most mothers are apt to ignore. A woman typically changes her underwear daily, unlike most men, I might add." Roland raised his eyebrows again, this time as if to say why look at me? "But a bra can be worn more than one day, in a pinch, pardon the pun."

Roland groaned. Will ignored him.

"Therefore, red bra, white panties. Mismatched. You corrected your lipstick on the ride in from the airport. There you are: semiotic interpretation."

All she could do was stare at him. In the space of ten minutes, he had discovered intimate and private details about her life, information that not even her best girlfriend knew. One thing she knew for certain. The man's reputation was deserved. He had read her like a book and this made her very nervous indeed. And then she felt a little sorry for him because she suddenly realized that this was exactly how most women must feel in his presence when they learned what he did for a living. She made a conscious decision not to let it bother her. They were, after all, professionals working together.

At this point, Roland interjected. "A remarkable demonstration of the power of observation and logical reasoning, and I'm glad you remembered everything I have taught you, but it's time to get Will back to Kaufbeuren and squared away at my apartment. I want the both of you to sleep out tomorrow and that is an order, Lieutenant. I need you both sharp so we can finally make some progress on this case, or Direktor Hauptmann will have my head, which I still have some use for."

As they stood to leave, Will whispered in Sylvie's ear just loud enough for Roland to hear, as he paid the bill. "His head is important to him because it has the lips he needs so that he doesn't dribble on his shirt when he drinks his beer."

Sylvie thought that was about the funniest thing she had heard. Perhaps working with these two might not be such a punishment after all.

Chapter Ten: The Fall

I N IDAR-OBERSTEIN, on a clean, quiet street lined with linden trees, without fanfare a small diamond shop opened for business. The building had once housed an electronics store selling stereos, VCRs, tape recorders, and the like. When the owner retired, he sold off his inventory and retired to the sunny beaches of Mallorca. After some refurbishing and repainting, the new store opened with a limited but selective stock of loose stones, rings, bracelets, necklaces, and other items one might expect for sale in a jewelry store. The front door, glass framed by oak, was flanked by two large display windows. The name of the company was stenciled discretely across the top of the left window. The street number, in bronze, was the only marking on the door. As the door opened, a little bell above it klingeled, alerting the person in back that a customer had entered the store. Glass display cases of rings, diamonds, earrings, and some crystal goods by Swarovski, faced the customer. Padded stools awaited the shoppers and placed them close to the brass lamps that provided the spot lighting for viewing the goods. It was not an impressive store in terms of decoration and décor; it was not ostentatious in any manner, nor was the staff effete or snobbish, as one might expect in other high-end shops. Only the alarms, video cameras, and security systems were state-of-the art, discretely placed so as not to intrude on the potential customer's need for privacy.

In the early days when the store was first open for business, other diamantaires occasionally visited, some to say hello and be introduced, some to pass along good wishes for success, others to check the competition's prices and the quality of the merchandise. Very few actually bought a stone for personal use, or brought a gem to be resold, but when they did, they got a good price, a handshake to seal the deal, and a hearty "mazel und broche," the ritual ending to the transaction that bestowed luck and blessing.

The consensus opinion was that the small concern did not pose a serious competitive threat to other similar interests and the wager among the established dealers in town gave the little shop less than two years. Customer traffic, according to their personal reconnoitering was minimal and, on some days, non-existent. This most likely was due to the high prices charged for the stones on display. They were clearly at the high-end, boutique prices really, and as competitors, they had little trouble matching the price or even beating it by five percent for similar goods.

The owner was always polite to his customers, in their experience, and treated his snooping cohorts with respect and deference, which often confused them. Unable to ascertain if he was Jewish, Indian, Lebanese, Dutch, Belgian, or even South African, all agreed he was knowledgeable and certainly knew his goods, but he was, alas, simply not a good businessman. Who could afford to pay such prices in Idar-Oberstein anyway? This was not Antwerp, or Amsterdam, or New York, where almost everyone in the business had a relative. Arabs and Japanese were occasionally seen exiting the little store, but they deserved to pay the prices charged if they were too lazy to walk down the street a block or two and find a decent deal.

THE FALL

There was a delicious little rumor floating around town, and keep this under your hat, that he dealt in outside goods, but who were they to say. None of the sight holders among them could recall ever seeing him on Pelikaanstraat in Antwerp where they received their legal goods from De Beers. Nor was he a member of the exchange in town, more than one hundred and fifty years old. However, good businessmen that they were, with a tip of the hat, the stroke of a beard, and a pull at the ringlets framing their faces, they acknowledged that everyone needed to move a smuggled stone now and then; perhaps a fancy from Tel Aviv; maybe a plaquette of illegal stones smuggled through India, which was making a real name for itself processing and polishing the lower-end of gem quality stones, and we could all learn a lesson from that. Their anxieties allayed and their interests cooled, the good diamantaires of Idar-Oberstein went about minding their own business and left the little jewelry store alone.

Every Wednesday the courier arrived, wrist chained to the diplomatic pouch, raised the bridge that lay across the counters and walked to the major's office. Whether the political situation in Sierra Leone stabilized or deteriorated, Samir remained the one constant even as the fighting ebbed and flowed and Captain Konema consolidated his gains in the diamond fields. Samir Ayoub provided a steady and reliable flow of diamonds from his broker's office in Koidu-Sefadu. Occasionally, he would include a swimmer in the shipment, a high-quality stone of ten or more carats, conspicuous among the hundreds of industrial-grade stones. The work of polishing and grinding the stones was contracted out to the laborers who lived in the villages surrounding Idar-Oberstein. The quality gemstones were mounted and displayed and sold to the public. The proceeds were used to support the daily operations of the business and Hain used the overages to pay his employees bonuses. A posting to Idar-Oberstein became a coveted position for the young, attractive female agents who worked behind the display cases during the day. The bonuses provided them the hard currency they needed to buy fashionable and modern clothes, handbags, and perfumes, and pay for the entertainment luxuries they did not have access to in East Germany.

It was a slow day and the leaves of the linden trees littered the sidewalks, a prelude to the coming of winter, when business would pick up again during the holidays. Rudiger Hain had given two of his female Stasi lieutenants the rest of the day off and they were happy to spend the afternoon shopping for shoes. He was a bit surprised but glad to be pulled away from his paperwork in the back office when he heard the bell jump as the front door opened. He put on his suit jacket and greeted the two customers waiting in the center of the room. The major was not used to seeing Chinese in the store, Japanese certainly, but rarely Chinese. The man appeared nondescript: black hair, brown eyes, black silk shirt and brown pants. He wore glasses with thick lenses that magnified his eyes and a tan blazer a bit too long for him in the sleeves, as if he had borrowed it from an older, larger brother.

The woman standing next to him was quite simply the most beautiful Eurasian he had ever seen. Her lips were full, dark and red, her glossy black hair pulled away from her forehead. With her hair tight within the jade comb at the back, she looked as though she had just emerged from a swim, but she was able to pull off the severe look because her features were of such perfect proportions. Rudiger could not escape the beauty of her jade green eyes. She broke the stare by averting her eyes as she bowed ever so slightly, enabling him to steal another fraction of a moment to look her over. The older man waited patiently as if he were used to exactly this sort of reaction. He opened the conversation with an apology for his poor and heavily accented German, which Rudiger accepted and silently agreed, and asked the man if he spoke English. He answered that he did; in fact, it just so happened that his niece was a graduate student in foreign languages and they were hoping to buy a stone to take back to Hong Kong if the price was agreeable to all. Rudiger assured him that he would do everything possible to satisfy them both and he noticed surreptitiously that she blushed into her perfect ears.

The man was interested in an unmounted stone, perhaps ten carats in size. Rudiger paused for a moment, mentally reviewing his inventory. He did not want them to leave. As luck would have it, Samir had sent along just such a stone with last week's shipment. It had been sent out for cutting and polishing and was returned only this morning. Surely, nothing more than coincidence, he thought to himself, her smile defeating the paranoia of his training. He then noticed the diamond ring on the man's finger, the only article of jewelry that he wore. She, on the other hand, wore only a robin's egg blue silk top with a mandarin collar and black silk pants with her sandals. Nothing more was required. To his naked eye, it appeared the ring on the man's finger ran to about ten carats also and most certainly was a synthetic. It occurred to him that the Chinese uncle, shrewd businessman that he was, had declared the fake diamond after he left Hong Kong and entered West Germany. Hain guessed that he would substitute the real diamond for the fake as he traveled home. This, however, was none of his business. He excused himself and went into his office and opened the safe where he had stored the diamond.

Hain returned and atop a crisp white sheet of paper, showed the diamond to the man and his niece and invited them to sit atop the stools for a better look. For more light, he switched on the brass lamp atop the

135

glass counter. It illuminated the diamond lying in repose in the exact center of the square white paper. He described the stone. "This is an emerald cut, similar to the stone in your ring." He used the tweezers to show all eight sides of the stone to best effect. "Emerald cuts are used to accentuate flawless stones such as the one before us." The man nodded. He had not yet reached out to touch the jewel, as most customers did unconsciously. "The flat top of the diamond is called the table; the bottom is the culet." He handed the man his jeweler's 10-power loupe and showed him how to place it in the orbit of his eye. The Chinese uncle carefully removed and placed his glasses atop the counter. As he looked into the heart of the stone, Hain continued his description.

"If the distance from the table to the culet is too great, light will refract out the sides and the center will appear black." He gave the man time to orient himself within the geometric center of the diamond.

He looked up with a pleased smile and said, "It does not."

Rudiger agreed. "That's because this stone is an ideal cut that follows the precise mathematical formula developed by the Belgian Marcel Tolkowsky. The radiance of a diamond is achieved by bringing out the stone's maximum brilliance for every facet's angle."

Very softly, as if not wanting to offend, the man said, "The stone has not been cut to achieve maximum brilliance."

Rudiger took a long hard look at the man, possible only because he was still examining the gem. "You are, of course, correct. One cannot achieve both maximum brilliance and maximum fire when cutting a diamond. A Tolkowski make gives us tremendous fire at the expense of a little less brilliance."

The man bowed his agreement. "One cannot be too careful. As you know, some synthetic stones today are nearly indistinguishable from authentic diamonds." He pulled at the ring on his finger, twisted it over the knuckle with some difficulty, and placed the ring next to the stone in the center of the white paper. "Would you tell me, please, if this stone is real."

"Certainly. May I handle it?"

"Of course."

He studied the emerald-cut gem under his loupe, then shined a hand-held laser into the stone. It was an excellent reproduction capable of fooling all but the most experienced eye. "I'm sorry to inform you, sir, that the stone is a synthetic, but a wonderful example nevertheless. Even as a synthetic, the fake is worth more than the ring and the setting. I intend no disrespect, sir, but the setting is poorly constructed and the band is merely ten carat white gold."

The man smiled at the corners of his mouth. "In other words, nothing here to draw the attention of a discerning eye?"

Rudiger smiled back. His initial surmise had been correct.

"If you will allow one more question, sir, before we agree to the price?"

"I am happy to answer whatever questions you might have. We offer a one hundred percent guarantee of satisfaction on our goods."

The Chinese uncle stood and bowed again and when she heard his next question, his niece hid a smile of embarrassment inside the cup of her hand. "Forgive the impertinence of the question, but how can I know for certain if the stone you are about to sell me is genuine?"

Rudiger nodded as if he had anticipated the question. He also made a mental note to raise the price. "An authentic diamond will fluoresce under x-ray light, if you care to have it checked. I will also provide you a certificate verifying the authenticity of the stone."

"Ah, very kind, but even commercial labs can be dishonest for a price and certificates can be forged."

Rudiger smiled again. This man was not an ordinary customer. He knew more about diamonds than he let on. He was either in the business himself or he had done his research. "For that reason, our diamonds are certified by the Diamond High Council, the HRI in Antwerp, Belgium. I can see to it that a certificate is issued for this stone."

"HRI?" he asked, carefully and deliberately enunciating the R.

"Hoge Raad voor Diamant...."

Before he could translate, she said to her uncle, "High Council for Diamonds."

"Indeed," Rudiger Hain acknowledged, pleased to be able to observe her again before her uncle commanded his attention.

"Would you be able to replace the synthetic with the genuine?"

"I can have it ready for you tomorrow at this time."

Without negotiation, the man agreed to the exorbitant price the major named and said his niece would come the next day to collect the purchase. Hands at their sides, they bowed as they said goodbye, and Rudiger walked them to the door. Once more he took the liberty of breathing in the scent of her perfume after they left, a heady mixture of opium and orchids. Before he closed the shop, he wrote out his report to Markus Wolf, his boss, and included it with the diplomatic bag that would be collected the next morning and taken to East Berlin.

LIEUTENANT GENERAL MARKUS Wolf declared to himself that Major Rudiger Hain's mission could now be counted an unequivocal success. Wolf received the diamonds he needed for East Germany's clandestine nascent nuclear missile program and for the more basic technological needs of industry. The direction of the MJOLNIR program, beyond securing diamonds for it, was no longer his concern. The diamond store located in Idar-Oberstein of the Federal Republic of West Germany served the dual purpose of providing him with a front behind which he placed some of his best Romeo and Juliet agents. The female Stasi agents, under the cover of working at the jewelry store, met, fell in love with, and recruited men and women with access to the intelligence secrets that had made Wolf and his agency the envy of the KGB, the BND, and even the CIA, although all were loath to admit it. Both the Bundesnachrichtendienst in West Germany and the CIA in the United States were aware that the Russians were smuggling diamonds into the Soviet Union through the auspices of Russelmag, their front in Antwerp manned by KGB agents. However, they had no idea whatsoever that Wolf and the Stasi were doing the very same thing under their collective noses and to such a degree of success that the Stasi were selling their excess inventory to the KGB at a handsome profit: another of the delicious little ironies of life that Wolf so much enjoyed.

Wolf permitted himself a chuckle of self-satisfaction as he read Hain's report at his desk at Headquarters. And because a fair share of the profit was channeled to his colleague Gottschalk at KoKo, everyone was content. Wolf continued to score string after string of intelligence coups, and he had the major promoted to colonel. In West Africa, Samir Ayoub became rich, Sierra Leone churned out diamonds and revolutions, a new term called 'blood diamonds' entered the international lexicon, and Captain Joseph Konema and the Revolutionary United Front moved down out of the hills and became a legitimate and dominant political force. One bright winter's day in 1985, Colonel Hain was called in from the cold by Lieutenant General Wolf himself.

Within the secure confines of his office, Wolf looked at the Colonel with pride. He considered him almost a son. "We have had a remarkable run, you and I, and you have served your country with distinction and honor." He took a sip from his glass of mineral water.

"Rudiger," he said with an air of finality and resignation, "I am closing the ADAMAS file forthwith." Without pleasure, he watched the shock spread through his top agent's face. "Listen to me carefully, Rudi, your life might depend on it. What I am about to tell you is highly classified and I doubt if three other people know it. I share this with you because you are a trusted comrade-in-arms and a dear friend. As you no doubt have anticipated, I will officially announce my retirement next year."

Rudiger shifted in the plush leather of the black chair and opened the last button of his suit coat. Wolf's retirement was inevitable and often whispered about, but it was also one of those issues no one wanted to address for fear of making the inevitable a fait accompli. He acknowledged the certainty of the Herr Direktor's decision. What he did not completely understand was the reason for closing down the diamond operation. He was in a position to continue the project even after Wolf's retirement. The consternation showed in his face. Hain understood that as the head of the Stasi, Wolf's decisions were final and did not require explanation, least of all to a newly promoted colonel. The circumstances leading to the lieutenant general's decision, however, were unusual and an explanation would help Hain understand the complexity underlying the action. His man deserved to know as much.

"As you know, it has been my intention to mentor and protect my best agents as I move into retirement." He thought it best not to mention the unfortunate exception of the Baroness, his top female agent lost in the West some years ago, an agent who had been used against him by the BND without his knowledge. "I have been made aware of information which may preclude my taking an active role in managing your career even from the distance of my retirement."

He turned and looked at the pictures on his desk of his latest wife and his beloved children. This is what it all came down to now: protecting the family. He had given his life, his energy, his talent, and his intellect to serve the greater good of the State, as had the younger man sitting before him. Now it was time to place personal interest above the public and the political. He dropped his bombshell, his voice quiet and steady, but intense. "I am convinced that within five years or so the East German State will fall. If this happens, and my analysis of geopolitical events convinces me that it will, then it is within the realm of possibility that the Stasi will be disbanded and all its officers discharged. It is more than likely that charges will be preferred against us for having done our duty." Wolf had never forgotten his service as a reporter at the Nuremberg trials. He stopped to let Colonel Hain comprehend the full import of what he had been told.

Rudiger took a deep breath. The man never ceased to amaze him, but this was the secret of his success through all these years. For almost forty years, Wolf had survived in a cold, cutthroat, backstabbing, sell out your neighbor to the State at any and all costs to protect yourself and your business, because he had a visionary ability to look into the future and discern not only what was to come, but also how it was likely to happen. "You think the Soviet Union will collapse and East Germany will reunite with the West, Lieutenant General?"

Wolf nodded. "Affirmative." Again he was pleased with how quickly Hain had drawn the correct conclusions. "Gorbachev is the chief architect here but I am afraid history will show that he tried to do too much too soon. However, I believe that his political vision for the Soviet Union will be realized. He knows all too well and our own research indicates that the Soviet Union is bankrupt and on the verge of economic collapse." He paused for a moment, ever the philosopher. "You and I understand that all great revolutions have their basis in economics. Marx, Engels, and Hegel taught us that. My dear friend Rudi...."

141

The colonel was astonished to hear the emotion in his mentor's voice and see the older man's eyes shimmer with tears. He looked suddenly very tired and vulnerable. Wolf turned away at that instant and dabbed at the corners of his eyes with his handkerchief. He did not apologize. When he looked again at Rudiger, he was composed and smiled. "It is the times we live in. Now listen to me carefully." The command voice and the steel in it were apparent once more. Rudiger unconsciously relaxed. "In two years or so I want you to follow me into retirement. This should give you a sufficient cushion before the West destroys the Stasi. If charges are brought against me for doing my job, they may very well seek out current officers instead of retired for their scapegoats. If the inevitable takes place, lose yourself in the West. Do not go to Russia."

It was wise and prescient advice.

WOLF RETIRED IN 1986 according to plan and Hain followed two years later, living off his modest pension and the monies he had saved from the diamond venture. In 1991, after the fall of the Berlin Wall, Wolf's predictions came true. Plans were set in motion to once more reunite East Germany with the West and the Stasi, as predicted became defunct. The Soviet Union disintegrated.

During the process of reunification, Markus Wolf, an avid reader and student of history, knew full well the fate of secret agencies that propped up the totalitarian societies for whom they worked. He took stock: at the risk of seeming immodest, he believed that his reputation within the clandestine community of espionage was unparalleled, and he hoped this would afford him a measure of protection against the cries for his head. The facts were that the CIA, the KGB, and even his archrivals, the BND, held him in the highest regard. Wealthy by any measure of status or fame, he was by no means a rich man according to western standards of luxury. The East German political regime had allowed him to live well, given his rank and position, and afforded him a lifestyle far beyond the ken of the average citizen in the German Democratic Republic. Nor was he embarrassed by how he lived or by the fringe benefits accorded him by the State in the service of his country. He was not an extravagant man and he saw to it that his family was well provided for. His greatest expense was his mistress but this was a tolerable allowance. The problem, to his mind, was the status of his pension. His savings and investments, such as they were, would not be sufficient to maintain even a semblance of his current lifestyle. Without his pension, he might become, and he appreciated this cruel irony, literally dependent on the new State as East Germany became absorbed into the West. He also faced the possibility of being charged with treason. His professional instincts told him this scenario was more probable than not.

Then Wolf's greatest fears were realized. After reunification, he was charged with high crimes against the State when he was merely doing his job in service to his country. Unfortunately, he had done it so well for so long that others decided he needed to be punished. This was the man who had given his entire professional and political life to the service of the socialist State, protecting and defending her against all enemies foreign and domestic, protecting and defending the ideals of the philosopher Karl Marx, whom he so admired. There was very little choice for him when the call from Beijing arrived at his private residence; in order to guarantee the financial future of his family and loved ones, former Lieutenant General Markus Wolf, former Direktor of Stasi, became a paid consultant.

In the meantime, he was forced to spend the immediate days of his life embroiled in a nightmare of legal battles defending his career and his service to his country. In the end, although he won some measure of reprieve, the legal battles left him impoverished. The winner of the Karl Marx Medal, the highest honor awarded for distinguished and meritorious service to the German Democratic Republic, was dishonored.

Rudiger watched the despicable proceedings from afar, hoping that the upswell of public opinion currently favoring the great spymaster might carry the day, but he had been enjoined by Wolf from making any contact. He knew it was for his own protection. He was disgusted and frustrated by the political posturing of the prosecutors, who should have known better, had they any understanding of duty and honor. The only thing Wolf was guilty of was doing his job with such a high degree of success that it embarrassed the leaders of the newly reunited Germany. Depressed, and his own future uncertain, Rudiger went to ground, unaware of the chain of events Wolf had set in motion during the process of reunification.

Under the established cover of having visited family in Schleswig-Holstein, he returned to Idar-Oberstein with the monies he had saved from his duty there, safely banked in Liechtenstein. He judiciously abandoned his meager pension in the East, carried with him all the papers supporting his identity as a diamantaire recently entered into retirement, and secured for himself a small but comfortable apartment on the outskirts of Idar-Oberstein, Bavaria. Late in 1992, he received, much to his surprise, a welcome call from a one-time but unforgettable customer, now a professor of foreign languages at the University of Munich. His next call was to Samir Ayoub and about eighteen months later his fortunes took a decided turn for the better.

Chapter Eleven: Synthetics

A FINE DIAMOND in a brilliant cut of fifty-eight facets can bring close to ten thousand dollars on the open market. There is very little intrinsic value in the stone itself, which is simply crystallized carbon. The worth of the gem is embedded in its origins. A hundred miles below the earth's crust immense pressures compress stone into a liquid state. Such pressures also force molten magma to seek the surface. An igneous rock, liquid kimberlite rises like a soufflé in a too hot oven. As gasses vent to escape the pressure, the soufflé collapses and more liquid rock flows into the pipe being thrust upward through the earth's permeable surface. There the kimberlite cools and solidifies into a blue-black color. Over time the tip of the pipe crumbles like an eraser and erodes and yellows with age. Most kimberlite pipes, some one and a half billion years old, others only a hundred million years old, are found in Africa. Like a fallen chocolate cake, Africa has settled some six thousand feet through the eons of time, further exposing kimberlite to the wind and the torrential rains that wash and sift the alluvial soil. A properly trained eye may discover on the exposed surface what appear to be pieces of broken, frosted glass. The miner, holding one between his fingers, would find it slightly oily to the touch and unremarkable in appearance. But he knows that he rolls on the table of his palm the hardest naturally occurring substance on earth. Now the diamond is becoming valuable.

THE ADAMANTINE HEART

The lucky miner, who has had the luxury of walking up to the stone, which is still possible in some regions of Africa, sells it to an agent for De Beers, the South African syndicate that controls between seventy-five and eighty percent of the world's fine diamonds. They send the stone to a cutter, a highly skilled artisan who determines whether the stone is to be cleaved or sawed. A cleavage cuts the diamond in line with the grain, sawing crosses the grain. Some rare stones emerge from the earth so well shaped that they require neither and are labeled 'makeable.' Stones requiring a cutter's skills are set before a diamond saw, paper-thin disks of phosphor bronze spinning at 4000 revolutions per minute. The edge of the blade is dressed with diamond paste and olive oil. Even a small diamond may take several hours to cut. Cutting shapes the diamond and maximizes its esthetic value. Typical shapes are the pear, the marquise, the rectangular baguette, the square, the oval, and the eight-side emerald. Emerald cuts are used to accentuate flawless diamonds. The stone is increasing in value.

If the stone is cut using the formula developed by the Belgian Marcel Tolkowsky, it is called an "ideal cut," which brings out maximum fire in each of the facets. Once cut, it is sent to be polished. For a brilliant cut, the 'cross-cutter' puts on the first eighteen facets, and then passes it along to the "brilliandeer" who works the remaining forty, if the diamond is in an Antwerp shop. If the stone has been sent to Tel Aviv, a Piermatic machine polishes the stone automatically. The hand of a skilled artisan adds greater value to the gem. By the time the diamond, once little more than pressure-treated carbon, has passed from the miner to the cutter, to the polisher, to the wholesaler, to the jeweler, and finally, from the jeweler to the client, the price of the diamond has risen more than six hundred percent.

Eighty percent of all mined diamonds have no use whatsoever in jewelry. A large portion of these stones, called "boart," is relegated to industry. De Beers happens to control most of the world's industrial diamond production as well. But this has been a more recent development in the diamond industry as more and more countries become technologically advanced. The modern industrial world would grind to a halt without diamonds. Now the intrinsic value of the diamond lies in its natural hardness, not in some relative, culturally determined esthetic based on cut, clarity, brilliance, or size. For instance, oil drillers need diamond tips to penetrate the toughest rock. Heat dispersion is another valued characteristic of boart and has applications in the space and missile programs of technologically advanced nations. The windows of some space capsules are not glass or plastic but are made entirely of highly polished diamond. Eventually, as demand increases and supplies are diminished, the world's store of industrial diamonds will be depleted. The only alternative is to produce synthetic stones.

Allmanna Svenska Elektriska Aktiebolaget (ASEA) pioneered synthetics in Sweden in 1953 but General Electric patented the process for production two years later. To this day, the details of this alchemical process remain a closely guarded secret, even though the basic recipe is public knowledge. A metal solvent is added to graphite, a common form of carbon, and then placed between tungsten carbide pistons. The pistons exert a sustained pressure of one million pounds per square inch, heating the graphite to temperatures of 2500 to 3000 degrees Fahrenheit. These quasi-natural stresses slowly convert the graphite into minute diamond crystals. The longer the heat and pressure are maintained, the larger the resulting diamonds. Unfortunately, one hour is necessary for even tiny industrial diamonds and a diamond of one carat requires an entire week under pressure. For this reason, it has been uneconomical to make gem quality diamonds. However, this changed when an American scientist in North Carolina rediscovered the work of a French physicist named Henri Moissan. The American developed a process for artificially producing large, single crystals of silicon carbide. The resulting lab-created stones were virtually indistinguishable from high-quality diamonds. The discovery was thought to be a closely guarded secret.

ON A BRIGHT and sunny Friday morning washed free of the oppressive humidity by the previous evening's thunderstorms, Dr. Samuel Bronson was right with the world and the world was right with him. The founder and chief executive officer of Carbon Research Technologies Incorporated, or CRTI, as they liked to call themselves, worked the early morning traffic of Durham, North Carolina with aplomb from behind the leather-wrapped steering wheel of his brand spanking new Lexus. The vehicle had been his gift to himself after last week's interview featured on CNN's financial news program, touting the up-and-coming promise of his small high-technology company. After the interview the stock jumped three-and-a-half-dollars and he had cashed in just enough to afford the luxury of the new ride. He breathed in the new car smell, ran his hand over the soft, shiny leather seats, and popped a greatest hits CD into the player. Christ almighty, he thought to himself, the damn thing sounds better than my stereo at home.

Bronson held a doctorate in material science from the prestigious Massachusetts Institute of Technology and after teaching there six years, moved on to work four years at General Electric in Worthington, Ohio as director of their Synthetic Diamond division. Twelve years ago, he resigned his position, gave up his security and his pension, mortgaged his house and raised enough money from family and friends to start up his new business venture. From the time he completed his doctorate at MIT, it had been his dream to produce synthetic diamonds. He intended to produce artificial diamonds indistinguishable from gemstones to the naked eye and sell them for a tenth the price of a natural stone. In the grand American entrepreneurial tradition, he wanted to do for quality simulants what Ray Kroc had done for hamburgers and Henry Ford for automobiles.

It had been a titanic struggle from the word go: raising the money nearly bankrupted him and put an enormous strain on his marriage. The fact that he worked twelve hours sometimes seven days a week during the early going did not contribute to the peace and harmony of his domestic situation. But those were the sacrifices one had to make and he had made them. Then De Beers swooped up out of South Africa like a demon wind off the desert sand and tried to blow him away. Only the intervention of the United States government saved his ass and he was not too proud to admit it. His new process for converting single crystal silicon carbide into diamond-like stones after two earlier failures had proven itself to the degree that both De Beers and Uncle Sam understood the potential. From De Beers' point of view, a flood of undetectable synthetics could corrupt their monopoly and destroy the pricing structure of the gemstone market. From the point of view of the U.S. economy, he could provide high-quality industrials inexpensively and substantially lower the costs of mining, oil exploration, and drilling. More significantly to the U. S. defense and space industry, the synthetics he produced in the lab could withstand temperatures over one thousand degrees centigrade. This made them invaluable for his country's space and missile programs.

When the money secured by the first loans had run out and he couldn't meet his payroll, the government had stepped in with a fresh infusion of capital; otherwise, he would have gone under. After the second failure in the lab, the stock of his company was delisted from the NASDAQ and was relegated to the pink sheets where penny stocks were traded by speculators. At that point, De Beers stepped in and tried to buy the company, but the government's lawyers were shrewd enough to help him structure his financials in such a way that he remained the majority stockholder. He was also prepared to swallow a 'poison pill,' thus thwarting the boys from Johannesburg in their black suits and white shirts in their attempt to take him over. With the shares held by the three members of his board pooled with his own, Dr. Bronson maintained an equity bulwark over which not even the diamond lords of South Africa could leap. He held the stock and he held the patents, protected by U. S. and international patent law, and finally De Beers backed off, not gone but waiting at a distance, ever vigilant and patient like jackals lying in the high grasses.

Now his time had come. After years of scrimping by on a salary less than what an associate professor made at a tier-three university, he watched the price of the company's stock jump up the chart until it quadrupled, then quadrupled again. The stock was relisted on the NASDAQ and when the short sellers got squeezed, his net worth, on paper at least, was suddenly in the hundred million range. This brought General Electric back sniffing at the edges, talking about a friendly takeover beneficial to both. Rumors of a buyout were being bruited by the financial press and the stock had jumped again today. It felt good being where he finally wanted to be, in a financial manner of speaking. The company was on good grounds but there was the nagging issue of the relational thing hanging over his head. All the hard work and sacrifice had paid off and he was still young enough to enjoy the coming rewards. Although he had married during his doctoral training, the marriage had produced no children and left him without much familial responsibility. He was thinking seriously of upgrading his relationship, much as he had recently upgraded his car from an eight-year-old Camry to a new Lexus. The cell phone snapped him from his reverie.

It was Carlton, his security chief. The heist had been quick, clean, and obviously the work of professionals. Although armed and in plainclothes, both the bodyguard and the courier charged with carrying the valise that held the first successful production run of artificial moissanite, had been overpowered as they walked across the company parking lot to the car. Carlton was smart enough not to bring up the fact that two years ago he had argued vociferously for a fence, a gate, and a manned security station. His proposal had been shelved as being too costly at the time. Bronson listened as he drove and as his mind raced to grasp the details of the story, he noticed that he had unconsciously increased his speed to match his rising anxiety. "I'll call you back in five," he said and replaced the handset in its holder mounted on the console. He got sick to his stomach as he digested the news.

He pulled into the parking lot of a small strip mall and found shade under a lone oak tree. He needed time to think and to get his stomach turned back outside in. The last thing he wanted to do now was vomit all over the Armani suit or on the butter-cream leather of the seats. He took off his sunglasses and replaced them in their protective case. He hit the buttons to lower the front windows to let in some fresh air. He could smell honeysuckle on the breeze. The cloying sweetness didn't help. He loosened his tie and unbuttoned the stiff collar of his shirt. He let the electric motors purr his seat into a recline as he sank into a more comfortable position. God, he had come a long way, and now this, he

151

thought, when does it ever end? He drove the acrid, choking panic back down into his stomach and ignored it. As he regained control of his breathing, his heart rate dropped and he was once again in control of his emotions. This time he let the panic transmute into anger. He had given too much of his life to let this thing beat him now.

As he waited for his head to clear and swallowed back the nausea, he took himself back to the early days of his research when he first discovered the track down which he would travel in pursuit of his life's work. It was hard to believe that he owed such a debt of gratitude to a little known and under-appreciated French chemist, outside of academia, anyway. For cryin' out loud, the guy won the Nobel Prize for chemistry in 1906 after discovering the element fluorine and nobody had ever heard of the poor bastard. His discovery of natural silicon carbide while poking into a meteorite found in Arizona's Diablo Canyon, no less, sent the two scientists, an ocean apart, careening down similar paths. Back at his lab, on the meteorite Moissan had found green, black, and brown deposits with a carbon crystal structure very similar to diamonds. In honor of Dr. Henri Moissan, the scientific world named the new stone moissanite. Bronson wrote his doctoral thesis on Moissan's discovery and in so doing came upon a lesser-known aspect of Moissan's work.

The discovery of fluorine in 1896 allowed him to obtain the professor's chair of organic chemistry at the Sorbonne in Paris. A bit of an iconoclast, very much like me, thought Bronson, Moissan also was regarded as the father of high-temperature chemistry. Pursuing this line of research, Moissan had invented a spectacular electric arc furnace capable of reaching extraordinarily high temperatures. And what exactly was his friend the French professor of chemistry and Nobel Prize winner cooking in his little furnace? It wasn't his evening dinner's asparagus soup.

One day while he was poking through Moissan's lab notebooks, Bronson discovered that Pierre had tried to convert carbon into synthetic black diamonds. Rumors at the time said he succeeded but his notebooks showed that he fell just short. Bronson had taken the end-point of Moissan's work for his own theoretical starting point, and with the advent of better, more efficient high temperature furnaces, laid out the process for artificially producing not diamonds, but moissanite. The genius of his process was that the resulting stones were so similar to real diamonds that it was practically impossible to tell them apart.

In addition to the beauty of the theoretical work, by coincidence a burgeoning need for such stones was emerging now that the personal computer revolution had taken place. Naturally occurring industrial diamonds, known as boart, could no longer meet the voracious needs of the marketplace. Bronson, in addition to filing patents for his new process, patented their application for use in laptop and calculator screens, for precision cutting blades, and perhaps most importantly, because they conducted heat like diamonds, showed how they could be used in the semiconductor industry. And let's not forget good old Uncle Sam's missile and space programs, he thought, thumping the top arch of the padded leather steering wheel with his palm.

The ability of his artificial diamonds to conduct heat made them so similar to real diamonds that only a highly trained expert, one familiar with the properties of both stones, could tell them apart. The problem for the diamond industry was that no one to date had been trained with both stones. In fact, very few individuals outside academia knew that synthetic moissanite even existed. His process was so good now, he thought with satisfaction, that the average jeweler on the street or any sight holder from De Beers, for that matter, would be fooled if a moissanite turned up in his plaquette. He knew this for a fact. He had taken one of the earlier prototypes from the lab to the best jeweler in town and the man had appraised the stone as a top-quality diamond. It had taken a real act of will to thank the man, refuse the money, and walk the stone back to the lab. But the seeds of a new idea had been implanted. The latest batch turned out so good he decided to sell them as man-made, gem-quality stones, but at a tenth of the cost of a real gem.

That's where the money was. That's what would make him rich beyond his wildest dreams and that had been the reason for the suffocating secrecy. He snapped his fingers: now it could be gone just like that. If the synthetic moissanites hit the street and were passed off as real and then the truth was discovered... well, he didn't even want to think about the consequences. At the very least, his reputation would be ruined. Ironic, wasn't it, that right now he had an ad campaign in the planning stages announcing his discovery and production of a stone so much like a diamond that virtually no one could tell the difference. And the gem would soon be available to the general public at a fraction of the cost of a true diamond. Everyone could now afford a diamond-like stone and could wear the look of luxury without having to go bankrupt to do it. Once the province of the rich, the look of wealth was now at hand for everyone. De Beers would be absolutely, positively, livid. And it would serve the snotty bastards right. Their syndicate had cornered the diamond market for far too long. Now the poor Joe working himself to death in the tobacco fields or down in the coal mine wouldn't have to scrape together three months' salary anymore just to impress his intended with a lousy half-carat sparkler for her fat finger. He looked at the five-carat stone on his ring finger casting a brilliant fire as he turned his hand to the sun. It was breathtaking, even to his jaundiced eye. Hell, he could hardly tell the difference himself and he had invented the damn thing. As the fiery light of the gem struck his eye, he had it.

There it was right in front of his nose. He would use the secrecy surrounding the project to his advantage. He brainstormed a while longer, looking into the adamantine heart of the stone, mesmerized by the hypnotic light, and formulated his plan of action. He called ahead to make the arrangements, rolled up the windows, put on his sunglasses, hit the memory button that put his seat back into its pre-programmed driving position, and keyed the ignition. As his mother used to tell him, when given lemons, make lemonade. He was about to put the squeeze on.

As requested, the security chief, the courier, and his bodyguard were waiting for him in the outer sitting room of his office, his one concession to the privilege of rank. He noticed all three were sweating in spite of the air conditioning. Good. He wanted them to sweat. He brought them in and seated them perfunctorily. While they waited, he went to his wet bar and poured himself a straight two-fingers shot of his best Kentucky bourbon. He did not offer the three men a drink. He took his time and made a show of sitting on the high-backed leather chair, swirling the bourbon in the heavy shot glass while he watched them squirm. He wanted them to think he was deciding their punishments. He knew all three feared for their jobs and he played the fear to his advantage. He let each man tell his version of the robbery and in hearing all three versions decided they had not been at fault. They had followed their protocols perfectly. They were good men with families, conscientious about their jobs, both ex-cops from New York. Their boss, the security chief, was a retired CIA spook. He looked ready to take the fall for the failure of his men. Bronson admired that about him. In the academic world, he was used to everyone covering his or her own ass whenever a screw-up happened. It was time to put his plan into action.

"The important thing," he said, "is that nobody got hurt." Both men visibly relaxed into their chairs and the chief dabbed at his upper lip with the silk handkerchief taken from the breast pocket of his suit coat. He looked at the moisture, refolded the silk cloth into a neat square, and placed it in his hip pocket. Now that their worst fears had not been realized, it was time to use their relief to enlist their loyalty. "As you know," he continued, "if this were to get out to the media, it could conceivably destroy our company and everything we have worked so long and so hard for. Everything we've accomplished so far will be lost." They nodded vigorously in agreement. He was careful to build his arguments so that they were inclusive. He wanted them to understand that if one fails, we all fail. They were getting the point. "What we do, men," he said exerting his control, "is treat this unfortunate incident as if it never happened." He waited for the surprise to register in their faces as they repositioned themselves in their seats.

"Right now, with the exception of the bastards who did the deed, only the four of us in this room know what happened today, and I intend to keep it that way." He looked at the chief of security for emphasis. He got the nonverbal confirmation he wanted. "The continued good fortune and future success of this company depends on the guarantee of our silence. We don't tell the police, we don't tell the press, God forbid, we don't tell the insurance company, and we sure as hell don't tell our wives or our girlfriends. Period. We eat the loss and go on. This is the cost of doing business. Are you with me?" They were resolute in their loyalty and he relaxed a bit himself, sipping from the drink. He got up and made three more. They drank to the health and stability of the company.

"What about the company for whom the first shipment was intended?" the security chief wondered.

"Right. We call them with our apologies. Quality control has detected a minor problem in the first batch and we could not in good conscience send them anything less than a perfect product. They'll understand. Here's what we do. Rewrite the invoices to show that the first production run was destroyed due to the flaws. The next run goes to them as soon as it comes off the line and we throw in a little sugar for their inconvenience. Problem solved... if we can keep our lips zipped."

They assured him again to a man that not another word about the incident would ever be spoken. When they opened the tan envelope containing their next paycheck, instead of the pink slip they were expecting, they found an early Christmas bonus that confirmed the wisdom of their decision. The unfortunate incident that nearly broke Carbon Research Technology, Incorporated was forgotten.

Interestingly enough for Bronson, the stolen goods never did surface, at least not in the United States, and if they did make it out to the street, they were so good that no one could tell they were fakes. He would never know what happened to his first commercial production run of artificial moissanite, but that was okay by him. Things at the company got back to normal and he was grateful for the routine and he began thinking seriously about that divorce thing again.

Chapter Twelve: The Courier

LSA MENDEL HAD been briefed, but she was nervous all the same. She sat at the foot of her bed, naked, smoking a cigarette, waiting for the topcoat of her fingernail polish to dry. The nicotine, more than the thought of the money, calmed her. The tremble in her hands subsided as she took another deep pull from the cigarette and forcefully blew the smoke away toward the open window. She didn't want the smell of it in her hair, which she had just washed and dried. It was time. Her courage was back up. She went to the desk, stabbed out the cigarette and checked her papers one more time. Passport, tickets, visas, all in good order and safely in sight. She went into the bathroom, carrying her purse. She closed the lid of the toilet and sat, her bag in her lap. She removed the plastic inserter and one tampon, already unwrapped. The only difference she could detect was the weight of it. It felt full and heavy, as if it had been presoaked. She loaded it in the applicator. She opened her knees and with her left hand felt for the opening of her vagina. She was dry, dammit, because of the nerves. She wet her fingers and quickly placed the plastic tube into the vaginal canal. She pressed the plunger and seated the tampon. She checked the string. Good. She stood and waited. She could feel the force of gravity pull at the weight of the tampon. She pushed it back in with her fingers and flexed the muscles of her vaginal canal. She flushed a bit at the tingle. The heavy tampon felt like a short, fat penis, she thought. She wondered if she could keep it in place for the duration of the trip. She opened her purse and checked the pile of four wrapped tampons. She was two weeks away from her period.

She walked into the next room and took a matching pair of white panties and bra from her suitcase. Once in the panties, she checked herself carefully in the mirror to make sure the string did not show. She leaned forward to allow her breasts to fall into the cups of her bra, and then smoothed the straps so they did not cut into her shoulders. One last look in the mirror as she patted her tummy, then she stepped into gray slacks and buttoned a blouse atop the bra. She stepped into sandals almost the color of her tan, checked her hair and her teeth as the phone rang. A taxi was waiting to take her to the airport. She thanked the concierge, gathered her purse, her carry-on, and her wheeled suitcase and looked over the room one last time. She had enjoyed her week on the beaches of Freetown, Sierra Leone but now it was time earn her money. The momentary twinge of panic bloomed across her stomach again and she reflexively clenched her muscles, holding the package in place. Papers and tickets in hand, she closed the door behind her and rode the elevator to the desk. Checkout was routine and efficient. She signed the credit slip and put the receipt in her purse. The black clerk, dressed in starched tropical whites, watched her walk all the way across the lobby and through the revolving doors to where her taxi waited. Beautiful blondes, these Germans, he thought, and went about his duties.

Aboard the Sabena flight, she endured the routine of seatbelt, exit, and oxygen mask instructions. She closed her eyes against the take-off and started when the big plane locked its wheels safely into its belly. The engineer from Wolfsburg in the middle seat next to hers popped open his laptop, put on his glasses and studied a schematic for rack and pinion steering. He attributed her nervousness to fear of flying and left her to the privacy behind her closed eyes. The flight attendants busied themselves with their service duties, pulling curtains, microwave trays, and dull-gray metal carts. It would be at least ten minutes before they reached her. They attended to the needs of the affluent fliers in the first class and business sections, mostly men in business suits already digging through financial pages in newspapers and glossy business magazines for the edge that would keep them flying at the front of the plane.

She went through it all again. She knew she was rationalizing. She promised herself this would be the one and only time. The easy money and his sense of competent professionalism had seduced her. He had made it seem so easy. And it had been fun really, everything paid for, the free week in exotic Sierra Leone, and now the expectation of the pay-off. The money would allow her to buy the Volkswagen Golf she had wanted for so long but could not yet afford on her teacher's salary. Only in her second year at the Volksschule, she did not have enough time in grade for her tenure, when the job would be hers for the rest of her career. In the meantime, she scrimped. The rent for her efficiency apartment in Augsburg took most of her paycheck; the evenings out with her friends took most of the rest. At the end of the month, she had barely enough for groceries and daily necessities. What she had though, was time. She was rich in time and as a teacher, could travel when school was not in session and this is why he had recruited her. Think about the money, she told herself over and over, and the mantra helped calm her. By the time the drink cart arrived, she had her breathing under control and she ordered a Courvoisier in one of those cute little bottles she liked to save as souvenirs of her travels. The engineer looked up from his maze of colored lines and equations just long enough to order a martini. She kept him at bay with the in-flight magazine and waited for dinner to be served. After dinner, and two more bottles of Courvoisier, she fell asleep behind her mask.

The interminable flight ran through so many time zones she could not remember them all, and combined with the alcohol in a potent concoction that numbed her senses. When the pilot announced that they were approximately twenty minutes from landing, she felt as if her entire body was vibrating at a very low frequency. She tried to repair some of the damage inflicted by the rigors of transcontinental travel but the fix did not please her. In the claustrophobic confines of the toilet, she lightened the bags under her blue eyes and touched up her lips. She pressed them together and cleaned the edges with a tissue. Her long blonde hair was an unruly mess and posed a real challenge to her limited time, space, and equipment. She attacked the deformity of her hair-do with a comb and a travel-size can of hairspray. Gradually, with determination and perseverance, she righted her coiffure and alleviated most of the damage done by pressing her hair into a pillow crushed up against the curve of the aircraft's bulkhead. Instead of refreshing her, the short nap after the last food service had left her even more disoriented than before. She looked once more into the mirror, sighed through her shoulders, and begrudgingly accepted what she saw. Besides, the sunglasses would hide her bloodshot eyes. She exited the toilet just as the fasten-seat-belt sign bonged and the captain announced they were on the descent path to Frankfurt am Main. He gave the weather report and she reclaimed her seat and made ready for landing as the attendants checked seat positions, seat belts, and secured trays and clicked shut the overhead bins.

The wait in the passport control line seemed interminable although there were actually very few travelers waiting to be processed through. When she was second in line, the nerves hit her again. She forced herself to breathe and when she handed across her green German passport she used a smile to divert the young customs official from the trembling in her hands. She had nothing to declare but he took his time with her as he did with most of the young attractive females who passed through his station. He enjoyed being able to look them over as part of his official duties from within his glass-framed booth, taking in each line and curve and letting his imagination fill in the rest. He returned her smile. She was pretty enough, this one, but she looked dead on her feet. When he noticed her point of origination as he checked her passport for visa stamps, he understood. Unlike most of the snobbish rich bitches he dealt with on a daily basis, this one did not ignore him behind a look of world-weary ennui. She was tired enough but seemed apologetic nevertheless. She wanted him to know that she was just too tired to flirt with him properly, even though she tried. He passed her through, having already decided he would like to pull aside and strip-search the brunette in the mini-skirt and heels, arms crossed under her breasts and blowing her bangs out of her eyes at the indignation of having to wait so long behind the tired blonde. Ilsa thanked him as he returned her passport and waved the next passenger forward.

She checked the gates on the overhead monitors and moved through the airport. Once away from the hassle of the passport and customs lines, where she had nothing to declare, she had to stop and sit for a minute and let the strength seep back into the muscles of her inner thighs while she waited at the baggage carousel. She had almost peed her panties. She returned from the toilet in good time to claim her suitcase off the conveyer. Luggage in hand rolling behind, she bought a Coke at a food kiosk and a warm, freshly baked pretzel. The salty taste of the pretzel and the caffeine in the soda gave her the jolt she needed to navigate the subterranean maze of tunnels that led to the

162

Bundesbahn station. She bought a one-way train ticket to Finthen and the gentle rocking of the train almost put her to sleep as they rolled from the artificial underground light out into the real light of day. She put her sunglasses on and managed to relax a bit. In a moment of panic, she felt the heavy tampon loaded with diamonds start to slide out. She clamped down hard, as if refusing a lover access, and the internal muscles at the opening of her vagina pushed the package back into place before it protruded up against the safety net of her panties. She spent the rest of the trip sitting with her legs tightly crossed. It wouldn't be much longer now.

She did not recognize the man sent to meet her at the small station in Finthen where commuters into Frankfurt changed trains for the many small villages that mushroomed around the outskirts of the big city. He held a hand-lettered sign, as she expected, with the name of the school where she taught. She walked up to him and spoke a prearranged coded sentence. He gave the appropriate reply and folded up the cardboard sign and pushed it into a garbage can. With one hand, he picked up her heavy, wheeled suitcase as if it were empty. She could barely manage to lift it with two. He turned and she followed. He wore his dark blond hair cut short, en brosse, and the line from his temples back behind his ears was shaved to the nape of his neck. Even his scalp was tanned. His sport coat was a poor fit and looked as if it had been made in Bulgaria. Beneath it, he wore a black polo shirt stretched tightly across the muscles of his massive chest.

Gennady Primakov did not dress to impress. He dressed for convenience and the sport coat was inconvenient so the first thing he did after loading her suitcase into the trunk of the Audi was remove it and throw it into the back seat. He had been told to wear it. He waited for her to buckle her seatbelt and as she stared at the size of his biceps, he backed out of the parking spot, paid the toll at the gate and drove away from the train station.

"Where are we going?" she asked, not to make polite conversation but to find out where they were going. She had no doubt that this one had no interest whatsoever in polite conversation. She had already prepared herself to ride in silence.

"I've been instructed to take you to the Gasthaus Waldenbruck in the Hessian forest. We will have lunch and you will visit the bathroom and place the goods in a plastic bag. We will take a short walk into the woods and you will give them to me. I will pay you and drop you off at the nearest bus station."

She could not quite place his accent but he sounded like a captain briefing his troops before a mission. As a member of the elite Soviet commandos called the Spetsnaz, Primakov had often done exactly that in Afghanistan and Angola. He was a warrior born and bred. When he could no longer bear the evisceration of his beloved Spetsnaz unit after the collapse of the Soviet Union, he became mercenary. He went to work for a time as an enforcer for the Russian Mafia at the casinos in Moscow and made enough money to come to the West. As part of his training, he spoke four languages, German among them. Given his combat expertise and facility with a wide variety of weapons, he was always able to find work. He liked his current job except for the stupid clothes he had to wear.

There was not much traffic this late in the day and they drove in silence on the winding roads tunneling through the dark firs of the Hessian forest. Silence was his preferred state before a mission; it provided him the time to mentally review his orders and visualize what he had to do. He disliked idle chatter, particularly between men and women, as he did not see the need for it. For him, conversation was meant to achieve practical goals, not to fill time that could be put to better use planning or reviewing battle objectives. People mistook his silence for brooding or some sort of philosophical depth; neither was correct. He was a simple man, a soldier, and he did not brood. He planned, and in his planning, looked to his survival. He saw the problem, analyzed the problem, and solved the problem. If unsuccessful, get on with it; if successful, get on with it. The winners were the ones who got to go home after the battles. He planned and drove in silence but he was aware of her at all times.

No, Primakov was not unaffected by Fräulein Ilsa Mendel. On the contrary, she was very attractive and smelled good. Simply put, he understood the effect she had on him, and his discipline as a professional soldier allowed him to compensate for it. He noticed that she fidgeted and stared at him. He ignored her. She broke the silence, unable to stand it any longer. "Why won't you talk to me?"

He grimaced and pointed to the radio. "You may play some music if you wish."

She shook her head emphatically. The movement of her hair sent another wave of perfume to his nose. "You haven't even told me your name. You could at least do me the courtesy of introducing yourself. What harm could that possibly do?"

Gennady Primakov, his mental planning done, to placate her made up a name. Unfortunately, this had the opposite effect. She used the introduction as grounds for more talk.

"You know all about me because you've been briefed by our boss. But I know nothing about you and I don't think that's fair. Why don't you tell me a little about yourself? After all, we are working together, aren't we? Come on," she prodded, "what harm can it do? I won't tell on you," she teased.

He considered what she said. Finished with his review of the plan and satisfied with its potential, he decided to patronize her for the good of the mission. It would be his gift to her. He started with a question. "Have you ever heard of the Russian Spetsnaz?"

She shook her head again, less emphatically this time but shifted in her seat, orienting herself to him. She pulled one leg up under the other. Of course not, she was only a young German schoolteacher. What could she possibly know about one of the world's elite fighting forces? It never ceased to amaze him how little most people knew about the Spetsnaz or anything related to the Soviet military for that matter, even after the fall of the Soviet Union. Then again, for many years everything about their group, including membership in it had been a carefully guarded State secret. During peacetime, they were often assigned to regular units within the Army and wore those insignia and uniforms but the older soldiers knew. There was something distinctive about a man when he became an elite soldier. He was smarter, stronger, better trained, more fit, more disciplined and highly motivated. He was Spetsnaz.

"Spetsnaz stands for Spetsialnogo naznachenyia. We were and are special purpose units of elite commandos like the U. S. Army Green Berets or Navy SEAL Special Forces, or those in your own German Kriegsmarine."

Her eyes widened with a newfound respect as she began to understand.

"I was a captain in the Spetsnaz before I came to Germany. I served in Afghanistan with Recon 66, an elite commando force assigned to ambush convoys smuggling weapons across the Pakistani border. I was a member of the 66th Jalalabad Paratroop brigade. We were famous for our HALO insertions, a technique, I might add, the U. S. Navy SEALs stole from us." He said it as a matter of pride rather than as an accusation.

"I'm not familiar with the term," she admitted, fascinated by the technical vernacular. She understood that she had to be careful now and tread lightly. Saying the wrong thing could shut him up immediately and for good. Her grandfather had fought as a soldier with the German Wehrmacht in World War II and rarely talked about his war experiences in the Army.

"HALO is another acronym and stands for high altitude low insertion. We were trained to jump from altitudes so high, around thirty thousand feet, so brutally cold and so devoid of oxygen, that we had to wear breather masks. We would fall through the dark, because we often jumped at night, and then at the last possible second popped our chutes, landed a second or two later, collected our equipment and went to war."

It amazed her to learn what some men did. She began to feel a bit proud about smuggling the diamonds, the pride supplanting the guilt. After all, she was risking her life too, in a manner of speaking. Her life as a teacher was on the line. She began to feel admiration and a newly found sense of respect for this quiet, powerful man who seemed so controlled and so competent. Her false sense of camaraderie helped displace the fear his physical presence engendered. She decided she wanted to know him better. She asked, "How many jumps did you make?"

He laughed suddenly, almost an inadvertent snort of derision, and she blushed. "Counting my training in the Fergama Valley in Uzbekistan, over two hundred jumps." Without another word, he pulled the car over to the side of the road and an icy chill came over her. He released his seatbelt as if it were a ripcord, walked around to the back of the car and took a manly leak by the roadside. She could see the arc of the yellow water in the mirror on her side. He returned and belted up.

She looked at him with disgust, in control of her feelings again. "And what if I have to go?"

He hadn't considered the possibility of her needs. "Go."

"I don't think so. I'm not Spetsnaz like you. I can't just raise my skirts and drop my shorts and pee by the side of the road with my ass hanging out for the entire world to see. I'll wait until we get to the Gasthaus, if you don't mind." She glared out the window.

He thought she was funny. "Suit yourself. And you're not wearing a skirt."

She wanted him to talk again in the short time they had left together but knew he would not initiate the conversation. She would have to prime him like a dry pump atop a deep well. "Have you ever killed a man?" She was certain that he had.

"Yes." he answered. "Thirty-seven."

He said it with the nonchalance of a star soccer player recounting the number of goals scored during his career. She felt the eerie chill again. She decided not to pursue that line of questioning. Instead, she asked, "What was it like in Afghanistan?"

"Fräulein, you don't want to know."

She got mad at him and not a little indignant. "I do want to know or I would not have asked. And unless you tell me, I can never know. I doubt that I will ever have the opportunity to fight in a war." She turned away again and looked out the window. He seemed not to notice that she was hurt.

To make it clear and simple as possible he said, "Afghanistan was our Vietnam." Now it was her turn to be silent but she turned back to him. "Our units were in Kabul early as 1979 and some of our Spetsnaz forces

168

carried out assassination missions. We were there to fight what some have called the hidden war but I can assure you that by the mid-eighties there was nothing hidden about it." He paused. "Except for the number of casualties our country reported to the rest of the world. The official count given to the media was 13,000, but when I was pulled out February 15, 1989—and I will never forget that day—I would say we lost closer to 30,000 soldiers."

"Why so many?" she wondered.

He shook his head. "I have asked myself the same question a hundred times. We were a superior force with superior materiel and training. We outmatched the Mujahedin in every regard. To my mind there is only one thing we lacked that the mug heads had...."

She had no idea what that could possibly be so she shook her head.

He looked at her and said with the absolute conviction of a soldier who has seen too much meaningless death, "A legitimate reason for being there. They defeated us psychologically. They would come down out of the mountains screaming that there is no God but Allah, as if we cared about that one way or the other, but we did our level best to speed them on their way to a warrior's death so they could get into heaven. They swarmed down out of the hills and the next moment they were gone. They suddenly appeared, usually in ambush and then like ghosts they were gone. That's what we called them, you know, dukhi. Ghosts. Disappeared as if the rocks swallowed them up."

He dropped his voice almost to a whisper and she had to scoot a bit closer to hear him. She sensed that he was confiding in her now, telling her secret information he had shared with no one else.

"Toward the end, morale was very low. Toward the end, about all we wanted to do was go home. We just wanted to do our job and then get back home in one piece. That's all I really cared about—getting my guys back home…." He smacked the top of the steering wheel with the flat of his palm with such force that it vibrated. She started at the sudden violence. He didn't apologize for startling her.

"Conditions there were so bad that a lot of the guys actually got hepatitis."

"That must have been awful," she commiserated but could not imagine what it would be like to get hepatitis.

"It was worse than that. Soldiers were drinking the piss of those who were already infected in an effort to get shipped home. Their choice was to go out in a body bag or get a medical ticket back home. It was disgusting but I can't blame them. Most of them were just kids."

"My god," she said, echoing his disgust.

"And when we did finally get rotated back to the Soviet Union we were met with stone faces and cold shoulders. It was as if we were criminals who had just been released from prison. The only difference between our soldiers and criminals was the color of our uniforms. All those medals I earned in combat I put in a box in my mother's house and I have never opened it again."

She could see that in him. He was unfailingly resolute. She was certain that when he made a decision there was no turning back. He would never again wear his medals. She considered that a real shame.

"Anyway, a year later I resigned my commission and got work protecting the owners of a casino in Moscow. Most money I ever made in my life. In one month, I could make more than I earned serving six years in the Spetsnaz. Now I'm in business for myself and now we're here." He turned into the parking spaces in front of the Gasthaus Waldenbruck, deep in the Hessian forest.

"Thanks for telling me that story," she said, genuinely moved by his experiences.

"Would you do me a small favor?" he asked.

She smiled. "Of course, anything."

"I know you're hungry and tired from the long flight but let's take a little walk into the woods before we eat so we can stretch our legs and take the mountain air. I hear it's supposed to be very good for your health."

She knew what he wanted. "Okay, but I absolutely have to go pee first and take care of a little matter. I'll be right back. I promise not to be long."

He let her go. In the Gasthaus, she asked direction to the women's toilet. She thanked the waiter and found the door without the stag's antlers. She removed the diamonds with a sigh of relief and shook them into a plastic bag taken from her purse. Even through the film of the plastic they were dazzling. As she peed, she wondered how much they could possibly be worth. She wiped herself and flushed everything else. She checked her make-up in the mirror, reapplied her lipstick and combed her hair. Spetsnaz or not, that was the best she could do for him.

A kilometer or so into the woods and under the hunting tower of the forest master she turned and raised her face to him under the expectation of a kiss. She never again opened her eyes. He made certain that it was a quick and clean kill. She deserved that much. When he felt her go slack under the ligature wound tightly around her neck, he experienced neither joy nor remorse. He was a professional hired to do a job. His only satisfaction was in the realization that she had not suffered. He owed her that much. He collected the baggie containing the jewels from her purse, then stripped and searched her. He handled her dead weight easily. Good girl. She was not holding out as many of the others had. But he understood that too. People stole. That's why

171

he checked each girl. He lifted the trouser of his right leg and pulled the commando knife from the scabbard strapped there. The orange bakelight handle felt warm to the touch, like a woman, and the razor-sharp AK-74 combat bayonet made short work of the butchery he was required to do. He didn't ask questions; he just did what he was told. With a quick flick of the knife, he checked everywhere. He cleaned the blade on the thin white material of her panties, once clean as bandages, and left her there under the tower that stood above her like a graveside monument. He gathered her shoes, placed her clothes in her bag and then examined the scene quietly for fully five minutes. Satisfied that nothing incriminating had been left, he returned along another path and did not look back. At the edge of the woods, he paused and only when he saw that the walk to the car would be unobserved, did he move back into the light of day. He got into the car and drove to Idar-Oberstein, threw her possessions into a public garbage can, and then handed the diamonds to Rudiger Hain, who was waiting for him at the office. He was paid for his work and given a bonus, which he had come to expect.

"Any complications?" he was asked, as always.

"None," he replied, as usual.

Chapter Thirteen: The Profiler

ROLAND DECLINED THE offer of a cigar from Direktor Hauptmann but signaled the waitress for another pilsner. Roland had just finished a bowl of clear chicken broth with thinly cut slices of Pfannkuchen, similar to a French crêpe, and the Direktor a platter of lunchmeats and cheeses. The sun was at just the proper angle so that the white and blue canopy above their white metal table on the sidewalk threw a blanket of shade over the tablecloth. Both men had seated themselves at the round table with a view to the passers-by walking up and down the city square doing their afternoon shopping. The shops once again were open after the mid-day break. Up the plaza, the fountain commemorating Kaufbeuren's history as a center of medieval commerce leaked water into the air. Occasionally a flock of pigeons circled until they could peck at the bread crumbs left for them by tourists without being accosted by their dogs or children. The early summer day was still cool enough to wear a suit coat comfortably although Roland had opted for his black leather jacket.

Having reaffirmed their friendship in taking a meal together, the Leitender Kriminaldirektor was enjoying his day away from the city of Munich, but both men were now ready to turn to business. "Bring me up to speed on Kommissar Schumann, if you will." He let Roland formulate his thoughts while he attended to the ritual of cutting the end from the cigar and rotating the tip into the flame of the match as he puffed it into smoke. This was just one of the things Rieger appreciated about his boss. Not only did he expect a man to formulate a cogent and articulate argument, he gave a man time to think about his response. Hauptmann was not afraid of silence, not afraid to wait while one thought, and not afraid to listen closely to what was said. More importantly, Rieger knew how crucial this oral report concerning Sylvie's performance would be. Unlike his idiot supervisor, who spent all his time reading reports and following the book, Direktor Hauptmann talked personally to the men and women under his command. Of course, the official evaluations would follow, but he placed little store in such documents. They were the provenance of the bureaucrats. Like the naval officer he once had been, he was a commander first and last. He was here to look a man in the eye and hear him speak. This would be the basis of his evaluation, not only of the officer being evaluated, but of the man behind the uniform as well. Roland appreciated the responsibility.

"When Kriminalkommissar Schumann was first assigned to me I could not have been more upset. This was nothing more than Steinmetz trying to get back at me for screwing his teenage daughter." Hauptmann smiled through a blue-white penumbra of cigar smoke. He never had to worry about Rieger's honesty or his directness, one of the reasons he got along so well with the man. "However, in the time we have worked together she has conducted herself professionally, knowing full well my feelings about working first with a partner and second with a female partner."

Hauptmann nodded. He fully understood the man sitting next to him. He refused to work with a partner because he was intolerant of incompetence. He refused to work with a female partner because he found them to be equally or often even more incompetent than males.

174

For Rieger, the issue was never one of sex but always one of competence. On this issue, he was unrelenting, to the detriment of his career. Kriminalhauptkommissar Roland Rieger, formally of the elite Grenzschutzpolizei, had always placed his public service to the Bavarian citizens he was sworn to protect above the advancement of his professional career. Hauptmann could not help but agree. The force was changing and changing rapidly and one of those changes just happened to be the addition of more female officers into the ranks. Unfortunately, the social re-engineering of the police force was a reflection of the greater society and they were stuck with it. Gradually, and here he advised Rieger to be patient, they were seeing a more highly qualified pool of female applicants filter through the ranks. It was his job to find the good ones.

"I am now of the opinion that she has the potential to become a competent officer, although she is not one yet. She is exceedingly bright, she absolutely knows her theory, and she is not afraid to work hard."

"Graduated top of her class," Hauptmann reminded him.

"Academically she has been very well prepared and she demonstrates enthusiasm for her work, but she lacks confidence and is not yet able to assert herself as she needs to. But don't get me wrong Bruno; I'm not finding fault here. Her confidence, I think, is simply a matter of her lack of experience in the field."

"Ah, but the question is," the Direktor added, gesturing with the cigar, "will she be able to gain that experience before she screws up a case or, heaven forbid, gets herself or someone else killed?"

"Now you understand my reticence in working with a partner. The stakes in this game are simply too high. The risks are too great." He finished his beer.

The Direktor looked at his watch. "Does she love the Job?"

"I think she is infatuated with the Job and certainly enjoys her status as a Detective Lieutenant in the Criminal Police. But really, Bruno, we can't expect someone so young and so inexperienced to love it as we do. If she survives and is smart enough not to get burned out, in time perhaps."

Direktor Hauptmann stubbed out the cigar. "One last question then before I leave. Will you keep her on as your partner?"

Roland knew immediately what the question entailed. If he said no, the Direktor would have absolutely no compunctions about assigning Schumann to another officer in another unit. "Given her performance to date, I am prepared to continue my work with her, Herr Direktor."

Hauptmann signaled for the waiter to bring him the bill. "Very well. I will see to it that she receives a positive performance evaluation, regardless of the paper that idiot Steinmetz pushes forward. And something for you, given your excellent work with the Lieutenant." He pulled a file from his attaché case and handed it to Roland. The confidential personnel folder contained an intelligence dossier on one Professor Doktor Osvald von Eltz, a member of the Bundeskriminalamt (BKA), the Federal Criminal Investigation Office at Wiesbaden. Roland knew better than to ask how Hauptmann had obtained the man's personnel file. This was also Hauptmann's way of reminding him of their agreement. To bring the Semiotician on board, they had to placate the bureaucrats in Bonn.

"Read it at your leisure and draw your own conclusions and please see to it that the file is returned directly to me post haste. A little something extra for our waiter today?" he asked, studying the addition.

Roland agreed and Hauptmann put down an extra Deutschmark atop the gratuity already figured into the bill. Roland thanked him for lunch and the opportunity to speak his mind. The Direktor said he wouldn't have it any other way and they shook hands goodbye.

PROFESSOR DOKTOR OSVALD von Eltz rode with Hauptkommissar Rieger and Will accompanied Lieutenant Schumann, who finally got to drive. Roland did not have much use for the man but his sense of duty and professionalism demanded that he control his dismissive attitude, despite his general dislike for pedants and didacts. This was the price he had to pay, he reminded himself, for bringing in his nephew, who seemed to be enjoying the attention of the young lieutenant in the car following. Rieger smiled into the rear-view mirror. Will reminded him of himself not too many years ago. He could see his sister in the semiotician's eyes, his father in the strong, square jaw and wavy black hair. If anything, the son was more handsome than the father, a detail that had not escaped Sylvie's highly trained notice and appreciation. She had very generously offered to take Will with her. The Doktor blew his nose with explosive force into a freshly laundered and scented silk handkerchief, wiped his reddened nose, and coughed his throat clear. He meticulously folded the handkerchief into a perfect square and placed it atop his thigh, waiting for the next sneeze to build.

"Sorry you're not feeling well, Herr Professor Doktor," Roland sympathized.

"A touch of allergies, Herr Hauptkommissar," he said dabbing the tears at the corners of his eyes for emphasis. He had let everyone know that he was fully prepared to continue, despite the debilitating pollen that had triggered the antihistamines in his nose. His suffering was valiant, bordering on the noble, and Roland thought his mother would have been proud. With the exception of his swollen face, everything about the man was perfect. His blue suit was freshly laundered and pressed and Roland could detect the faint smell of the cleaning liquids used by the dry cleaners even through the piney scent of the man's cologne. He wore his thin, limp hair combed straight back and pulled into a knob of a ponytail, which Roland thought looked ridiculous on a man. He was a thin man to the point of emaciation, his high nervous energy and his general distaste for food, the allergies again, combining to produce a gauntness that bordered on emaciation. He was quite proud of his thinness, really, which he took to be a svelte elegance, the very words his mother once used to describe his figure. Roland said he looked fine, when Sylvie whispered in his ear how thin the man seemed, for being just two weeks out of the grave and the Lieutenant was forced to turn away as she tried to hide an inadvertent laugh.

There was no doubt in the man, no uncertainty whatsoever. Everything from his lips fell with absolute, unfailing exactitude. He was a professor and a doctor and an expert and when he spoke it was as if he expected every word to be written down and underlined. So far, most of what he had to say Roland had ignored. He stood quietly in the background at the press conference when Direktor Hauptmann introduced his new team to the media. Sylvie was nervous and blushed as she presented her credentials, proud of her training but embarrassed by her lack of experience. She was a striking figure of feminine power in her dress uniform. Will had fielded the reporters' questions in German and immediately won over the room of photographers, journalists, news anchors with too much hairspray, cameramen and crew, jostling and shouting for a chance to question the American criminologist who spoke with confidence and good humor. He yielded the microphones with grace and a generous introduction of his colleague, the Herr Professor Doktor Osvald von Eltz .

Von Eltz, both a thin and a short man, seemed dwarfed by the physical size of the tall, muscular American. He waited to speak until Will sat down. His hands trembled as he gripped the sides of the dais, but there was no quaver, no indecision in his voice. He bent the microphones forward and looked out over the crowd, chin thrust forward. My god, Roland thought, he thinks he's Mussolini talking to the loyal Fascisti.

"Within the week..." he started cryptically, and repeated the phrase. Now there was dead silence. To Roland's chagrin, he repeated, "Within the week, this case will be solved and we will have your killer."

As the crowd erupted with questions, Roland looked over to his commander who smiled back under raised eyebrows. No doubt about it, the Professor Doktor was in his element and handled the news crews as if they were fawning graduate students come to worship at the feet of the great scholar. And then he shut them down with an imperious wave that signaled the news conference was over, for the team was this very moment preparing to depart, ready to begin their investigation. He stepped back and blew his nose with admirable ferocity.

One week, Roland thought, shaking his head as they entered the green of the Hessian forest. Sometimes it takes me that long simply to type up a requisition for an unmarked police car. He shook his head, unaware that he was doing so and von Eltz said, "Herr Hauptkommissar?"

"Oh, nothing. Excuse me. Merely thinking about the viciousness of the killings."

"Don't worry. I will see to it that you get your man," he said obsequiously.

Purely as a matter of courtesy, Roland thanked him instead of saying what he really felt.

179

THE ADAMANTINE HEART

A HUNTER, SCOUTING the deer trails in advance of the season, had come upon the body and reported it from the Gasthaus Waldenbruck. The local SCHUPO had done a good job securing the crime scene and keeping all non-essential personnel outside the yellow cordon. Given the striking similarities in the case, Roland's team had been given jurisdiction over the matter. The authorities of the Rheinland-Pfalz were more than happy to wash their hands of the affair. Let the yodeling, beer drinking Bavarians have it.

They parked at the Gasthaus, waited for Sylvie to use the bathroom inside, and then hiked into the forest to the crime scene. The SCHUPO sergeant noticed Roland's Kriminalpolizei medallion but also checked his identity card before allowing the team to pass. Roland waited patiently and then commended the young man for doing his job thoroughly. He did not introduce the two criminologists. Technical and forensic services had already finished photographing the scene, taken hair and nail samples, and conducted interviews. As usual, the victim was found naked, strangled and then mutilated, her clothes cut and ripped from her body. Bagged and tagged, everything had been sent for analysis to the crime lab. The sergeant reported to Roland that no one had seen anything and the time of death was put at the day before, given the lividity of the blood in the body. "A pretty girl," he said, shaking his head. "I hope you catch this guy." He had a daughter about the same age. Roland thanked him for his good work and let the profiler take charge. Professor Doktor von Elz was off the leash muttering a mantra to himself: "behavior reflects personality, behavior reflects personality."

Von Eltz literally ran to the crime scene and circled the body two or three times, stopped, then circled counterclockwise. The entire time he propped his right arm at the elbow atop his left hand, the left arm crossed at the chest. The index finger of his right hand lay against his cheek. Throughout his circuit he umhmmed to himself. He did not stop to touch the body or move it. Finished with his observations, he walked away and stopped, then turned his back to the other three. He clasped his hands tightly behind his back and looked up into the clouds as if he were reading them for signs.

Sylvie looked at Roland, questions in her face. He held his finger to his lips, indicating silence. "Let him work," he said. "We enter into this with an open mind."

Will touched his shoulder to his uncle's. "An open mind can also be indicative of a hole in the head," he whispered just loud enough for the two to hear. Five minutes passed, then ten. Suddenly Professor Doktor von Eltz spun about-face and waited expectantly.

"I assume he wants us to come to him," Will observed.

Roland was losing his good humor and patience in the face of the man's posturing. He was skeptical of academic types to begin, present company excepted, and this man was notorious for building his cases without the benefit of fieldwork. It was a miracle that he had come along to observe the body this time, most certainly a result of the media coverage. Now working for the federals in Bonn, he was originally a teacher at the university in Frankfurt and he rarely ventured out of the classroom to a crime scene. As a theoretician, he kept his shoes clean and his hands unbloodied. As the three approached, he straightened his tie, shot his cuffs to the end of his bony wrists for dramatic emphasis and told Sylvie she would probably want to take notes. He was wrong, but diligently she took out her notebook from her satchel and stood at the ready. When Will, Roland, and Sylvie faced him in a half-circle, Sylvie with her pen and note pad in hand, Doktor von Eltz began his lecture.

"I see three motives here: domination, manipulation, and control. All three are evident in the fact that the victim was brought here, stripped, killed, and then brutalized. I deduce that our killer is of the unorganized type in that he has killed his victim here rather than killing her elsewhere and disposing of the body here."

"What did he do with her clothes?" Roland asked.

"He's a trophy taker. I would not be at all surprised if he kept the panties or bra in addition to taking pictures of his work."

Sylvie shook her head. The thought was morbid.

"We see it all the time," he assured her.

Will and Roland nodded their collective agreement. He was right about that. They let him continue.

"The multiple stab wounds are indicative of piquerism. Piquerism denotes extreme anger. This man hated women, most likely his mother, a theme I intend to revisit," he said, as if making them a promise.

Will asked a question. "Why do we see signs of vaginal penetration but a complete lack of semen?"

"I was coming to that. He obviously wears a condom so not to leave physical evidence."

"But wouldn't this be a sign of an organized killer."

The Doktor considered the logical possibility, then dismissed it as too blatant. "Sexually violating the corpse after death is certainly indicative of a disorganized personality."

Will and Roland looked to each other, both wondering the same thing. How did he know the sex was post mortem? They held their silence as the psychiatrist continued to expostulate.

"A clear-cut case," he assured them, misinterpreting their skepticism for worry. "Classic really, for all intents and purposes. Your killer is a white male, late twenties, early thirties. He is the product of a dysfunctional family and probably still lives with his mother. He has a job that allows him to travel, hence the victims in different locations. He has a girlfriend, but the relationship is unsatisfying to him and most likely she dominates him, as does his mother. Let me know if I'm going too fast," he said to Sylvie. She shook her head but did not look up from her pad. "Very well, I continue. He is shy with women and possesses a low self-esteem. I would expect that he is disheveled, nor does he attend to his personal hygiene." Here he sniffed self-disgustedly, affronted by the very idea that anyone could possibly be so offensive. It was almost un-German.

"He suffered from enuresis, bed-wedding," he translated for Sylvie's benefit, "late into his teens." She glared at him, but he was lost in his oral dissertation. "This lack of control was compensated for by starting fires. I suggest you look for individuals who were arrested for petty arson as juveniles. You will also find that he stole and tortured small animals, probably the family dog. This was the experimentation phase of his emerging psychopathology that now allows him to carve up his victims. Symbolically he is seeking to learn about women, for whom he has no understanding..."

"Or compassion," Will interjected.

Von Eltz ignored him. The point was irrelevant.

Roland asked, "Why does it appear that there is little or no struggle? It appears the victim came willingly if not under threat."

"Good question," Eltz allowed, but said it in such a way as to appear patronizing. "Many of these killers, in addition to having excellent intelligence, are charming if not highly articulate." He forestalled Roland's next question. "Moreover, these individuals are fascinated by the police. Many have tried to become police officers and failed, so they take jobs related to police work. I predict, accordingly, that our man most likely will have a job that requires him to wear some sort of uniform. I also predict that he has all the accoutrements of police work in his possession: handcuffs, side arm, badge and identity cards, all faked, of course. This is what enables him to walk his victims into the forest, strangle them, and then mutilate their corpses. Therein lies the psychopathology. All the anger and hatred he has for his controlling, dominating mother is displaced on these victims. The killing is a psychodrama. These unfortunate girls are stand-ins for the perverse relationship he has with his mother." He stopped to breathe and wipe his dripping nose. He was having difficulty breathing.

Sylvie used the break in the monologue to pose a question. "Why does he hate his mother?"

"Abuse," he said in one word, his short rasping breaths insufficient to the needs of a longer sentence, so he repeated the word for emphasis. "Abuse. Almost all serial killers suffered either physical or sexual abuse and, more often than not, a combination of the two, during their early formative years. I have no doubt that our killer was sexually violated by his father, beaten if he did not obey, and thus hates his mother for the very simple reason that she did not protect her child. She looked away and chose to ignore her husband's late-night visits to her little boy's room. In this, she spared herself the drunken beatings she could expect from her lout of a husband and thus kept peace in the family. And there you have it. Behavior reflects personality. I invite you to focus your search for an individual who fits the profile I have described and you will shortly have your man. I suggest, furthermore, that you restrict your search to the local area as these killers, fairly early in their career, kill in what is known as an area of comfort. No doubt he roamed these woods and others like it as a child to escape the horror of his childhood and he feels confident in such areas, hence the killing here.

He walked up to Sylvie and offered his arm. Out of politeness, she took it. "Come my dear, I will escort you back to the Gasthaus and share with you my most recent psychological analysis of the relationship such killers have with their mothers. You will find it entirely fascinating."

Sylvie looked back over her shoulder to Will and Roland, unable to disguise the look of desperation on her face.

"You two go ahead," Roland suggested. "Will and I need a moment or two to fully appreciate the Professor's tour de force analysis."

This appeal to his vanity produced a smile and he graciously took his leave, towing the lieutenant along.

Roland turned to Will. "Well, what do you think?"

Will shrugged. "I think they have a future together if she plays her cards right."

"I had the profile in mind."

Will knew from the tone of his uncle's voice that it was time to leave the levity aside. "To be honest, he knows his stuff. In fact, I agreed with some of what he had to say..."

Roland prodded him. "But..."

"But you could have gotten the same thing out of a textbook. My problem with the profile is that it's so general as to be almost useless. It's the same cookie on the sheet with thirty others."

Roland smiled. "Exactly my thinking. And this is not, I repeat, not a disorganized killer. Everything about this guy reeks of professionalism. This guy is a pro and he's not doing this to get his jollies. And that's what triggers my personal alarm. Something about all this does not ring true. I hear a crack in the bell."

He signaled to the officer waiting outside the yellow tape that they were finished and relinquished back to him control of the crime scene. "Just between you and me, Will, what's your read on these killings?" Roland asked, as they walked the trail out of the woods and up the hill to the Gasthaus.

"I have no doubt that the unknown subject, or the unsub as my colleagues at the FBI are fond of saying, very likely fits some elements of the profile the good Doktor described. But so do you, and so do I; well, you more than me. But my analysis so far tells me your instincts are correct. This is not the work of a serial killer."

Roland nodded, satisfied that his conclusions had been substantiated by his nephew. He was also interested to learn where Will's analysis would lead them. "If this is not the work of von Eltz's psychopathic serial killer, who then?"

"An assassin," Will said simply and clapped Roland twice on the back.

Curious, thought Roland as they walked across the parking lot, he had already arrived at precisely the same conclusion.

Chapter Fourteen: The Profile

ROLAND PUT SYLVIE in charge of making the arrest for no other reason than to give her the experience she needed. Not only would she get to wear off some leather from the bottom of her new shoes, she would learn the organizational skills necessary to conduct such an investigation. Working with the profile drawn up by Professor Doktor Osvald von Eltz, she became a hunter of men. Her weapon of choice as she stalked the killer was the computer and once immersed in the morass of the various criminal databases, she was truly and fully in her element. She spent hours in front of the computer terminal in Roland's office at Headquarters running local, regional, federal and Interpol searches, checking whatever correlations emerged from the databases.

She began by developing a geographic perimeter, a circle within which all the murders had taken place. She followed von Eltz's assertion that most serial killers work within an area of comfort, that is, in a location they know, often an area where they grew up or lived for some time. The area within the circle was still daunting, covering the Hessian forest at its northernmost point and the Voralpen region of Bavaria at the southernmost. The common element here was the forest. All four victims were found deep in the woods. Her contribution to the profile included searching for a man who was an avid outdoorsman, a hiker perhaps; even better, a hunter.

Gradually she was able to narrow her search. According to the profile, she was looking for a white male in his late twenties to mid-thirties. He lived with his mother but probably in a downstairs apartment where his comings and goings could not be monitored. He was probably in a tempestuous relationship and quite possibly had broken up recently with his girlfriend. This was the necessary trigger event that pushed him to the killings. He worked a meaningless job for which he was overqualified and resented the fact. He would have a fascination for the police and at one point might have tried to become an officer, but failed. He was a loner and spent a great deal of his time fantasizing about women. He needed to control them, a compensation for his sense of inadequacy and low self-esteem. He was addicted to bondage and sadomasochistic pornography. Von Eltz had offered to go through representative samples with her, but she politely declined, citing the overwhelming workload Roland had assigned her.

As Sylvie factored in the elements that constituted the profile, the list of suspects narrowed to three. When she brought up prior records for sexual assault, pyromania, and juvenile delinquency, she had her man. She remembered one of her criminal justice professors saying that the computer was an amazing crime fighting tool. As she read the profile of the man on the screen, she became a believer. She called Roland, sitting with Will in a café downtown, and informed them of her findings. She asked for and received permission to interview the man.

Matteus Falck worked as a busboy and general maintenance man at the Gasthaus zum Hirsch in Germaringen. He lived with his invalid mother in a small apartment above the Gasthaus. He had just turned thirty-one, his brown hair was long and dirty and Sylvie wrinkled her nose in disgust at the man's body odor. He had obviously not showered or cleaned himself in a number of days. She identified herself and the

188

two male SCHUPO bull officers brought along to make the arrest. She was stunned when he invited them in and said, "What took you so long?"

Upstairs he introduced them to his mother, sitting up in her bed watching TV. The woman was old and frail and clearly in her mid-seventies. She stared at them vacantly, unsure of the cause of all the commotion. She turned her eyes to her son, as if pleading for help. In an act of tenderness, he leaned down and kissed her cheek and said that he had to go out for a while. She patted his hand and returned her attention to the yodelers on the Bavarian variety show she was watching. She hummed a little as the music caught her ear and lost herself in the memory of a young girl growing up in the Alps at Oberjoch. Bringing home the cattle with the distinctive tinkling of the bells and daisy wreaths around their necks, she walked the trails down the hills to the barn where her father waited to milk the cows.

"She had a stroke," he explained, "just last year. She's been nothing but an anchor around my neck ever since." Sylvie was shocked at the callousness of the comment. Then he said, "Sometimes I just want to strangle her by the neck and get it over with."

She recorded the comment in her notebook.

His room looked like a laundry bag had exploded in it. There were dirty clothes everywhere and the room stank of acrid sweat and musty sheets. The walls were plastered with posters of the SS during World War II. Three pair of handcuffs lay in plain sight atop his chest of drawers. At the computer desk, she found clippings from newspapers and magazines that reported the killings. When they checked the hard drive on his computer, it was filled with images of rape, bondage, sexual torture and sado-masochism. That explained his pierced nipples and penis ring, of which he seemed inordinately proud. He offered to put in a ring and show it to her. She just glared at him, trying to decide if he was serious or not. She decided he was serious when she saw the collection of rings on a tissue next to a bottle of denatured alcohol atop his chest-of-drawers. His offer rebuffed, he stood there watching them sheepishly, hands stuffed in the back pockets of his dirty jeans, wondering what would happen next, embarrassed by what they were finding. Sylvie called Roland on the cellphone and brought him up to date. He told her to bring Falck in.

Matteus Falck, who seemed strangely pleased at this turn of events in his life, was arrested on suspicion of murder and transported by the SCHUPO to jail in Kaufbeuren where he was held for questioning the following day. After work, KRIPO Kommissar Sylvie Schumann went immediately home and took the hottest shower she could stand, literally rubbing her skin raw with the loofah as she tried to scour the man's stink from her. She couldn't believe that he had asked her if she wanted to see his penis ring. He meant that he wanted her to watch him put it in first and then show it to her! The mental image disgusted her. After the shower, she sat on her bed and cried for herself and for all the pretty dead young women who reminded her so much of herself.

The next day Roland and Will took her to lunch and it really helped as they listened while she told them the whole story and she only cried once, which embarrassed her but the men let her cry and waited until she regained her composure. When she returned to the table, Roland asked a favor.

"Will and I have discussed this and we want you to make certain that von Eltz gets full credit for capturing Falck."

She protested. She had done all the fieldwork.

Roland agreed. "You did a fine job Lieutenant, but you have to trust us on this one."

She didn't understand. Why should she give up her share of the credit? An arrest like this could make or break a career.

Roland said, "That's exactly the point. Make certain that von Eltz gets the credit and downplay your role in the arrest. If anything, emphasize the fact that you were simply following his profile."

She looked at Will.

He nodded. "Let this be the Professor Doktor von Eltz show."

She folded her napkin and sighed. "I don't understand but I'll do as you ask."

"Trust me on this, Sylvie. You're doing the right thing," Roland assured her.

As expected, von Eltz called a press conference but Roland and Will did not attend, called away to assist on a stabbing in Kempten. Sylvie did her duty as the arresting officer but suffered through it and, although von Eltz thanked her publicly, he introduced her as Sylvie Schubert. When she quietly corrected him, he replied in all his gallant charm that he preferred Schumann to Schubert anyway, and this produced a round of polite laughter from the media. Von Eltz then launched into a ninety-minute exposition wherein he detailed point-by-point how Falck matched every aspect of the profile that he, von Eltz, had constructed for the Kriminalpolizei. At the end, there were no questions for Lieutenant Schumann, only for the brilliant profiler von Eltz, who had solved the case exactly as predicted.

Sylvie walked away from the conference disheartened and a bit confused, wondering if she had done the right thing until nine days later the body of another young woman, slain under similar circumstances, was discovered. Von Eltz was unavailable for comment on this stunning turn of events. A spokesman from his office in Bonn indicated that he was currently en route to Luxembourg, consulting there on the case of a serial rapist. Now Sylvie understood why Will and Roland had been so adamant about assigning credit for the apprehension of Falck. They knew he wasn't the killer. They were only trying to protect her. She blew the bangs from her forehead. If it wasn't Falck, who then?

Matteus Falck was brought into the interrogation room looking none too worse for the wear. If anything, Roland noticed, he enjoyed being the center of attention. The SCHUPO sergeant uncuffed him and seated him at the round table, stepped out of the room and informed the Hauptkommissar that the prisoner was present and ready for questioning. Roland thanked him and said they would wait ten minutes or so in order to sweat him. Roland decided the best way to get this guy to talk was to take as much control from him as possible. He wanted to send the man a clear and unequivocal message that he was in control. They watched him fidget. He rimmed his lips with his tongue as if he were parched. He drummed his fingers. He sneezed into his hand and wiped the mucous on his prison denims.

"It's not a very pretty sight," Will quipped and Sylvie laughed nervously. There was something eerie about that man, something in the eyes that didn't seem quite right and she could feel the hair stand at the nape of her neck. She rubbed the goose pimples on her forearm.

"Respect and trust that feeling, Sylvie. It might save your life one day," Roland said.

"Do they all give off such strange signals?" she asked.

Roland nodded. "Most of them do."

"Part of their sense of alienation is a function of their inappropriate nonverbal behaviors. You just saw a couple. He would do exactly the same thing in the presence of others. Prepare yourself for the stare," Will explained.

"Oh, god," she said, covering her mouth protectively.

Will nodded. "He will look into you as if you were a computer screen."

"What should I do?" she asked.

"Stare back," Will suggested. "He does it unconsciously as a means of visual control. The subordinate male in a wolf pack will always avert his glance first. The alpha male controls him merely by the intensity and duration of the stare."

Roland added, "Men have been known to kill each other in prison when one gives the other what they call a 'hard look'."

Will stared at Sylvie and she immediately looked away, and then pushed him with both hands on the chest.

"Stop that!" she admonished and he grinned.

"Come on, children," Roland directed, "let's go to work."

Roland sat directly across from Falck, Sylvie and Will on either side of the man. They did not give him the luxury of looking at Sylvie. Will scooted his chair close enough so that his shoulder touched Falck's, invading the man's private space. Will made certain that the smaller man was aware of his imposing physical presence. Falck immediately sat up in his chair, coming up out of his nonchalant slouch. Chief Detective Roland Rieger of the Criminal Police did the introductions. Sylvie, of course, he had met. At the mention of her name, he reached down and squeezed his penis through his trouser legs for her benefit. Will reached over and gripped the man's wrist, nearly crushing the bone and the man's penis before he placed the man's hands atop the table. He glared at Will, then turned his attention to Roland. "I know you," was all he said.

"I am well known," Roland agreed.

"I knew you were coming for me."

"You've been following the case."

Falck nodded. "It took you longer than I thought. And why did you have to send this rookie bitch to get me?" he asked derisively but with the subtext of a child's petulance. "Why did you send this bitch to arrest me?" He wanted the honor of being arrested by no one less than the redoubtable Hauptkommissar Rieger.

"You were too good and too careful. That's why I had to call in Doktor von Eltz, the world-famous psychiatrist and criminal profiler."

Falck swelled up at the praise. He was now getting his just due. He felt he was among equals again, except for the pussy lieutenant who could use a good fucking, he decided. Will slapped him lightly upside the head, startling Falck. "It's impolite to stare at a lady."

Falck immediately mumbled an apology.

"Tell me about the cases," Roland said, using a tone that suggested here were two colleagues comparing notes on an investigation.

Falck launched into a description of his careful planning, his modus operandi, he actually used those words, and his brilliant control of the crime scene, his words.

"Why these particular girls?" Roland asked, looking to motivation.

Falck studied the question. He had often pondered the issue of motivation. "Those bitches needed to be fucked."

Roland made a note. Very quietly he asked, "Did they need to be killed?"

Falck dropped his eyes and seemed to sink into his shoulders. He began to rim his lips again with the moisture of his tongue. He looked quickly at Sylvie and then back at Roland. He lapsed into a sullen silence.

"Lieutenant Schumann," Will said sharply and she started.

"Yes?"

"Would you be so kind and bring us the beer and sandwiches we were expecting?"

She looked at Roland for confirmation. He nodded and she rose. Will said, "It shouldn't be more than fifteen minutes, right?"

She looked at her watch and said, "Fifteen minutes."

Roland smiled at her and Falck watched her walk all the way out of the room.

After the door closed, Falck sat up again. With the Lieutenant gone, he opened up.

"They had to be punished for being sluts. Every one of those bitches came on to me. You know how women are." He looked quickly at the door Sylvie had just closed.

Roland nodded. "I know how women are."

"All talk and no action. Nothing but tease and come on. I had to teach them a lesson."

"What did you teach them?" Roland asked.

"If you screw with my feelings, you die."

"You just wanted a relationship and all they wanted was slutty sex."

Falck looked at Rieger with admiration. Here was a kindred spirit who understood.

Roland took a minute to leaf through Falck's record. As a juvenile, he had been arrested for starting more than twenty small fires around the neighborhood where he lived. After his father left the house under the suspicion of having sexually abused the boy, Falck was arrested for killing and skinning the neighbor's pet dog. He was doing it for a biology project at the Volksschule, he told authorities. He was released early from his military service under allegations of homosexual activity. In his late twenties, he was caught twice peeping into the bedroom window of a fourteen-year-old girl while masturbating.

Roland looked up. "When did you break up with your girlfriend?"

The question caught Falck by surprise. He hadn't mentioned any girlfriend. "About six months ago, just after my mother's stroke."

"Because she wouldn't play along?"

195

Again Falck was caught unawares. She thought he was getting too perverse and the cuffs scared her. Once he had choked her just a bit too long before sex and she had passed out. When she awoke later, she discovered he had taken the opportunity to explore her anally. After the doctor stitched her up, she decided she had no future with Falck. Falck finished the story with raised eyebrows and a shrug to indicate can you imagine that. He thought she liked it rough. Will and Roland both shook their heads and Falck took it as a sign of commiseration instead of disbelief.

"How did you kill them?"

The question puzzled Falck. Everyone knew from the paper, the newsmagazines, and the TV reports that the girls had been strangled. He decided the Hauptkommissar was merely checking his story for consistency. "You know. I choked those bitches till they twitched." He made choking gestures with his hands.

Roland looked at the notes Sylvie had prepared for him. "I see. Just as you would choke your mother."

Falck pouted and fell silent as Roland wrote a note to himself. At this point Sylvie returned with a bag of sandwiches and beer. As they ate, Falck told them the story of his father's sexual abuse from the time he was nine until he turned thirteen. His mother, fearing the drunken beatings she suffered, said nothing and looked the other way. A counselor at school picked up symptoms of abuse in the despondent boy, already acting out his anger and frustration in his fights with other boys his age, and reported her suspicions to social services. And that was the last he ever saw of his father, now stuck with a mother who vented all her hate and vitriol on the son, the image of his father.

Roland looked to Will. They had heard enough. The interview was over. As Falck stood and placed his hands behind his back to be cuffed,

Roland said to him, "I will personally see to it that you get the help you need," and Falck was led away.

They went to Sylvie's office. She slumped into her chair and laid her forearm across her brow. "That was the most incredible thing I've ever experienced. I am absolutely beat."

Roland popped the top off a Weihenstephaner pilsner and handed it to Will. "Those guys do suck the energy out of you."

Sylvie declined the offer of a beer. Her stomach was upset and she wasn't feeling so good. She shuddered inadvertently. Will noticed.

"Still feel his eyes on you?"

She nodded. "That guy gives me the creeps. I was amazed at how closely he fit the profile."

"That amazed me too," Will admitted. Roland burped politely and said "sorry" without being sorry.

"Pig," Sylvie accused him, and then blushed as she realized what she had said without thinking, and to whom.

"You're quite right," Will acknowledged. "The man is completely devoid of any social skills."

Roland burped again in agreement. "Unfortunately, Master Matteus Falck is not our killer. He is a very disturbed young man who has created an elaborate fantasy for himself."

Will picked up where his uncle left off. "He has created for himself a fantasy world that matches the profile von Eltz drew up because young Master Falck has read everything written in the popular press about serial rapists. Unable to bring himself to actually commit the acts because of his overpowering sense of inadequacy, fostered and maintained by his rather unhealthy relationship with his dear mother, I might add, the devious little dog skinner has stolen the credit for the murders."

197

Sylvie could not believe what she was hearing. She had been absolutely convinced beyond a shadow of any reasonable freaking doubt that Falck was the killer. She felt naked and vulnerable as if she had been stripped of her convictions and beliefs. How could she have been so utterly and completely wrong?

"Don't feel bad, Sylvie," Roland consoled his charge. "The guy is a master of deceit. He's a chronic liar who builds webs of deceit and lives within the lies."

Will agreed. "I have no doubt that in a year or so, when the fantasy of living vicariously through the killings by the real murderer begins to lose its edge, he might one day summon the courage to actually do it himself. And he will start with his mother."

Roland nodded. "So, you have done a good thing, Sylvie. You have saved a life and Matteus Falck will finally get the psychiatric care he so desperately needs. And we have eliminated quite a list of suspects. No. Don't you worry a bit about this. You will see that you have actually brought us closer to the real killer."

Sylvie was almost at the point of tears but Roland's words brought her back to composure. She dropped the veil of hubris, admitted to herself that she had been wrong, and in that instant of self-realization, took the first step to becoming a competent detective.

"How did you know?"

"The media were told all the victims died of strangulation, but we did not mention the method. Falck assumed that they had been strangled by hand, which fit the fantasy murders he saw himself committing. He naturally assumed that's how the strangulation was effected. Your note about his desire to choke his mother to death was the symbolic clue that led us to our conclusion. That's why we have Will here."

Sylvie blew her bangs off her forehead. "That von Eltz really is a pompous idiot, isn't he?"

They all laughed. As Roland locked up his briefcase with his notes and files, Sylvie once again had tears in her eyes. Both Will and Roland stopped their preparations to leave.

"I just want to thank you two for what you did for me. You stopped me from making an utter fool of myself out there at the press conference. I couldn't wait to get the credit and take the glory."

Roland put his briefcase down on the table. "You have learned to trust your partner and in so doing, will become a good partner. More importantly, you have learned to trust yourself and in so doing, will become a fine detective."

"Where do we go from here?" she asked, having recovered her infectious grin.

"Victimology," Will answered.

"Victimology?" she asked.

"Victimology," Roland assured her. "Pick you up at your house at ten tomorrow morning for a little day trip and a conference between the three of us on victimology."

Chapter Fifteen: Crosswords

THEY WERE BOTH fatigued from the day and too tired to go out to eat, so Roland served a bowl of beef broth with knödel, a German dumpling that Will's mother had often made for him. Under the three large knödel that rolled and danced in the soup, he found tender chunks of beef from the bone that had given the soup its wonderful flavor. After dinner, they left each other in the privacy of the diversions necessary to take their minds off the case. Roland sat on the couch, where he slept as often as not, working through a crossword puzzle, sipping the Crown Royal Will had brought as a gift. The puzzle was almost completed save for one section in the upper right hand-corner. He needed two words. The clue for the word that blocked him was 'chutzpah.' He had the last four letters, E R V E, but not the first. Finally he had it! VERVE. "Damn!" he muttered aloud. Although the V fit the down word, it transformed the word in the top line to gibberish. But it had to fit. He could not think of a possible word that included the V for the clue across. Roland slapped the magazine down atop the coffee table and finished the whisky. He was beaten.

Will looked up from reading a classic German pornographic pocketbook set in the 19th century describing the sexual adventures of a famous Viennese actress of the time. He figured this area of his vocabulary needed broadening. "What's up?" he asked his uncle.

"One goddamned word keeps me from completing this monstrosity of a puzzle. I've been working on it for three days."

"Let me see it."

Roland flipped it over to Will in his chair at the foot of the couch and directly under the green canopy of the spider plant hanging from the ceiling. He pushed a dangling vine aside as he caught the flapping magazine. He studied the corner causing all the problems. He detected no errors, no mistakes that he could see in Roland's answers to the clues. But it was obvious that the V in VERVE did not fit into the belly of the word atop and across it. Therefore, he concluded, it must be wrong. Instead of trying to solve for the word across, he re-examined the clue 'chutzpah.' He handed the puzzle back to Roland.

"Not VERVE, NERVE. Try it with an N."

Roland slapped his forehead with the open palm of his hand. What an idiot. That was it. Puzzle solved. It fit perfectly. Now it seemed so easy once he saw it black on white. He stood up and poured himself another shot of the Canadian whisky and then decided his nephew deserved one as well.

Will took the shot glass of amber fluid from Roland carefully so not to spill a drop of the precious liquid. And at the prices the Germans charged for booze, it was precious indeed.

"That's exactly why we can't solve this case, if you ask me," Roland suggested. "The clues point us to an answer that fits the clues, but has hindered us from arriving at the correct solution. Let's apply the same chain of reasoning you used to solve the puzzle and assume that although the answer fits the clues, it leads us to an incorrect solution. We have arrived at, and are thus forcing the idea that these murders are sex crimes and the work of a serial killer."

"I see what you mean," said Will, nodding his agreement. This is actually the work of an anti-serial killer."

Roland looked over at him. There were still times when he could not tell if Will was being serious or not.

Will explained. "Not anti in the sense of against— anti in the sense of anti-matter. A positron is the anti-particle of an electron. The only difference between the two is the charge. An electron has a negative charge and a positron is a positively charged electron. They are similar but for the charge and that makes all the difference in the world—it changes the solution."

"So, what you're saying, Will, is that we have what appears to be a serial killer, but we need to find the one factor that changes our conception of what serial killer means."

"Right!" he agreed emphatically. "A semiotic analysis is really about determining meanings. All murders mean something. They are interpretable actions. In other words, someone could very well have designed those murders to lead us to the conclusion that this was the work of a serial killer, thereby leading us to what we perceive is the correct solution when, in fact, our gut instincts and the anomalies are trying to tell us something different." He pointed at the magazine on the table. "It's just like the crossword puzzle. The answer to the clue took us in the wrong direction at first."

"Hmmm," said Roland as he pondered the entirely new possibilities this line of thinking opened up. "What we have then is a killer not motivated by some convoluted quasi-Freudian psychopathology but a devious, calculating, intelligence that has scripted a puzzle with certain clues designed to lead us away from discovering him."

"I agree," said Will. "What we have is a man who wants us to think the killer is a convoluted quasi-Freudian sexual psychopath. That's the

202

man we're trying to catch but that's not the man doing the killings. What we need to do now is go back and focus on each and every one of the anomalies and try to make sense of them."

Roland nodded. "What we have now is a piece of paper used in the diamond industry. This is the anomalous sign we must interpret. We will use it to help contextualize the killings and this will set us back on the right track."

Will beamed at his uncle. "You're starting to sound like a semiotician."

Roland grinned back. "At least we're rid of that idiot von Eltz."

"I'll drink to that," said Will, offering his glass for one more fill. "But let's push our reasoning just a bit more and see where else it takes us." The smooth fire of the whisky had stoked the dry tinder of his analytic mind. Roland settled back on a pillow, put his feet up and waited for Will to finish his thinking. When it came, it would be fast and sharp and he wanted to be ready.

"Einstein can help us here. A photon is both a particle and a wave. In other words, based on the perspective of the observer, a photon has the potential of being perceived either as a particle or a wave. But the photon as an entity is not either-or. It is both. It manifests itself as either-or only as a function of the observer's perspective."

Roland was not sure where Will's dissertation on the physics of light was taking them.

"Here it is. The correct solution to this case equals the photon. Our current perspective as observers of the crimes has led us to conclude that we perceive a serial killing by a sexual psychopath."

"Right." Roland was back on track.

"Let's equate that perspective with the view that the photon is a particle."

"Got it."

"Now if we were to change our perspective, our observation will yield another conclusion, equally correct, but different. This new conclusion we will set equal to the idea that a photon is a wave. But remember, a photon is not merely one or the other; it is both. Seeing the photon as solely a particle or solely a wave gives us an incomplete understanding of the nature of the photon."

"Aha," said Roland. "The real killer is analogous to the photon. Our current observations have given us the perspective that our man is a sexual predator."

"Yes," said Will, the excitement in his voice undeniable.

"So, what we need," continued Roland, although his head was starting to ache, "what we need is that second perspective that will allow us to understand the man both as a serial killer and as one who has designed the murders to look like serial killings."

"I am absolutely convinced this is how we must proceed. When we discover this aspect—let's call it the wave perspective of the case—we will then have a more complete understanding of the man who committed these crimes."

Roland nodded. "One thing we know for certain. Matteus Falck is not our killer, although he may very well fit the profile for a serial murderer. He is the forced solution in the same way I tried to force the answer to the crossword clue. Tomorrow we start fresh. I don't care whom Sylvie has to screw to find the real killer," he said with finality. "All in the line of duty, of course."

SYLVIE WAS A summer girl. She had watched her favorite season arrive in the Alps with the exuberance of a young girl prancing in a new dress. Everywhere she looked, the colors were new and fresh. The needle tips of the conifers that stippled the hillsides looked as if they had been dipped in blue-green paint. Entire fields were swathed in yellow. Purple and red edged the fields in the borders between the meadows as they gave way to the stand of forests. White clouds scraped their gray bellies across the barrier of the Alps pushing granite up into the blue sky. The day was clear and bright, rinsed clean by a morning mountain shower that further delineated the colors of the growing seasons. Roland was at the wheel of the BMW and seemed in a particularly good mood. His face glistened from the closeness of his shave, but last summer's tan was no longer able to disguise the scars earned in the course of his duty. Will rode shotgun, casual and comfortable in a blue polo worn above khaki slacks. He wore his shirt open at the neck. Sylvie was in back, using the cover of her anonymity in the rear to study the two men. Seated behind Roland, she stretched her long legs, crossed at the ankle, across the median of the car and rested her feet behind Will's seat. She kicked off her black pumps. Her step-in, zip-at-the-hip leather skirt was fashionably short, but she had the legs to make it work. A beige V-neck sweater, false cashmere, was just right for the cool of the mid-morning. She observed that Roland was in his ubiquitous black slacks, which spent the evening hanging outside on the iron railing fronting his apartment's balcony. He brought the freshened pants in just before the first of the big rain drops spattered the glass door. His black leather jacket was rolled at the cuffs, as were the long sleeves of a field shirt, epaulettes at the shoulders. The coat was too long in the arm. She knew that to fit the coat across the muscles of his chest, he must buy one size larger and he compensates by rolling up the sleeves.

Roland had a destination in mind but his route today is circuitous by design. It is still too early for him to have his first meal of the day so he has decided to drive away the time. He took them through the postcard beauty of his beloved Allgäu, a region of Bavaria renowned for its spectacular vistas and natural splendor. As much as he appreciates his American citizenship, Will was inwardly proud that this is the land of his birth. In all his travels, he tells Sylvie, who has only been to Switzerland and the Benelux countries, he has found few places that can match the Allgäu, none that can surpass it.

Roland took them off the state highways and onto the country roads barely wider than a hay wagon, even though they are usually paved. Here the farmers ride their tractors from the villages into the fields and bicyclists pedal the two or three kilometers between the neighboring towns. Will watched a gray stork rise majestically from a stream bank on long bony wings, a trout wriggling in the capture of its long stabbing bill. Roland slowed the roll of the car so they can all watch the enormous bird turn into flight above the treetops. They drove on past wide-eyed Bavarian cows the color of fawn, bells tinkling under their necks as they turn to watch the car. They stare at the vehicle with a mixture of curiosity and distrust. It is too soon for milking. They return to cropping the fresh grass and clover that sweetens their milk. Roland mooed at them but was ignored.

Down they went into the valley near Oberegg, the BMW nosing into the tight turns and switchbacks that mark their descent to the Katzenmühle, a refurbished four hundred-year-old mill now serving as a restaurant. They got out, stretched their arms to the sky, and walked around the grounds until blood circulated back into their arms and legs. Roland went off to speak with the owners and renew old acquaintances. Will and Sylvie commandeered a table under a broad umbrella stretched to protect them from the sun. They wanted the best view of the stream running through the meadow beside the forest that grew up the side of the mountain before gradually fading away into stone. They looked around. They were the only ones there.

"Service should be good, Will observed dryly, as a Dutch door to the mill was pushed open. He remarked how short and squat the building looks. Four hundred years ago he would have seemed a giant, Sylvie tells him. Their waitress was young girl. Eager to be fifteen, she was resplendent in a Bavarian folk costume called a dirndl, which showcased her newly rounded breasts. She came for their drink order and unashamedly flirted with Will. Still too early in the day for beer, Will asked for tea with milk and sugar, and Sylvie for coffee with milk and sugar.

"I think you've made a new friend," Sylvie observed.

"I think she's just practicing," Will countered.

The young girl, just rounding out of her chubbiness, returned with freshly baked rolls, butter, a selection of lunchmeats and sausages, and a basket of black bread and confitures. Will went first for a slice of the dense, sweet-smelling, black bread, fully an inch thick through the middle and weighing nearly a quarter-pound. By the time he finished layering it with fresh butter, three or four slices of smoked Bavarian ham, tomato slices, and sprinkled it with salt and pepper, he needed two hands just to maneuver the deli raft to his mouth. Sylvie watched him in awe and marveled at his appetite. She broke a roll in two daintily, buttered the side in hand and topped it with orange marmalade. A mountain breeze cooled the tea and the coffee and turned up the edges of their napkins. She put a strand of blond hair back into place, disarranged by the momentary wind. Will noticed she was staring at him.

"What color panties do I have on today, Herr Professor Doktor?" she asked defiantly.

Interrupting a bite, he said without hesitation, "Black," and gave her a short false smile at the corners of his mouth before he resumed chewing.

She stuck out her lower lip in a classic little girl pout and spent the next ten minutes trying to figure out how he got it right. Had she asked him, he would have told her that an essential element of accurate interpretation is perception and perception requires observation. He prided himself on his powers of observation like a scientist, or a painter, or a poet, especially when the object of his observation was lovely as Sylvie Schumann. What made it even more fun was that she was still somewhat uncertain of her attributes and the degree to which they appealed to men. She had not yet discovered the full measure of her potential power as a female. This endeared her to him.

It's not that she was naïve; her training as a police officer had obviated any lingering schoolgirl naïveté. Even so, she was yet something of an innocent, a quality that distinguished her from most American women of the same age. American girls of her age had been stripped of feminine innocence by too much exposure to hedonistic, superficial popular culture. It was one thing to know about life, he mused as she tried to figure out how he knew. It was another thing entirely to callously distrust all men and perceive them as untrustworthy nemeses for the simple fact that they were males, because that's how attractive young women behaved in the soap operas or in the movies. Sylvie did not distrust him, or other men for that matter, because he was a man; rather, she was somewhat disturbed by his power and sense of self as a man, attractive but intelligent, strong but gentle, intense but affable. A fully competent, confident male, Will was an enigma, a puzzle for her to solve, and certainly a challenge worthy of her attention. She cared very little if she stumbled and blundered a bit as she took on the challenge of understanding him. And this was a part of her strength that Will found irresistibly attractive. She did not seem to be afraid of him. She reserved that for Roland.

The Hauptkommissar strolled up, his schmoozing done and with an uncanny ability born of thousands of hours closely observing people, immediately sized up the situation. He tugged gently at Sylvie's lower lip, still out in a full power pout and affected a false paternal tone. "Is he teasing you again?"

She wanted to be angry but he had such a dramatic look of false concern on his face that she laughed aloud. He was the consummate actor, her Roland, and in that instant realized this was how she now thought of him: her Roland. And the fact that she could laugh at herself so readily and naturally endeared her to both men.

"Don't think I'm finished with you," she admonished Will, pointing her long elegant finger at him so there could be no doubt. Will just looked at her, slowly chewing, face devoid of all emotion. As Roland removed his leather coat and draped it over the curve of his chair back, she again said to Will, "Well, are you going to tell me or not?"

He chewed mechanically.

"I expect," Roland observed, "that if he is not milked soon, he will begin to moo."

That cracked Will out of his stoic mime's face and he choked as he swallowed. Sputtering, he washed the false swallow down with a gulp of tea.

"Now children, behave while I finish my noodle soup, which darling Pia has just brought me, steaming hot from the kitchen of her dear sweet mother, Frau Daufratshofer. Then we will do some important work if you can be persuaded to turn your attentions from each other and refocus them on our case." Roland tasted the soup from his spoon, sipping elegantly from the side as his father used to do and, as usual, found it to be excellent, nearly as good as his own.

Chapter Sixteen: Victimology

FINISHED WITH LUNCH, the three got down to cases. Roland was perfectly content to give Will the lead. Besides, it would allow his nephew, in the grand tradition of Rieger men, to show off for Sylvie while he sat back, observed, and objectively listened to the facts of the case. Unused ashtrays were repurposed to hold loose documents under the breeze that teased at the papers from time to time. Sylvie had her notebook out again, this time less as a recorder and more for her personal interest in the new attack they were planning. She wrote down the word victimology and underlined it. The word had a false ring to it, as if it had been invented for the purpose of word play. The more she thought about it, the more the word made sense.

Will began in English, after taking a sip from his beer to clear his throat. "I want to go back and re-examine everything we know about the tower killing. This time, however, I want us to focus on the victim and not the killer. Our theory is that as we understand the victim we will, in turn, learn about the killer. Victim and killer are related in the sense that every word in a sentence depends on every other word in that sentence for its meaning. That's why von Eltz's profile failed. He gave us a dictionary interpretation, so to speak, one general enough to fit any number of individuals. What we need to do is limit the range of interpretive meaning until we arrive at one specifically relevant to this crime. For lack of a better term, we are going to disambiguate the crime."

Roland produced a stage groan but Sylvie wrote the word into her notes with a flourish. Will passed around the photos of the crime scene.

"One more thing before we get started, so bear with me. I also want us to focus our analysis pragmatically this time."

"Pragmatically?" Sylvie asked, looking for a definition. Her English was good, but not that good.

"Broadly speaking, pragmatics is the study of meaningful human action. It derives from the work of Ludwig Wittgenstein and the ordinary language philosophers who were interested in studying language in use. They pushed the study of language meaning beyond semantics of word meanings into pragmatics."

Roland could see there was no stopping him now, so he let him run. And to be honest, he admitted to himself, despite the vocabulary he found Will's ideas interesting. In his mind, he was already leaping forward trying out potential applications. No, the young scholar and criminologist was clearly in his element and it would do them good to hear this new perspective.

"Pragmatic meaning is derived from the action of using language. Since our text for analysis is not language but the crime, we should focus on the actions of the crime, specifically as it relates to the victim. I want us to ask the question, what does it do?"

Sylvie and Roland mulled the question over. She looked to her superior, saving her question. "What does this crime do?" Roland offered, taking the lead.

"It kills this woman," Sylvie said, pointing to the victim in the picture; then she was embarrassed for stating the blatantly obvious.

Will shook his head affirmatively. "Shaking my head this way is an action. You interpret that action to mean 'yes.' That's also a pragmatic interpretation. My method suggests that we can do the same for a crime. However, we have to challenge every one of our assumptions, even those that appear to be standard or obvious. Ask the next question."

Roland asked the next logical question. "What does killing this woman do?" Almost before Roland could finish, Sylvie blurted out,

"It silences her."

Will looked at Sylvie with amazement. "Perfect. And what does silencing her do?"

"Two things," Roland said, "It protects the killer's identity and prevents us from understanding his motivation, if we assume that his motivation is not psychopathological."

Now Will was impressed with them both. "We have now made her silence meaningful. She knew what she now cannot tell us. This will be our key to finding the motive."

At this point, Sylvie asked a question that would have qualified her for graduate studies, Will thought. "But don't all killings result in silencing the victim?"

Roland turned to Will, very much interested in how he would answer her pertinent question.

Will Introduced a measure of respect into his smile for Sylvie. "Of course, they do. But there are pragmatic motives other than silencing the victim. We have now laid the groundwork for exploring them, so let us proceed."

He motioned to Sylvie, writing furiously. "Let's leave this line of thought for a bit and come back to it a little later. Of all the many ways to kill a person, she was killed by the use of a garrote."

They studied the photos again. This time Will asked the question, "What does using a garrote do?" He let them think. Roland's greater experience came into play.

"It kills fairly quickly, silently, does not leave a weapon per se at the crime scene, is relatively unmessy, but requires a certain amount of skill to be used properly." He emphasized the last phrase, now thoroughly involved in the direction Will was taking them.

"Every one of the victims was killed this way," Sylvie pointed out for them to remember.

"So now we have a killer using a garrote, effectively and efficiently from the very first murder. This is not the case of a sociopath who gets better and learns as he goes."

"An assassin?" Sylvie wondered aloud.

"Or at least a professional," Roland suggested.

Sylvie put down her pen. "This can only mean that the killer was hired to do the killings."

"Not necessarily," Will cautioned. "The killer might be working to serve himself and we cannot overlook this fact. But the other elements of the context of the crime suggest to me, at least, that you're on the right track."

Roland nodded. He had arrived at the same conclusion.

"Next question. Each of the victims was killed in the woods and forensics tells us they were not killed and subsequently dropped there. The crime scenes were not dump areas, which true serial killers often use. Nor do we see any other signs of force that would indicate the victims were physically coerced to come along. What does this do?" Will asked.

"It tells us they either came willingly or were coerced in some other non-violent fashion."

"Both scenarios are possible," Will admitted.

"Let me make a case against the second," Roland said, "and let's see if we can eliminate it. We know from the tire tracks that these events were not stalk and kill. So, in each instance the victim first got into the car with the killer. We've had no reports from citizens or the SCHUPO of anyone in the local area reporting the use of force or a struggle between a man and a woman, at least none that were not domestic disputes. Assume then she got in willingly, and it looks like they all did." Following Will's lead, he turned the conclusion into a pragmatic question. "What does willingly getting into a killer's car do?"

"It shows us that they trust the killer, at least enough to get into the car with him," Sylvie said, shaking her head at the thought.

"And what does trusting the killer tell us?" Roland continued.

"That they were either working together or somehow knew each other," Sylvie added.

"Bravo," acknowledged Will. "We're getting farther and farther from von Eltz's profile. But to be objective, we must also address the other aspects of the case, particularly those that recur. A pattern is also meaningful. To be honest, a symbolic interpretation of the technique used for asphyxiation is possible and, in this instance, appropriate.

"Why appropriate?" Sylvie wanted to know.

"Because our interpretation is pragmatic and not psychoanalytic. So, we are permitted to do symbolic interpretation so long as we stay within our context of pragmatics, not psychoanalytics. Accordingly, using a garrote not only symbolizes the need for silence, but also the need to be professional. What does this do? It tells us this is a trained professional and trained professionals usually take pride in their work."

"No," he said shaking his head for emphasis, "this cannot be the work of a disorganized psychopath. Von Eltz got it wrong."

Will took another drink from his beer and let the conclusion settle among them. Again he motioned to Sylvie.

"Make certain that we do not forget to ask what kind of trained professional."

She nodded as she wrote the question and starred it.

"What do the stab wounds, the piquerism, do?" Roland asked.

"They confound us," Will said, and the others laughed. Will was nonplussed. He had not intended his answer as a joke. He pointed out to them that they had incorrectly interpreted his language action of saying 'they confound us' as a joke, instead of a statement of fact. He made his point that pragmatic interpretations can also be ambiguous.

"That's the purpose of the action. The stabbing, which the coroner agrees is not the cause of death, is designed to confound us by leading us to a false conclusion: the conclusion that this is the work of a psychopathic serial killer. These are false signs, like kids switching the directional signs on a highway. Such misdirection again points to a highly trained professional who has thought his actions through, or...," and here he paused for dramatic effect, "is following orders."

At this point Sylvie looked at Will with eyes wide and blue as the Bavarian sky.

"What does using the knife do?" Roland asked, pushing the issue, undaunted by the expected brilliance of his nephew.

"Again, a misdirectional sign that forces us to do a symbolic analysis. Psychoanalytically, the knife is a classic representation of the penis. We're back to the serial rapist. But let's make our question, 'What does creating signs that misdirect us do?'" He threw the question back at Roland as Sylvie watched the two engage in an intense, intellectual sparring.

216

"Aha," said Roland, "I see where you're going. It suggests the planning behind the murders, and possibly again, a mastermind behind the crime."

Will simply nodded. His semiotic method was helping them arrive at inescapable conclusions.

"There are still two things that trouble me the most," Sylvie admitted, looking closely at the photos. "In all the cases, the nipples are cut off, and in all cases, the vagina is ripped open with a very sharp knife capable of splitting the pubic bone."

"Very good," said Roland, "I was wondering when we would come to that."

"I haven't forgotten that either," Will said. "In fact, they are central pieces in our interpretive puzzle. The nipples are false signs again, I'm certain of it, but there is again a legitimate symbolic significance that might apply here, given our new context of pragmatic analysis."

Sylvie tried, "He hates women and this is his way of defeminizing them."

"I thought of that too," Roland said, paying her a backhanded compliment. "But that would fit our old psychoanalytic context of the classic serial killer."

"Right," Will said, emphatically. "But in our new pragmatic context, it could mean a professional, or a warrior, let's say, taking a prize from his vanquished enemy."

"Seems a bit of a stretch to me," Roland said.

"Indian scalps, heads taken by headhunters, American soldiers in Vietnam taking ears from the Viet Cong."

"My God," said Sylvie, as she listened to Will recite the last. "You think this guy is a soldier?" she said in the form of a question.

Will reached over the table and took her face in both hands. "I could just kiss you. Write that down. No, no, not that I could kiss you but that he might very well be a soldier. It fits, Sylvie, it fits."

"And not an ordinary soldier, Will. A commando of some sort," suggested Roland, the excitement in his voice evident.

"A commando hired to kill?" Will posed the question but and they left the answer for later. There was still the issue of the mutilation of the genitalia. "Again, it's polysemous." Will said.

"Poly what?" Roland asked incredulously. Sylvie just stared at him and waited patiently.

"Hey, you guys hired me." He grinned, and then returned to earning his pay. "Words that can mean more than one thing at the same time. Polysemous. Every single one of these crimes has been designed to hide their true meaning behind a plausible but false meaning. Now, especially now, we have to address the question of what does mutilating the vagina do?

"I follow," said Roland, "It both draws attention to the vagina and it hides evidence, potentially."

Will looked at his uncle with respect. Roland held up his hands in mock defense. "Just don't get any ideas about kissing me. You can write that in your little book, Sylvie, for my protection."

She giggled.

Will directed his attention to her. "You're the expert here."
She wasn't so sure and she was having difficulty framing the question. "What does the vagina do?" she offered tentatively.

Both men smiled but did not laugh.

"For the purpose of our argument let's accept the obvious," she said with a sigh of relief. She wasn't quite the expert they thought but such secrets were hers alone, for now. What else could a vagina be used for. The answer came to her in an instant. "To hide something."

Roland slapped his forehead and Will just grinned.

"Why go to such lengths?"

"Smuggling," Roland said.

"Smuggling, but what? Not a hell of a lot of room in there, in my experience."

Roland ignored his attempt at humor and pointed a finger at him. "Diamonds."

"Of course. The diamond plaquette found at the other crime scene."

"You guys have got to be kidding," Sylvie countered, but she said it without conviction. "Diamond smuggling? Anyone can just go and buy a diamond."

"Wait a minute. Five victims so far and that assumes we have found them all. How many diamonds, let's say one to five carats, might fit in a woman's vagina?"

This time it was Sylvie's turn to say, "Don't look at me."

"Just a guess," Will continued. "Two hundred total?"

Sylvie turned to Roland. "Can you get me fakes?"

He nodded.

She would do the test herself, for the sake of science and the Bavarian State Criminal Police, but more importantly, for each of the five brutally murdered women.

ROLAND WAS EXCEPTIONALLY pleased with the new orientation of the case, although he did not let on. He decided to conduct the investigation in accordance with the new theories they had developed. He felt a sense of excitement as he reviewed the work they had done together. This was good. For the first time since the discovery of the first body in the woods outside Mooshütte, he felt they had a chance to solve the case. What he needed now was time to himself in order to organize the procedural, the daily grind of field investigation on which so many cases depended for their solution. This was the grunt work of being a detective, chasing down leads, knocking on doors, interviewing hundreds of people, most of whom didn't give a damn and could care even less. This required searching license and vehicular databases, tracking credit card histories, getting telephone records, and writing absolutely everything down.

His work now, before he sent his troops into the fray, was similar to a battlefield commander. It was his duty and obligation to prepare the strategies and the tactics for the investigation to follow. In this situation, however, the unsub, or the unknown subject, still held the advantage. Now, even more than previously, it was imperative to gather information and compare it to the theoretical model. The information that fit would be kept. What didn't fit would also be kept but in a separate file in the very real likelihood that the theory was wrong and the model would have to be reworked. The possibility of this alternative caused him an instant of despair and left him with a sour stomach. He knew in his gut that if they had to rework their theoretical paradigm again, most likely, the case would be left unsolved, and he would have failed. Despite his history of success, his career could not afford such a failure. He put the idea aside.

It was that time in the case to begin using a form of logical reasoning called the method of residues. Despite the daunting terminology, the method was quite simple, really. All the data they collected would be collated, correlated, sifted through, and reduced, until only one possible solution remained. Through this process of distillation of the facts, a picture would emerge like a photograph developing within its chemical bath in the darkroom. They were ready now to begin the process of constructing a killer using the theoretical template derived from their inductive observations and subsequent deductive analytical reasoning. In the absence of physical evidence, they were forced to rely on the sort of semiotic interpretation Will had contributed to the case. Otherwise, they had to depend on the guy walking in off the street and confessing his crimes to clear his conscience but the odds of that happening were about as good as Hitler coming back to start a fourth Reich. They were stuck with what they had and would have to make the best of it. He could not remember a case when he had less to go on.

He sent Will and Sylvie on a walk, sensing their restlessness and their need to get to know each other better. They seemed glad for a chance to get away and talk about something other than the case, but they worried about leaving him alone. He welcomed the opportunity to think without interruption. He gave them his assurances and watched as they took the path along the reservoirs that held back the natural spring waters full of trout for the restaurant's menu. They were a striking pair and he felt the pang of regret that he would not have the opportunity to know her as his nephew most likely would, if he was any judge of women. So much the better; it would avoid all sorts of potential problems and this was one of the reasons why he had decided to avoid fraternizing with female colleagues. He had no doubt they would be gone for an hour or so as they climbed up the hillside into the forest, plenty of time for him to organize his plan of attack and lay out the assignments.

After accepting another beer from the waitress, from his black leather valise he took out a notebook and created an outline of the incontrovertible facts of the case. Next to information that had been validated by one or more independent sources, he penned the letters

221

KTBT, which stood for known to be true. He was certain that the solution depended on being able to separate the facts of the case from the assumptions, not that assumptions were always or necessarily bad, but in this instance, there was very little latitude and not much time left for stumbling down blind alleys. For an old pro like himself who had handled nearly two hundred investigations during his career, that part was easy enough. The hard part was supporting good assumptions with reliable facts rather than treating the assumptions as facts. That's where most cases failed, in his experience. His list of facts known to be true was disturbingly small, but no matter. One iota of reliable information, like a single seed of nacre that an irritated oyster worried into pearl, could be enough to make the beginnings of a solution to a case.

There were five murders. All the victims were female and forensics placed their ages in the same range, mid-twenties to late-twenties. All were teachers and all were single; strike that, all were unmarried according to legal records. All were murdered by strangulation, stripped naked, their bodies sliced and mutilated. All were left in the woods, hidden but not buried, as if their discovery were of little importance to the killer. And so far, he had been right. Oh, oh. That part was an assumption and he erased it and rewrote it in the Assumptions column. Aha! What was developing was a clear and unvarying modus operandi and this linked the cases, but this too was an assumption, albeit a good one. However, he adhered to his protocol and wrote it in the appropriate list. Still missing, even as he delineated the m.o., was the killer's motivation. Von Eltz had done a good enough job screwing that part up so he decided to leave motivation for another time.

There did not seem to be any chronological regularity to the killings. It was not as if the guy got off work on Friday afternoon, stalked the bars all night and the bodies turned up Saturday morning. There were no distinct intervals between the killings. Good, he thought. At least we have eliminated any sort of chronological pattern. Method of residues. What he had was a date for the discovery of the first body and the last, which did not necessarily imply the actual sequence of the murders. He did not consider this to be problematic to the case, only incidental. A more reliable time-line would emerge during the course of the investigation and then it could very well prove to be valuable information as they developed their list of possible subjects.

He continued his work, concentrating intensely, lost in the stream of ideas and annotations and it startled him when he looked up to find a fresh pilsner within reach. He paused to drink down a third of the beer, relishing the coolness of the liquid. Thinking was thirsty work. He was almost finished with his notes. He glanced at his watch. Older couples arriving for an early dinner and a walk were being seated and shortly he would either have to give up his table or order dinner. He looked up the path trailing into the woods, expecting Will and Sylvie to emerge at any moment. He decided the two would probably want dinner together, without the intrusion of his company. That suited him. He had other plans for the evening, anyway.

When they did come down the path twenty minutes later, holding hands and grinning like guilty teenagers, he had just finished his analytical work. Sylvie, he noticed, had reapplied her lipstick, not altogether successfully in the dimming light. He decided to have some fun with the two, secretly pleased that they had finally acknowledged their attraction for each other.

"That shade of lipstick flatters you," he said to Will, who grinned a little more foolishly and thanked his uncle for noticing.

"We knew we wouldn't be able to hide anything from you, master detective and super sleuth that you are, so we decided the prudent course of action would be to publicly proclaim our love."

"Love?" Sylvie questioned. "That's certainly news to me."

"Don't believe a word of it, Roland. The hussy couldn't keep her hands off me. German girls are embarrassingly easy."

Sylvie defended her honor and the honor of her slighted countrywomen with a slap to his shoulder that made the early diners look up from their soup, but Will stood and took it like a man. Roland waited for the horseplay to end and as they seated themselves, handed out their assignments. When he informed them that they were on their own for dinner, they grinned beatifically, as if they just had been ordained in the same order, and he knew that he had guessed correctly about the two angels sitting opposite.

"Start Monday," he said, giving the rest of the evening and the next day to them. "I have to see a man about a diamond," he added cryptically as he picked up the check, his little present to them in honor of their newly discovered love.

Chapter Seventeen: The Investigation

MONDAY CAME SOON enough after the quiet day, or Ruhetag, Roland had given them. Will remembered such days from his youth and appreciated this aspect of Bavarian culture. Similar to a siesta, it lasted the entire day and gave him time with Sylvie. Sylvie was an unexpected pleasure. In the security of her own bed, she demonstrated imagination and showed a willingness to indulge herself. In equal measure, she gave back everything she received. When he left her bed for his own, he was still somewhat weak in the knees, tired but sated, satisfied but already looking forward to the next time they would be together.

She said she understood as he dressed and made ready to leave. He assured her that his return to Roland's apartment to sleep was not a decision lightly made. In this regard, he shared his uncle's idiosyncrasy. Both men had decided early in their relationships with women that it was best to sleep alone. For them, sleeping was a singular and private activity and they did not give up their beds merely to satisfy a social convention. Even so, she did not want him to go. That was it, not the sleeping together but the leaving. He sat on the bed with her, combing his fingers through the muss of her blonde hair. He wished her sweet dreams and she begrudgingly kissed him goodbye, acknowledging his need to sleep without her, but not without a little-girl pout that made her seem even more beautiful.

When her bell rang the next morning at ten, she buzzed him in, stripped him at the door and they resumed where they had left off the night before, refreshed and eager to continue their exploration of each other. They hurried because they had a full day of work ahead. Roland was sending them north to the Hessian forest again for another round of interviews with the owner of the Gasthaus there. This would give Rieger time to make some phone calls and talk with colleagues about the case on the offhand chance that the detectives had overlooked a link.

As Sylvie and Will drove through the countryside back to the Gasthaus in the forest, they reviewed the important aspects of the case, making a pretense of professionalism in an attempt to prove to each other that nothing about their working relationship had changed. In this, they were both wrong but joined each other in the mutual construction of the denial. He could not help but admire the sleek elegant length of her legs, sheer and smooth within the nylon. He now took the liberty of caressing her thighs as she drove. She had the lithe, muscled legs of a professional figure skater, the muscles of her thighs and calves working as she alternately pressed the clutch, the gas, and the brake pedals. Even her toes were pretty and well formed, although she admitted to him that she hated the size of her feet. She also had told him during an interim cuddle the night before that she thought her breasts were too small and he shook his head no emphatically. Women.

If anything, her breasts were in exact and proper proportion to the height and slimness of her figure and perfectly shaped. The beauty is in the shape and proportion, he told her, kissing each breast for emphasis, not in the size. For him personally, he assured her, large sloppy breasts were nothing but a turn-off and this surprised but secretly pleased her. She was under the impression that all men were biologically attracted to women with breasts larger than her own, the bigger the better, in fact.

He thought about it for a minute and said she was correct after all and he graciously offered to pay for the implants. She slapped him on the top of his silly head, grabbed him by both ears and put him to work where he could do the most good.

It was a pleasure to watch her drive. She was quite good really, and she handled the shifting with aplomb, even in her stockinged feet. She had slipped her pumps off, toe to the heel, right foot first, then left, without apology or self-consciousness. It certainly did not hinder her driving, he observed, after the first few doubtful minutes and it certainly added to the length of her already long legs as she arched and pointed her foot to work the pedals. He reclined his seatback a notch or two so his head would not hit the roof. Both already had the seats of the BMW rolled back as far as they would go, and he was content to let her point out the landmarks and areas of interest along the way after they had finished their oral review of the case. In the parking lot of the Gasthaus on the outskirts of the Hessian forest where the last murder had taken place, she swung her knees around to him as she pulled her pumps back on, deliberately allowing him a peak up her skirt.

"Voyeur," she called him, gathering her purse and notebook, and as he reached again for the inside of her thigh, she fended him off and escaped out the door of the BMW. She was merely testing his vaunted powers of concentration.

The owner of the establishment, the Herr Wirt, was none too pleased with the recent turn of events affecting his restaurant and hotel. The murder in the forest surrounding his place of business, and this was the high season, had not increased the flow of traffic to the degree he expected. He cleaned the water spots from the beer glasses with a white towel and placed them upside down on a clean cloth atop the bar. A murder in the area was one thing. A murder that did not increase business, well, that was intolerable. Impressed as he was with Lieutenant Schumann's credentials, to say nothing of the size of her smiling colleague standing next to her, Heinrich Erbst was in no mood to answer another round of questions, even for the criminal police. When Sylvie assured him that they would take up as little of his time as possible, he put down the polishing rag and the beer glass he was working on, came out from behind the security of the bar, and invited them to sit at a table not yet dressed for service atop the fresh white linen. He decided that cooperation alone would get the cops out of the place so he could go back to readying the dining room for the lunch hour. Otherwise, they would just stand there waiting. What else did they have to do all day but drive around bothering hard-working people just trying to make an honest living? He had forgotten about the poached deer he brought in through the back door or the payments under the counter to the liquor supplier so that neither had to pay the government tax.

On the day the murder took place, he was working in the back room taking inventory, so unless anyone came and asked for him specifically, he would not have seen anyone entering the restaurant. Who might? He thought back to the day and time. The wait staff would not have arrived yet and the cooks would be busy with prep. His Croat man, Broz, responsible for setting up the tables might have seen someone or given directions. In fact, that happened frequently. Why was this not mentioned in the report to the Schutzpolizei during the initial interviews? How was he to know? Maybe nobody asked that question. Anyway, that was Broz over there, working at the far end of the room by the windows that looked out onto the forest. They watched a small man in black pants and white shirt meticulously laying out the silverware and glasses, carefully folding napkins, and slapping crumbs from the seat cushions of the chairs with a towel. He came over immediately at the request of the Herr Wirt, towel draped over his shoulder like a serape.

He was nervous and sweated into his moustache. His swarthy skin glistened with perspiration. His hands shook and he hid them behind his back after tugging at the buttoned collar just below his prominent Adam's apple. Sylvie was certain that he was in the country illegally, working without the proper papers. She told him they were investigating the case of the unfortunate young woman found murdered in the forest.

"The Herr Wirt had mentioned that you might be able to help us with the case."

The man sighed so heavily in relief that they could smell the garlic wafting off his breath. Even as he promised that he would do everything within his feeble powers to help, he continued to sweat profusely, staining dark semi-circles under each arm. "Yes, a pretty young woman had come in that day asking to use the restaurant's toilet." He examined the photo Sylvie placed on the table. He bent down to examine the shot, afraid to pick it up. "No." He shook his head emphatically.

Sylvie showed him the next picture. Again he bent down to look more closely and Will caught the smell of work and fear and garlic combined in a shirt that had been worn the day before and should have been changed.

"Yes. That was her! I showed her the door for the women's facility Yes. She seemed in a hurry but she was also in there quite a long time." He tried to make a little joke out of it but when Sylvie did not smile, he was embarrassed almost to the point of desperation.

It did not help that his boss, Herr Erbst, simply glared at him for prolonging the interview. Broz excused himself and asked for a glass of water, dry voice cracking in the effort. Sylvie pushed out a chair for him to sit and looked over at the owner with just the proper amount of innocent expectation. He got up grumbling to himself under his breath and returned with a glass of water. He had not bothered to ask Will or Sylvie if they wanted anything so Will said if it wouldn't be an imposition..., and smiled serenely into the rage reddening the restaurant owner's fat cheeks. When he returned with a pitcher of ice water and two more glasses with a thoughtful slice of lemon in each, Sylvie kindly thanked him and then dismissed him rather curtly, telling him that would be all and he could return to his work behind the bar. He left without speaking and watched from behind the vantage point of the bar, taking up the rag and making a pretense of wiping out the glasses.

No one else had come in with the woman, Janos Broz remembered, but there was someone waiting for her in the car. Her husband, he guessed, but he could not see him clearly through the lace trim and engraved figures of the restaurant's glass windows that looked out onto the parking lot.

"The car? A Volkswagen Golf, blue with two doors," he said with pride. "I hope to own such a fine car one day. No, I noticed nothing unusual or out of the ordinary." He sipped at his water gratefully.

Everything seemed normal that day. He had seen a woman hurrying to use the bathroom after a long trip in the car, the husband waiting patiently outside. Yes, she had been carrying a purse but he could not remember the color, only that it was dark. The only thing that struck him as unusual was the amount of time she spent in the bathroom, he repeated. He took another drink from the glass of water, draining nearly half its contents with one gulp. He was calm enough to begin speculating now. Perhaps she was having stomach problems.

Sylvie agreed and said that was probably what happened and thanked him for his cooperation. When he did not leave, she thanked him again and said he was free to return to his duties. He stood, begging their pardon in heavily accented German, then thanked them profusely and gave them each his wet hand to shake. He continued to mutter to himself in Serbo-Croatian as he left, so great was his relief that the ordeal had come to a good end.

The Herr Wirt, now suddenly grown gracious, escorted them to the heavy double doors of the Gasthaus and gallantly showed them out. He extended an invitation to come for dinner after the investigation was finished and they thanked him for his generous but false offer. Sylvie walked Will directly to the parking spot where Broz had seen the blue Golf. She checked the angles for line of sight back to the window of the building, verifying the man's story. Only then did she allow herself to breathe through her nose again and when she noticed Will doing the same, turned to him and they laughed, taking in cleaning draughts of the cool, sweet pine-scented air, refreshingly clean and clear.

Sylvie wanted a walk, but not in the direction of the crime scene. She said more as an observation than an apology, that some of the recent immigrants into Germany had not yet learned the same standards of hygiene and cleanliness as the locals. Will apologized and promised he would be more careful about changing his shirt in the future. She walked away from his feeble attempt to be funny, hiding her smile. She needed time now to talk out the results of the interview. She was curious to learn what Will thought. He had been quiet throughout the interview, letting her ask all the questions, and she had been proud of her performance. Suddenly she shook her head, a gentle remonstration of self for so quickly trusting this man whom she hardly knew.

"What would your mother say?" Will teased. He read the shocked surprise on her face as she stopped dead in her tracks, astounded that

231

he had guessed correctly once again. She wanted to know how he had intruded into her innermost and private thoughts.

"And don't you dare say elementary, my dear," she warned. "In fact, I don't want to hear it."

In this instance, he decided that discretion was the better part of valor and said only that semiotic analysis can also be applied to reading emotions and let it go at that. Outside the view of the Gasthaus and within the cover of the woods she surreptitiously slid her hand into his, looking for comfort. He was smart enough to remain silent and kiss her at just the right time. After the kiss, she took him fully into the embrace of her arms and placed her head on his chest, letting him know that everything was okay and that she had made her decision to trust him without regret. He wanted just one more kiss before they resumed their walk.

"Do you think the Croat was telling the truth?" She knew that her questions during the interview had allowed him the luxury of carefully studying the behaviors and actions of the two men.

"I think he was desperately telling the truth in order to avoid being arrested."

"I was thinking the same thing," she agreed. "What does that give us; rather, what does that do for us?

Will did not answer immediately. A few paces ahead they found a bench and sat on the weathered wood, listening to the birds sing, watching the squirrels work in the pine boughs overhead as they scurried and chided them for the interruption from below. Sylvie took out her notebook.

"We can say with assurance now that if the driver is indeed the killer, he is a male, something we have previously assumed."

She nodded and made a note. This was an obvious and simple fact but their protocols demanded that they check every item of information, no matter how obvious or simple.

Will continued. "It also allows us to conclude that to some degree he was known to her, even if they were working together for only a short period of time. That in itself may be significant; I mean the idea that they were working together. The fact is, she had a chance to escape into and through the restaurant had she been kidnapped or otherwise held against her will. But she did not. She returned to the man waiting in the car. That is also significant."

"Why would she do that?"

"Remember, they are working together."

"We assume they are working together."

He looked at her. "Right. Let's keep it as a working assumption, but one with a high level of probability." He waited for her to finish the notation. "They walk into the woods together but only he returns, gets in the car and drives off. A transaction of some sort has been completed—I'm theorizing know—and he no longer requires her services, so to speak."

"Why so long in the bathroom?" Sylvie asked.

"Maybe Broz was right. Maybe it was gastrointestinal."

They looked at each other one heartbeat and simultaneously said "No!"

"Okay," he said trying again, "she relieved herself in good time but then took extra time to prepare something or to do something."

"Of course," said Sylvie. "If we theorize that her actions are consistent with our previous scenario, then she is taking the extra time to remove the diamonds from her vagina and puts them in her purse. Once into the woods, she hands them over, expecting to get paid for her troubles, but she gets killed instead. He gets the money on top of the diamonds and stages the murder scene to look like a serial killing."

"That's what I'm thinking," Will said, simply.

"So, our next move is to catch up with him. But where to start?" she mused, thinking aloud. She turned to face him as the answer dawned on her and she could see that he had been waiting for her to say: the car. It was time to take another ride. The nearest airport was Frankfurt am Main and that's where they would check the car rental agencies for a late model, blue, two-door, Volkswagen Golf.

They hurried back to their own car. At speed, they just might arrive in time to question the staff working the appropriate shift.

The speed at which Sylvie drove on the Autobahn terrified him.

As usual, construction at the Frankfurt International airport delayed vehicle traffic coming in and out of the massive facility, one of the primary gateways for Germany and Europe. Traffic slowed to a crawl, in-bound access limited to a single lane marked by orange traffic cones. Construction cranes towered above the horizon, lifting materials and moving them elsewhere. He heard the powerful thrum of the big diesel engines as the cranes turned and repositioned their loads. Black smoke hung in the air and the stink was compounded by the unseasonably warm weather that forced commuters to roll windows down to escape the heat. This further contributed to a rise in tempers, frustrated illegal honking, and a series of gesticulations that appeared comical when viewed from afar.

"The monkeys are angry in their little cars," Will said to Sylvie. They were fully stopped now in a line so long he could see neither end.

"Welcome to German rush-hour traffic at its finest," she said.

"Can't you invoke some supreme civil authority or fire up your emergency lights and get us out of this mess?"

She considered the request, but where would they go? Straight up? "Just be patient, big boy, and consider this more quality time spent together. Let's talk about us," she suggested.

He groaned. "My mother warned me about women like you," he told her. "All they care about in the world is their damned relationship. Everything is us, us, us, we this and we that. They see the world only as a couple. It's as if they have become some kind of freakish binary unit, forever joined to their partner at the hip. No longer two distinct individuals, they become a pathetic perverse form of relational life called a "We.""

Sylvie laughed at his dramatic rant, a happy and melodic soprano note that infused her voice with a certain amount of unrestricted youthful glee. "My god," she said, "you've just described most of my girlfriends. It's sad, really. They think they're so happy but their happiness is a straw house. When the guys leave, they're devastated. Their quaint little house of happiness collapses in a heap around them. But the funny thing is, Will, they wind up mourning the loss of the relationship more than they do the loss of the guy."

Will looked at her with genuine surprise, amazed at her perspicacity. As the traffic once again inched forward, she quickly turned the ignition key and they slowly followed and actually made second gear. "How did you get so smart about relationships?" he asked.

"Oh, I don't know. Just lucky, I guess. You're my first failure, really," she teased. "Can I ask you a personal family question," she asked, "even if it's about Roland?"

"Why not?" he allowed. "But you have to realize that he is a very private man and I might not know the answer to your question."

She nodded, but she had to know. "Why does he never go into his office?" She asked it with such innocence that he could not help but laugh.

"He says there has never been a murder committed in his office. His work is where the crime takes him, and it rarely takes him back to the office."

This made eminent good sense to her and she accepted the answer. Fifteen minutes later, they finally arrived at the rental agency. In one regard, the Stau, or traffic jam, was a boon as most of the arriving passengers had already picked up their luggage, booked their rentals, and were merging into the creep of traffic away from the airport and onto the Autobahn. The efficient staff at the rental counter reduced the stream of passengers to a trickle until the next round of flights arrived. Sylvie walked right up to the counter, flashed her credentials so that even the three or four people already in line at the counter could see them, and asked to speak with the manager.

The alarmed manager hurried them around the counter as quickly as he could within the boundaries of courtesy, and seated them in his small office, beyond the view of the curious glances from the waiting customers. Her request was not unusual. He had worked with the KRIPO on numerous other occasions. He made certain she knew that. He wanted to do everything possible to keep them on the good side of his agency. In fact, he had special, unadvertised discounts for the police and they used his agency exclusively as an acknowledgment of his cooperation and his generosity. This was just his way of showing his gratitude for the fine work done by his friends in uniform. What could it hurt? Will leaned in to Sylvie's ear and whispered conspiratorially, "There is corruption all around us."

She tried hard not to laugh.

THE INVESTIGATION

The manager had turned his back to them in order to face his computer screen, and missed the little aside. It took him only a couple of keystrokes as he paged through the screens on his terminal. He had the date, an approximate time, the make and model of the vehicle. He hit the print key and the printer lurched, fed down a sheet of paper, chattered for a bit, and gave them a record of rentals for the day in question. The list was limited to customers renting a Golf. When the color was factored in, the list was further narrowed. When two female names were excluded, they were left with the names of five persons who on that day had rented a blue, two door Golf. Only one had returned the vehicle later the same day. Will looked at a figure he had written on a piece of paper. The mileage figures of that particular rental roughly coincided with a trip to and a return from the Gasthaus Waldenbruck in the Hessian forest. Sylvie asked to speak with the agent who had rented the vehicle.

At the end of her shift, she was anxious to get home. It had been a particularly hot and busy day and she had been hounded and pestered for upgrades she did not have. Her uniform had lost its crispness and her hairdo was going limp, the unseasonable heat and humidity defeating the inadequate cooling system at the agency. She pulled herself together in front of her boss and tried not to stare at the gorgeous man with the police lieutenant. Sylvie looked at the woman's nametag, and asked Fräulein Kessler If she remembered any of the customers named on the printout. She studied the list diligently as she had been taught in the vocational school, and then pointed to a name, delighted that she recognized it.

"This one."

It was the same-day return.

"Why that one?" Sylvie asked.

The young agent standing, giggled and crossed her legs. "His coat didn't fit very well."

"What do you mean?"

"The muscles of his chest made the lapels stick out. His hair was cut short, you know, so that it stood up like the bristles on a hair brush?"

"Like a skinhead?"

She shook her head no.

"A military haircut, then?"

She pulled at the lower lip, momentarily flustered. "Well, not like a German or Dutch soldier." She tapped her chin with her index finger. "More like an American Marine." She smiled at Will, happy to see that she had pleased him with the information. After all, that was the best part of her personality and one of the reasons why she got this job. She liked to please people. Then Sylvie re-directed her attention from pleasing Will to the next question.

"Did you notice anything else unusual about the man?"

She nodded and then deliberated a moment. This was actually getting to be quite fun. She had never been interrogated by the KRIPO. She couldn't wait to tell her roommate how cute the guy was. She might even get her name and picture in the *Frankfurter Allgemeine*, not that she ever read it. She combed her fingers through the mess of her black hair, disgusted at what it had become in the heat and humidity of the day. She wouldn't want them to take her photograph in this condition. Definitely time for a new cut, and maybe a new color like the blonde asking most of the questions.

"Hilda!?" Her boss startled her back to the issue of the question.

"Oh, I remember now," she said completely unaffected, completely used to having others bring her attention back into the conversation and out of the many happy places inside her own head.

238

"He spoke German like an Ausländer," she said. "His German was good but he spoke with a foreign accent that I couldn't quite place. He did something nasal with some of the vowels but I thought it made him seem cute, really." She looked to Sylvie for female substantiation. "But he wasn't an attractive man by any means, don't get me wrong, certainly not as handsome as your colleague."

Sylvie recrossed her legs, unconsciously moving closer to Will. Sylvie nodded at the privilege of this girl-to-girl information, understanding full well the attraction of a woman to an ordinary looking man who possessed other attributes sufficient to holding a woman's attention, like a powerful physique, a fast car, or a charming accent.

At this point Will said "Spetsialnogo naznachenyia" and watched the young agent's eyes widen in surprise.

"Yes," she gushed, unable to disguise her amazement, "that's exactly how he sounded, you know, Spanish or something."

"Russian," he gently corrected and Sylvie fought hard not to laugh.

"Russian," Sylvie repeated, "probably stationed in East Germany at one time. That would explain his knowledge of German."

She asked Hilda if she would work that evening with a police sketch artist and when the agent looked helplessly at her boss he said, "It is our duty as citizens, Fräulein Kessler, but make sure you log the hours and I'll see to it that you are paid." The thought of the extra money cheered her into cooperation once more and she agreed to do her onerous civic duty. Her friends at the local would have to wait.

Sylvie made the arrangements, thanked first Fräulein Kessler, and then her boss Herr Finsterwald, called for the police artist and left him the number of her office fax machine and her cell phone. She looked at her watch as she folded her notebook and placed it in her purse. She couldn't believe how hungry she was.

239

"Dinner?" asked Will

"Love to," she said, "and for once you're buying."

THE INFORMER

Chapter Eighteen: The Informer

THE UNSUB HAD made such an immediate and indelible impression on the mind of Fräulein Hilda Kessler—the young woman who worked at the car rental agency—that the police sketch came together with startling detail. Based on her description of the subject, the police artist had taken the composite, enhanced it on the computer, and using his knowledge of facial structures and racial characteristics, produced a rendering that seemed more photograph than portrait. Roland had copies made for distribution after Sylvie and Will brought over the original computer-generated composite.

At Roland's apartment the next day, Will did not take his usual seat in the corner of the living room under the hanging spider plant. Instead, he sat on the couch, Sylvie next to him, forcing Roland to take the chair that had once been the favorite of Will's grandfather. After they finished the business of rebuilding case files with the attached portrait, Roland made a quick trip to the kitchen. He shouldered through the door to the living room, three glasses in one hand held upside down by the base, a late-harvest Riesling from Piesport and a corkscrew in the other. He let Will uncork the wine and smiled with satisfaction when his nephew recalled that this was his father's favorite wine. Will poured three glasses of the golden wine, its perfume filling the room, while Roland opened the cabinet along the far wall where he kept his better books, records, videos, and lately, a small collection of compact discs. He found what he was looking for: Domingo singing zarzuela arias, his favorite disc of the moment and a present from Will. As the first dramatic notes of the Spanish guitar floated from the speakers, he adjusted the volume for background listening, came to the coffee table to pick up his glass of white wine, and settled into the comfort of his father's old smoking chair.

The wine was cool and excellent but too sweet for Rieger's palate. Will's father had always preferred late harvest wines for their luxurious mixture of sugar and acid. Roland preferred something just a bit more dry, but he was happy to indulge his nephew, who had inherited his father's preference for French Sauternes, special ice wines from Germany, or even November-harvested Moscatos from Italy. Will told them the story of the time he drank a rare five puttonys Tokaj from Hungary, a luscious, sweet, honeyed bottle of a wine. After the story, Roland looked over at the two on the couch and shook his head.

"I'm really disgusted with you," he said to Will, referring to his intimate relationship with Sylvie. "I thought my sister had raised you better than that." He tsk-tsked his displeasure, then sighed at the inevitability of it all.

Will hung his head, properly chastised, and confessed his shame. "It was that uniform. I'm just a sucker for a long-legged blonde in a uniform." He managed to deflect most of the elbow strike to his ribs.

Roland nodded his sage understanding. There was indeed something about a woman in uniform. He forgave Will his indiscretion. "But you, Sylvie, I expected that a partner of mine would surely have better taste than to fall for someone like Will."

Sylvie reassured him. "Don't worry, Roland. I'm only using him for his body. Just a temporary fling. Nothing more." She sipped her wine with cool indifference.

Will turned to her and they clicked wineglasses, toasting the superficiality and meaninglessness of it all. "Here's to shallow, short-lived relationships based entirely on biochemical sexual attraction and genetic pre-determination," Will offered as a toast and they drank, happy to have anything to drink to.

"To men and machines and the climaxes they cause," Sylvie contributed, already feeling the effects of the alcohol.

The two men looked at her, feigning shock. "That's really embarrassing, Sylvie," Will chided, but she was uncowed and not the least bit chastened.

"I can't help what I'm like and I can't help what I like." She paused. "Did I say that right?"

"Well said," complimented Roland, as Will poured their glasses full for another round. "Let's all drink to what we are and hope no one else finds out."

Before he sent them to bed, they saw off three more bottles of wine and capped the night with shots from the Crown Royal. Will told stories of his days as a professor at university; Roland contributed hilarious tales from his early days on the Job, and his relationship with Will's father. Sylvie, well into the second bottle, allowed the men to ask about her first sexual experience, which she offered only after they promised to tell the same. Then Roland recanted and said he would have to invent his because he was still a virgin, saving himself for the right woman. After that startling revelation, the conversation degraded and the hilarity increased.

THE ADAMANTINE HEART

The two men stood on the balcony taking in the fresh night air, tinged with high mountain cold as it traveled across the serrated peaks of the Alps. Unable to wait for Sylvie, who had claimed first rights to the bathroom, they watered the grasses three stories below. Suitably relieved, they proclaimed in kinship and camaraderie that life was good. They had a long day waiting for them with a trip into Munich a necessity. Roland took the couch, where he enjoyed sleeping anyway, leaving the queen-sized bed for Will and Sylvie, who fell asleep in the comfort of his arms. Half an hour later, Will slipped from her side, stole a pillow, and stretched out on the rug beside the bed.

Two hours later, the insistent press of the wine against her bladder roused her into just enough groggy consciousness to know she had to pee. She threw off the sheet and swung her bare legs over the side of the bed. As she rose, she stepped on his stomach and as he grunted, she screamed. He sat bolt upright in alarm, wondering who kicked him in the gut. They collapsed in a laughing heap on the floor when their senses finally came together enough for them to realize what they were doing. Will pressed his finger to her lips, commanding silence. They listened to the night sounds of the darkened apartment. In the midst of all the commotion, Roland had not so much as stirred.

They were up relatively early, particularly for Will, not too far removed from a professor's hours and habits: afternoon or evening seminars and late evenings spent grading papers or writing research articles. Roland, too, was still a bit sleepy and grumbly, having not fully slept out the effects of the wine and the late hours. They begrudged Sylvie her fresh-faced alertness and bright eyes so early in the morning. She wanted to talk, eager to pursue the new level of intimacy that had developed between the three. At the breakfast table in the kitchen, the two men preferred to sit in silence, but they were polite enough about it. When

244

required to speak, they rarely managed anything more than monosyllables.

"Butter?"

"No. Thanks."

After the food hit their systems and their blood sugar perked up sufficiently, they became livelier. Roland whistled an aria from a Lehar operetta and Will sang the song, taking advantage of the excellent acoustics of the stairwell. Sylvie was surprised at the quality of his voice and even more surprised that he knew all the words to an aria that most Germans would recognize but could not sing. In the car, with encouragement, but not much, he sang "Che gelida manina," the famous aria from Puccini's *La Boheme*. His voice broke at the high C and he apologized, a bit embarrassed and explained that he had not been singing much lately so his voice was out of shape. Then he sang the very same aria again, only this time in its German version, "Wie eiskalt ist dies Händchen." Roland joined in, his pleasant baritone singing along to the section that did not demand such a high tessitura. This time Will attacked the high C, and he hit it, although his voice thinned with the strain and he laughed at the result. "There," he said, "as good as anything Peter Schreier ever sang."

Sylvie smiled. Schreier was a famous German tenor whose last name in German meant screamer. She settled back into her seat enjoying the ride through the countryside into Munich. She listened with genuine interest as the two men amiably debated the merits of German tenor voices from the last fifty years. Fritz Wunderlich was the clear and decided choice of both. Once in the city, Roland double-parked and jumped out at the entrance to the English Gardens and told them to take the car, see the sights of the city center, have lunch and pick him up at three at the same location. He handed Sylvie into the driver's seat, admiring her legs as he did so, shut the door after she gathered herself into the car, and he was off into the park for his meeting.

One of his favorite parks in Munich, the English Gardens bloomed next to the Isar river. He walked from Ludwigstrasse where he had left the car for Sylvie and Will, past the Japanese teahouse and the Chinese pagoda, until he reached the center and the heart of the park, Kleinhesselhoher Lake. He found an empty bench, checked it carefully before he sat, and watched the daily routine of a mother duck teaching her ducklings how to paddle all in a row. It was a clear day and warming and he could see the skyline of Munich nearby and the skyline of the Alps in the distance. He saw the half dome of the Amphitheater where open-air plays were performed during the good weather of the summer.

The mother duck honked her youngsters into a tight turn-about and brought her waddling brood out of the lake and onto the shore, shaking the water from their tails. She waited to be fed. Roland held up his hands to show that they were empty, and he confessed to her that he should not have come without breadcrumbs to feed them. She listened patiently but when he produced no food, she scolded her crew back into the waters, paddling down the shore toward the next bench where they might have better luck. After watching them paddle their tails smoothly out of sight, he rose and walked to the north end of the park.

Raisa Borodinskaya was already dressed for work. She had come from the hair salon and she felt good about herself. The weekly pampering never failed to elevate her mood, even if the weather was dreary, as it often was in Munich, particularly during the early part of winter before the snows came, or late in the spring when the rains washed the city clean. Two hours at the salon invariably corrected even the darkest Russian brooding, but today the weather matched her mood perfectly. Bright, but still cool on the skin, she gave her face to the sun, closed her eyes and waited for its warmth to plump her cheeks. She crossed her legs under her miniskirt carefully; she wasn't required to show for work at the nearby FKK club called the Oasis until three o'clock and it wouldn't do to advertise when she was still off-duty.

She had arrived about half an hour early and sat near the Biergarten at the northern end of the park. The wind was a cool touch on her freshly waxed legs, the sun illuminating the shine in the oil used to finish the treatment. She hated her legs; too short and too muscular. She starved herself to keep the fat off her thighs and to stay the creep of cellulite that made her ass look like a loofa. Thank god, her face remained youthful and her breasts were still holding up; that's where she made her money. She crossed her arms to hide her nipples, stimulated by the brush of the breeze, and listened to the sounds of the park that reminded her so much of home.

She heard the excited screams of children as they ran and fell, the shrill call of mothers diverted from their gossip, but mostly she listened for the birds. For an instant, she was a young girl again, spending the afternoon in the park with her father, proud in her new Sunday dress pink as her cheeks. His attention was entirely on her. She was happy to be in the hand of her father, so strong and so handsome in the uniform of a Russian sailor. He was a submariner visiting his homeport, and she was absolutely thrilled that he was on leave, spending the day in the park with her and listening to every silly little thing she had to say. That was her fondest memory of her father. One day shortly after her tenth birthday he went away as usual, called to the sea, and she was so sad to see him off.

Her father was a sailor in service to the Rodina, and his duty to mother Russia required that he spend long months under the sea, patrolling the waters of the Atlantic. She had wondered even then if the extra kisses or the hug that seemed a bit longer than the others foreshadowed what was to come. She was jealous of mother Russia and did not give her father over gladly to the great Soviet Navy. She remembered the tiny ball of fear that grew in the emptiness within her stomach like a new walnut in its shell on the day he put back to sea. She remembered how the walnut of fear shattered and swept over her the day her mother said her father would not return, dead at sea, the result of a reactor accident aboard the nuclear submarine. The fear was always with her, capable of re-emerging and sweeping her away in a paralyzing wash of anxiety and dread in the same way her mother had been swept away in the wash of vodka, her mother's only means of containing her own fear. Only as an adult was she able to recapture that fear and keep it in the place behind her stomach where it had been born. At sixteen, Raisa sold the diamond ring her father had given her on her tenth birthday—his mother's wedding ring—and used the money to escape the emotional ghetto of her mother's despair. In her school dress and bonnet with the red ribbon, she traveled by train from her home in Novosibirsk to Moscow and eventually to Paris, and no one thought to bother the pretty young redhead, diligently studying her textbook.

In Paris, when her money ran out, she discovered that men would pay for the sexual use of her body, and she consigned herself to the work of sex for pay, giving up romance for capital, thus ensuring her existence. She bounced from Paris to Amsterdam, where she made films and an obscene amount of money from the low-quality production of bestiality porno so much in demand by the Japanese. She saved her guilders and used the money to finance her move to Munich and the legalized prostitution of Germany. She couldn't decide which was worse, the incessant, remorseless humping of the black labs in Holland or the same from the bored, rich college students at the university. These were the scions of the German economic miracle. The sons had supplanted the fervent political nationalism of their fathers and grandfathers from the first half of the century with an equally ardent pursuit of wealth during the second half. Their fathers had substituted capitalism for militarism and the sons of these wealthy tycoons were her best customers, and Karl Marx, born in Trier, Germany, no doubt spun in his grave like the spindle in the gear shaft of a wheel moving the factory line forward.

Her worst customers in the FKK sauna club were expatriate Russians, members of organized crime making a killing in the smuggling and the selling of the best parts of the dismantled Soviet military to minor countries in the Balkans or the Middle East. Howitzers, tanks, even a MiG jet fighter, all was for sale if the price were right; small arms, shoulder-fired missiles, mortars, all manner of ammunition and explosives were available. Whatever the well-equipped liberation army required, it could be had along with technical expertise and personal training.

Members of this new caste of mobsters, the Russian Mafia, came to her with unbelievable swagger, unbelievable stories, and almost as much money as the spoiled brats at the University of Munich. She tolerated their coarseness and cheap cologne and listened, converting her store of information into intellectual capital because she was at that point in her working life where she was no longer the first chosen from the presentation line or the bar at the club. At twenty seven, even her sexual expertise was no longer a sufficient substitute for the loss of her youth. She forced herself to think back again to a special Spring day in the park by the banks of the Ob river so many years ago, her father resplendent in his submariner's uniform, and the fear was once again contained.

"I understand it's still quite cold in Novosibirsk this time of year."

Her concentration caught up in the rapture of her reverie, she jumped and gasped at the sound of his voice. For an instant, she thought she had heard her father's voice. She had been completely unaware of the man who was now sitting next to her. She placed her hand across her chest for protection and looked over at him.

"You pig!" she accused him in her Russian-accented German. "How long have you been sitting there watching me?" she demanded.

"Just long enough to appreciate a Siberian beauty in such a gorgeous natural setting," he said. "Red looks good on you, Raisa," he added.

She had recovered sufficiently to accept the compliment. "Do you really think so?" She was worried that the auburn tint covering the first wisps of gray was too much for her complexion. He reassured her. He knew she was now at the age where she was once again susceptible to flattery.

"It's been too long, Raisa. I've missed you."

She crossed her legs toward him but turned away at the shoulder. "You only come to see me now when you want information."

He waited for a moment, thinking of the right thing to say. "It's the Job, Raisa. Things are not good now. Steinmetz is all over my ass about this Forest Killer, as the press has so unimaginatively named him. It's my career, this time, not just loss of rank." He was being honest and there was just the right hint of resignation in his voice to convince her.

Prostitute, porno star, paid police informant, at the core she was a woman and she could not resist the man in spite of their professional relationship. For this reason, she had become one of Hauptkommissar Roland Rieger's most dependable sources of information about southern Germany's dark side. Her knowledge of the activities of the Russian Mafia was encyclopedic. He knew her information would be reliable, but he also knew enough to have the money ready.

"I've been following the case in the media," she told him, all business now. "In fact, everyone on the street is talking about it. Some of the other girls are scared to death. It's bad for business, you know. In a strange sort of way, they're all rooting for you to catch this guy."

He nodded and pulled the computer-enhanced composite from his coat pocket and handed it to her.

"I know him," she said. "His name is Gennady Primakov." She told Roland that Primakov was known among the Russian community in Munich, and although she thought he did not work in organized crime, word on the street had it that he was a specialist with services for hire. "Definitely ex-military," she said, "probably a paratrooper or some sort of commando." She had heard the term for it once but could not remember it, although it was on the tip of her tongue.

He tried a word as she searched her memory. "Spetsnazovet."

"That was it," she said slapping his thigh for emphasis. She had just confirmed Will's reasoning that the killer was a member of some army's special forces. Now Roland knew it was the Soviet Spetsnaz. She did not know for whom he worked, but rumor had it that he took assignments from time to time, once actually leaving the country, and he seemed to be well-paid for his work, although she certainly hadn't seen any signs of it.

Roland took her to mean that Primakov was tight with his money and did not spend it on clothes, cars, or the ladies. Most likely, as an ex-patriot, he was saving his money for a return to mother Russia after the chaos subsided. A man like Primakov, who carried his patriotism in his heart, would not easily give up or forget the customs of his homeland. That meant he drank and probably frequented a favorite watering hole.

"Nikita's," Raisa said.

He reached into the coat pocket of his leather jacket for an envelope containing her fee and handed it over, slipping it carefully between the space in the small of her back and the curve of the park bench. She reached behind her for the package and without opening it, slipped it quickly into her purse. Roland knew she would have the money in the bank before she went to work at the Oasis. He also knew how uncomfortable the pay-off made her. She had no qualms about being paid for sex, her profession, but being a paid informant did not sit well with her Siberian code of ethics that forbade giving information to the police or any government official. She had convinced herself she was doing it out of friendship. As always, he knew exactly what to say.

"Please accept this as a small token of gratitude on behalf of the free state of Bavaria for your loyalty and assistance in this extremely important criminal investigation."

Merely the fact that he put it so officially calmed her apprehensions. She was making a contribution to her adopted country and helping to bring a murderer to justice. More importantly, she was doing it as a favor to him.

She looked quickly at her watch. She still had about an hour before work. "Rolli," she purred, "come back to the apartment with me, for old time's sake. As always, lubimyi: no charge for you."

Although they had not been lovers for some time, he gallantly offered her his arm, prepared to make any and all sacrifices, no matter how large or small, as a loyal servant in the service of the once royal and now free state of Bavaria's criminal police force.

Chapter Nineteen: The Apprehension

H E HAD THE same feeling he used to get walking up the trails of loose scree on the side of some unpronounceable mountain in Afghanistan. The hair on his arms and at the back of his neck rose and he had learned to trust his war fighter's instincts. Twice it had saved his life. Each time he had felt the vague sensation of danger, he had stopped and put his men behind whatever hardscrabble cover they could find. Each time the Mujahedin had been prematurely forced to fire from behind their ambush points, screaming their high shrill war cries over short staccato bursts from their semi-automatics. Their mortars brought the loose rock rolling down the sides of the hills as the concussions cannonaded back and forth between the high peaks flanking each side of the valley. He could still hear rocks ping off his helmet and taste the stone dust in his mouth. Then they were gone and the valley crashed into silence.

Even through the vodka-induced haze he felt the sensation emerge again, as if he were back with his unit, fighting for the high ground and waiting for the Mi-24 attack helicopters to save their asses. The fear died down when the first of the Crocodiles, so-called because of the camo paint schemes, popped up and fired their missiles into the slopes ahead of his men. He threw back the last of the ice-cold, pepper-flavored spirit. As it burned its way down his throat, he watched the door to the street. It was still too early in the day for the regulars to come into the Russian bar. The old man in back did a reasonable job with the food when he was sober enough to see it, and he kept the prices cheaper than the standard German fare. What really brought the expatriates in—not counting the girls interested in hooking up with dangerous men—were the fifteen different flavors of vodka stored in the freezer behind the bar.

From his table at the back of the room he could watch the flow of traffic in and out of the place. There was nothing behind him except a wall on which a tinny speaker rattled out ludicrous Russian folk music played and sung by members of the Soviet Army. What a laugh that was. Why couldn't he have gotten a duty assignment like that? From the moment they walked through the door he could tell they were police. The tall blonde was a real beauty and he would regret having to kill her. Patience. They might not be here for him. The oldest of the three bulls called the bartender over and showed what looked to be a photo. In an instant, Primakov knew someone had given him up, but he did not panic, letting his training take over as he regulated his breathing and started to plan. Despite the bartender's dismissive denial that he had never seen the person in the picture, his body language said otherwise. As their eyes adapted to the dark inside the bar, they spotted him. They approached the table cautiously, the blonde beside the older cop, the younger male standing off to the side, watching intently. That one was likely to give him trouble. He looked fit, relaxed and confident. He knew the look. He had had it once himself during better days when he marched with the troops on parade through Red Square.

"Gennady Primakov?" he was asked.

He nodded.

THE APPREHENSION

"You are wanted for questioning by the Bavarian State Criminal Police in regard to a capital case. We have a car waiting to take you to Headquarters."

He nodded again and watched as all three tensed when he reached for his wallet and left a small tip on the table. Good. He wanted them to relax as he stood. He asked them what this was all about, slightly slurring his words. He came out from behind the table, clumsily, as if the alcohol were having an effect. As he stumbled toward her, Kommissar Lieutenant Sylvie Schumann stepped back reflexively. She barely saw the short powerful right hand that struck her just to the left of the curve of her chin, instantly knocking her unconscious. Only the fact that she was already moving back and away from the line of the punch saved her from suffering a death blow. In the split second when the two men were still stunned by his actions, Primakov reached for the old Walther PPK strapped to his ankle. The older cop, already in a defensive crouch, was reaching for his Glock 20 ten millimeter. He knew that pistol could do some serious damage. It would be close.

Primakov didn't have time to settle into a balanced shooting stance so he fired immediately as he brought the gun up. There wasn't time to watch the big guy. The pistols roared simultaneously and he thought that his had misfired. The older cop's bullet caught him in the left shoulder, spinning him completely around. The kinetic force of the round pushed him backward onto the table where he had been drinking and it collapsed under his weight. He noted with satisfaction that the cop had been hit and was down too. Primakov was almost there; two down, one to go.

He still had his weapon in hand. Good. The adrenaline kept him from feeling the first flush of pain from the round centered in his left shoulder. As the younger guy came at him, Primakov scrambled to a knee, raised the firearm and started the squeeze. The man kicked the weapon from his hand just before the weapon fired and the bullet plowed into the ceiling. Primakov admired the beautifully executed wheel kick as he fought through the fog of shock starting to envelop him.

Almost every day of his life since the age of eighteen, he had put his body through the rigors of advanced physical training. After his qualification and acceptance into the Spetsnaz, he became a master of Sambo, a combination of various martial arts and fighting styles with a heavy emphasis on wrestling techniques. He came up off the floor and shot a one-leg takedown attempt but the big man countered by moving in to his rush. He was forced to release the hold and lost his advantage when he took an elbow strike to the ear that hurt like hell as his eardrum ruptured. Enough of this shit, he thought, I'm in no mood to dance with this guy. He reached for his blade. He feinted a high slash to the eyes, hoping for the reflexive blink, then lunged out of his crouch with a thrust up through the ribs and into the heart. But the man turned his right shoulder into Primakov and caught his wrist before the blade could bite into his chest. He felt the steel grip of the man twisting his arm out and down with such force that he felt the bones in his arm snap. He heard the clatter of the commando knife as it fell to the wood floor. The last thing he remembered was an explosion of light at the back of his head as if a grenade had exploded above and behind him in the darkness of night, the red-hot shards of metal ripping jagged trails of light through the sky. He could not hear the whistling of the fragments but he thought he tasted beer as he passed out.

Sylvie stood above the prostrate commando. The only thing left of the heavy one-liter beer Krug was the handle, shaking in her hand. She was still wobbly on her feet but a look of absolute, murderous rage suffused her face. She reached for her weapon, aimed at his head and prepared to fire.

"Sylvie," Will said gently. "It's over. He's finished. He can't hurt you anymore. Holster your weapon and put him in handcuffs. I'll see to Roland."

As she knelt behind the man, now bleeding from shoulder and scalp, her rage turned from disgust to concern for her partners. "Are you hurt? I don't know how bad Roland was hit."

At that point Roland struggled to his feet, saw that the situation was under control and tried to keep pressure on the inside of the biceps of his left arm. He managed to slip out of his coat, sodden with blood, and Will ripped the sleeve of his shirt off. Roland's arm was still bleeding. Will looked at it closely.

"I think you'll live. Looks like a flesh wound but I don't think it hit the brachial artery. Should leave you with a rather nice scar though." He used the torn shirtsleeve as a bandage and had Roland apply pressure with his other hand.

"What about him?" Roland asked, nodding his head toward Primakov, hands now cuffed behind his broad back, but still unconscious at Sylvie's feet.

"I don't know. I saw him take your round in the shoulder, I felt his arm break, and Sylvie brained him pretty good for a girl... I mean she cold-cocked that bastard."

Sylvie looked at Primakov and then grinned. "I did lay him out, didn't I?"

"Probably saved our lives," Will admitted.

"I don't know," she said somewhat ruefully. "You looked like you were holding your own. Where did you learn to fight like that, anyway?"

"Black belt in Tae Kwon Do; further training in Krav Maga at the FBI academy, but really not a match for a Sambo Master like this guy. I was lucky to block the knife thrust. The fact that he had been drinking and was shot first slowed him down enough for me to react."

"I think we all got a little bit lucky today," Roland acknowledged as he looked over the mess. The entire incident had lasted probably less than fifteen seconds and the place looked like a war zone.

"By the way, and I don't mean to sound stupid, but what is a Sambo Master?" Sylvie asked, mumbling through the swelling of her jaw.

Will looked to Roland, who took the question. He too had been exposed to the fighting arts during his time in the Grenzschutzpolizei who patrolled Germany's borders.

"It's not stupid at all, Sylvie," he told her. "I wish our personnel today received anywhere near that level of instruction in hand-to-hand combat. It's a Russian form of self-defense taught to their commandos like the Spetsnaz. If I remember correctly, Sambo stands for samozashchitya bez oruzhiya, which means self-defense or self-protection without weapons, but it's really a synthesis of the best of all the martial arts in all their lethal forms," he explained.

In the distance, they could hear the sound of the ambulance and police cruisers.

"The cavalry are on their way," Will noted.

Two minutes later the paramedics arrived and properly bandaged Roland's arm. He was advised to take stitches at the hospital. Sylvie got a bag of ice for her swollen jaw, unbroken but throbbing, no teeth dislodged. After Will thoroughly searched the man, Primakov got stuck with an IV needle that he could not feel and rode out of the bar strapped to a stretcher. After Roland dealt with the arriving SCHUPO officers, Will drove his crew to the hospital, following in the wake of the ambulance's siren. At the hospital, Roland let the doctor sew the tear in his bicep, and after Will and Sylvie admired the doctor's handiwork with needle and thread, Roland called the SCHUPO Watch Commander and made certain that Primakov was placed under twenty-four hour guard.

The surgeon informed him that Primakov would require surgery to remove the slug from his shoulder. You can see it there on the X-ray quite clearly. And he would also need a couple of staples to pull the scalp at the back of his head into place. The skull fracture would heal on its own, given time, but there was the concussion to deal with. Roland asked to be called as soon as Primakov regained consciousness and the surgeon assured him he would make it so.

"By the way, if you don't mind my asking, what did this one do?"

"Murder," was all Roland said, but the surgeon was satisfied. This was not his first rodeo, as the American soldiers stationed in Bavaria liked to say.

THE DRAB COLORS of the hospital room seemed a perfect reflection of Gennady Primakov's mood. He hurt, in fact, he hurt all over and he had a splitting headache, but that was not the problem. He had been shot in action before and he knew the pain was temporary. His wounds would heal in time. Primakov's problem was that he saw the hospital as a prison. He could not get out and the worst thing possible for a soldier, with the exception of being killed, was being taken prisoner. To his highly trained military mind, it meant that the enemy had defeated him. He had lost face.

There was no honor in capture. He wanted to die fighting. He had secretly admired this aspect of the Mujahedin; they were willing to die in the service of Allah. Their death as heroes guaranteed them passage into heaven. He had no god to die for, no one to certify his heroism, no one to serve proudly, and no hope of escaping his prison. The worst possible thing had happened: he had lived. He was in no mood to be pestered with questions. He just wanted to die.

The lieutenant was a real beauty even by cold hard Russian standards. It was almost worth living just to speak and be in the same room with her. He realized now why she was the one asking the questions as the two men sat back and listened. They were appealing to his male vanity. He shifted up higher on his pillows to get a better look at his interrogator. No wonder he had staples holding his head together. She was tall and sleek and the muscles of her legs stood out as she crossed them. With the vision of her darkening on his retina, he could die gladly. But she persisted with the damn questions. He cleared his throat, dry from the medication, raw from the breathing tube strapped to his nostrils. It was time to put an end to this torture.

"I want to make a statement."

"Go ahead," she said. "Do you want a glass of water?"

He shook his head. He did not intend to speak long. "My name is Gennady Primakov. I was formerly a soldier; a captain in the most elite of the Soviet commandos called the Spetsnaz. I wear the Order of Lenin given for heroism. I served my country with honor and distinction." He paused for a moment and tried to swallow. He accepted the glass of water from her. He drank half and handed it back to her. She placed it on the tray next to his bed. "I am not a freak, or a perverted rapist, or a demented serial killer. I was hired to do a job and I did it. I disguised the murders to look like the work of a psychopath. I take full responsibility for what I have done. I have nothing more to say."

That was the extent of his statement. With one last look at Sylvie, he closed his eyes. He accepted no deals, no offers of leniency to name the person who had hired him, offered no insight into his motive or purpose beyond his terse statement. He lapsed into a silence profound and deep as a coma. There was nothing left for them to do but leave. As they exited the room, Hauptkommissar Rieger took the clipboard from the SCHUPO officer on guard and initialed next to his typed name, then let Will and Sylvie do likewise. He reiterated that no one not on the list was to pass through that door for any reason without calling the attending physician for permission. And Roland had given the doctor permission to admit no one. They worked their way out of the maze of passages, following the lines painted on the floor through the smell of antiseptic, and arrived back on the street.

Will said, "Once he gets out of the hospital, Primakov will try to kill himself. He is a man who has lost all sense of who and what he is. He won't want to go on like this."

Roland nodded.

Sylvie asked, "Why now and not earlier?"

"He sees himself as a mercenary, a professional soldier for hire. He failed in his mission. He lost his unit, his army, his country and, most importantly, his sense of manhood. He is ready to die."

"I'll see to it that he is watched as well as protected," Roland said.

"We don't want to take a chance with him. He may yet decide to accept some sort of deal."

Will looked doubtful and Sylvie just didn't know.

THREE DAYS LATER the head of hospital himself called Roland with the bad news. The morning shift nurse found Primakov dead in his bed. No, he had not tried to kill himself. Someone had done that for him, he said with a certain amount of embarrassment. Two minutes before the attending physician was to see Primakov on rounds, a female nurse, or at least a female impersonating a nurse, he corrected himself, walked up to the guard and informed him that Nurse Oberfeld had been called to an emergency—not an unusual circumstance in the hospital—and she was taking her place. The guard, although she was in hospital scrubs right down to her sterile booties and even wore a stethoscope, did not want her to pass. She told him it would take less than a minute—a simple injection to help Primakov with the pain when he awoke and he was welcome to come in and observe. Well, that did it. The SCHUPO officer said she went in, swabbed Primakov's muscular arm, palpated the vein, inserted the hypodermic's needle, pushed the plunger, dabbed at the spot of blood when she removed the needle, put a Band-Aid on and said, "All done."

She asked the guard to open the curtains to let some light into the room, and we surmise that it was at this time she switched off and then disconnected the heart monitor. She walked out, initialed for the attending nurse, and she was gone. She could imagine the poor boy's surprise when the real nurse showed up two minutes later and asked who had signed her name to the sheet. They immediately called the physician on duty to set the record straight, because the poor guard was now unwilling to let anyone pass. By the time they pushed past him into the room, Primakov was dead and they were not able to resuscitate him. The imposter had injected an air embolism into his arm, and he died when it reached his heart.

"I'm sorry, Hauptkommissar," the physician said, "but there was nothing we could do. Oh, one thing further, and I'm certain that the young SCHUPO corporal will include this in his formal report. The woman impersonating our shift nurse was possibly Asian; Chinese is my best guess."

Roland thanked the good doctor and assured him that he had done everything possible. He relayed the information to Will who did not seem very surprised by the sudden turn of events.

"I had a hunch there was yet one more layer of this onion to be peeled. It looks like we still have some work to do."

Roland could only agree. "Things are about to get even more complicated around here. Excuse me just a moment. I have to call Direktor Hauptmann." He stepped into the hall vestibule, closing the door behind him.

The Direktor answered his personal line after the first ring. Roland briefed him quickly and efficiently. When Roland finished his report, Hauptmann said, "Let Steinmetz handle the press conference. He will state publicly that the case is officially closed. Say nothing to the contrary. Take one week's leave and see to it that Lieutenant Schumann does the same. In fact, it would be best if all three of you went off together. Upon your return, you will find an administrative order above my name transferring you, Schumann, and the services of your nephew temporarily to my offices. We will use the guise of having your team write up a training manual describing the semiotic techniques that Dr. Sheridan used to solve this case. This will get Steinmetz out of your hair and off your back and you will be able to further your investigation under my official imprimatur. Any questions? Good. I'll speak with you again at the press conference. And Roland, excellent work. My compliments to you and your team."

STEINMETZ DID AN excellent job with the press conference the next day. His office even arranged a press kit to hand out. It contained bios of Roland, Sylvie, Will, and of course, himself. A brief dossier of Primakov was also included. He announced precisely on time that the case of the

Forest Killer had been solved; a suspect had been taken into custody, and had unfortunately died as a result of injuries suffered during his apprehension.

"We can consider the case officially closed," he told the media crowd, "thanks to the assistance of our American colleague, a consultant to the Special Crimes Unit at the FBI."

He waited for the applause to die away and opened the floor to questions. After handling the media's redundant questions with good humor and official aplomb, ever the dutiful commander, he stepped aside and brought the three investigators forward to the microphone in the five minutes left to them. Roland had been instructed to wear his sling whether he needed it or not, and Sylvie was told to go lightly on the make-up as if anything less than whitewash could hide the massive multicolored bruise that covered her face from jaw to cheekbone.

The questions started up again and the reporter from *Der Spiegel*, Germany's equivalent to *Time* or *Newsweek* in the States, seemed quite interested in the semiotic analysis Will had brought to the case. The man had actually done his homework and was familiar with the "dead file," or cold cases Will had solved while a professor at university. Shortly thereafter, Steinmetz again took control at the podium, and introduced Leitender Direktor Hauptmann, who had just arrived. Hauptmann wasted no time.

"I want to thank Polizeirat Steinmetz for his persistence in continuing the investigation when almost everyone else thought the case had been solved. My special thanks to the investigative team led by Erster Kriminalhauptkommissar Rieger, Kriminaloberkommissar Schumann, and our esteemed colleague from the States, a Professor Doktor Sheridan. All are to be commended." He paused deliberately, waiting even after the applause ended.

THE APPREHENSION

The astute associate editor from *Der Spiegel* piped up. "In my notes and in the bios, I have the ranks of the two officers as Kriminalhauptkommissar and Kriminalkommissar."

Leitender Kriminaldirektor Hauptmann grinned now. "You may wish to amend your notes to reflect the promotions of our two officers and you are all invited to join us in celebrating their accomplishments."

To another round of overwhelmingly enthusiastic applause and cheers, he took the fourth gold star from a velvet case and pinned it to Roland's bar of three. Then he placed a second star on Sylvie's epaulette and shook her hand, kissing her cheek. Will was presented with a special gold medal honoring his service to the citizens of the free state of Bavaria.

To the media, to the good burghers of Bavaria, and to those with special interests in the affair, it appeared that the case of the notorious Forest Killer had been solved and the file officially closed. After the party, Direktor Hauptmann wrote the orders that would place all principals on leave and directed them to report to him in one week's time for reassignment to his office. He held the orders just long enough to allow them time to finish their investigation of Primakov's apartment.

Chapter Twenty: The Apartment

THE COMMOTION QUICKLY died down. The press moved on to their next titillating, fast-breaking, hard-hitting news story. This time the wife of a high-ranking government official caught him in bed with a young boy. Spurned and now vindictive, she found herself suddenly possessed of a higher moral purpose. She gently closed the door to the tryst in the bedroom, ran and got her automatic thirty-five-millimeter camera, and when she returned, managed to shoot enough film of the two surprised lovers to keep the tabloids happily supplied with photos for the next three months.

In the meantime, now out of the glare of the harsh lights of the cameras, the normal routine of everyday police work gradually reestablished itself. Roland was tired, and his arm, although healing without complications, hurt during even the most mundane activities. Getting dressed in the morning was a trial for a one-armed man. Pants and shirts were manageable but try putting a sock on your left foot with your right hand. He endured and every day the arm got better. He used the time to catch up on his paperwork and, more importantly, his thinking about the case. Sylvie and Will helped by entering his documents, written in longhand, into the computer and with all three working on the project, it wasn't long before they were caught up.

Roland was happy to have the promotion and the extra money it brought at the end of each month. It would become even more valuable when he retired and started to draw his pension. Glad as he was to have the money and the rank, it still rankled him because he knew full well he should have been promoted five years sooner, but that certainly was not Hauptmann's fault. He returned to signing the documents Sylvie and Will had printed out for him. He enjoyed writing his new rank in full on the signature lines. He was most pleased with the work Sylvie had done and his private report to Leitender Kriminaldirektor Hauptmann made her contributions to solving the case absolutely clear. Despite her inexperience, her organizational skills and natural intelligence perfectly complemented his investigative style. In the report, he mentioned that he would consider it a personal and professional favor if Kriminaloberkommissar Schumann remained his partner. There were additional investigative skills she could still learn from him.

In the report that would be made public, Roland highlighted Schumann's contributions but also brought attention to the fact that the case most likely would not have been solved without the analytical skills and new perspective Will had brought to the investigation. Using Will's semiotic perspective had allowed them to treat the crimes as a text that had to be read and interpreted. The meaning of each element could be understood only in relation to and within the context of all the other elements. Granted, to a large degree this was how he had evolved his own investigative style as a matter of instinct, training, and experience, but to actually have the methodology laid out like a template had proven invaluable. He appreciated the irony of the fact that by working within the confines of semiotic analysis, they had been able to think outside the lines, so to speak, and this move had brought them to the second layer of meaning under which Primakov had been hiding.

Within the memory of his experience, this was one of those rare crimes layered like an onion. To be frank, most murders were so routine that they were boring. In such cases, there was no duplicity in the act. Somebody wanted to kill somebody else and did it without the benefit of much planning. Maybe they rearranged the crime scene somewhat to look like a suicide, but the average person's idea of suicides and murders was largely influenced by what they had seen on television or at the movies, and this was always a dead giveaway. Pardon the pun, he thought. He remembered a famous painting he had once read about, although he could not for the life of him remember who the painter was. No matter. The art experts had discovered that the original painting was buried under two layers of paint, each a carefully executed painting, one painted atop the other and hiding the one below. Strip the first layer of paint and a new painting emerged. Strip the next layer of paint and, lo and behold, there was the masterpiece. Only an expert would have known to look more deeply into the canvas. This had been Will's second real contribution. He had not allowed himself to be fooled by surface appearances. His semiotic interpretation of the crimes had allowed him to peel back the onion, to scrape away the top paintings until they found the hidden criminal masterpiece.

One thing remained as Roland finished his review. They had yet to locate and capture the mastermind, the grand designer of the elaborate deception. Will was already hard at work trying to understand the actions of the prime mover and Sylvie was using the computer to track and trace back Primakov's electronic transactions. She had searched phone records, credit cards, banks statements, and official documents; anything that had been put in a database and contained his name. The next step was to visit his apartment and check his computer for any information they might glean from the files he kept there. Roland knew they were getting closer to discovering the identity of the man behind the scenes. He wondered who they would find as they scraped and peeled off the last layer of paint.

PRIMAKOV LIVED IN a small, efficiency apartment in a three-story building on the outskirts of Munich. The elevator, just large enough to transport all three of them at once, lurched to a stop on the top floor. Roland used the passkey obtained from the superintendent of the building. The rooms were almost Japanese in their economy of space and Will wondered how anyone could live in something so small. A leather coat depended from one of three plastic coat hangers in the short foyer. Ahead lay the kitchen, to the right a diminutive living room, to the left a bathroom and then on to a single bedroom.

"No doubt this guy was a soldier," Will observed. "In the States, I've seen single rooms in graduate student housing with more space than this place. I guess once you've lived in the Soviet Army's barracks, even this seems like a little piece of heaven."

Sylvie wondered what the hell he was going on about. She had girlfriends who would kill for such an apartment. It was clean, modern, and orderly and everything was squared away. Will opened the door to the half-sized refrigerator. Butter, eggs, apples, sausages, two pork chops bought the day before according to the wrapper, and three bottles of mineral water. In the small freezer compartment, an unopened bottle of vodka lay on its side. Will opened a cabinet above the kitchen table and took down three shot glasses. He broke the seal on the bottle and poured himself a generous shot. Sylvie looked at him reprovingly.

"Isn't that what burglars do when they break in—sit down and have a sandwich and something to drink after they finish looting the place?"

Will smacked his lips, savoring the cool fire of the liquid in his belly. "That's right, Fräulein Kriminaloberkommissar. Thusly, I demonstrate my disdain for the son of a bitch who tried to slip a professional pig sticker between my ribs; thusly, I show my utter and complete contempt for the bastard who so very nearly took my loved one away from me."

Sylvie blushed her embarrassment at the words.

"I'm talking about Roland."

"You idiot," she said, taking the bottle from him. "This is unprofessional behavior."

Roland came in at that moment and told her to pour one for him too while she had the bottle down.

"It's hopeless," she said, giving in to the inevitable. She poured one for him and one for herself. "I advise you both to seek help for your alcoholism."

"We are," Roland explained, accepting the drink and clinking his glass to hers. "And this is just a small first step."

Roland understood what Will was doing and even if Sylvie did not, she took part. It was a symbolic act, standing in the confines of the dead man's kitchen drinking his vodka. It was a celebration, a ritual acknowledgment that the Spetsnaz commando had not defeated them. They had survived and emerged as a team, confident in each other. Roland had dispensed with the sling as soon as he got home from the news conference. The swelling in Sylvie's jaw had subsided into a bruise so dark that even make-up could not cover it. The doctor warned her that the force of the blow had bruised even the bone of the mandible. They were battered and a little worse for the wear, but now they were a functioning fighting team.

Will took one last shot from the bottle and swallowed the realization of how close he had come to losing them both. "Mumble that you love me," he told her, patting a wisp of drool from the corner of her still numb jaw.

"American freak," she said to Roland, showing him that she did not blame him for that side of the family, but she accepted the medicinal kiss on her throbbing jaw all the same. Roland was thoroughly amused by their interplay and he looked at her with helpless resignation. After all, she had unmade her own bed and taken Will into it. Now it was time to get some work done. They took their drinks and went into the living room and sat on the sofa.

"Primakov was first and foremost an elite soldier," Roland said, stating the obvious for the purpose of getting them back on track.

"Which means he followed protocols and maintained his attention to detail," Will contributed. "I don't expect that we will find anything hidden behind a box on a closet shelf or buried in a file cabinet in the wrong folder."

"What do we do?" asked Sylvie. They both looked at Roland.

"Follow the money. We know that he wasn't acting on his own. He was working as a professional, a mercenary for hire, so to speak, hired for his commando skills. Somebody paid him and he put the money somewhere. It isn't under the mattress. I checked."

"It was easy enough to get his bank records," Sylvie reminded them.

Roland shook his head. "He might have an account but you won't find the payoffs there. He knows it would be too easy to trace a paper trail."

Will agreed with Roland. "This was the kind of guy who probably didn't trust banks in the first place, given his experience back in Mother Russia. But I still think the money is in the bank."

Sylvie looked at him and saw that he was serious. Primakov would not trust others to handle his money. He would want it kept safely, yet still under his control. The money would be at the bank. Then she had it. "A safe-deposit box."

"You got it," said Will.

Roland held up a small key.

"Ooooh," Sylvie cooed. "You guys are good! Where did you find it?"

"Cookie jar," said Will with affected pride.

"He was looking for a cookie," Roland explained, so Sylvie would not think too highly of their accomplishment. "This gets us the money," Roland allowed, "and confirms our suspicions. But it doesn't get us to the source."

"But I know what might," Sylvie said, getting up from the couch with an assist from Will. "Follow me." They came obediently.

In the bedroom large enough only for a double bed and a small desk, Sylvie pulled out a chair and sat in front of a personal computer atop the nondescript prefab desk. She pushed the power button and the monitor brightened and the printer ready light came on. She waited for the software to load. She brought up the file directory and scrolled through the names. They were all in Russian.

"Damn! Now what?"

Will reached past her shoulder, took the mouse and clicked open a folder. He clicked again on one of a series of icons that appeared. A picture came up on the screen.

"Those can't be real," Sylvie said under raised eyebrows.

"How can she breathe without choking?" Will wondered aloud.

"He doesn't seem to care," Roland noted.

Will clicked another icon. More of the same: standard pornography downloaded from the Internet. He gave the mouse back to Sylvie. If he's downloading jpegs off the Web, he probably has email too."

THE APARTMENT

A couple of clicks later and Sylvie was in his email program. "Damn!" she said again, only more forcefully this time. She was getting impatient at being thwarted so easily. "He's got the damn thing encrypted."

Although the email they found for him that day had been encrypted and sent anonymously, Sylvie and Will discovered that the encryption was a fairly standard commercial software program. The hardest part had been to figure out the key word that enabled the decryption/encryption process.

"Semiotics can help us here too," Will assured her when he saw the frustration working into her face. She was prepared to run a program that would try at lightning speed every word in the German language from A to Z until the key word was recognized, but it was still time-consuming. They had already tried the obvious: his name, his mother's maiden name, his birth date, his identification number, and numerous combinations thereof. They even thought to look under the keyboard on the off chance that he had written the key down and had hidden it there, but to no avail. They found nothing in his personal papers. What they did have was a photograph of Captain Primakov pictured with four other soldiers in full combat regalia standing in front of a Soviet Hind attack helicopter, fully armed. Will studied the picture. There was something that shone with crystal clarity through the man's eyes. Pride.

"What was the most important thing in this guy's life?" he asked Sylvie, thinking aloud.

"His mother?" Sylvie tried, taking him for a typical male.

"Not in your life," Will kidded. "His."

She looked at him with false exasperation. "We know he was a soldier so he probably loved the Soviet Army."

"I'm not so sure," Will said, slowly shaking his head. "This guy was more than just a soldier. He was about as elite as you can get, similar to

273

a Green Beret, or a British SAS, or a German Kriegsmarine. This guy was Spetsnaz and lived and died for his unit. Not only is it a Russian word, it's also an acronym. At the keyboard, Sylvie tried it, Will watching over her shoulder. As she typed, she asked again what it stood for.

"Spesialnogo naznachenyia," he told her.

She misspelled it the first time and Will corrected her: "S P E T S N A Z."

The encryption program accepted the key word and automatically deciphered the encrypted email messages. There was absolutely nothing in them of any help whatsoever.

Sylvie turned and looked up at Will, unashamed to share her sense of helplessness. Will thought for a minute. He had Sylvie instruct the computer to display the entire routing header for the last message. "There!" he said, pointing significantly.

Sylvie looked immediately but did not know what to look for. "Where...? What am I looking for?"

Will touched the screen with his finger, using it as a pointer. "Look. Although the sender is anonymous, we can still track the message back to its origin. He used a series of gateways and routers running through universities and businesses but the key link is the mainframe at the University of Frankfurt am Main. See that?"

She saw it now and nodded. The movement of her hair off the nape of her neck released a whiff of her perfume and he bent down to kiss her.

She pushed him away. "That gives me goose pimples."

He ignored the rebuff, busy with other things. "Aha," he said, "and there's the point of origination. The Internet Service Provider for the computer he used is in Idar-Oberstein."

274

"And why is that significant?" Roland asked, having heard the excitement in their voices from the living room.

"I have no idea," said Will, now out of the throes of his initial excitement. I assumed the sender was using his personal computer, but he could just as well have been using an open terminal in a library, or in a computer lab at a university. At the very least, it might tell us this is where he lives since all the messages have come from that location."

Roland shook his head. "Don't sell your analysis short. Idar-Oberstein, although not too many people outside the city know it, is one of the oldest diamond bourses in Europe."

Will smacked his forehead with the heel of his palm as he remembered the obvious.

Sylvie looked back over her shoulder at Roland. "The piece of paper we found at the crime scene."

Roland nodded. "A Russian plaquette used for wrapping and transporting diamonds. It's called a sight. Things are beginning to fall into place."

"Looks like our next excursion might be a trip to the diamond center of Germany known as Idar-Oberstein, the town that can't decide about its name. And don't you get any ideas," Will said to Sylvie, pointedly. She gave him a grin Mona Lisa would have coveted.

"Wait a minute!" Will suddenly commanded, staying Sylvie's hand just before she clicked the mouse to get out of the email program. He had noticed something. The system was automatically checking for new messages and at the bottom right side of the screen a small warning icon signaled that a new, unread message waited. Sylvie went to the program's in-box. The new message read: 'Reply if all is well.' There was no signature.

"When was the message sent?" Roland asked, sensing that this might be their man.

Will checked the header. "The same day we got to Primakov."

Roland stood up and shot his cuffs. The trail was cold but it was a trail nevertheless. "Can we track it back to its source?"

Sylvie brought up the routing headers. "It's been anonymized but there is the service provider," she said pointing to the screen. "It's the same one out of Idar-Oberstein. We can subpoena them and that should get us his real name."

"Good work, you two," Roland said. "I'll write the orders and you two can execute them." He looked at his watch. "It's getting late. We have to stop at the bank before it closes." He patted the coat pocket of his blazer. The sheaf of documents there gave him full and legal access to all of Primakov's possessions and assets as they related to the investigation.

"One more thing before we go," Will said. He hit the reply box and typed: "All is not well," and sent the message.

"Let's get out of here," Roland directed. "And I don't want to go to Idar-Oberstein until you can give me a pretty good idea of the kind of man we're looking for."

"Already working on it," Will said.

Sylvie shut down the computer, picked up the files she had downloaded to a disk, and turned the machine off. She waited until the screen darkened and then put the disk in her purse for safekeeping. She turned the lights off behind her. Will had washed the shot glasses and replaced them. They gave the apartment one more good look over and prepared to leave. Will stuffed the half-finished bottle of vodka into the pocket of his black leather coat and winked at Sylvie. They would finish it later. In the elevator to the ground floor, Roland informed them that they would need to pack a suitcase for a short working vacation. They would be leaving the next day.

Chapter Twenty-one: In the Wachau

DIREKTOR HAUPTMANN GAVE them a week, nine days if you counted the weekends, and they were far enough along in the investigation that Roland felt he could justify the time off, if they made it a working holiday. It would give them time to heal, to recover, and to plan as they got closer to the man behind Primakov. A short trip was in order, so they headed first south toward Garmisch-Partenkirchen where they saw the famous Zugspitze, the highest mountain in that part of the Bavarian Alps. Roland also pointed out the Eagle's Nest where Hitler had kept his summer retreat. Will couldn't see it from the road but admired the massive thrust of the granite that towered above them. He let Roland take a picture of Sylvie by his side, the Alpine peaks in the background glistening with snow.

They stayed off the Autobahn to avoid a hundred car pile-up earlier that morning when fog had blanketed the road and reduced visibility to less than a car length. For most German drivers who did not consider themselves bound by the laws of physics—which they treated largely as an inconvenience in their finely engineered high-speed touring machines—this hardly qualified as a reason for reducing speed below 160 kilometers per hour. Accordingly, their cars accordioned into each other, one domino being pushed into the next until the entire curving line lay flat and smoking, jammed horns blaring down the line.

IN THE WACHAU

Roland knew the alternative state roads from his early years of service as a SCHUPO officer on the highway detail and he expertly guided them around the mess with only one turn back. They were eastbound for Linz and the border of Austria. The Wachau was their destination, more poetically known as the Niebelungengau, the region of the mythic Niebelung warriors celebrated and romanticized in Richard Wagner's monumental operas. Here they intended to hike, see the sights, and drink the wine. The Wachau, if not Austria's most famous viticulture region, was certainly the most beautiful and picturesque. They followed the Danube, Europe's second largest river after the Rhine, and Will, ever the wise guy, wanted to know when it was finally going to turn blue, disappointed at the brown tinge to the water.

"Hell, if I wanted to see muddy water, I could have stayed home and admired the Mississippi," he grumbled, playing the American tourist. From the backseat, where Roland sprawled reading his guidebook, he was told to shut up and drive.

At Krems, known as the doorway to the Wachau, a typical lower Austrian city of about twenty thousand inhabitants, they stopped for gas and Sylvie took off to find a restroom. Roland made him stop at half a tank and Will understood why when he converted the Austrian schillings into D-Mark and then into dollars. Gas was close to five dollars a gallon. No wonder most of the cars on the Autobahns were so small. Sylvie came back with the groceries, bars of chocolate, and bottles of carbonated lemonade for everyone. It was cold, not too sweet, and hit the spot. Once everyone was back in place, buckled up, and in control of their chocolate, Will took Roland's BMW back into the traffic weaving its way along the outside of the twists and turns forced into the road by the Danube.

Rieger was quite content in the back and more than willing to let the younger pair handle the driving. There was a time when he would have enjoyed taking the wheel himself, but given his injury and the good hands at the wheel, he relaxed and became a tourist, taking in the sights. A short while later they were in Melk. He had Will pull over, Sylvie got out the map for this region of Austria—they were less than eighteen kilometers from Vienna—and had her locate a little village of about three thousand inhabitants named Loosdorf. It took her a minute or two to find it on the Aral map; she showed it to Roland, who agreed it was indeed Loosdorf, and Sylvie directed Will onto the correct route.

Roland repacked his DK guidebook for Austria, and in the five minutes or so remaining in the ride, he mentally reviewed what they needed to do in order to push forward the investigation. Tomorrow would be an important day and he intended to use it to develop a method for getting them next to Primakov's boss. He was certain that their first stop after their return to Germany from the Wachau would be in Idar-Oberstein. They found the city sign at the outskirts of the village and drove through the hamlet of Loosdorf. They passed through the quaint village square and past the high steepled church whose bell called all true believers to worship every Sunday, even if the Austrian national football team was playing on television at the time. They turned onto a road that paralleled the town's outskirts. Four or five newer houses stood in a line-up, entrances facing the village. On the other side of the street, a hay meadow lapped up against the gardens of the main houses of the village. Roland had Will stop in front of the driveway of the second to last house in the row and checked the number on the door against the one on his reservation booking slip. "This is it. Go ahead and pull into the driveway. Looks like the owner is home, if that's his Mitsubishi parked there."

IN THE WACHAU

Roland had booked them an accommodation in a private home in the little town near Melk. Peter Mautner and his wife Paula owned the home, a modern two-story house on the edge of the woods. Mautner worked for the Austrian rail service and commuted into Vienna. The downstairs section of the house was built as a self-contained apartment. Mautner showed them in through the door that opened at the side of the house at ground level. He was an affable man and seemed genuinely happy to see his guests. Will suspected that Roland had stayed here once before under different circumstances. The location and the terms were simply too good to be coincidental. Will's suspicions were confirmed when Roland opened the door to "my room," the first door off the hall and on the left. A queen-size bed dominated the room and sat before a massive freestanding oaken closet, large enough to hide a horse inside. A portable color television sat on a table at the foot of the bed.

Mautner pulled up the slats covering the windows and let them look into the garden of the backyard. For the guests, a wooden picnic table with pine chairs awaited and provided a quiet, pastoral setting for late breakfasts or after-dinner drinks while watching the sun drop into the forest just beyond the white half fence at the boundary of the back yard. Across the hall, Will and Sylvie had their room. Will was instantly pleased to see the two beds, each covered with a fluffy, goose-down feather bed. Their room also had a TV, two large mirrored chest-of-drawers, and a writing table in the corner. Everything seemed new and clean. They dropped their luggage and Herr Mautner showed them to the WC, which also contained a bidet, then opened the door to the shower and wash sinks next to it.

"I think I could be very happy here," Will said, for all to hear and Herr Mautner positively beamed.

THE ADAMANTINE HEART

He waved them up the stairs to the main floor. He simply had to introduce his illustrious guests to his wife, if they would not consider it too much of an inconvenience so shortly after their long journey. Mautner shuffled out of his street shoes and pushed his feet into his house slippers. Roland, Sylvie, and Will walked down the hall and into the kitchen in their socks. Paula Mautner was delightful, a perfect complement to her husband, rosy-cheeked and round-faced, not a touch of make-up to mar her chubby cheeks. She pushed at her brown curly hair and shot her husband a glance for not giving her due warning, but he just grinned under his mustache like an imp, happy with the mischief he caused. She immediately untied her apron, put it on the counter next to the sink, and curtsied ever so slightly as the introductions were made. Will couldn't tell if she was more impressed with meeting a Professor Doktor from the United States or a German woman who just happened to be a Kriminaloberkommissar. Introductions done, Paula Mautner, using only her twinkling blue eyes, directed her husband to take their guests into the living room and seat them. It would be impolite to refuse their hospitality, so they went but Will noticed something out of the corner of his eye as he left the kitchen. He turned to Frau Mautner.

"Is it possible that I see before me a world-famous Viennese Sachertorte?"

Frau Mautner nodded enthusiastically. Will swore to himself that her smile was identical to her husband's. It was as if they had practiced grinning together.

"This is absolutely my most favorite desert in the entire world," Will said dramatically. "I love it even more than the Blackforest cherry cake my grandmother used to make for me in Bavaria. The first time I tried an authentic Sachertorte in Vienna, I thought I had tasted a slice of heaven."

IN THE WACHAU

Paula Mautner touched him lightly on the forearm. She looked dismayed. "Please forgive me, Herr Professor. I would immediately invite you to have a piece, but alas, I have made this one for our annual charity to support our local volunteer fire department. There is a big dance tonight on the outskirts of town. You might have seen the banners announcing the event as you drove through the town."

"It sounds like a most worthy cause and I have no doubt that your beautiful creation will add considerably to the evening's contributions."

She blushed through her grin although she dropped her eyes like a young girl just about to be kissed. He let her escort him into the living room. Mautner had already taken down a bottle of apricot Schnaps from the liquor closet and handed a glass to Will and his wife as they entered. He toasted his guests. "To a pleasant and relaxing stay in the Wachau."

They clinked glasses all around and Will drank half of his shot. The burn of the liquor took his breath away and he inadvertently gasped. They laughed politely at his discomfort and he played to them. "Roland, please go out to the car and get me the fire extinguisher."

Mautner immediately poured his glass full. Will sniffed the liquid fire carefully for self-protection. In the clear liquid, he smelled sun-ripened apricots, as if their very essence had somehow been distilled into the glass.

"Amazing," he remarked. This time, better prepared for the effect, he took the liquid down properly, made a show of taking the last drop from the shot glass and set it atop the coaster on the coffee table with authority. "AAAH!"

Mautner was there again with a refill. "A local product called Marillenschnaps, you see, made from apricots grown in our local orchards. We're quite proud of it, really."

283

They drank for another half-hour before Roland stood and announced they still needed to unpack and prepare for their walk into town, where they would have dinner at the local restaurant. Upon hearing this, Herr and Frau Mautner immediately rose and stood side-by-side. Before he showed them down the stairs to their rooms, Peter Mautner formally invited them to attend the festivities at the volunteer fireman's ball later that evening. Roland accepted and Mautner said he would be sure to save them places next to him at the long tables under the festival tent. They went down the stairs to their respective rooms, laughing and giddy from the schnapps. Roland said he would come for them in thirty minutes, if that was enough time. They looked at each other and shook their heads no in unison. Not a minute more Roland said as he carefully closed the door behind them. Sylvie fell backward onto the cloud of the feather bed, pulling her blouse out of her skirt, pulling Will on top of her. They were still dressing hurriedly when Roland knocked precisely thirty minutes later.

THEY WALKED INTO the village and found the restaurant in a little Gasthaus that advertised five rooms to let with regrets that they were all taken. At the tail end of the dinner rush, the place was crowded with revelers looking forward to the festivities at the Volunteer Fireman's Ball and most wore traditional costumes, dirndls for the women and lederhosen for the men. Just as they arrived, a table opened up overlooking the street and they were promptly seated. As the waitress presented them with menus, Sylvie asked Roland if they were going to the dance.

"Of course," Roland assured her, understanding the young woman's need to see and be seen.

IN THE WACHAU

The waitress was back with beers for the men and a glass of the local white wine, a Grüner Veltliner, for Sylvie. She waited patiently while they dove once more behind the tall broad menus. Will spotted something called a Hussar's cutlet and ordered it for the name alone. Sylvie settled for a schnitzel in the Viennese style, being so close to Vienna, she giggled, and Roland, in the mood for something spicier, selected a veal schnitzel with a cream curry sauce. The Hussarnkotlet was a marvel to behold. The chef had evidently taken a quick peak from the kitchen and determined here was a man of sufficient size to handle the immense portion that overpowered the dimensions of the plate.

A veal cutlet had been pounded, but not as thin as the more delicate Wienerschnitzel that Sylvie was breathing in. About half an inch thick, it was folded over on itself like an omelet, seared and then sautéed to a golden brown. The center, Will discovered with his first bite, was stuffed with salami and pepper cheese. He could taste the spice of red pepper and paprika. In a separate ramekin, the waitress had brought whipped herb butter redolent of fresh garlic and Roland indicated this was to be smeared atop the cutlet while it was still warm from the pan. The mixture of the herb butter with the juices of the cutlet was exquisite. Will savored another bite. It was so delicious he could not speak. The cool, golden pilsner was a perfect accompaniment to the paprika, pepper, and garlic flavors.

"Absolutely sensational," Will said to the others. "If your meal is anywhere near as good..."

"Let me try a bite," Sylvie demanded.

Will pushed her hand away and shook his head. "Too good to share," he mumbled through another mouthful, then relented and cut her a very small piece to taste.

She ignored it and cut herself a generous portion with her own knife and fork. Roland declined the offer of the first taste, satisfied with his own meal and not wanting to mix flavors.

After the last of the dinner plates were cleared away, Will patted the muscles of his stomach. "I understand now where Mautner gets his cute little belly."

"Three or four hours on the dance floor will take care of that," Sylvie promised.

Will looked at her in horror.

After Roland paid the bill, waiting for the receipt at the table, they walked out into the night air down the cobblestone streets to the outskirts of the village. They followed the hand-lettered signs directing them to the Volunteer Fireman's Charity Ball and shortly they were in the flow of people heading in the same direction. The locals were dressed in folk costumes; the women wore dresses called dirndls, low-cut, lace-trimmed bodices that showed off their breasts; the men wore lederhosen, leather shorts that showed off their legs; and finely embroidered white shirts and knee-high woolen socks. The youngsters, boys and girls alike, were modern in their dress, choosing to wear the colors and names of their favorite sports teams or superstars, many of them American football or basketball players. In this cultural mélange of persons, ages, and styles, the three detectives blended in and were swept toward the nexus of all the excitement, a freestanding red barn, timbers above stone walls, decorated with banners proclaiming the event, welcoming one and all. Adjacent stood an immense brightly colored festival tent. Inside the tent, portable tables were covered with the baked goods to be sold by the women, breads, pastries, and cakes of every conceivable size and shape, color and configuration. Those who drove from neighboring villages followed the guidance of volunteers whose flashlights pointed them to park their cars in a loose semblance of order in the field surrounding the barn. The loose weathered timbers of the massive barn could not contain the heavy brass notes of the oompah-pah band, and Sylvie, as if responding to some internal cultural compulsion, took Will by the arm and skipped a couple of steps in perfect time to the music. As they neared the huge, double-wide doors, they could see the band blowing and banging, people dancing, others laughing at the dancers, people at the tables clapping in time to the music and spilling a lot of beer. At the door, a volunteer firefighter in a highly polished chromed helmet took their schillings and admitted them.

Along one wall of the ancient structure, surely an old hay barn at one time that was now converted to a civic center of sorts, they saw a row of tables covered with red and white cloth where the baked goods brought by the women of the village were set for sale. Soon as the pastries, pies, and the like were sold, fresh goods were brought over from the stores under the festival tent, replenishing supplies in the barn. They spotted Frau Mautner in a red and white apron, and she waved and pointed them toward one of the long tables that ran the length of the barn. Amidst the crowd of people eating and drinking, they located Herr Mautner, standing on a bench to be more clearly visible and he waved them over. Roland sat next to him, Will and Sylvie on the other side across the rough, oaken tabletop. The waitress came and off-loaded her cargo, deposited six sloshing liter Krugs of beer at the next table of locals, accepted payment, returned change, and after she stashed her payment in the pockets of her sodden apron, asked for their order. Roland ordered newly bottled Riesling from last year's harvest. This was an ancient tradition in the Wachau, similar to the vin nouveau of Beaujolais in France with the exception that the wines were white, not red.

After the Heurigen wines arrived and were tasted and the vintage pronounced exceptional, Sylvie pulled Will from his bench. "Up! Up!" she commanded and led him to the dance floor.

The band, arrayed in traditional folk costumes, consisted of an accordion player, various horns, tubas, and trumpets, not all played at the same time, and there was even a guitarist and a drummer, and a zither player. A rather eclectic musical mix, Will thought, but they were good and loud, enthusiastic, and seemingly indefatigable. Under Sylvie's rather expert lead, Will found himself immersed in the frenzy of a polka and could not resist adding his voice to the band during the yodeling. They danced until Will begged to be released, claiming an immense Bavarian thirst, and as he sat and revived himself with the fresh, tart apple fruit and crispness of the new wine, Sylvie captured Roland and danced him into the storm of revelers. He lasted only a third as long. Even Mautner was called to take a turn, stepping into a reasonable facsimile of a high-country waltz.

As difficult as it was for Will to keep up with Sylvie on the dance floor, he had even more trouble drinking with the Austrians and trying to fathom their heavy local dialect. In many ways, it seemed almost Bavarian, but he was forced to listen carefully and some of the idioms required Roland's translation. He was trying hard to hear under the din of the band and make conversation with those sitting next to him. On his left sat the village cobbler and local shoe seller who took an inordinate interest in Will's New Balance running shoes, a brand he was unfamiliar with.

"What's the largest size you carry?" Will asked the man.

"Ten and a half, maybe a few in eleven," he answered.

Will reached down and slipped the sneaker off his foot and handed it to the man, whose mouth dropped open in amazement. "Size 14," Will told him.

The cobbler looked at the shoe from every possible angle, studying it like a Roman artifact. Before Will got the use of his shoe back, it was passed down the table on his side, crossed at the end, was admired by everyone on the opposite side, until it was handed back down the row of people across from him. Will was not the least disconcerted by the journey his shoe had taken. He was unaffected by the gasps of surprise or the unabashed laughter when comparisons were made with smaller feet. He was nonplussed by the giggles of astonishment as the shoe made its way from hand to hand down the entire length of the old hay barn. When he finally got his shoe back, he greeted it like a long-lost friend, and made a show of putting it back on his shoeless foot. He did not have to pay for another drink the entire evening.

As they danced and drank away the night, the long day eventually caught up with them. Will was numb with fatigue. The long drive had drawn his energy down. The concentration it took to meet new people and the careful attention he needed to understand the lower-Austrian dialect had all conspired to drain him. He was riding the wave of Sylvie's youthful enthusiasm and he drew from her seemingly limitless energy. He cobbled together the strength for one more dance before he intended to pull her away from the admiring mob of men and women alike, out into the dark where he could have her for himself on the walk back home. During the slow dance, she rested her head on his shoulder and he felt the deep sigh. He lifted her chin up to look into her cerulean blue eyes, the exact color of the Bavarian porcelain in his mother's kitchen cabinet.

"Anything wrong?"

"I don't know," she admitted. "It's just a feeling."

"What sort of feeling?" he asked, still not too concerned, thinking she was finally getting tired and would be ready for bed soon.

"I don't know," she said again, but he could tell she was not trying to be difficult, so he waited and held her a bit more tightly.

"I know it probably sounds silly but I have the feeling that someone is watching me."

He wanted to laugh and say of course everyone is watching you, because you are the most beautiful woman in Austria. Instead, seeing that she was serious, he carefully scanned the crowd, using the rhythm of the dance to make a complete but unobtrusive turn about the floor. Nothing seemed out of the ordinary. All he could think to do next was comfort her. "Of course everyone's looking at you. You're the prettiest girl in the place."

She looked up into the comfort of his reassuring eyes, looking to see if he was telling her the truth. Then she kissed him, even if he did have a tendency to exaggerate just a little bit. "I'm just getting tired," she decided. Maybe we should leave in a little while?"

"I'm all for that. Roland seems to be slowing down too. I'd rather dance another set," he lied, testing her to see if she believed him, "but I'll suggest to him it's time for us all to head for home."

He made her dance one more song just to show he could and then they walked out into the cool and quiet of the night, navigating their way under the stars up and down the narrow streets into the pitch-black darkness of the other side of town. Roland wobbled down the center of the street, hands in pockets, whistling a little folk tune to himself, and Will and Sylvie followed his lead under the Austrian starlight, giggling to each other that they were completely and utterly lost and didn't have a clue as to where their rooms were.

Chapter Twenty-two: Aggstein

TORN FROM SLEEP, now he could feel the vague slop of consciousness pulling at him like the tide taking sand out to sea. He tried desperately to swim back to the shore of sleep but it was no use. He could not resist the persistent tug that pulled him further up onto land and into the light. He was both frustrated and angry until he heard her voice.

"Get up, lazy bones. We have work to do."

He choked and groaned and begged her to have mercy and let him drown again in sleep. "Just fifteen more minutes will do," he lied. His head was spinning on the axle of his neck and somehow his tongue had grown fur and swollen overnight to the size of a beaver tail. He showed it to her and that's all she needed to see. She let the rolled slats down at the window blocking all light from the room and he disappeared into the darkness, sucking on the pacifier of his own tongue, smiling like a baby.

At noon, she tried again, two hours after the first abortive attempt. This time he responded, and she noticed he was lucid enough to understand human conversation. She enticed him with a little mystery. "Frau Mautner, your new girlfriend, has something waiting for you upstairs. She'll be insulted if you don't come up for lunch. Roland wants to do some work while we eat on the back porch and then we're going to take a drive. Come on big boy, you can do it. Once we get you into a hot shower, you'll start to come around." She pulled the comforter

291

down to his big feet, exposing his full length. "Oh, excuse me. Looks like somebody is already up."

He shuddered at the thought of water touching his body, but that Sylvie, she was sly as a fox, and he wanted to see his new girlfriend and most of all he wanted his surprise.

He survived the shock of the water on his skin, not surprised in the least that his body was resisting anything not alcohol based now that he had replaced his blood with booze. The extra two hours of sleep had helped and he was starting to burn down the poison in his system. He figured another two weeks and he would be back to normal. He shaved and brushed his teeth but could not taste the toothpaste. He looked at his tongue in the mirror, and then decided that was not such a good thing to do after all. His aftershave smelled funny and he had to fight back an overwhelming urge to drink some of it. At that point, he swore to himself that he would never drink again. That seemed a little harsh. He promised himself he would never drink to excess again; oh, what the hell—drinking wasn't so bad if he would just stop when he knew he had reached his limit. His negotiations with himself successfully concluded, he dressed and presented himself upstairs.

Paula Mautner had risen early to bake and construct a Viennese Sachertorte just for him. She cut him a slice that must have weighed just short of a kilo and when she saw this was exactly what he wanted she smiled for the rest of the day. She sent him out to the backyard where Sylvie and Roland were having their brunch.

"Look Roland, he brought us both dessert. How kind of you."

"I don't think so," Will said, immune to any and all sarcasm but he did sit apart from them at the table so they could not reach his plate.

Roland chuckled as he sipped his tea. He understood excess. But that really was a big piece of cake, even for an American. Before Will went into a diabetic coma from all the sugar and chocolate and cream, Roland started building the profile of the man pulling the strings.

They had decided on the metaphor of a puppet master. They saw him as a man working behind the scenes to manipulate the action out front. Since they could not see their criminal wizard behind the curtains, they decided to work from the outside in, much the same way Will attacked his giant piece of Sachertorte. Will explained his method of reasoning as he scooted his chair into the penumbra of the shadow thrown by the umbrella above the table.

"We're working with shadows, in a sense. All we see and all we have are the shadows. We can't see the umbrella casting the shadow; what we have to do then is infer it. After all, a shadow cannot exist in the absence of the object blocking the sun."

"I don't see how you can even talk after eating that massive piece of cake. And I can't believe you wouldn't share even a bite," Sylvie complained.

He smirked. "Paula made it especially for me."

"Oh, so it's Paula now?"

"Yes, we're very close now that we've shared Sachertorte. It's a bond more powerful than love, really. Someday you'll understand that," he said, sagely. He stirred his cup of tea, which Roland had poured for him, added cream and two more sugars. When he had the mixture just right, he resumed his dissertation. "Physicists talk all the time about elementary particles of nature like the Higgs boson as if they exist. However, and keep this under your hat, no one to date has ever seen a Higgs boson, or a pi meson, or a neutrino, or a..."

"We get the point," Roland assured him.

"The problem is that they are too small to be observed."

"How do we know they really exist then," Sylvie asked, "if we can't actually see them?"

He shook his teaspoon at her. "That is a very bright question. What we observe are the manifestations of their behavior. We see signs that they exist. The shadow we're sitting in is a sign of the umbrella that casts it. A paw print of a bear in the snow is an interpretable sign. We observe its characteristics, compare it to any other known signs, thus reducing the possibility for alternative interpretation, and then we develop what the famous American philosopher Charles Sanders Peirce—spelled Peirce but pronounced 'purse'—called an abductive hypothesis."

"I followed you right up to the philosopher. What the hell is an abductive hypothesis?" Roland wanted to know. "And spare me the 'that is a very bright question' routine."

Will put his spoon back in his teacup. "Let me see. How can I put this so even a KRIPO chief of detectives can understand? An hypothesis, as you know, is a statement about the relationship between two or more variables. Usually these are given as causality statements where in a certain context or condition x is said to cause y."

"Smoking causes cancer," Sylvie offered.

"Right. But abductive statements are based in probability, recognizing that we cannot know with absolute certainty that smoking causes cancer every time. If you'll allow me to digress just a minute?"

Roland made a show of looking at his watch.

"We can't observe all cases of cancer, all cases of smoking, or all cases where cancer appears after smoking. This is called the problem of induction. We make our statements about the world based on some reasonable number of observations and then extrapolate to the general population. What we are really saying is that there is a high probability that smoking causes cancer."

"Ah," said Sylvie, "that's why some people can smoke all their lives and not get cancer."

"Yes, like my mother. Some people fall outside the range of probability due to genetics or some other factor."

"So, what we're doing is building a logical syllogism based on inductive reasoning," suggested Roland.

"Exactly!" Will was getting excited again and Sylvie watched his enthusiasm with bemusement and not just a little admiration. His passion for such issues was infectious and he had a certain talent for making complex theoretical concepts easily understandable. She wished her teachers at university had been so good.

"Because we can't observe all cases, we are left with making a probability statement, not a statement of absolute truth, as some scientists would have you believe. Getting back to our puppet master…"

Roland looked at his watch and shook his head. Will had gone over his allotted minute, but pressed on undaunted by artificially imposed limitations.

"We can only develop a probability statement about who he is, in other words, an abductive hypothesis. We reason from the manifestations of his existence in the same way the tracks of a neutrino through a bubble chamber tell us something about the characteristics of the particle beyond the fact that it was indeed there."

"Let's do it," said Roland, ready to move from the theoretical to the practical, from the realm of the conceptual to the realm of the real.

"I think our puppet master metaphor would probably be a good place to start," Sylvie offered.

Will nodded emphatically and took another sip of his tea, which was growing cold in the open air. "There can be no doubt that the man is a manipulator."

Roland picked up the thread. "He is also a master strategist; he's the one who scripts the action in addition to pulling the strings."

"He's a professional and not merely an amateur doing this as a hobby," Will added. "More than likely he is or was highly trained at what he does."

"Highly educated, too?" Sylvie wondered aloud, thinking about Will and the possibility that the man might also hold a Ph. D. in something.

Will shook his head. "I don't think so; at least not in the classical sense—and I'm not just being catty. I don't doubt for a moment his expertise." He looked over at Roland who was drumming his fingers quietly atop the table. Will watched him straighten out his mustache with an outward sweep of his thumb and index finger around the corners of his mouth. He looked over at Will.

"If we rule out the formal university education of the sort that has perverted your mind, then we have to ask which institutions or organizations are capable of providing the kind of training that would allow our man to manifest the sorts of behaviors we have been observing."

Will nodded and waited. Roland had asked exactly the right question and wanted to share the answer he thought would fit the question.

"BND," Roland said.

"Bundesnachrichtendienst?" Sylvie echoed incredulously. You think he's a spook in our federal intelligence service?"

"He might very well be a rogue spy," Will suggested, liking the idea.

This time Roland nodded. "All the signs point to it if we consider them from the standpoint of some sort of training; spycraft, they call it.

296

Subterfuge, the way he has protected himself, the elaborate and carefully planned scheme, all suggest a highly trained agent."

"I think you're on to something," Will admitted. "A rogue agent is let go after the Cold War. He feels disaffected and decides to put all that valuable training and expertise to good use enriching himself."

"Of course," said Sylvie. "We get reports all the time from Interpol of the same thing happening in Russia with ex-KGB. They align themselves with the Russian Mafia to put rubles in their pockets."

"I don't approve of calling it the Russian Mafia," Roland interjected, "it gives the Mafia a bad name."

Will chuckled and pushed his teacup away. "I have to agree with you there. Organization is not exactly their strong suit; at least not yet, anyway."

"Not to change the subject," said Sylvie, doing exactly that and getting them back on track, "but our guy decides to smuggle diamonds instead of turning agents or stealing State secrets. He insulates himself by using young teachers on holiday for his mules." She thought for a minute and then grinned sheepishly. "About fifty, on average, depending on the carat size of the stones."

The two men looked at her and then to each other for help. Then they got it.

She explained. "Depending on the carat size, you can get about fifty diamonds inside the largest size of a hollowed-out tampon. But it weighs a ton and you have to squeeze like hell to keep it in place, which is not an altogether unpleasant exercise, if you know what I mean," she added.

"They're called Kegel exercises; used to strengthen the internal muscles of the vagina," Will offered.

Sylvie looked at him, flabbergasted. "Now how could you possibly know that?"

"Years of intensive gender research."

Roland had his calculator out during the interlude and was working the numbers. "Conservatively, since we don't know the carat size of all the diamonds, let's say three to five million, U.S." He turned the calculator so Will could read it.

Will blew out his cheeks in a long slow exhale. "Time for me to think about another line of work—that is, if I can get Sylvie interested. On a professor's salary it would take me a hundred years to earn that much."

Sylvie agreed. "But it would only take you ten years on the salary of an Erster Hauptkommissar," she said teasing Roland.

"Five," he said without batting an eye.

They all laughed at the hopelessness of their financial situations and at how ridiculous it seemed for one man to make so much money illegally in so little time. They turned and watched as Paul Mautner drove up in his Mitsubishi, clearly the pride of all Loosdorf, and they waved him a hello. He greeted them all warmly and said he had taken the rest of the day off and if they had no plans for the afternoon and early evening, they were invited to an outing in the Wachau. They accepted with pleasure.

MAUTNER DROVE THEM through the wine villages along the Danube into the heart of the Wachau. In the little Dorf called Aggstein, he paused before a sign giving directions to the ruins of a castle that sat on the hill towering over the Danube. Tourists, instructed to leave their cars, parked in the lot below the sign, and walked the paved, one lane access road up to the ruins. With all the aplomb of a highly placed cabinet minister, Mautner ignored the "No vehicles beyond this point" warning and blithely began the sharply twisting ascent to the top. As the pedestrians moved out of the way ahead of the sound of the oncoming car, he maintained the demeanor of an official carrying important persons on important business. He waited patiently for the stragglers to move aside, stop, and watch as the car passed them by wondering who was so important that they could ride when all others must walk. Just below the ramparts of the castle, Mautner stopped in a small parking lot of three spaces reserved for the ticket takers who worked the booth at the entrance to the attraction.

"Too hot to spend an hour walking all the way up here today," Mautner explained, "especially when we can drive it in five minutes. And there was very little traffic."

His guests could only agree and marvel at how right he was. They did not buy the tour, opting instead for passes that allowed them to explore the crumbling fortifications on their own. They enjoyed scrambling atop ramparts already old and in disrepair when Columbus set sail from Europe for the first time. They climbed ladders, walked atop walls, peered into small dark rooms and took pictures of the breathtaking view afforded them by the climb to the very top of the castle. The panorama of the valley and the Danube twisting through it provided an exhilarating backdrop against which Will posed Mautner, pleased to be in the picture, with Roland, Sylvie between them for balance. Then Mautner graciously offered to shoot the three travelers. He was meticulous about setting up the shot to take full advantage of the splendid vista. A castle wall to the left, and a conical turret above, framed the misty panorama of river and vineyards in the distance. After the photo opportunities were exhausted, Roland offered to buy Mautner an ice cream and he accepted. Will and Sylvie arranged to meet them half an hour later by the ticket booth.

They clambered up and down a few more ladders and found themselves mounting the steps inside the cool dark cone of a watchtower.

"It really is a spectacular view," Will admitted looking through the stone aperture built into the wall. Sylvie took his hand tightly and leaned up against him.

"Tired?" he asked her, brushing back a lock of naturally blonde hair misplaced by the wind. "If you let it grow you could be my Rapunzel and I could be your prince. Would you let your hair down for me so I could climb into your tower?"

She ignored him although she liked the idea of what he was saying. At the moment, however, she was preoccupied with something else. "It's that strange feeling again. The same one I had last night. I think someone is definitely following us, or watching us."

Will watched the tourists moving through the ancient structure, in and out of rooms, up and down the wooden ladders, standing, taking pictures or posing for them, reading their guidebooks for explanations. "I'll keep an eye out," he promised, and that's all she needed to hear.

A quick kiss lightened her somber mood and she cheerfully helped two young Japanese women identically dressed in a white blouse and pleated blue skirt over white knee length socks and blocky black shoes. Students from Osaka, they explained in broken German, and she found the on-off button of the Minolta without too much trouble and snapped the picture of the two giggling girls. They bowed their thanks and hid their smiles behind cupped hands when she replied "Do itashimashte" to their "Domo arigato."

"I didn't know you spoke Chinese," Will joked, happy to see her back in good sorts.

300

Mautner and Roland had finished their ice cream treats and were disposing the cups and wooden spoons in the wire receptacles that thanked them in four languages. They piled into the car, passing the huffing, puffing walkers, straining and sweating from the forced exertions of climbing the hill. A few watched the car with suspicion as it descended the steep incline. Mautner, his years as a civil servant with the Austrian rail system holding him in good stead, properly and politely ignored their stares.

He drove them for an hour or so through the famous Niebelungen forest, pointing out items of interest, an old church here, a Roman stele there, and they made the appropriate comments, all the while impressed with his knowledge not only of the place, but its history as well. They could not have asked for a better-informed professional guide. Mautner had planned their route so that they arrived in Dürnstein, where Archduke Leopold of Austria had held Richard the Lionhearted for ransom. They decided to forgo a visit up the hill to the ruins of Castle Dürnstein where Richard waited desperately for money to be raised until the fateful day he heard the song of the faithful minnesinger who had traveled over lands far and wide to find his liege lord. After all, Roland pointed out, the ransom had been paid and Richard was no longer there. In the light of this information, they elected to walk the cobblestone streets of the little town instead. Mautner apologized and explained that he had business at the local train station and hoped It would not inconvenience them too greatly if he left them for an hour or two. He made arrangements to meet them for drinks at the local Pensione across from the church at 5:30. He left them at the famous blue church and they paid the price of admission to see its collection of mummified saints and martyrs laid out in their Sunday best on display in glass coffins.

"Creepy," said Sylvie, looking at all those shriveled wrinkles and stringy white hair. "They all seem so small, as if they were very old children."

"Very little protein in the diet," Will observed, ever the professor.

"Not too many of them lived past forty-five," Roland added, thinking of birthdays not too far in the future.

Will feigned concern. "You are looking a bit peaked today," he said, looking carefully into his eyes.

"What do you prescribe, Herr Doktor, in the short time left to me and before my fortune rapidly diminishes?"

"I suggest that you spend half of all your money on old wine, young women, and romantic songs..."

Roland nodded at this sage advice.

"And the other half, you should spend foolishly."

Sylvie laughed in spite of herself at the childish antics of the two men, defiling the sanctity of the mausoleum with their sinful irreverence. "You two are really too much."

"Exactly what part of the prescription do you disagree with?" Will asked. Medically, he has a right to know," he said. Roland waited expectantly.

She took them each by one arm and shepherded them through the massive doors of the church back out into the light of day. "I've heard you both sing and you would be wise to spend your money on wine and women, and look, we just happen to be at the Pensione, and as a pretty young woman I could use a glass of wine to cut the medieval dust from my throat."

They took a table on the sidewalk, agreed on an Austrian wine to share, a special designated wine called Smaragd, named after the emerald lizard found in the vineyards of the Wachau region of Austria. As they waited for the bottle to arrive, an impeccably dressed man in a navy-blue Hugo Boss double-breasted suit approached the table, excused himself and said, "I believe you might be looking for me." He paused and then introduced himself. "Colonel Rudiger Hain, formerly of the East German Secret State Police, at your service."

Roland indicated an empty metal chair at the table next to theirs. "Feel free to join us."

Chapter Twenty-three: The Offer

SYLVIE MOVED HER purse from beside the leg of her chair up into the security of her lap. It was a conscious movement that put her Sig Sauer at hand. Roland pulled his right leg closer to his chair, giving him easier access to the Glock automatic pistol strapped just above his ankle; this too was a conscious movement. Will observed the tension at the table and noted with interest that Hain too had taken it all in.

"No need to worry," he said behind a wry smile, opening his coat with both hands. "I am unarmed, but I am dangerous," he said, with a wink for Sylvie. She refused the smile.

"What can I do for you, Colonel Hain?" Roland asked, getting down to it.

"Place me under arrest."

Roland could see he was serious. He had not intended the request as a joke. Roland wanted to know what was behind it. "We're on holiday, as you are no doubt aware, having followed us here from Germany. I can put you in touch with my Austrian counterparts, if you wish. In the meantime, let me recommend a glass of the Grüner Veltliner. This year's harvest was particularly good."

"I think I will join you for a glass, but your other offer is respectfully refused." He pulled out a chair from the table next to theirs and sat so he could face Roland.

"Suit yourself," Roland said nonchalantly, and signaled for the waiter. As they waited for the bottle to arrive, Hain addressed Will.

"I've read your papers on the application of semiotic theory to solving cold cases. Excellent work, if you will permit a layman to compliment your scholarship."

"Not at all," Will demurred, "a compliment is a compliment. I'm pleased when anyone reads my work."

Sylvie frowned at him, wondering why anyone would want to make polite conversation with such a man, no matter how elegant or polished he seemed. She shuddered just a bit through the shoulders, saved by the arrival of the waiter with the bottle, another Smaragd. He conducted the ritual of opening the white wine and poured all the glasses half full. He waited for Roland's assurance that the wine was acceptable and when no further orders were placed, he turned his attention to other tables. Hain took a sip and savored the wine.

"Very good, indeed. In fact, far superior to the swill I had to drink in the East." He paused for a moment, habit forcing him to check the other tables with quick, efficient surreptitious scans. Evidently, he was satisfied with what he saw. He addressed himself to Roland, realizing that Sylvie was not about to lend a sympathetic ear. He spoke as one professional to another. "I prefer to surrender myself into your custody for a variety of reasons. I determined you were within a week of tracking me down upon your return to Germany and the credit might as well go to you and your team sooner than later."

Roland interrupted none too politely. "Enough with the flattery, Hain. You didn't just come in from the cold and offer yourself up because you suddenly developed a new morality. No, I think you're here because you have something to trade in hopes of improving your situation."

Will understood where Roland was headed. "I get the feeling that Colonel Hain is about to make us an offer we can't refuse."

Hain removed his sunglasses and Sylvie was shocked to see the soft fawn that made his eyes seem so attractive. What startled her most was not the color but the incongruity of the underlying intensity. This was a man used to being obeyed. She was afraid of this man, now more so than before. She felt Will's hand rest lightly atop hers and she remembered to breathe, but she kept her purse in her lap all the same.

"As the Americans say, I will put my cards on the table. I do have a story to tell and I think it is in your best interests to hear me out."

Roland shrugged, a man on vacation with time enough to indulge such a request, now that his wineglass was full again.

"In 1984, my boss, now retired Colonel General Markus Wolf, approached me with a plan he had conceived. Working with the Bereich Kommerzielle Koordinierung, the Division of Commercial Coordination, which we called KoKo in-house, Wolf arranged for me to be trained in the Soviet Union as a diamantaire for the purpose of establishing a diamond pipeline that ran from West Africa to Europe. I was provided training, funds, and given the contacts to establish myself behind the false front of a diamond concern in Idar-Oberstein. This gave us legitimacy and proximity to the diamond exchange there. To be frank, the old man's idea was brilliant, although I later learned that the KGB had done essentially the same thing with their business called Russelmag, working out of Antwerp."

"There were some rumors to that effect," Roland acknowledged.

Hain nodded. "We had a perfect set-up. We had practically an inexhaustible supply of goods coming in from Sierra Leone. Wolf was getting the hard currency from the sale of the better stones and used it to finance the purchase of the secret technologies we so desperately needed because of the embargo. The technocrats were getting the industrial boart they needed for their projects." He decided not to mention the MIJOLNIR project, East Germany's push to develop independently its own strategic nuclear missile capability, thus freeing itself from dependency on the Soviets. He knew he would have to play that card at another table.

Roland was interested in getting to the heart of the story and the offer that would no doubt follow, so he prompted Hain. "And then the Wall came tumbling down, the Soviet Union disintegrated and the two Germanys were once more reunited. We know that story, Rudiger. We saw it on TV."

Hain folded his sunglasses and put them in the inside pocket of his suit coat. "Wolf, whose analysis predicted these events, called me home to Lichtenberg in East Berlin, shut down the operation and retired shortly thereafter. As you know," he said with an inflection of disgust coloring his voice, "Wolf was charged with treason by the West, was convicted and sentenced to jail—all for simply doing his job."

Roland had been a secret but begrudging admirer of Wolf and the way he had led the Stasi to innumerable intelligence coups. He knew that Wolf's accomplishments were the envy of the BND, the CIA, and even the KGB, with whom he often shared his good fortune. He personally considered what the government had done to Wolf a political travesty, but he decided to reserve his personal sentiments for the time being.

"The case was appealed and the sentence overturned," Roland said, somewhat clinically.

"The damage had already been done," Hain argued, unable to keep the irritation from his voice.

Sylvie had no doubt that Colonel Hain felt the same way about his leader as she did about Roland. For him to turn like this and come to them must involve something of great importance. She was now interested in what he had to say.

"A couple of years ago a rather handsome Chinese couple came into the store, an uncle and his niece, they said, and bought two or three very good stones from us. I did not realize it at the time, but they were both agents for the Chinese and were casing our operation. It seems that imitation is also a sincere form of flattery in the Orient."

"That's it!" Will interrupted.

Sylvie jumped, startled.

"Sorry," he said to Sylvie first and then to Hain, who just smiled. "The missing letter that completes the puzzle; but it's not a letter at all—it's an ideogram," he said, turning to Roland.

Neither Hain nor Sylvie was quite sure what he was talking about but Roland seemed to know, so Hain continued.

"They contacted me after I went to ground and asked me to reestablish the store in Idar-Oberstein and reopen the pipeline to the diamonds in Africa. However, without couriers who had diplomatic immunity, I couldn't bring the diamonds in under the cover of a diplomatic pouch. I had to figure out another way to bring the gems into the country undetected. In the same way that we used to recruit West German students to work for us as double agents, I recruited German schoolteachers on holiday to smuggle the stones."

"Why did you have to kill them?" It was Sylvie's turn to interrupt.

"I deeply regret that aspect of the operation," he said with sincerity. "But I killed no one. Primakov killed those women, without clearing it with me, I might add. I accept the responsibility because I did not stop it."

"You didn't want it to stop," Sylvie accused Hain.

He looked away from her. "For the deception to work, I allowed the killings to continue. And if it had not been for the work of the good Professor Doktor here, we would have gotten away with it." He said it not as a matter of pride but as a statement of fact, a compliment to Roland and his team. Roland knew he was right on both accounts.

"So, you did not kill Primakov," Roland asserted, jumping ahead.

"I did not."

Sylvie did not believe him. It would be in his best interests to silence Primakov. She asked, "Who did then?"

Hain turned to Will, waiting for him to speak.

"The Chinese," Will said, with certainty. The report that the nurse who had killed Hain was Asian now made sense.

"Yes."

"And that's why you're here," Roland concluded. "You believe they're after you next."

"Yes," was all Rudiger Hain had to say, with no uncertainty in his voice. He finished the last of his wine. He was now ready to make his offer. "I am willing to explain in detail all aspects of the Chinese operation. I will name agents and expose their plan for obtaining top secret technological information from the West to support the growth and development of their own nuclear weapons program."

Roland took a quick look at Sylvie. She was now convinced that Hain was telling the truth. He could see that she believed him. She looked at Will. He was poker-faced. Roland took the opportunity to ask, "What do you want in exchange for the information, keeping in mind that I am merely the investigating detective and do not have the authority to make a deal."

"I want to be placed in a witness protection program similar to what the Americans offer. In fact, that's where I want to disappear, Herr

309

Erster Kriminalhauptkommissar. And my congratulations on the well-deserved promotion."

Roland nodded absentmindedly. He had suspected as much.

"There's still something you're not telling us," Will said emphatically.

Hain took a deep breath, held it, and then let it go as he removed a white packet from his coat pocket. He unfolded the blue-white Russian paper atop the table and exposed two diamonds casting brilliance back to the late afternoon sun.

"Go ahead and examine them," he offered to Sylvie, handing her a jeweler's loupe. She fitted it to her eye with some difficulty and held it in place with her right hand. With her left, she groped for the diamonds.

"Keep your left eye open until you are ready to examine the stone," Hain instructed.

"That helps," she said. She found one of the diamonds and looked deeply into its adamantine heart. "Absolutely beautiful," she said. "It looks as if the heart of the diamond is on fire." Finished with her examination she passed the gems to Roland and then to Will for inspection.

"Yes," Hain agreed, "it's what we call the adamantine heart. My problem, and the reason why I'm here today," Hain continued, as he watched the men peer into the stones, "is because one of those gems is not a diamond." He paused to take full advantage of his dramatic revelation. "Even a highly trained diamantaire from Antwerp has been fooled by the artificial. He folded his hands in front of him, leaving the gems to sparkle in the sunlight. "And that's all I have to say until Rieger calls his contact in Department Four of the BND."

Sylvie looked over at Roland. He continued to surprise her. She was unaware that he had dealings with or knew anyone in the Bundesnachrichtendienst. "Who do you know in the BND?"

310

THE OFFER

Roland looked over at Will and smiled.

"Uncle Erik," Will said.

"My younger brother Erik," Roland confirmed, "Assistant Director, counter-espionage, Federal Intelligence Service."

Rudiger Hain folded the diamonds back into the square of their protective paper, an oversized Russian brand, and replaced them in his coat pocket. He relaxed back into his chair, an almost imperceptible sigh of relief at his lips. It did not escape Will's notice.

At that moment, Mautner drove by in his blue Mitsubishi, looking for a parking space. The tables at the café were filling with tourists ready to take an early meal and give their feet a rest.

Roland wrote a number on the back of his card. "Call me tomorrow at ten. And be prepared to travel to Vienna, and from there back to Munich."

Hain studied the number on the card and handed it back as he stood. "It was a pleasure meeting you," he said, bowing specifically in the direction of Sylvie." He disappeared into the flow of tourists looking into shop windows, reading posted restaurant menus, or simply trying to remember where they parked their cars. Sylvie was the first to speak. She shuddered again as if she had just caught a chill.

"Oooohhhh. That is a very dangerous man."

Roland just raised his eyebrows, deep in thought.

"Well, what do you think, Professor Doktor?" she asked.

"It's nice to see someone with Old World manners and charm."

She shot him a searing look, but then was forced to laugh. "Imbecile," she said as Mautner drove by again.

This time he stopped, backed up, and double-parked illegally in front of the café. His smile arrived before he did. When he saw the serious

311

expressions all around, he dropped the smile and asked, "Anything I can do?"

Roland looked at him for a moment, choosing his words carefully. "Very good of you to offer, Peter," he said using the familiar form of address to indicate how much they appreciated what he had done. "This is a police matter that requires our attention and a certain amount of discretion if we are to resolve it successfully."

"Rest assured that I am entirely trustworthy," he said, in all humility.

"That goes without saying, dear Peter. Please take a seat as I have a rather urgent call to make."

Mautner seated himself in Hain's chair and smelled the lingering presence of the man's expensive cologne. He asked Will if there were still real, live Indians in America. Will nodded and regaled him with the story of how he once had to shoot a bear in Idaho not twenty miles from a reservation where the famous Nez Perce Indians lived. With appropriate embellishments, Will was able to stretch the story the entire twenty minutes Roland needed to make his arrangements. When he came back to the table, his mood had lightened.

"Everything is in order."

Mautner drove them home to Loosdorf through his beloved Wachau. Will had to answer questions the entire way, more from Sylvie than Peter, who could not bring herself to believe that in this day and age someone would still have to shoot such a beautiful and wild creature as a black bear, an animal that once had the roam of Germany's black forests, but was seen now mostly in animal sanctuaries and zoos.

"It's very dangerous out West, even today," Will said, and she could only agree: for the poor bears.

Chapter Twenty-four: Acceptance

COLONEL RUDIGER HAIN, ex-Stasi agent and former diamantaire, awaited them outside the restaurant in Loosdorf. As the church bells rang the hour, he commended them for their punctuality. Will commended him for his civility. They agreed to leave his car and take the BMW. Hain sat in the back seat behind Roland at the wheel. He did not offer to shake hands. Sylvie was in front, having insisted that she would not sit next to the spy. To placate her, Will had given up the comfort of the extra legroom the front passenger seat afforded. Roland had let them work it out.

As they got underway, Hain placed an expensive Hermes leather attaché case on the seat between himself and Will, shouldered into his seat belt, careful not to wrinkle the drape of his dark blue suit. He had the look of a sophisticated international executive prepared for a trip into the center of Austrian commerce. Will noted with just a hint of self-serving satisfaction that Hain had used too much cologne even as Roland upped the fan a notch in the BMW. They made small talk the twenty or so kilometers into Vienna, discussing the sights, and then the relative merits of the Porsche versus the Ferrari. Hain drove a Porsche.

They arrived at a nondescript government office building near the Prater, Vienna's world-famous amusement park. They stopped to watch the slow rise and fall of the enormous wooden cars of the Riesenrad, the gigantic Ferris wheel that afforded the best look over the rooftops of the city. At the behest of the German government, Austrian officials had prepared a large office. Agents in plainclothes checked their credentials before they were led to an elevator. When the bank of lights on the elevator wall indicated that they had reached the top floor of the building, the car paused, the agent riding with them inserted a key, turned it, and they ascended yet another level. They were handed over to another agent who escorted them down the marble hall and were passed through an unmarked door. Erik Rieger and two other men talking quietly sat at the round conference table. He rose and came first to his older brother, shaking his hand generously. He turned up the legendary Rieger charm when introduced to Sylvie. He hugged Will with unabashed affection.

"I thought you were still in Prague on a case," Will said.

"Until the moment of Roland's call," he explained. "You look fit. Germany agrees with you," he said, looking with pleasure at Sylvie.

Will beamed.

Roland introduced Colonel Rudiger Hain and the two shook hands. "I've long admired the work of your boss," he said, saying exactly the right thing to put Hain at ease. "Roland tells me you have something of importance for us," he added, indicating where they all should sit.

He introduced Special Agent Robert Campbell of the CIA and Label ben Duvid Feinberg, a representative of the International Gemological Institute, a noted expert on diamonds. Introductions finished, they took their places and Erik poured from a beaker of sparkling water and explained that the meeting was being videotaped. Hain seemed not to care, as if he expected nothing less. He looked at Assistant Director Rieger and the thick manila file folder on the table before him, his official Stasi dossier from headquarters at East Berlin. This unnerved him somewhat and he took a careful drink from his glass after Rieger invited him to begin.

"Since you have no doubt been apprised of my background and my bona fides, I will forgo a review of the events that have brought me to the table, so to speak, and present my offer. In exchange for a new identity and a new life in the United States, I am prepared to give you the names of the agents working for the Chinese Ministry of State Security, in addition to the details I have gleaned concerning espionage activities in support of their nuclear weapons program." He paused and took another drink. He needed it.

Both Rieger and Special Agent Campbell were taking notes.

"May I interject a moment?" Will asked his uncle.

"By all means," Erik allowed.

"Although I accept the reasons for Colonel Hain being here today, there is still something that troubles me, and I know that Roland shares my concern. I would hope that one of the conditions of accepting your offer is that you allow us to tie up any loose ends regarding our investigation."

Roland nodded his support and Sylvie saw they had discussed the matter without her. For a moment, she was angry, but thought better of it. She had learned to trust the two men. If Will had been certain of his conclusions, he would have discussed them with her. The fact that he had not led her to believe that the two men were taking a chance. She remained silent and listened carefully.

"Whatever I can do to help," Hain offered magnanimously.

"You can tell us the real reason why you came to us."

"I see. You don't think the Chinese are trying to kill me to keep me silent."

Will looked at him for a full minute before he replied. "I don't doubt they are after you, but something tells me, based on your history and your behavior, that your motives are not as pure as you would have us believe."

Hain smiled as he shook his head. "I admit as much. The truth is that I have been less than completely honest with my Chinese cohorts. My concern is that they have discovered my deception and are now intent on eliminating me, not to assure silence but to avenge their sense of honor for having been duped."

"Well, what exactly did you do?" Campbell wanted to know.

Hain placed his attaché case on the table and opened it. He unfolded the white packet that contained the two stones he had shown them yesterday in Dürnstein. He pushed them across to Feinberg, whose interest was now measurably piqued. From the brown fold-over briefcase at his side, he removed a jeweler's loupe and screwed it into his right eye, where it almost seemed to click into place beneath the bony ridges of his brow.

"High quality goods and excellent workmanship. Each stone properly mounted in an expensive setting would probably bring about twenty-five thousand retail."

Hain looked at Roland as if to say, "See, I told you the truth." Instead, he said to everyone at the table, "One of the two stones is not a diamond. It is, in fact, a man-made artificial."

Feinberg blushed all the way from his bearded cheeks up into the bald spot covered by his yarmulke. "Impossible," he muttered under his breath. He took an instrument from his briefcase, a standard thermal tester. He checked the thermal conductivity readings and both stones registered in the range for diamonds. He looked up and pushed the

316

tester around for all to read, using the numbers as vindication of his expertise.

"Now you know why the Chinese were fooled," Hain said. "If you will permit me..."

He took another device from his case. "This is a Model 990 tester, produced by an American firm in the United States, and until very recently, a highly classified piece of technology."

He was glad that no one asked how he happened to have the unit. He placed the first stone against the fiber optic probe and maintained contact. An alarm sounded and a green light illuminated.

"The alarm indicates the stone is a diamond." He placed the probe against the second stone and they waited. Nothing happened. "We can now say with certainty that the stone is not a diamond. The device tests for the absorption of ultraviolet light. Diamonds transmit UVs, but this stone strongly absorbs at those wavelengths. The stone, gentlemen and lady, is a lab-created artificial diamond called a moissanite."

Feinberg took the stone and tested for specific gravity. "Incredible," he said in his Hebrew accented German. "I must apologize. The stone is indeed an artificial." He adjusted his skullcap, removed a clean white handkerchief from his black suit coat pocket and mopped his sweating brow. "After thirty-five years in the business one develops an eye for goods and labors under the belief that one cannot be fooled. This stone," he said, nudging it with his finger, "has defeated me. In my defense, I can say only that very few people outside the diamond industry and few within know of its existence. This is because the Americans have kept its development under very close guard." He looked to Campbell for help.

Agent Campbell shook his head. "Even I was unaware of the existence of such a stone."

They all looked at Hain, who was smiling.

"That beauty is part of the first flawless production run stolen from the manufacturer in North Carolina. For obvious reasons, the company did not report the theft. I have not allowed the stones to appear in the usual retail marketplace."

"What have you done with them?" Assistant Director Erik Rieger asked.

Hain allowed Will to answer the question.

"After the Chinese bought the first shipment of authentic smuggled stones from Sierra Leone, he substituted the moissanite, which cost a fraction of the original diamonds and kept those stones for himself. He could then sell the diamonds on the open market, thus profiting twice. But now he believes the Chinese may have discovered his duplicity, and he may be correct."

Hain nodded graciously.

Will now had the final piece of the puzzle in place.

"In exchange for what I have told you, I ask for immunity from prosecution and placement in a witness protection program."

"I have a different proposal," Sylvie said, angry that the man might succeed in getting away with his intricate and elaborate deceptions. "Why don't we just give him over to the Chinese, let justice be done, and wash our hands of the whole sordid affair?" She was thinking of the five pretty girls who had been so callously murdered.

The suggestion was met with stunned silence, but all the men except Hain were forcing back smiles. He was about to speak against the plan when Erik Rieger held up his hand.

"I think we've heard enough. This meeting is concluded and Colonel Hain is now officially in the custody of the BND. Roland, if you have a minute, I would like to speak with you briefly before you go," he said to his brother.

Hain came over to Will as Roland and Erik stepped outside for a private word. "If you don't mind my asking, how did you know there was something more?" He shook Will's hand as he asked the question.

"There's always something more," Will said, not caring to hide the satisfaction in his voice. "I just didn't know what it was."

Hain brushed it off and turned to Sylvie. "Just between you and me, Oberkommissar Schumann, you have been a most worthy adversary. I would have been proud to serve with you in the Stasi. Please allow me the courtesy of a proper Russian farewell."

She was aghast at the man's endless audacity, but agreed reluctantly, uncertain why an East German agent would want to say goodbye in the Russian-style. Despite her misgivings, she permitted this last strange request.

He leaned in to kiss her, first on the right cheek, then her left, then the right again. The other men looked away briefly as she instinctively closed her eyes to receive the kisses. The smell of the man's expensive cologne held her close as she forced herself not to pull away.

At this point, Erik and Roland returned to the room and Hain finished saying his goodbyes to the men responsible for his capture. Erik thanked Feinberg, the diamond expert, and CIA agent Campbell. He signaled to two men in suits to accompany the men back to their hotel in Vienna. At his signal, another two young agents of the BND took custody of Colonel Rudiger Hain. Meanwhile, Erik promised Will they would get together in a week or so and properly celebrate his return to Germany. Once again on the street, the three detectives stood for a minute or two before walking to the car, glad to be out in the fresh air, each sorting out their private thoughts.

Sylvie, explicably, quietly began to cry.

"What's the matter?" Roland asked, knowing she needed to talk.

"He got away with murder," she said, putting voice to what they all knew but could not say. "They're going to let him get away with it, I just know they are. I don't care if he didn't actually touch those women—he is just as much responsible for their murders as Primakov."

Will gave her the comfort of his arm as she looked to Roland for an explanation.

"Just between you and me, I also think it stinks, but the CIA and the BND have taken it out of our hands. It's no longer a police matter. The case is closed. We did our jobs. We solved the crime and we brought the murderers in. And Erik informed me in confidence that we uncovered an extensive Chinese spy satrap that reaches from Beijing to Berlin to San Francisco, and I'm telling you this out of friendship. Don't beat yourself up over this Sylvie. We just got involved in a game with players a bit out of our league. Take the positive and walk away from the rest. That's what we have to do."

She sniffled and dabbed at the tears with the handkerchief Will had gallantly supplied. "I know you're right, but I still think it stinks."

"It stinks to high heaven," Will agreed, "but sometimes the best way to get rid of the smell of the manure pile is to bury it deeply." He handed her into the car as Roland offered her the keys and took the back seat. She put Will's wet handkerchief into the pocket of her linen blazer and drove them toward Loosdorf.

Ten minutes out of the clty, Will noticed with dismay that Sylvie was again silently crying. The tears rolled over her cheeks and spilled onto her blouse. Will reached for her hand and tried to comfort her.

"Don't worry, sweetheart. It may look like Hain got away with it, but he will forever be a prisoner within the system. Being placed in the

Witness Security program is no easy life. He will be watched by U. S. Federal Marshals. In a sense, he will be in a prison without bars," he said, somewhat overstating his case for her benefit. "And the information we will get from him will benefit both our countries."

To his chagrin, his words of comfort served only to increase the force of the tears, although she made a valiant effort to hold them back. Will looked to Roland in desperation.

The Erster Hauptkommissar knew that Sylvie wasn't worried about Hain. With the case closed, she knew that Will would be leaving. She was crying because she was afraid she would lose him. He watched her reach into her jacket pocket for the handkerchief Will had given her. Instead of the linen cloth her fingers expected to find, she brought out a white, folded paper plaquette. She held it up for the men to see.

Will took it and opened it. Folded in the center was a flawless, blue-white diamond of at least ten carats. Will handed it back to Roland in the rear seat.

"Now I wonder where did this come from?" Will said facetiously, and then answered his own question. "Hain must have slipped it in your pocket while he was slobbering all over you."

"What I want to know," Sylvie said, her tears once again under control, "is what in the world should I do with it?"

Roland refolded the oversize plaquette around the sparkling stone and handed the package to Sylvie.

"I'll tell you exactly what you should do with it. Have it mounted in an antique setting and if anyone ever asks, say it was a family heirloom given to you by your dear, sweet and generous mother. In the meantime, Will has another two-kilo piece of Sachertorte waiting for him and we have a vacation to finish."